TRAVELS

COLONY SIX, BOOK 3

BOOKS BY TEYLA BRANTON

Colony Six
Insight
Sketches
Visions
Travels

Unbounded Series
The Change
The Cure
The Escape
The Reckoning
The Takeover

Unbounded Novellas
Ava's Revenge
Mortal Brother
Lethal Engagement
Set Ablaze

Imprints
First Touch
Touch of Rain
On the Hunt
Upstaged
Under Fire
Blinded

UNDER THE NAME RACHEL BRANTON

Lily's House
House Without Lies
Tell Me No Lies
Your Eyes Don't Lie
Hearts Never Lie
Broken Lies
No Secrets and Lies
Cowboys Can't Lie

Finding Home
All that I Love
Take Me Home

Other Books
How Far

TRAVELS

COLONY SIX, BOOK 3

TEYLA BRANTON

This is a work of fiction, and the views expressed herein are the sole responsibility of the author. Likewise, certain characters, places, and incidents are the product of the author's imagination, and any resemblance to actual persons, living or dead, or actual events or locales, is entirely coincidental.

Travels (Colony Six Book 3)

Published by White Star Press
P.O. Box 353
American Fork, Utah 84003

Printed in the United States of America
ISBN: 978-1-948982-12-2
Year of first printing: 2019

DEDICATION

To my readers who have encouraged
me to keep writing. Thank you for your
support!

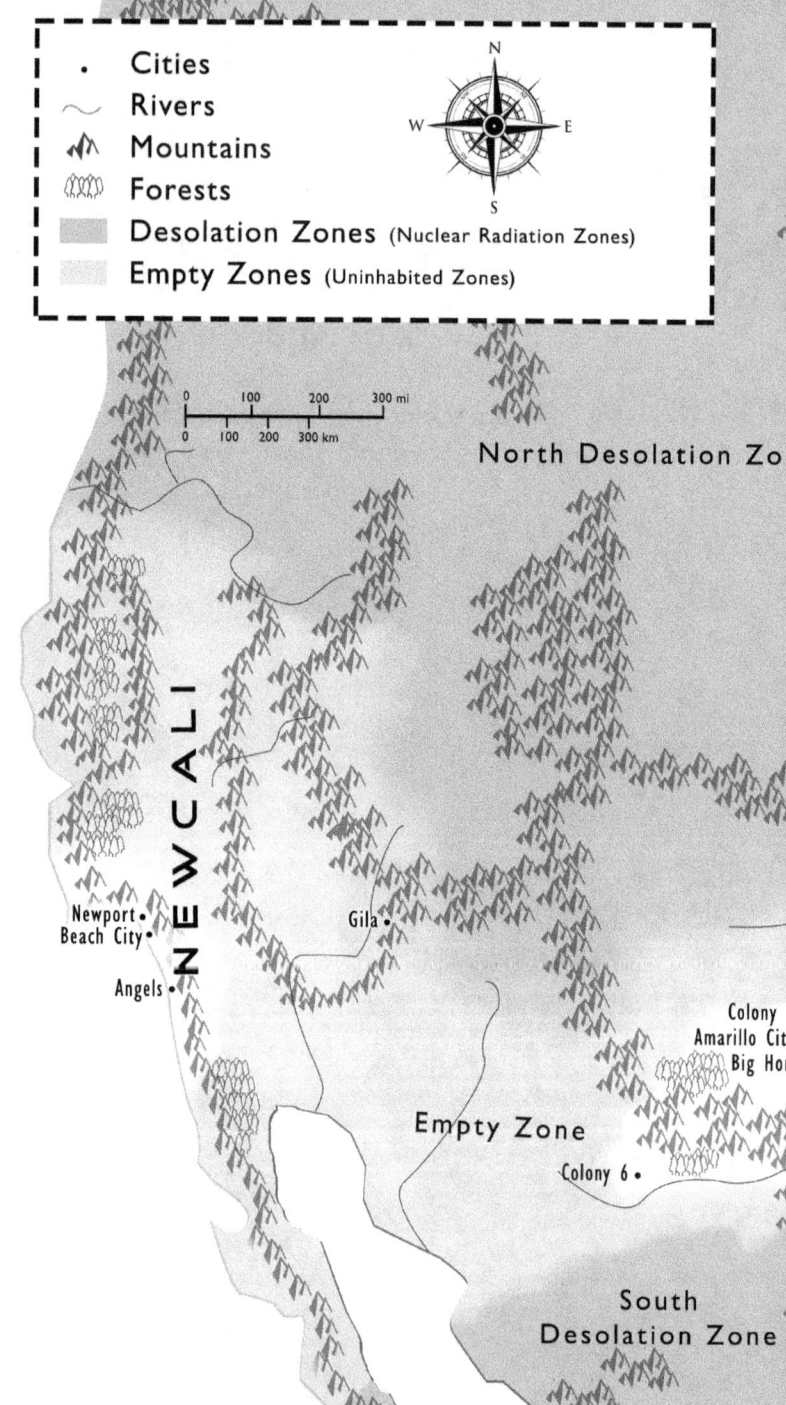

Cities
Rivers
Mountains
Forests
Desolation Zones (Nuclear Radiation Zones)
Empty Zones (Uninhabited Zones)

N
W E
S

0   100   200   300 mi
0   100   200   300 km

North Desolation Zon

NEWCALI

Newport •
Beach City •

Gila •

Angels •

Colony 5
Amarillo Cit
Big Hor

Empty Zone

Colony 6 •

South
Desolation Zone

WELCOME TO THE CORE: COMMONWEALTH OBJECTIVE FOR REFORM AND EFFICIENCY

PROLOGUE

In the year 2198, nuclear war and economic failure devastated the population in a horrific event later known as Breakdown. Twenty years later, the CORE (Commonwealth Objective for Reform and Efficiency) was born, and six welfare colonies were created to help the poor and displaced. The formation of these colonies was first hailed as the best and most compassionate act of humankind, but what they eventually became was enslavement.

For sixty years, three hundred thousand people were kept behind the walls. They, their children, and their grandchildren believed the lies about eventual integration with society, not knowing that the system created by the Elite depended on their continued slavery.

When a secret experiment carried out upon the unwitting citizens of Colony 6 resulted in amazing abilities that always ended in violent madness, ten thousand people were exterminated. Only a few gifted—sixers—survived. Six of these were childhood friends. As a young crew, they protected each other in their struggle to live. Now reunited as adults, their unusual abilities and their unfailing loyalty is the CORE's last hope for freedom.

CHAPTER I

Location: Amarillo City, Dallastar
Year: 2278, 80 years after Breakdown

Lyssa Sloan peeked into the alleyway next to the sauce bar that was already doing a steady business, even this early in the day. The December air was mild compared to past years, but she felt cold inside. Dead. Following Ty Bissett was not something she'd planned to do on this day off, but here she was trailing him.

Again.

And hoping today wasn't the day he was destined to die.

She'd met Ty for lunch, as they sometimes did during her days away from division. He'd been complaining about not seeing her enough, and she'd put him off because as much as she was beginning to like him, she couldn't tell him the truth. Not about her ability, her underground activities, and certainly not about the illegal existence of her daughter. She understood that her secrets required her to draw the line, and if they couldn't have truth between them, she didn't have much hope that they could overcome something as important as his impending death.

Still, she'd followed him, because she did care about him. Enough to regret that she couldn't move in with him away from her twin and her brother-in-law, Kansas, the only father her child would ever know. Lyssa wished she'd never have to see Kansas again, but even if she could admit to being Tamsin's mother, she wouldn't take her from her beloved father.

Instead of returning to the enforcer division where they both worked, her in dispatch and him in personnel, Ty had hopped a sky train and come to this northwest part of town. Not exactly a rundown part of Amarillo City but definitely not the nicest. Not a place they'd ever gone together.

Teev surveillance was apparent in the cameras mounted on the building next to her, but none faced the alleyway where Ty had disappeared. Which meant whatever he was doing, he didn't want a record of it. This wasn't just handing a few cash credits to a sauced man outside a bar, as she'd witnessed him doing on other times she'd followed him. Ty had to know this alley didn't connect to the feed that watched everyone in the CORE, and she'd worked in the darkness far too long to believe the choice in location was an accident.

Fear shot through her, tingling to her toes and making it hard to breathe. What if this was it? What if this was the moment Jaxon had seen in his visions, the moment Ty died? Those visions were the reason she'd started following Ty in the first place, worrying that her work with the underground had put him in danger. But her secrets weren't why he was here today.

Another emotion crowded in on the first. Anger that he hadn't shared his own secrets with her. He had no right to want more from her when he wasn't willing to tell her why he had been skulking all around town.

Squelching her reaction, Lyssa moved closer to the tall building where she wouldn't be as visible to the camera. There, she removed her iTeev from her bag, unfolded the screen, and pretended to study the display, which was currently off. Her back was against the wall now, the solid feel of it comforting. She wished she'd taken a camera disrupter from the underground conference room, but she would have needed permission, and she hadn't told any of the others about Ty's mysterious movements, or how he'd sometimes vanish when she was following him.

Almost as if he knew he was being followed.

Glancing up and down the street, she saw nothing out of the ordinary. Several groups of people headed toward the sky train station at the end of the block, a pair of men were getting into two different public shuttles, and a woman came from the bar and went into the readymeal store next door. It appeared to be an ordinary Tuesday afternoon in Amarillo City.

Lyssa peeked casually around the corner of the building, every muscle tensed as she anticipated having to draw back quickly. Instead, a huge recycling bin blocked most of the space in the alleyway. If Ty was there, it hid him completely.

Grimacing, Lyssa slipped her iTeev into her bag, made a show of fastening her long coat against a nonexistent breeze, and turned into the alleyway. Once there, she sprinted to the end of the bin. A rotten smell wafted out at her, and her stomach clenched. Their pre-Breakdown ancestors hadn't been able to get rid of the need for trash bins, and in the sixty years since its formation, the CORE hadn't either.

Taking a shallow breath through her nose, she touched the bin and peered around the side. She was rewarded by a side view of Ty's narrow face, his black hair reaching halfway down his neck, grown longer just for her. He was talking animatedly to someone out of Lyssa's view behind the metal bin.

His excitement alone was unusual, as he was generally more reserved.

Cold bit into her fingers, and she pulled them back from the metal and tucked them under her arms without moving her head. Ty had turned a bit, and now she could partially see his companion. The stranger was a good head taller than Ty, and his dark brown hair was longer. He didn't look like one of the punks Ty usually passed cash credits to, and the longer hair meant he wasn't Special Forces.

Lyssa didn't know whether to be relieved or worried at this knowledge. Special Forces were enforcers under the direct order of the Controller, and he was after the sixers—those born in Colony 6 with unusual abilities—so it was good Ty wasn't meeting with them. But an unknown could be just as dangerous.

Maybe Ty was helping people who had refused to be implanted with the new CivIDs. The underground had seen a lot of those people in the five weeks since the implants became mandatory in Dallastar—as they had been in Estlantic for years. Most of those people hadn't been ready to drop their lives, however, and go into hiding, so El Cerebro, leader of the underground, had turned them away. It was just as well. As Special Forces cleaned out the empty zones in Estlantic and refugees fled to Dallastar, the underground was experiencing a severe overcrowding in the pre-Breakdown subway tunnels.

This vein of thought was getting her nowhere. She couldn't hear what they were saying unless she exposed herself, and she couldn't save Ty if the man turned violent—if it was even possible for anyone to save him from his destiny. She and the rest of her Colony 6 crew had theorized that millions of choices could affect the outcome in any situation, and what Jaxon experienced in each of his visions was the most likely occurrence, the most likely average of every possible outcome.

Which meant there might be a lesser number of other possible alternatives. But so far his visions always came true, or with a slight variation, and no one marked with such certain death had ever been saved.

Despair threatened to fill Lyssa's chest, but she pushed it back with the skill of long practice. Tamsin, her daughter, was the most important thing in her life. The loss of anything else could—and would—be endured.

Lyssa considered her options. Short of sneaking down the side of the bin, or climbing on top of it, which wasn't possible without equipment, she couldn't hear the conversation. Her ability of projecting her conscious thoughts to another location allowed her to travel incorporeally, but to date she'd only been able to travel to where her twin sister Lyra was physically. Lyra could do the same with Lyssa. That meant one of them already had to be present, and if the situation was dangerous, as it could be today, that wasn't a good thing.

The underground doctor they worked with couldn't find any reason for the limit, or even why they could only visit each other. He thought it would be possible to eventually "travel" to anyone they were close to—and that should include Ty. Clenching her jaw, Lyssa concentrated on the side of his face. She remembered his kisses and the way his warm hands felt on her skin. How for those moments he made her forget the other man she wished she didn't love.

The air around Lyssa seemed to convulse. She felt a surge of triumph. She could feel herself starting to travel. She crouched down to make sure she wouldn't become disoriented and fall.

The next minute, Lyssa was standing in school next to her daughter. Ten-year-old Tamsin sat at a table with three other children in her technology class, examining a holographic representation of a building the children were putting together like a puzzle. Tamsin's small face was eager, her forehead wrinkling in concentration as she dragged each of the pieces across the holo screen with a finger.

Lyssa gasped at the impossibility. She'd never been able to visit her daughter unless Lyra was with the child—and not for lack of trying. Lyssa craned her neck, scanning the room, but Lyra was nowhere in sight.

Tamsin's gaze on the holograph faltered as she glanced in the direction where Lyssa stood. Her eyes squinted as if trying to focus on something just beyond her sight. Lyssa swallowed, wavering in indecision. This was a huge breakthrough in her ability, and she longed to speak to her daughter, to see if she could hear her as Lyra could, but even being there put Tamsin in danger, especially if she started talking about people who weren't there.

The girl shook her head and went back to her schoolwork, removing a piece that a classmate had placed during her distraction. "No," she said firmly. "We tried that last time and it fell in the earthquake. Remember?"

Lyssa came back to her body with a start, her hand automatically going to the Enforce .380 she carried in a waistband holster. Working for division, she had clearance for it, even if she wasn't an enforcer like most of her crew. But Ty hadn't moved, and she anticipated that her trip had taken mere seconds.

Even as she watched, Ty's body language changed. He edged away from his companion in clear indication their meeting was concluding. Lyssa pulled her head back behind the bin, jumped to her feet, and hurried back to the main street. There wasn't time to call the private shuttle that her brother-in-law's job at the transportation department allowed her, or to get far enough down the road that Ty wouldn't recognize her, so she ducked inside the bar.

Seconds later, through the glass at the top part of the door, she saw Ty pass, his head bent as he hurried down the street in the direction of the sky train. He'd be on his way back to division now, already late. It wasn't likely he'd be in danger on the sky train, not with all the cameras and people around. She could relax. Maybe she'd give him a call and tell him she'd changed her mind about not seeing him tonight.

She was about to leave the bar when the door swung open and a man filled the doorway. He reminded Lyssa of El Cerebro's underground guards—not big, but definitely strong. It took only a heartbeat to recognize the man Ty had been with moments before. She started toward the counter, barely flicking a glance at him.

"Chotks," she told the bartender, slipping onto one of the transparent seats that instantly molded to her backside.

The heavyset man behind the bar gave her a real smile, a testament that chotks was a lot more expensive compared to the synthesized sauce that most came here to drink in this part of town. Asking for it made her stand out, but not enough to endure the sauce.

He poured her a glass as she pulled out her iTeev to transfer the credits with a couple taps of her finger on the screen. She pretended to focus on her glass as the strange man sat on another stool.

"Double chotks," he said, not glancing at her or any of the other customers and barely acknowledging the bartender. His voice held a hint of a New York accent.

She let her eyes wander in his direction. He wore a long black coat that covered all of his clothing except his black boots, which glistened as if they'd been shined recently. The coat and boots looked like rare leather rather than synthetic, and the way he downed his chotks told her he was accustomed to the good stuff. He was tall, with a powerful neck and a broad face. His hands were big, useful. His eyes held intelligence, but he was definitely not a man who called the shots. Rather, he was a trusted underling. She'd worked at the Amarillo Enforcer Division and with the underground long enough to recognize the type. Whatever information this man had received or given to Ty Bissett, it hadn't been initiated by him.

Did that mean he worked for Ty? Lyssa was unable to wrap her mind around that. Ty was intelligent, to be sure, and shyly witty and doggedly determined. If he was capable of owning a man like this, what was he doing in a relatively low-level job like personnel?

Before Lyssa had time to consider, the man finished his drink and headed for the door. Lyssa drank the rest of her chotks, welcoming the pleasant buzz that gave her courage, and followed him to the door. He didn't go toward the sky train station, and she hesitated only a minute before falling in after him. If she couldn't get answers from Ty, she'd get answers from him.

Maybe.

She'd only gone a block when the man turned a corner and disappeared. The only place he could have gone into was a restaurant, but when she went inside, he was nowhere to be seen. Obviously, he suspected something, or maybe he routinely practiced ditching people behind him. She was nearly back to the door when an arm snaked around her neck, and she was dragged into a large dark alcove off the entryway. She tried to scream, but the arm around her neck was too tight. Her toes barely skimmed the floor as he pulled her along.

"What do you want?" her attacker growled in her ear. "Who are you?"

"Let me go," she managed to gasp. Black dots began to pepper her vision. Her lungs screamed for oxygen. She had to do something—and fast. There was no way to reach the gun in her back holster, or even the iTeev in her bag.

She willed herself to her sister. It was as easy as a step, as if the thirty kilometers between them didn't exist. Lyssa appeared in dispatch, near Lyra, whose fingers played with menus on the TAD-Alert's holoscreen that made up the entire walls of dispatch. The Teev Aided Dispatch Alert System was a super Teev that aided them in sending the right enforcers for each emergency call. The system was also linked to other TADs in various dispatch offices across the CORE. Lyra looked up and saw her, a smile beginning on her face.

"Activate my iTeev with the TAD," Lyssa ordered, surprised that her mental voice showed none of the strain she'd felt when her physical body tried to talk. She wondered fleetingly what would happen if she died while out of her body. "Hurry! There's a guy. He's choking me."

"What?" Lyra blurted, drawing the attention of the other employee who was working dispatch.

"Activate my iTeev!" Lyssa shouted, but her sister was already pulling up the correct menu.

Despite community belief that CORE authorities could only monitor personal iTeevs or Teevs that were connected to the feed, the TAD could also activate any device unless it was disconnected from the feed completely. How often citizens were monitored without their knowledge, Lyssa could only guess, but given what she'd learned in the past few months, her iTeev spent more and more time off the feed.

She jumped back to her body as her iTeev, still in her bag, squawked a warning sound. "This is the TAD-Alert," boomed an authoritative voice that had been patterned from the CORE's first Controller. "What is the nature of your emergency?"

Lyssa felt the man's grip relax slightly, and she sucked in desperately needed air. As she did, a Teev built into the alcove where they were standing activated a holoscreen in the middle of the space, depicting Lyra's face framed by long ebony hair.

Which meant her sister had not only tracked her down but also searched for onsite Teevs to get eyes on the situation.

"What is the nature of your emergency?" Lyra echoed the original question from the iTeev. Her voice was calm but her face radiated fury.

"Saca!" cursed the man. He reached for something in his pocket and the image of Lyra vanished, the holoscreen showing only a brilliant light that made Lyssa squint.

"Don't follow me," the man snarled. Then Lyssa was falling to the hard floor, made of some kind of pre-Breakdown rock substitute. She hit hard, rolling to mitigate the impact. By the time she recovered, Lyra's face hovered over her again on the holoscreen.

"You okay?" Lyra asked, the corners of her slanted eyes creased with worry.

Lyssa nodded.

"What happened?" This husky question came from their co-worker Gemma Drexel, whose round face appeared in the holo behind Lyra. The woman's curvy figure belied the masculine sound of her voice.

Lyssa shook her head, knowing Lyra would understand that she couldn't explain, not over the feed and not in front of Gemma. "Must have wanted my credits," she said. "Or my iTeev. Can you track him?"

Lyra consulted a display Lyssa couldn't see. "The TAD's lost him," she said. "I'll track his CivID. We got a glimpse of that. It's probably counterfeit, though."

Gemma nodded, her medium brown hair falling over her shoulder. "Maybe he's one of those fringers like the ones they've been catching in Estlantic." She shivered. "In my opinion, Special Forces can't get here fast enough to clear out our empty zones. They're getting too bold."

Lyra exchanged a meaningful glance with Lyssa. The

sisters were fighting to protect fringers—and to free the three hundred thousand people imprisoned in the six welfare colonies. But admitting to that over the feed was as good as asking for medical enhancement.

"Thanks for your help," Lyra said pointedly to Gemma. "I can take it from here." The other woman smiled and backed away until she vanished from the holo. When she was gone, Lyra asked, "Are you sure you're all right?" Worry remained apparent in her brown eyes. Lyssa knew because it was the same expression she saw in her own every morning when she looked in the mirror.

"Yeah. I'm good." Lyssa climbed to her feet. She'd expected that the restaurant personnel would have heard the commotion, but so far no one had ventured in.

"I'm sending Eagle to your location," Lyra continued. "Meanwhile, you'd better check your messages. There's a meeting, and he's been trying to reach you."

A meeting meant she was supposed to go to the underground conference room where there was no chance of being overheard by someone who could report to the Elite. Lyssa nodded. "Okay, thanks."

Lyra studied her, obviously alert to some subtle nuance in her face. "Is there something else?"

There was something, of course. Lyra needed to know that she'd traveled to Tamsin today and also the rest Lyssa hadn't yet told her about her daughter. Lyra was Tamsin's registered mother, just as Kansas, Lyra's husband, was Tamsin's registered father—a fact that indebted Lyssa to them forever. They were the only reason Tamsin had legal status and Lyssa hadn't been condemned to a colony for an illegal birth. Even more than that, they'd helped raise Tamsin, and were as much her parents as Lyssa herself. As such, they deserved to know. But not over the feed.

"We'll talk tonight," Lyssa said.

"Tonight then. Eagle's almost there. Look for the enforcer shuttle."

As Lyssa left the alcove, a restaurant employee came into the entry from a back room. She wore her dark hair in an impossibly high bun, covered with a net of rainbow lights that matched the lights on her very short white dress.

"Only one for lunch?" she trilled.

"I've changed my mind."

"Very well. Have a nice day." Shrugging, the employee removed her iTeev from her pocket, unfolding it to fit over her eyes. The plastic molded comfortably onto her face. "Resume program," she said, unlatching the built-in earbuds and pushing them into her ears.

No wonder the woman had heard nothing of the man's attack. Shaking her head, Lyssa went into the street, grateful that the man who'd attacked her was nowhere to be seen. Would he report the incident to Ty—or to whoever else might employ him?

Minutes later, a silver, tetrahedron-shaped enforcer shuttle raced down the street, the black and red stripes on the side flashing emergency. For once, Lyssa didn't mind the resentful stares that followed her as the panel doors slid opened and she dived into the passenger seat.

"There you are," Eagle said from the other front seat, his mouth twisting into a hint of a grin on his narrow face. His registered name was Randal Jensen, but he'd been Eagle Eyes Jensen to her all their growing up years in Colony 6. As usual, he wore his special dark glasses that contained iTeev tech, but also so much more. Without them, he was nearly blind. With them, he saw more than she could ever dream to see, as they enhanced his special sixer ability. Instead of enforcer blues, the division weapons expert sported black linen pants and a thick matching jacket without a collar.

"When you didn't answer your iTeev, we started worrying," he added.

"Sorry. It was silenced."

"What happened?" The shuttle started forward on automatic drive as he spoke, and Lyssa knew he'd used eye movements to communicate with the onboard Teev.

Lyssa didn't answer, debating how much she should say. "We'll need to track him down," she said finally. "Did my sister get a good visual?"

"No. He must have been wearing an identity blocker, though it was apparently programmed to let his fake Civ-ID be recorded by cameras so the warning program wasn't alerted."

"Of course he did. I'll have to ask Reese to draw him."

"Why don't you tell me what happened?" Eagle prompted. "He didn't just attack you out of the blue. And tell me the truth." He leaned his lanky form back in the driver's seat. "You're better than most at lying, but not even you can hide changes in your body temperature from me."

She sighed. "I was following him, and he got the jump on me."

"And why were you following him?" Eagle cupped a hand between them, wiggling his fingers in encouragement for her to spill more details.

"I was following Ty first, and they had a meeting in an alleyway. It was the first meeting I've witnessed that I can't write off to helping derelicts and punks."

Eagle frowned. "That doesn't sound good. Maybe we should put him under official surveillance."

Lyssa felt happier at that. "You think Captain Brogan would go for it?"

"The man attacked you, so that endangers everyone." Eagle paused for a moment, raising his hands and swiping invisible screens in a way that told her he'd activated the iTeev holo features built into his glasses and was searching for something. He didn't need to use his hands, as initiating the shuttle had proven, but it was easier as well as polite to give her warning that his attention was elsewhere. Otherwise, it was impossible to tell what he was doing under those dark glasses.

"Well, Ty's back at division now, safe and sound," he said after a moment.

"Yes, but for how long?" Lyssa couldn't help the bitter words. "I shouldn't have gotten involved with him. Jaxon warned me." She'd just been so lonely, living with Kansas and Lyra. Lonely in knowing that even if Kansas had wanted her, Lyssa would never cross that line with him. He was her sister's husband and the best father a child could have. That is where it started and ended. Period. Unfortunately, her heart hadn't seemed to get the message.

Eagle's hands dropped to his lap. "Even if you weren't involved, he'd still die. So from his point-of-view, it's good you got involved. You've made him happy, and maybe finding out who that man is will help." But they both knew it was a long shot. Ty Bissett would die of a broken neck, and given the usual timeline of Jaxon's visions, Ty was already on borrowed time.

"Speaking of Brogan," Eagle said. "He's called a meeting in the underground. That's why I've been trying to contact you. He sounds worried."

Lyssa pulled out her iTeev, turned on the screen, and disconnected her link from the feed. There were signal blockers in the ancient subway tunnels that were home to the underground, and those were always activated during their meetings, but all of them were extra careful when approaching or while in the tunnels. Especially these days when so many fringers were fleeing Special Forces in the eastern empty zones. Eagle would even take the shuttle off feed before they arrived at their destination.

Like the others in her crew, Lyssa had fought to survive her youth in Colony 6 and had grown into a responsible citizen—but the Elite who ruled the CORE still wanted her dead. She was a sixer, a person who had developed a special ability from the experimental viribus drug placed in their water. Now only Captain Brogan's rewriting of her past prevented her capture by Special Forces. If they knew she was working with the underground, she'd be doubly wanted. It paid to be careful—and to suspect everyone.

"It's got to be about Nova," she said. "Maybe she's back from Newcali."

Eagle gave his customary uneven shrug, his right shoulder lifting slightly before the left. "I guess we're about to find out."

"If you ask me, using Brogan's niece as a security deposit for use of Newcali's hovercraft was a mistake, even if it did save Jaxon's life. They've had the shuttle back for more than a month now, and we still don't have Nova."

The edge of Eagle's mouth twitched as if he found her response amusing. "Hopefully, she's just been gathering information."

Lyssa knew what he wasn't saying—that every day Newcali didn't return the child was one day closer to trouble. Nova's father had died from radiation exposure sustained while retrieving tech from the desolation zones in exchange for his daughter's release from the colony where she'd been born. Brogan had taken care of Nova in the four years since, and he wouldn't sit idly by if he discovered she was in danger.

They left the shuttle in a public parking lot near the edge of town and made their way down a blind alley to a derelict apartment building in the adjoining empty zone. In the basement, they found a well-hidden staircase that led into the subway.

Before she'd started working for the underground—first by coercion and then under her own will—Lyssa hadn't known of the existence of an ancient underground train system, much less heard rumors of tunnels still existing. The solar-powered sky train had crisscrossed the territory before Breakdown, and one of the CORE's first activities after its formation had been to restore as many main lines as possible. With the addition of the blue public shuttles, nothing else had been needed. The centuries-old tunnels were now home to hundreds of undergrounders, who had fled CORE society for one reason or another.

Lyssa knew her way to the underground conference room, but she was glad to have Eagle with her. His ability to recreate a mental 3D rendition of anything he experienced or could imagine made it impossible for him to lose his way from any of the several entrances, even without his glasses that transmitted all kinds of information directly to his brain. If the tunnels had new cave-ins, he'd simply circumvent and find a new path that would get them where they needed to go.

"Here." Eagle pressed something into her hand, and she realized it was a light. She put the strap over her head, adjusting its position until it hung heavy and reassuring on her upper chest, bathing the tunnels with illumination. She knew he didn't need the light, so he'd brought it for her.

"Thanks." She adjusted her coat under the light, making sure the magnetic fasteners were locked tightly. Since it was December, the tunnels would be frigid until they arrived at the inhabited stations.

"We'd better hurry. Reese and Jaxon left division before I did." Eagle grinned before adding, "And if you aren't there, Lyra can't fly over. She's too busy to leave division physically."

"Traveling isn't flying," she said, but the comment lightened her spirits. Truth be told, sometimes it *was* a little like flying.

They had gone a half kilometer when Eagle raised his hand in a signal for her to stop, his head turned attentively toward a tunnel they were passing. Lyssa was about to ask if he'd detected a cave-in when he motioned her forward past the intersection. Then he stopped again, unzipped his jacket, and drew a gun from his shoulder holster.

"What is it?" she whispered.

"About a dozen people are down that tunnel, and they can't be undergrounders. No one sets up this side of the guards. It's too dangerous."

The underground had an elaborate warning system that Lyssa hadn't bothered to research, but Eagle would know what he was talking about. "Okay," she said. "But be careful."

"They won't turn on their lights for a while. I'll get the drop on them. I'll shout when I need you."

He retraced their steps, quickly disappearing from view as Lyssa watched, careful to aim her light forward and not back at him. Minutes ticked by as she waited. Her body felt hot despite the cold in the tunnels. She should have gone with Eagle. She was trained in marksmanship and hand-to-hand combat—Captain Brogan had insisted on that for both her and Lyra. Reese and Jaxon would never have let Eagle face a dozen people alone. If her ability worked properly, she could have at least traveled mentally with Eagle, but here she remained, useless. She didn't know if he needed backup. He could die, and she'd still be waiting here like a target with this light on her chest.

She waited a minute more. Still nothing. What if he'd run into Special Forces? Or fringers who weren't numbered among their allies? Worse, the heat signatures he'd seen could belong to a group of radiation-crazed monsters that typically roamed the desolation zones.

Taking a deep breath, she whisked the light from her chest

and put it down on the rocky floor of the tunnel. She started back the way they'd come. She'd only gone a few steps when she changed her mind and went back for the light.

Switching it off, she began to feel her way along the wall. *Hold on, Eagle,* she thought. *I'm coming.*

CHAPTER 2

B eing able to detect the full range of electromagnetic emissions gave Eagle a real advantage in total darkness—or rather, in what appeared to be total darkness. To him, various infrared emissions were clearly visible. Before his eyesight had gone completely, he'd still been able to see the full light spectrum without aid; now his glasses transmitted that information directly to his brain, bypassing his near-useless eyes. Anyone who didn't know about his Colony 6 background thought the glasses were responsible for his acute observations, but it was his sixer ability that allowed him to decipher the signals. He could also accurately judge distance, velocity, depth, weight, and more with a simple glance. He only had to traverse a path once and the 3D map would be so clear in his mind that it was better than seeing.

When they'd passed the tunnel intersection, he'd very clearly "seen" thermal emissions in the form of bodies cowered against the walls. These emissions were still there as he entered the second tunnel, moving slowly and steadily to avoid kicking rocks or making sounds that would alert his prey.

The fact that they were hiding told Eagle the intruders weren't the arrogant Special Forces, who were more likely to shoot first and ask questions later. The figures also weren't the huge, violent monsters that lived in the desolation zones—animals who had been changed over generations by the radiation. That left either stray kids who had stumbled onto the tunnels or fringers. Fringers was the CORE term for anyone who wasn't a legal citizen. They lived illegally on the fringes of society eking out their survival however they could. Most fringers, he'd learned, hated the CORE Elite and their rules, and if caught by enforcers, they usually ended up medically enhanced or sentenced to a colony.

There were rewards for turning in the "crazed fringers," though only a few actually lived close enough to a desolation zone to be damaged by the radiation, and these were as crazy as their animal counterparts.

A cool breeze wafted toward Eagle as he worked his way down the tunnel, and tendrils of a new light—still invisible to the naked eye—came with it, telling him there was another entry nearby, or maybe a cave-in somewhere in the empty zone above them. He wished he were wearing his enforcer uniform, with its built-in climate controls and bulletproof material, but with the influx of new people fleeing Estlantic and seeking refuge, it was no longer safe to come here dressed as an enforcer. Too many unknown eyes to sell them out. At least he was using a vest—a lighter, stretchy version of the regular enforcer uniform. Not full coverage but just as bulletproof. Lyssa had no such protection, which was why he'd made her stay behind.

A sound came from up ahead, one that was immediately silenced. Eagle paused, waiting for a very long time, but he heard nothing more. He moved forward again. The visible light was growing brighter now with every step, though it would still be dark to those without his ability. That these intruders were waiting so long to make sure he and Lyssa were gone meant they were intelligent and experienced. So not local teens, but fringers, ones not crazed by radiation, and probably strangers to Amarillo City because they obviously didn't understand that their lives were in danger this close to El Cerebro and his underground guards. Maybe they thought they could steal from him.

He paused to study them carefully, looking for weapons. A figure crouched among the others, his head reaching taller than most, and in the light, Eagle recognized him. He knew the shape of his face, his height, and the angle of his shoulders. No two humans were ever alike. Even the identical twins Lyssa and Lyra held themselves differently. As impossible as it seemed, there could be no doubt. But the boy he recognized was supposed to be brain dead.

Joy swelled inside Eagle, sharp and unexpected. For the first time in weeks, his shoulders felt lighter. He hurried forward, care forgotten, mouth opened to speak. But before he could utter a word, he felt the cold metal barrel of a gun pressed against his neck. His neck and not his back, where the protective vest might have given him the opportunity to whirl and defend himself.

"Toss your gun to the ground," came the guttural voice of the shadow person.

Eagle's breath caught in his throat as he craned to see who was behind him. There seemed to be nothing, the infrared light angling around whoever carried the gun. Yet, even the darkness gave him an outline, a big, wide one, as if the person—or thing—was terribly fat. Thick arms stretched up at an awkward angle, holding the gun which slightly reflected the light, as if whatever darkness that held the figure didn't quite mask the gun.

Eagle saw where he'd gone wrong. This figure had been farther down the tunnel from its companions, crouched behind one of the old metal control boxes that littered the subway tunnels. He'd thought the darkness was part of the box itself, not a person. Or thing.

"I said drop it!" The voice was harsher now, anger seeping from the words.

"Wait," Eagle said as a light came on in front of him. He nearly gasped at the brightness, though his mind reported that for most people, that tiny bit of light would be far too dim to illuminate much. With a few eye movements, he blocked some of the signal coming from his glasses. He'd turned them up far too much on his way down the tunnel. "You don't understand," he added.

"I understand that you'd better hold still, or our friend is going to make a permanent hole in you," said the man who held the light. The people with him were standing up now. They looked like a ragged bunch that had traveled fast and far with too little food.

"Okay." Eagle leaned over and gently tossed his gun, careful to make sure it landed too far away from any of the people in front of him to easily find in the dimness. "There."

"You'll take us to El Cerebro right now," came another voice from the group, a younger voice. Eagle's mouth curved into a smile, despite the gun at his neck. His brain hadn't deceived him. The boy was alive.

But if Eagle wasn't careful, he was going to get himself killed. "Okay," he agreed. "I can do—"

A flood light went on behind him, cutting his sentence short. Eagle was grateful he'd turned down the signal on his glasses. He turned it down further, watching the group in front of him cringe and blink as they squinted at the brightness.

"Hands up now," Lyssa's voice called out from somewhere

beyond the figure that held Eagle captive. "Slowly. No sudden moves with the gun, or I'll shoot you and a couple of your friends. Feel that? That's a nine mil I won't mind emptying into your back—or whatever I'm pressing it against."

Eagle still couldn't see the figure, and Lyssa wouldn't be able to either, but she must have noticed the dark outline. The thick appendages pulled back from him slowly and raised the gun in the air.

"Wait," Eagle told Lyssa. "Don't shoot. One of them is the boy who died."

"The boy who died?" Lyssa sounded confused, which was totally understandable since none of the people in front of them were dead.

"Yeah, in Santoni. Nova's friend, Thane." While he was talking, Eagle didn't take his eyes from the illuminated people in front of him, especially the tall boy.

"Eagle?" Thane—or Thaniel, as his father Silas had called him—separated himself from the other fringers and came toward Eagle. He looked dirty and exhausted, but he could have been crawling and he would have looked a lot better than when Eagle had last seen him five weeks ago, the day Dr. Kentley had resuscitated him far too late. "Is that really you? I can't see with that light in my eyes." The teen sounded happy that it might be Eagle, as if he didn't remember his death had been Eagle's fault.

"It's me," Eagle said, as Lyssa angled the light away.

"No wonder you could come down the tunnels in the dark. I bet you have them all memorized. You can probably even see everything. Well, except Shadow there." To Eagle's surprise, Thane hugged him, though they hadn't really been that close. Certainly not hugging close. Not even during the last torturous hours when Eagle had first saved Thane's life and then gotten him killed.

"Oh, you mean he's the boy whose father is with the underground in Santoni," Lyssa said, as she took the gun from the shadow figure.

"It's okay," Thane told the other fringers. "Eagle's a friend. He saved my life. Twice."

Eagle didn't think now was the time to remind Thane that Eagle had been the one to put the teen in front of the bullet that had killed him. "Why are you here?" Eagle asked him. "Is something wrong in Santoni?"

Thane nodded. "Enforcers found our tunnels. They've found old subway blueprints and are forcing us all out. There are more of us on the way, but we came ahead to remind El Cerebro of the debt he owes my father for helping your team when you were in Santoni. Can you take us to him?"

Eagle debated for only a second. Usually, they took refugee fringers to a building they'd cleared out in the empty zone, where they'd be given supplies and a suggestion of where to set up camp. But El Cerebro did owe Thane and his father a favor, and it would be easy enough to take them to the underground lair by a circuitous route that none of them would be able to retrace. Then El Cerebro could decide what to do with them.

"Okay." Eagle cast a look at the shadow behind him before retrieving his gun.

Thane caught his glance. "Shadow's from Colony 6. Like you."

A sixer? Eagle studied the black figure, whose shortness was emphasized by the large girth. He still couldn't see anything but black, so it made sense that this person had an ability.

"Shadow, drop it," Thane urged. "I told you, he's a friend."

"Then why does *she* still have a gun on me?" came the gravelly voice.

Thane looked at Eagle, who nodded at Lyssa. She stepped back, lowering her weapon slightly but not holstering it.

The darkness in front of them gradually lightened and then became a person as it faded away completely. Before Eagle stood an incredibly attractive woman with long brown hair, a freckled face, and unusual blue eyes that stared out at him challengingly. She was as dirty and stained as Thane, but now she glowed brighter in the dim tunnel than anyone else. She wore a furry bulk that Eagle would have thought was a bear if all of those hadn't gone extinct during Breakdown. He suspected instead that the fur had come from some radiation-crazed beast like the one Thane and his friends had kept in a cage in the empty zone near Santoni. Maybe even the same one. They'd released it on the enforcers who had been chasing them, and it would have been a danger running free. By no stretch of the imagination had it been a pet.

"Eagle, meet Shadow," Thane said. "I guess you can see what her ability is." He laughed. "Or not see it, rather."

"Hello," Eagle said, holding out a hand.

Shadow nodded but didn't take his hand. Instead, she pressed a box on her throat which Eagle assumed was a voice modulator that had made her sound so gruff. "So, are we going to stand here all day and talk?" she questioned. "We're all tired and hungry." Her actual voice was soft and husky—and more than a little accusing.

Eagle determined that she was exactly point zero three percent brighter than anyone else in the tunnel, which meant not only could she repel light, she could gather it to her as well. He wondered if she was aware of the second part of her gift and how much light or energy she could gather.

"We can go now," Eagle said, "but you'll have to turn over your weapons. You can gather them now or let El Cerebro's people take them when we get closer. If you give them to me, you'll get them back. You have my word."

A low grumble went through the crowd, but Thane moved

into the group and began talking with the grizzled man who seemed to be their leader. Eagle picked up and holstered his weapon as a show of good faith, but he kept his hand near it in case there was trouble. He didn't much like guns, which was odd for a trained enforcer turned division's weapon's expert, but he was a good shot by nature of his ability. Given a choice, he preferred explosives.

"So when did you level out of school and leave the Coop?" he asked Shadow.

Her eyes narrowed as they met his. "They had stopped letting anyone out before I finished."

In theory, any colony child who finished school could integrate into mainstream society. That's what the public believed. In reality, they were moved around in the colony where they were born and kept to work for the rest of their short lives. For only a brief time, CORE Elite had allowed limited numbers of young people from Colony 6 to integrate into society as a part of the experiment that had caused the sixer abilities, but when madness had begun to claim the gifted, both in society and inside the colony walls, most had been exterminated by Special Forces. Eagle and his crew had been one of the last groups included in the integration, and they were thirty, so that put Shadow probably somewhere in her mid to late twenties.

"Then . . . how?" He was curious about her. Maybe more than he should be, but she was interesting.

Her lips curved in the first real smile he'd seen from her. "I left on my own. Walked right onto the sky train, the line that leaves the city. It was winter and stormy, early in the morning. Dark enough that they didn't see me."

"Nice." He hesitated several indecisive seconds before adding, "Just a word of caution, though. You might want to keep your ability to yourself down here. Until you decide what you want to do, I mean."

This time her dazzlingly bright smile was mocking, but it made her more lovely, at least to Eagle. His ability gave him so many options when looking at a person. Light changed people, and with Shadow, the changes were more pronounced.

"You mean someone might use my ability? Ah, I'm touched that you care." Her husky tone dripped sarcasm. "Don't concern yourself with me. I know how the world works. I know that no matter who I end up working for, my ability will be my best asset. As long as whatever I do helps bring those whore wrangling, pus bag Elites to their knees, I'll be happy." Her chin lifted as if daring him to contradict her.

He only nodded, because that was also his goal, even if he didn't see an opportunity for success in the immediate future. The Elite had fourteen thousand enforcers and Special Forces. The underground had a much smaller guard to protect an untrained, frightened populace that had been conditioned all their lives to obey. Anger could only take them so far. They needed a solid plan.

Seeming satisfied, Shadow tucked a strand of dark hair behind her ear, and Eagle watched in fascination at the light that shimmered around her entire body. Shimmer would be a better name for her, but he knew that was something he should keep to himself, at least for now. When she moved away, he noticed a severe limp. Eagle studied her left leg, noting that it glowed with the reddish color that always indicated pain. Obviously, she'd been hurt at some point, and he hoped Dr. Kentley could help her.

A short time later, Thane broke from the group and returned with a rifle, three pistols, and four knives, which wasn't much between a dozen fringers. A tug of pity for them pulled at Eagle. They were hiding more, of course, but this offering was enough to assure him they weren't going to shoot him in the back. And El Cerebro could easily deal with the rest.

"Okay, let's go." Eagle turned and started down the tunnel, motioning to Lyssa in hand signals to take up the rear. He didn't need the light up front, and if she carried it, she could illuminate everyone's path and keep an eye on the fringers.

Thane walked with Eagle while Shadow dropped back with two women, one who looked vaguely familiar. Before Eagle could place her, Thane bumped his shoulder to gain his attention.

"I'm glad it was you we ran into," he said. "Seriously, it took so much effort to get here, and everyone's jumpy. Enforcers have cleaned out half the tunnels there, and the ones they can't reach, they burn out."

"I can't imagine there'd be much left to flame," Eagle commented as he turned down a tunnel that actually led away from the underground headquarters. A few circles and he'd lead them back to one of the two guarded sections that signaled the real beginning of El Cerebro's underground domain.

Thane's foot sent a rock skittering in front of them. "That's what I thought. But they have this guy who makes things hot. Really hot. If people are in a tunnel he's clearing, they burn. And not just their outsides. He can even melt the metal and rock."

Eagle felt suddenly cold. "What does he look like?"

"Shorter than you and me, but big. Square face."

"Did you hear his name? Is it Queran?"

Thane stared at him. "Yes. You know him?"

"Ran into him at Headquarter Enforcer Division some weeks back. I recognized him. He's definitely a sixer from the Coop—from Colony 6, I mean. He was a few levels above me in school. He was mean, even then."

"Well, he's killed a lot of people. We had to leave before he found the rest."

"Why didn't you send us a message?"

Thane snorted. "We *are* the message. The others are coming more slowly with the kids. But there's nothing you can do. We've been a target since your visit." The teen didn't sound bitter, but Eagle was sure some of his people would blame them. If Eagle and his crew hadn't gone to protect Dr. Kentley, maybe only he would have been captured. But they'd needed to save Kentley. He was the only sixer who could stave off the madness for them, as well as keep people alive with his ability. At the time, it had seemed like the right decision. Now he didn't know.

They walked in silence for a long moment, and then Eagle asked, "What happened after we left? How did you recover?"

Thane chuckled. "I have you to thank for that. And Kentley."

"Me? I'm the one who got you killed."

"That's not what Debs says. You remember Debs, right?"

"Yeah. The old woman who watched Dr. Kentley's kids." Eagle and Thane had been trying to save her grown son when Thane had been shot. The man had lived at the price of the boy. Or so Eagle had thought.

"Debs said everyone wanted to leave me behind after I died, but you got me to Kentley, and his ability brought me back." He grimaced. "It nearly didn't, though. I was out an entire week, and they were debating using my organs for transplants when I woke up." He flashed a grin at Eagle. "In my book, I owe you my life twice, since you got us away from the enforcers in the first place."

The burden of guilt Eagle had been carrying all these weeks lightened. "Nova will be happy to know you're okay."

"How is she anyway?" Thane's voice was so eager, Eagle guessed the boy had been wondering how to bring her up. Eagle couldn't very well tell him because he wasn't sure.

"Last time I saw her, she was fine. Well, mostly. She didn't take your death well."

"Really?" Thane grinned like a lovesick idiot. "Then I can't wait to surprise her."

Eagle hoped he'd have the chance. But after she'd been in Newcali for so long, he was expecting the worst.

After another short bout of silence, Thane said, "Debs is here too. Did you see her?" He glanced behind them. "She should have stayed back with the others, but her son was one of those that Queran guy cooked from the inside out. She hasn't been the same since. Kind of touched in the head, you know? We brought her in the hopes that being with Kentley's kids would shake her out of her grief."

The irony of that information hit Eagle hard. Debs had chosen to leave the children she'd helped raised from infants to stay with her son. If Eagle hadn't saved the son and gotten Thane killed, he could have spared her and the children that separation.

He looked back and saw Debs now, walking with Shadow. Her head was covered with a scarf, and the already impossibly deep wrinkles on her face were deeper now. She walked with her back bent and shoulders hunched. No wonder she'd only seemed familiar. This wasn't the same strong, proud woman he'd met five weeks ago.

"You won't be able to stay here. You know that, right?" Eagle asked Thane. "Well, *you* might, with your connection to Nova, and Debs because of Dr. Kentley. But not the others."

Thane bristled. "El Cerebro owes us. We helped you."

"Yeah, but he can't support everyone down here. We've had dozens of people arriving from the empty zones in Estlantic as well. He's begun placing people in the empty zones here instead of bringing them down to the underground."

Thane's lip curled. "And what happens when Special Forces begins clearing those out too?"

"I don't know. We're working on it."

Something had to give—and soon. Eagle knew that for as many fringers who arrived in Amarillo City, many more were captured and either killed or sent to a colony. The influx of refugees had kept them so busy, there hadn't been much time to work on the main problem of overthrowing the CORE Elite.

Frustration waved through Eagle. It all seemed so impossible. They fell into an uneasy silence that completely eradicated the former ease between them. By the time Eagle finally brought the group to the right tunnel, the fringers were beginning to droop. Four underground guards stepped out from the crevasses along the tunnel, appearing behind and in front of them. More and more guards were necessary with the increased number of fringers seeking out El Cerebro. Eagle had a password, but it wasn't needed because the guard recognized him.

"Don't resist. They'll need to check you for weapons," Eagle said, passing over the weapons he'd collected earlier. "Make sure they get these back," he told the guards. "I promised."

After the group was relieved of more knives and another gun, two of the guards accompanied them past the conference room and farther down the tunnel until they reached the main gathering place that had once been a huge station platform. Eagle went up the cement stairs and motioned for Thane and the others to follow. The newcomers stared at the mismatched rows of couches and eating tables that were teeming with people. Along the back wall, enterprising undergrounders had set up tables and booths, selling anything from eggs and fresh vegetables grown in secret greenhouses to jewelry and knockoff iTeevs.

"I have a meeting now with El Cerebro," Eagle told Thane. "I'll tell him you're here. In the meantime, stay with these guards and get yourselves something to eat." He pulled cash credits from an inner pocket and gave them to Thane, motioning at two readymeal vending machines in a corner. In the old days, food in the underground had been gathered and shared by all, but with the influx of people, they'd resorted to rationing, even for those who were permitted to stay. That was accomplished by using cash credits given out by El Cerebro.

Lyssa hadn't come onto the platform, and when he joined her back in the tunnel, he frowned and said, "I don't like how this place has changed. Something's going to give."

She nodded. "I know. It's too many people in one place. Come on, they're waiting." She motioned back down the tunnel to the entrance of the conference room where Captain Vic Brogan, in his guise as the fearsome underground lord, El Cerebro, had emerged from the room and now stood with two others in their sixer crew, Reese Parker and Jaxon Tennant, both detectives on their division's Violent Crimes Unit. They wore civilian clothes and looked more like the two underground guards standing near the conference room door than CORE enforcers.

"Glad to see you could make it," Brogan said. With the skin-like mask over his face, his mild tone, and the relaxed stance of his muscular body and barrel chest, it might have been hard to tell if he was upset at their tardiness, but the heat radiating from his body told Eagle he was seriously annoyed.

Eagle felt a wave of unease. As Captain of the Amarillo City Enforcer Division, Brogan had assembled their original Colony 6 crew for his underground purposes, and so far he had been powerful enough to protect them from the searches of the Special Forces. But they all understood that in his role as El Cerebro, he couldn't allow any of them to renounce his cause.

Our cause, Eagle amended, because he was in this to the end, whatever that turned out to be. The Elite were quickly leading the population of the CORE into slavery, and he'd rather die than go back to life as it was in the Coop. That was why he was here, and as long as El Cerebro was fighting the Elite, Eagle would stand with him.

Brogan didn't speak as he set his palm on the door's lock pad and opened the huge room that was off limits to anyone except the crew and El Cerebro's most trusted guards. But once they were inside, he removed the face mask with the C tattoo inked into the fake cheek, followed by the black beanie and the brown hair. He left on the shoulder pads that made his broad shoulders even wider.

"I have a mission for you," Brogan said, raking a hand through his black hair. "I think it's the only way we'll find a solution to our problem with the Elite. But what I'm asking you to do is something no one has done before, and I can't guarantee you'll make it back alive."

CHAPTER 3

As Captain Brogan made his dire pronouncement, Lyssa reached mentally for Lyra and traveled briefly to her side. "It's time," she told her. "Join us when you can."

Lyra stood with an expression of relief, and Lyssa experienced a slight guilt that she hadn't checked back in with her sister before now. Lyra must have wondered what was taking so long, but she'd hear about Thane soon enough.

"I'm going to take my break," Lyra said to their co-worker Gemma. "Text me if it picks up to more than you can handle."

Lyssa didn't hear Gemma's reply as she returned back to her body. She didn't need to follow Lyra to the bathroom or wherever she was going to find privacy.

"What's the mission?" Reese was asking Captain Brogan as Lyssa returned to her body. As usual, a drawing pad lay on the table in front of Reese, and the fingers of her left hand wrapped around a pencil. An image was slowly appearing on the page. By profession, Reese was not only an enforcer detective in the Violent Crimes Unit but also a sketch artist—except her sketches were images taken directly from witnesses' minds. It gave her a distinct advantage over other detectives.

Lyssa needed to remember to ask Reese to sketch the man she'd seen today and run it through the database for a match. The scene was still replaying vividly in her mind, when she let it, but Lyssa couldn't begin to put it on paper.

"I'm not sure you should sound that excited," Jaxon grumbled from his chair on Reese's left. Not only were they partners, but they'd been dating since their last mission, and sparks of attraction radiated from them at every turn. It would have made Lyssa nauseated if she hadn't been so happy for them. It was about time. Even as children, they'd been inseparable.

Reese switched her pencil to her right hand and continued drawing with barely a pause. Her left hand touched Jaxon's shoulder. "Why, did you have a premonition about it?"

"No. Nothing like that. At least, I don't think. It's just that the last time in Estlantic, we almost didn't make it out."

That was true, but Lyssa couldn't fault Reese's enthusiasm. They'd had five weeks of doing nothing except stashing refugees in the safest places they could find in the empty zones. Until now, she'd had no idea there were so many people surviving on the fringes of society. No wonder the Elite were getting worried. They might rule with an iron fist, but with radiation-crazed beasts encroaching on the borders, and with supplies in the empty zones dwindling, thus forcing the fringers to steal from citizens in the CORE, things weren't exactly going smoothly for them.

Lyra appeared near Lyssa in her usual chair, as if she were there in person. Eagle, near the foot of the table, turned to stare momentarily in Lyra's direction, his head cocked to the side, but he didn't say anything.

"Lyra's here," Lyssa announced. "If we were waiting for her."

All eyes fixed on Captain Brogan, sitting at the head of

the table, even Lyra's incorporeal ones. Brogan's black hair was slightly longer than regulation standard, and with his compact frame and broad shoulders, he looked like a born fighter. His angled face almost overshadowed the brown, heavy-lidded eyes that could be both deeply compassionate and hard as steel like they were today.

"As you all know, we are quickly reaching a crisis here," he said. "We don't have enough supplies to continue feeding the refugees that Special Forces is clearing from the empty zones. I thought that after what we did in New York to free Dani and her brother, we'd be able to make headway on our cause, but we're barely staying afloat. The truth is, even if we weren't overwhelmed, I'm not sure we could come up with a plan on our own. At least not one that doesn't include arming all these fringers and getting them killed."

"We always knew it was heading toward that," Eagle said. "But I have to agree with you. Every scenario I come up with leaves them slaughtered and the Elite passing more rigorous controls over all the people. Most CORE citizens are too afraid to do anything to help us."

"My aunt's been hearing talk about another welfare colony being created," Reese said, "and people are wondering who's going to populate it. She has connections, so I'm inclined to believe there might be something to the rumors."

Brogan nodded. "I heard it too—and from official channels. It's taken me time to track down the rumors, and that's also part of what has me worried. They're going to offer birth orders to anyone who wants to live in the new Colony 7."

Lyssa glanced to find her sister sitting ramrod straight in her chair, her narrow face pale. Being rejected for birth orders time and time again was taking a huge toll, and Lyssa knew it was her fault for using up Lyra's one chance to be a mother.

"They'll do it," Lyra said softly. "Thousands of women. Couples." No one else could hear her, so Lyssa repeated the words, and then added without looking away from Lyra, "If they build one new colony, why not another?"

For a long time, no one spoke. "When you think about it, it makes sense," Brogan said finally. "With limited resources, what better way to create more goods? A relatively cheap workforce who will export luxuries for the Elite. I'm guessing in the beginning they'll sell it as different from the other colonies, a paradise. The houses will probably be a little larger. Or maybe there'll be apartments. But the end will be the same. We have to stop them."

"How?" Lyssa asked, dragging her gaze away from Lyra's now-wilted shoulders.

Brogan stood and began pacing the front of the room, as if his thoughts were too large to contain in a chair. "Usually when I decide on a course of action, I look to history to see what worked best. But I've scoured the database, and we just don't have enough pre-Breakdown history to look back on. We've recovered news films and entertainment clips that cover most of the events leading up to Breakdown, but nothing before that. Nothing that resembles our current society. Anything we try is new ground—and we don't have much margin for error. That's why I think we need to look into forging a stronger alliance with Newcali. Unlike all the other fringers we've met, they have a government, an army, and assets."

"Dani did say they'd be willing to take the fringers." Jaxon leaned back in his chair, folding his arms across his chest. "And speaking of Dani, where is she?"

Lyssa wondered the same thing. Dani was the sixth member of their Colony 6 crew, and also some kind of commander among the Newcali people. While Lyssa and the others were relatively new to the underground movement, Dani had created her own movement and had been fighting Special Forces in the colonies and smuggling people out of them for the past decade.

"Dani will be here later," Brogan said. "I asked her to begin arranging transport to Newcali so that I could talk with you alone."

"Are you saying you don't trust her?" Lyssa believed Dani would die for any of them, but she also knew Dani's involvement with Newcali left her with a dual agenda. "Or is it Newcali you don't trust? They did help us with the hover in Estlantic."

"It's not that I don't trust her," Brogan said, sitting abruptly. "But I can't send refugees to Newcali if I don't know anything about their government. As for what happened with their hovercraft, that's part of why we need to act now. Dani told me today she received word that Nova doesn't want to come home, and they refuse to force her."

Lyssa gaped at him, understanding only too well what it would mean to her if it had been Tamsin. "That doesn't make sense. We all know how Nova loves it down here. She loves you."

Brogan's jaw tightened, as did the muscles in his thick arms. Lyssa could imagine that his hands under the table must be clenched with fury. "The fact that she's not here to report about life in Newcali is exactly why I'm worried," he said. "She knows the importance of an alliance with them. She wouldn't choose to stay. At least, I don't think she would."

"Maybe she's still upset about Thane." Eagle's voice was gentle. Lyssa had seen how his guilt about Thane had eaten at him, so maybe he understood more than anyone what Nova had gone through.

Brogan nodded. "I'm sure she is. But she would have at least spoken to me personally about it." For a brief second, Lyssa heard the naked pain in his voice, but when he spoke again, the emotion was masked. "That makes me suspicious.

So your mission is two-fold. Three, actually. I want you to find out more about their leaders and what ideas they have to offer. I also want you to see if they have any access to pre-Breakdown history. As far as we know, we're the only ones left on the planet, but in the past two or three thousand years, some country somewhere overcame their oppressive government. If they did it, maybe we can find a way to do the same without killing the rest of humanity."

"You think the Newcalians are going to give us access?" Reese asked.

Brogan nodded. "After the empty zones, they're the Controller's next target. Dani has already told me they want a meeting, so I'm giving it to them. Which brings us to your last assignment: bringing Nova home."

"What if she doesn't want to come?" Jaxon asked.

Brogan's glare was cold. "She's a child. She doesn't have a choice. I'm not her friend. I'm her uncle and guardian. I can't be either of those things with her so far away. She might choose differently when she's an adult, but for now, her place is here with me." His gaze circled the room as if daring them to refute him. Lyssa would be the last to do so. In her opinion, Brogan had already let Nova run wild for far too long.

"Of course, with things the way they are down here right now, I can't leave myself," Brogan continued. "If something went wrong, my possible death or capture might set back the underground movement indefinitely. I can't risk that for anyone."

For the first time, Lyssa realized that while they were all trapped in this fight, so was Brogan. He perhaps more than anyone else.

"I'm going to need all of you there," Brogan said. "But I won't force you. If anyone wants out, let me know now."

Silence reigned for long seconds. "Of course we're all in," Jaxon finally answered for everyone. "We're a crew."

Nods all around, except for Lyra, who no one except Lyssa could see.

Brogan's gaze settled on Jaxon. "You'll be lead on this mission."

Lyra shook out of her slump and turned to Lyssa. "We'll need an excuse to tell Kansas and figure out care for Tamsin," she said. "Maybe a dispatch seminar?"

Lyssa nodded and relayed a version of Lyra's comments to Brogan. "A seminar would probably work as a cover story for Lyra and me."

Brogan's thick brows gathered in thought. "I'll have Hammer arrange that," he said. "I'm sorry to take both of you, but neither of you can 'travel' that far apart from each other, and we may need your ability." He paused and added, "I know you've been working on stretching that distance, but how are you coming along with projecting yourselves to other people?"

No way was Lyssa going to say anything about visiting Tamsin today. That might be of interest to the crew, but protecting her daughter was more important.

"No luck," Lyssa muttered at the same time Lyra said, "I've traveled to where Kansas is."

"What?" Lyssa stared at her. Lyra had traveled to her husband's location? "When? Why didn't you tell me?"

"It began about six weeks ago." Lyra gave her slight shoulders a shrug. "I've been meaning to tell you, but we've been so busy. At first it happened only in the apartment, and it isn't all that big, and you were home every time, so I thought it was a matter of being close to you. I wasn't sure it meant anything."

"Of course it means something. I've never been able to leave your sight. How many times are we talking about?" Lyssa was aware of everyone listening to her side of the conversation, but they could wait for the full explanation.

"Three times in the apartment, and he was always sleeping.

But yesterday I traveled to his work. He couldn't see or hear me, though."

Lyssa felt jubilant. That meant the theory of them being able to travel to others was a reality. They just needed to figure out how.

Lyra stood, sliding eerily through the arm rest of her high-backed chair to hover beside Lyssa. "It happened too with Tamsin," she said in almost a whisper, darting a wary glance at Brogan. "But I didn't want to bring her into it."

"Of course not." Lyssa shook her head, feeling stunned and more than a little left out that her sister had been able to visit Tamsin too, probably before she had. As if Lyra were every bit as close to Lyssa's child. Or closer. But Lyssa knew she had no right to feel that way. Lyra had saved their lives, and Lyssa owed her everything. Every breath that Tamsin took, every hug Lyssa gave her—all that was because of Lyra and Kansas.

"If you're finished, can you fill us in?" Brogan's thick brows drew like a V above his eyes.

Lyssa nodded. "Lyra's been able to travel to her husband, Kansas, at his work in the Department of Transportation."

There was a collective gasp and then smiles. "So it is possible," Reese said.

"He couldn't see or hear her, though."

"We always knew that would be likely, even if you could travel to other people," Brogan said. "Seeing you is not their gift. But being able to watch anyone you wanted and report back would be a huge bonus for us—and no risk to either of you."

"Maybe one of the madness preventive treatments would help," Jaxon said. "The minute traces of viribus could trigger something. Doc Kentley still has a few, last I checked."

Ice seeped into Lyssa's veins. Dr. Kentley had used old water skins from the Coop to extract enough viribus to create a limited number of treatments to control the madness that afflicted sixers. Without more of the drug, he couldn't find a cure, and once the treatments were gone, they'd have nothing except Kentley's healing ability. As long as even a few doses remained, there was some security.

"We might need it more later," Lyssa protested. "Until we get our hands on a decent sample of viribus, that's all we got. What if one of us goes mad?"

Brogan considered a moment. "Lyssa, Lyra, and Dani's abilities are physical, and Kentley thinks using them should keep the madness away for a while. Same with Reese and her drawing. Eagle's very blindness protects him somewhat, and he should remain safe as long as he can download his 3D images to the Teev. It's a release of sorts."

"So you're saying I'm the one with the problem," Jaxon said. "And that we need to save the treatments for me?"

"Well, taking the juke to get more visions didn't help now, did it?" Reese retorted dryly.

Jaxon frowned. "I'm fine now."

Brogan raised a hand for silence. "I'll talk it over with Kentley. I'm meeting with him after this. He has a list of medical supplies he'd like us to bargain with Newcali for."

"He's not coming with us?" Lyssa asked.

Brogan snorted. "Absolutely not. They'd never return him. Even Dani admits to that."

"When do we leave?" Reese set down her pencil and ripped a page from her drawing pad.

"In the morning." Brogan reached for his El Cerebro mask. "Just make sure you bring Nova home, whatever it takes."

"There's something else that might help with Nova," Lyssa said. "I mean, if it really was her decision to stay."

Brogan arched a brow, his fingers pausing on the mask. "And that is?"

"Thane, her friend from Santoni. He's not dead or in a coma like we thought. Eagle and I found him and a dozen others in the tunnels just now. That's what took us so long to get here. He's part of an advanced group coming from Santoni to claim the favor you owe them for helping us there."

"What do they want?" Brogan didn't sigh audibly, but exhaustion was clear in his voice.

"Eagle might know," she said. "I didn't really talk to him."

Eagle gave them his uneven shrug. "Food, shelter. The usual. We'll have to set them up in the empty zone with the others."

"I was thinking Thane could come with us," Lyssa countered. "If Nova's staying there because she feels guilty about him, seeing him alive might convince her to come home."

Eagle stood abruptly. "And what if we get him killed? Again, I might add. Staying out of contact isn't like Nova—we've agreed on that. So taking Thane will only put him in unnecessary danger."

"Staying here isn't exactly going to be a piece of cake," Jaxon reminded him. "I say let the boy come. He can see for himself if Newcali is somewhere his people will want to seek refuge. They can't all stay here, and Special Forces is coming for them—for all of us. And if he helps us with Nova, that's all for the better. We know how stubborn she is." He nodded apologetically at Brogan as he spoke the last words.

"Give him the option," Brogan said. He reached for the mask and pulled it over his face, instantly transforming his features with the pale, unlined flesh. The C on the right cheek made him almost as recognizable as the CORE's most prominent leaders. "I'll talk to the boy and make a decision." He settled his brown wig over his black hair and pulled on the beanie before standing. Then, with a wave of his hands, he brought up the holoscreen covering one of the side walls and peered at his image that appeared there, larger than life. He made a slight adjustment to his beanie and the hair under it before adding, "Anything else I should know?"

Eagle sighed and sat back down. "That sixer we learned about when we were in Estlantic, the one who nearly burned us to death?"

"Queran?" Jaxon scowled.

"Right, him. He's helping Special Forces clear out the tunnels in Santoni. And if they know about those tunnels, it's only a matter of time until they bring him here."

Brogan's masked face showed no emotion, but his voice was utterly cold as he said, "Then we'll have to kill him."

A breathless silence fell on the room. Lyssa didn't remember anything about Queran from the old Coop days, except that he'd been a few levels ahead of them in school. But he'd been an unsuspecting part of the experimental drugs, just as they had. He hadn't asked for any of it. Now he worked for the Controller in exchange for the temporary cure. If driven to madness, would she have done the same?

"Thane's group also brought a sixer with them," Lyssa said, pushing the disturbing thoughts aside "One who can repel the light or something. She's called Shadow. She repelled it so well, not even Eagle could see her in the tunnel."

"She can gather light too," Eagle said, surprising her. "It's probably not noticeable to anyone, but she can. I don't even know if she's aware of it, or how much she could gather if she tried."

Brogan nodded in appreciation. "That could be useful."

Jaxon arose and came over to the head of the table next to Brogan. "Are you sure you'll be able to deal with the fringers while Reese and I are gone?"

"It's never going to be an ideal time to have you leave," Brogan said. "If we can't make a stronger alliance with Newcali or come up with a plan, the Director will continue to tighten control, especially as long as she has the Controller and his Special Forces doing her dirty work. We'll survive until you get back. Just come back with some ideas." Turning, he strode toward the door, opening it with his palm print. His closest guard knew his real identity, but most undergrounders had no idea, so their meetings were always behind locked doors.

Lyra waved at Lyssa and vanished. They'd talk later, but the vivid unhappiness in her sister's eyes made Lyssa think of her birth order application. Lyssa wasn't married, so it was unlikely she'd be chosen by the Regulator, especially with people living longer and fewer birth orders needed to maintain the population of two million citizens. Two million because that was the magic number of people the welfare colonies could sustain with their labor.

Deep in her thoughts, Lyssa didn't notice Reese had dropped back from following the others to the door until a drawing was shoved into her hand.

"What's this?" But the words turned to ash in Lyssa's mouth as her eyes fixed on a drawing of her attacker.

"I heard about what happened," Reese said. "I caught this sketch from you earlier, and I'm guessing this is him."

Lyssa nodded, her heart beating more rapidly. She was relieved at least that Ty wasn't in the picture. This sketch was from later when Lyssa saw the stranger enter the restaurant. "Thank you. I guess I'd better do a database search."

"Yeah, do that." Reese glanced ahead at the others through the open door. "The captain knows you were following Ty. If he's involved with something, you can't protect him."

Lyssa nodded, thinking of Ty's happy grin as he'd kissed her after lunch. "I know."

Reese clapped a hand on her shoulder. "For what it's worth, I'm happy things are going well with you and Ty. I hope it works out."

With a broken neck in his future, working out really wasn't an option. Besides, things weren't working out. Until Tamsin was an adult, or Lyssa found a man she knew she could trust with her daughter's life, a real relationship was out of the question.

In the tunnel, Brogan in his El Cerebro guise was already talking to Thane and his group. Dr. Sam Kentley approached them from behind, holding the hands of his children, Gwen and Probert, who were five and six respectively.

"Doc!" Thane greeted the tired-looking man enthusiastically. He leaned over to speak to the children as well, but they ignored him, pulling away from their father.

"Debs! Debs! Debs!" they shouted, thrusting themselves toward a bent old woman who had slumped on the ground against the tunnel wall.

"You came!" Gwen threw her arms around the old woman, uncaring of her dirty clothes or the unpleasant aroma Lyssa had noticed around all the newcomers.

"Dad!" Probert called back to Kentley. "It's Debs. She's finally come."

The scarf around the old woman's head slipped, revealing a closely shorn head. Tears slipped down the lined face, but her sagging shoulders lifted as her arms wrapped around the children. "I've missed you two so much," she said, her voice gravely to the point of being incomprehensible.

Kentley immediately strode toward the woman, bending over to grasp her hands. She stared at him in gratitude, the tiredness leaking from her as Kentley's ability to heal worked its magic. But Lyssa suspected it was the kids and their obvious joy at seeing the old woman that made the real difference.

"Take Debs back to our place to rest," he told the kids.

"But," Debs began to protest. "I stayed with my son. I let you down." She paused. "He's dead."

Kentley shook his head, his expression compassionate. "You did what you felt you had to. I'm sorry about your son. Very sorry. But you will stay with us now. We can take care of each other. I'll clear it with El Cerebro."

Debs nodded and let him help her to her feet. The children, one on each side, led the old woman away. Lyssa turned from observing the happy reunion to head topside, only to find Eagle at her side.

"I'll go with you," he said. "You have to pick your daughter up soon, right?"

Tamsin was more than old enough to ride home from school alone on the sky train with the other children, but Lyssa and Lyra wouldn't allow it. Not when they had so many secrets. When neither of them could be there, the aging sitter picked her up and watched her until one of them came for her. But on Lyssa's four days off she was there, front and center, waiting outside the school.

"Yes. And thanks." She was always happy to have Eagle's company through the subway tunnels. "I'll go with you to division before I meet Tamsin. I have to drop off a drawing Reese gave me for Hammer to look at. I was going to run a search myself, but he has that backdoor into the database, and I don't want the drawing to flag anyone who might be watching." Evan Hammer was the Crime Scene Investigation unit leader at division, as well as one of Brogan's operatives, though he wasn't a sixer.

"Good idea."

She waited until the others were out of hearing before saying, "I'm sorry about Thane." She hoped her suggestion to bring him along didn't get Thane killed for real this time.

He shrugged. "I think we'll be okay. I trust Dani—probably more than Brogan does. She never let us down in the Coop. I just didn't want to worry about Thane."

"I understand that." She was grateful Tamsin would be nowhere near Newcali. "But I've been wondering something. Back in the conference room, could you see Lyra? I thought you reacted to her when she first appeared."

Eagle's head swung briefly in her direction. "I did see something. A change of light."

"Has that ever happened before?"

"Not that I've noticed. I was thinking if I did a little tinkering with my glasses, I might be able to see when you travel."

"Really? That would be helpful."

He grinned. "Not as helpful as you finding someone besides Lyra. Her traveling to Kansas is a real breakthrough."

"If only I knew how we did it."

"We?" Eagle was quick to pick up on her slip.

"The collective we," she said lightly. "If Lyra can travel to her husband, I should be able to do it as well."

Eagle seemed to accept that, but her light emissions were probably all over the place. Yes, she was hiding something that had happened weeks ago with Tamsin. She'd hidden it even from Lyra, but that would end today. Lyra had to be told about what Tamsin could do.

CHAPTER 4

Work slid by slowly for Lyra Bateman. There had been more emergency calls to dispatch than normal during the day, as if people were already gearing up to be upset at the outcome of the birth order announcements scheduled later this week. Lyra had been rejected the last time, so she and Kansas had to wait six months to reapply, and then wait three more months for the next announcement. That meant an ironic nine months between chances for permission to have a baby.

The opportunity to visit Newcali put a new spin on everything. If life there was as she hoped, maybe she'd stay and raise her own child. But would Kansas come with her? And what about Tamsin? Lyra couldn't fathom leaving her behind. Tamsin might be Lyssa's daughter, but she was a part of Lyra too. And Kansas adored her. It all seemed so impossible.

Impotent anger rose inside Lyra, and it was all she could do not to scream.

When her shift finally ended, the shuttle Kansas had made available to her waited outside division. Ever since they had spotted people following them back in Estlantic, before the move to Dallastar, Kansas had insisted, and she couldn't very well tell him the men had belonged to El Cerebro, who'd been keeping an eye on her and Lyssa to make sure they weren't murdered like so many other sixers from the Coop. Besides, she could never forget that they were still in danger here, even with altered records, because the Controller had access to the real population database, the one that included all the murdered and missing.

She found Lyssa and Tamsin making dinner in the kitchen when she arrived at their shared apartment. They weren't simply heating readymeals but using genuine produce and real eggs they had stopped to buy from an expensive store. Lyra's mouth watered in appreciation.

Tamsin ran to her, her skinny brown arms wrapping around her tightly. "Hi, Aunt Lyssa." Out in the world, Lyra was known by her true name and Tamsin was her daughter, but here in her own home, Lyra and her sister changed identities. That meant she was Lyssa here, aunt to Tamsin instead of mother. They did this so Lyssa could raise her own child and for Tamsin's safety rather than expect the child to keep a secret that wasn't her fault.

Tamsin also didn't know that Kansas wasn't her birth father and was really married to Lyra and not her mother. It made being alone with Kansas difficult for Lyra, even now that they'd put in a hidden adjoining door to their separate bedrooms. With how tense things had been between her and Kansas, the awkward pretense almost didn't matter. Too often, Lyra found herself wondering if she should walk away, if she should give up her life and let Lyssa become her in reality. She knew how her sister felt about Kansas; maybe in time he could return her feelings and they could make a real life together without her.

Numbness set through Lyra as it always did when she

thought about leaving Kansas. She welcomed it, because otherwise, it hurt too much.

"Hi, sweetie," Lyra held on to Tamsin for a second too long, and then kissed her forehead. The ten-year-old didn't seem to mind.

"Mom says you guys have to go out of town for a few days. I wish it wasn't both of you."

"Daddy will drop you off and pick you up at Rebecca's," Lyssa said. "It'll be fun, just the two of you."

Tamsin's face brightened at the prospect. "Yeah, I guess. Can I watch the Teev?"

"You have any school work?" Lyssa and Lyra said together.

Tamsin gave an exaggerated sigh. "Yes. I'll go finish it." She stomped off dramatically to her bedroom while the women stifled laughter as they watched her leave.

All mirth fled when Lyssa sat at the small rectangular table. "You traveled to Tamsin?" Her black hair was pulled back in a casual braid, but besides that, looking at her sister was like looking at a Teev image of herself. Both were petite, with the slightest Asian tilt to their eyes, even after centuries of mixed blood.

Lyra scooted a chair closer and sat. "Yes."

"I did too. Today. But there's something more." A line of concern marred the smooth skin between Lyssa's eyes. "Five weeks ago, before we left for Estlantic, Tamsin traveled to me when I was at Ty's."

Lyra clutched at the table. "You saw her?"

"No, she told me about it later. She thinks it was a dream, and so did I, but she described a painting of the Freedom Fountain on Ty's wall. It's in his bedroom."

Lyra jumped up from the chair. "We have to explain it to her. She needs to know. What if she does it in school?"

Lyssa grabbed her hand and pulled her back to the chair.

"It was at night, when she should have been sleeping. I told her if it ever happened again to think of her body. And since then, she hasn't had the dream again. As far as I know."

Lyra had never heard of second-generation ability without use of the viribus that had been given to them in the Coop, but the idea that Tamsin shared their gift was both amazing and terrifying. Would she also eventually go insane like all the other sixers? Lyra knew of the madness only too well. Yesterday, she had finally broken down and asked Dr. Kentley for a treatment, because she'd felt the madness encroaching and she was afraid of what it would do to her family. To Tamsin, especially, but also to Kansas. She'd almost admitted about the treatment at the meeting, but Captain Brogan would learn about it soon enough from Kentley.

"They can never know about Tamsin," Lyra said. "Brogan and the others."

"No," Lyssa agreed. "But maybe there are more examples of second-generation abilities. We were put in Colony 6 for our family's propensity toward extrasensory abilities, so why wouldn't Tamsin inherit it from me?"

"What about her father? Was he a sixer?" Tamsin had been conceived in the days before mandatory birth control implants. By the time Lyssa found out her required weekly pill hadn't worked, she had already broken up with Tamsin's father.

"I don't think so, but I guess he could have been, just not from our school. It's not like I went around telling anyone where I was born."

"Maybe you should look him up and ask."

"If he's a sixer, he's probably dead. Besides, it's too risky."

Lyra sighed. What kind of a world was it when searching for your baby's father might get you and your child killed?

"I have to go see Ty tonight after Tamsin's in bed," Lyssa said, "but I won't be staying long."

Lyra studied Lyssa's face, her concern for her sister over-coming her desire not to know. "Is Tamsin the reason you haven't been seeing him as much?"

"Well, yes. That and the fact that he's going to die." Lyssa looked as if she wanted to say more, but she didn't, and Lyra was momentarily glad. She still had to tell Kansas about their leaving, and he wasn't going to take it well. She didn't know if she could shoulder Lyssa's burdens as well.

Even so, Lyra gripped her sister's hand. "I'm sorry."

Lyssa nodded. "How did you travel to Kansas? I mean, if Tamsin has started to manifest the ability, that might be why we can travel to her. But Kansas doesn't have it."

"I took one of Kentley's treatments," Lyra admitted. "So maybe that was it. I felt like I was . . ." Tears filled Lyra's eyes. "Like I was losing myself."

Lyssa stood and pulled Lyra up with her, and for a long moment, the sisters clung to one another. "Then Jaxon was right," Lyssa said finally.

"Maybe not." Lyra said. "I think it cleared my mind enough that I could rest, and that helped me focus better. Maybe more of the drug can trigger traveling, but where we go, I want to believe that's up to us."

Lyssa gave her a wan smile. "I hope you're right."

Lyra sat on the couch in their small living room, trying to find the energy to get up and go to bed. Lyssa had already gone to see Ty, and Kansas was in Tamsin's bedroom playing the guitar and singing a lullaby that his father had once sung to him. Instead of rising, Lyra pulled a blanket over her, shut her eyes, and let the ever-lurking weariness take over. Things were bad between her and Kansas, and most nights she'd escape as soon as she could to the privacy of her bedroom, but maybe tonight she'd get up the courage to change things.

Her body lightened. The next minute she was traveling, the world around her blurring until it reformed itself into Tamsin's bedroom. For long moments, she watched her husband's fingers strum the cords on his old guitar. She loved the strength of his hands, the way his short black hair curled at the edges, and the brown eyes that seemed deep enough to drown in. Kansas was gorgeously bronze, darker than most people in the CORE. His nose, cheeks, lips, and eyes were perfect, except the dark, thumb-sized birthmark near his left eye that never quite went away even with medical treatment. His voice was like honey, soft and sexy, and she couldn't help gliding closer and stroking his hair. If there was any doubt that she loved him, for this moment, it was gone.

Kansas didn't see or feel her, of course, and the texture of his hair only came from her imagination, but when Lyra glanced at the bed, Tamsin was looking right at her. Sleepily, though, as if she wasn't sure of what she saw. "Love you, Mommy," she whispered. Obviously, the girl assumed she was Lyssa, and just as obviously, she really could see Lyra.

Instantly, Lyra was back in her body, sitting up on the couch. Lyssa had said that Tamsin had traveled when she should have been sleeping. Yesterday, Lyra had also been taking a nap after seeing Dr. Kentley for the treatment when she'd traveled to Kansas at his work. Maybe that was the key to their ability. Maybe it wasn't focusing but letting go that allowed them to travel to someone new, until they learned their feel . . . or whatever it was that helped them find a particular person. Of course, it was rather hard to will yourself somewhere when you were sleeping.

Lyra rose and stumbled sleepily down the hall to her

bedroom. Her hand was on the doorknob opposite Tamsin's when Kansas emerged from the child's room.

"Lyra," he said softly, longingly.

He sounded like a stranger, and for a moment, Lyra was again fighting tears.

"What's wrong, honey?" He pulled her close, and she didn't resist, though having him this near when she couldn't officially have his baby was a strange sort of delicious torture. "Is it about the seminar in Estlantic? I still don't see why Captain Brogan needs to send both you and Lyssa. Especially for three days. Tamsin's going to miss you."

For a bleak moment, Lyra wished she could tell him everything. About her involvement in the underground, how the welfare colonies were really work camps, and how Special Forces was killing sixers and fringers alike. But doing so would put him in danger. Was she willing to risk that?

"I'm not happy about going, but I have no choice," she said. The trip might even end up lasting longer than three days, but she wasn't going to tell him that.

His hands slid up her back tentatively, and when she didn't draw away, he bent and nibbled the spot under her right ear where a tiny mole on her neck set her apart from her twin. This solitary physical difference from Lyssa was the thing he claimed to love most about her. It had been over a month since he'd last kissed it, since they'd made love. And much longer than that since they'd done anything but hurt each other.

When his lips finally found hers, she kissed him back, desire beating through her pulse. He groaned and pushed his body against hers. Seconds later, he was opening the door to her room, pulling her inside and leading her to the bed. All the while, he continued kissing her, stroking her. Her own hands explored his back and stomach and neck, as if they had minds of their own. Nothing else mattered.

They fell to the bed, his body a solid and welcome presence over hers. All she knew in that moment was Kansas. Her love for him. Her need for him, and his need for her. Passion consumed her, hot and urgent. This was what it had been like between them in the early days. Before her yearning for a baby had put a wedge between them.

After their lovemaking, she lay in his arms, feeling sated and content. He leaned his head closer and kissed her cheek. "I love you," he said. "So much."

For reasons she found hard to understand, that made tears come to her eyes. At the beginning of their relationship, there had been so much promise, even after they'd offered to pretend Tamsin was theirs. They hadn't known then what that would mean to them, either the good or the bad.

They lay together for a long moment, limbs entwined. Lyra expected her exhaustion to take over, but she felt wide awake. She hadn't expected this tonight, and with where their relationship was, maybe it was a mistake.

"Kansas?" she said.

"Hmm?" he returned groggily.

"Would you consider leaving the CORE if it meant we could have a child?" Her hand flitted to her lower stomach.

For a moment, he gave no response, and then he moved, pulling his arm out from under her and turning to face her, his head propped on one elbow. He waved the lights on with his other hand, but Lyra had disconnected the Teev feed in here as she had in the kitchen. Working with the TAD-Alert had made her all too aware of how any connected Teev could be activated without her knowing, and she didn't want it in her bedroom.

He rolled to turn on her bedside lamp instead, and then faced her again. "Leave the CORE? What are you talking about? Sweetheart, there's nothing but the CORE. And now that they've passed the law making it illegal to go into the empty zones without a permit, there's really no other place to go. No one survives in the desolation zones."

"What if I learned about another place?"

"You mean with the fringers." He frowned. "They're crazy. How could they not be? They live in the empty zones, or did before enforcers started cleaning them out. You know what living so near the radiation has done to them."

"Not all of them are damaged by radiation," she insisted. "There are still places on this continent that CORE Elite don't control."

He studied her for the space of several heartbeats. "Is this when you finally tell me you're working with the underground? Because I've known for months now. And I'm betting you and Lyssa aren't going to attend a dispatch seminar, are you?"

Lyra stared at him. "Why are you saying this?" What she was really asking was how much he had figured out, so she could know how much more to keep from him. Because that's what they were doing, living a lie.

"It's kind of hard not to notice when your wife brings home a gun. And her sister too." He sat up, yanked on his undershorts and sat again, his back against the headboard, knees bent, feet on the bed. His hands fisted next to his hips, a sure sign he was angry.

"We work at an enforcer division now, so we're allowed. It's for safety."

He blew out an exasperated sigh. "Other dispatch workers aren't carrying guns. Then there's times when you suddenly leave during the day or even overnight. And what about disconnecting rooms in our house from the feed? A guy sometimes wants to watch a Teev holo when he eats. What's going on?" He unclenched his left fist and brought that hand to his knees. Now his arm seemed to be a barrier that blocked her out. "And tell me the truth. I need that. Our relationship needs it. Or all the great sex in the world isn't going to save us. What is so important that you are willing to risk our family?"

He fell into an expectant silence. She recognized that expression. She had to give him something. Maybe all of it. She sat up and with her legs tucked under her, she faced the headboard so she could see him better. She gathered the sheet around her, wrapping it around her chest and tucking in the corners. Maybe that was her barrier.

"I don't know where to start," she said. "And I don't know if you're still going to love me if I tell you everything." If he betrayed her, Brogan would have no qualms about eliminating him. She couldn't allow that.

"You don't trust me, you mean."

She couldn't deny that. He hadn't been all that sympathetic with her yearning for her own child. It was different for him. Tamsin might not have come from his genes, but he'd had every other experience a father could have with a child. She hadn't. Lyra longed to feel her baby kicking inside her body, and later tugging at her breast as she nursed. Even if that wasn't possible, and they applied instead to adopt an illegally-born child, it would still be hers. Hers and Kansas's. Just their own. With no Lyssa taking precedence in the child's heart.

The silence between them now felt louder than screaming, but Lyra wasn't sure what to do. Maybe if she kept quiet, he'd let it go.

"I took Tamsin as my own," he said finally. "I bribed people in order to get us that birth order. I've been patient with Lyssa having to live with us all these years, though I begged her to give us Tamsin and walk away. I petitioned shuttles for you and Lyssa when you suspected men were following you. What more can I do to prove myself?"

He was right. He had done a lot, and if his part in Tamsin's birth was discovered, he'd be sent to a colony just like her and

Lyssa, or maybe sent in for medical enhancement. And there was no doubt in her mind that he would continue to love Tamsin regardless of what happened between them this night.

"You know I grew up in the Coop—Colony 6. I told you that when we got married." She gazed at him earnestly.

"Yes, and I know you and Lyssa have some sort of strange psychic connection, and you've hinted that it was because of experimental drugs you were given in the colony."

She nodded, pursing her lips as she chose her next words carefully. "But what you don't know, what I only learned a few months ago, is that Colony 6 is the only colony that ever integrated people into society, and only a few thousand over a ten-year period. All the other colonies . . . the people never leave. Ever. They work sixty-hour weeks and ship all their products to the CORE in exchange for inferior readymeals and houses barely larger than our kitchen."

"No, that can't be. We're helping the poor, teaching them to be responsible." But his hand went down from his knee, as if his barrier were also dropping.

"Maybe that's the way it started out, but now we live off them. The Elite have enslaved three hundred thousand people in the six colonies. But it's worse than that." She took a steadying breath. "Now they're planning to build another one."

And then because she'd wanted to for so long, she told him the rest, about the sixers and the madness, the ten thousand murders and the people still missing from Colony 6, the spying capability of the TAD-Alert, and the supposedly official citizen database. When she'd finally run out of words, he began shaking his head, staring at her incredulously as if she had spilled a pile of garbage in his lap.

Finally, he took one of her hands. "Even if this is all true, what can we do about it? Anything we try puts us at risk."

She sighed. "Maybe not if we went to Newcali."

"The fabled territory of the fringers?" He grimaced. "I know you said your childhood friend has been there, but if it does exist, it's just a tiny village in an empty zone Special Forces hasn't found yet. It's a place people want to believe in when they don't agree with the government. And, yes, I understand why people are upset. There have been a lot of crackdowns lately."

"It does exist—and it's not just a village. They have a lot of people and superior technology. I've ridden in one of their hovercrafts. It actually flies above the ground, and that's where I'm really going tomorrow, to Newcali in a hover, to see if they can help us figure out how to make things better for everyone. That's why I was thinking . . . if it's everything I hope it is, maybe we could move there."

His face flushed, anger covering the disbelief. His hand pulled from hers. "Are you serious? Do you have any idea how dangerous leaving the CORE is? Not to mention the risk of radiation. If you're wrong, we could lose Tamsin. We could lose everything."

Tears welled in her eyes and started down her face. "Just the fact that you have to be afraid of learning more or about leaving is reason enough that we should try. Right now we only live at the will of the Elite. If we do nothing, how many more will die?"

He scooted closer to her. "You and Tamsin are my family. That's all that matters. Think of Tamsin."

"I *am* thinking of her. And the babies we could be having. No one but us should have the right to decide if we have a baby. Things are only getting worse in the CORE. Can't you see that? We have to do something."

"No, we don't. We have a good life, good jobs. I know you want a child, but you can't let that desire destroy what good we have." He set his hands on her shoulders, his eyes boring into hers. "Whatever else you're doing, you need to stop. Now."

Was he really that blind? Or did he simply not care?

"No," she said. "I can't. This isn't just about the right to have a child. This is for all my people still imprisoned in Colony 6. It's for the future. A free future for everyone."

His hands dropped from her shoulders. "I won't let you take Tamsin."

"I'm doing this *for* Tamsin."

"No, you're doing it for you." With that, he stood and strode toward the wall, moving aside the hanging tapestry to reveal the sliding door that led to his own bedroom. It opened with his handprint, and he disappeared inside.

"You're wrong," she whispered as the tapestry fell back into place. But she wasn't really sure. She liked to believe that she'd fight for the colonies and freedoms, even if the restrictions didn't affect her so intimately. But maybe she wouldn't. Maybe if not for her desire to have a baby, she'd be like Kansas and cling to her own safety despite the ever-tightening noose of the CORE.

She hated him at that moment. Both hated and loved him. Lying down on the bed, she clasped her hands over her lower stomach. Would she trade her husband for a child of her own?

She thought she knew the answer, and it broke her heart.

CHAPTER 5

Lyssa drove to a bar to meet Ty instead of accepting his invitation for a romantic evening alone in his apartment. There had been a note of irritation in his voice when she'd made the bar suggestion, but she used her trip the next morning as an excuse, and he'd capitulated. Truth was, she'd only been to his apartment a few times since Tamsin had traveled there. Seeing her mother with a man that wasn't her dad had brought up too many questions, even if Tamsin thought she was dreaming.

Lyssa had hoped she wouldn't need to tell Tamsin the truth about their lives before she leveled out of school, but if the child was traveling, she'd have to be told sooner rather than later. Lyssa remembered only too well her own fear the first time she'd traveled while awake on the day she'd been in labor with Tamsin. Before then it had happened only while she'd been asleep or nearly so, and she'd been sure it was a dream. For weeks after the first time, she'd lived in horror that she was going mad—and that had been long before any symptoms of the sixer madness had set in.

The chosen bar was an enforcer hangout, and as usual, the street was crowded with enforcer shuttles, enforcer scramblers, and a few rare private vehicles. She parked half a block from the bar before hurrying to meet Ty at a small corner table he'd secured for them. He was dressed in black pants and a blue shirt that opened at the neck. He looked great, and when he stood to kiss her cheek, she noticed he smelled even better.

"Are you all right?" Ty asked, after they'd finished their first drink. Like her, he'd eaten at home but he was having a chocolate bread drop as a snack. Lyssa loved the drops, but her own fresh dinner had filled her up, so she'd ordered a second drink instead.

"I'm great," she said. "Just a little tired."

He laughed. "And I thought days off were for resting."

"Tamsin and I walked along the river after I picked her up from school, and then we made dinner. I don't want her to think that food only comes from a carton. And her homework was impossible tonight."

"Food does come mostly from a cartoon," he joked. "Seriously, though, Lyra's lucky to have your help."

"I like doing it. Tamsin's a great kid."

"It's good practice for when you have your own."

Lyssa's smile became real. "Maybe."

Ty's expression changed to one she didn't recognize. No, she had seen it on his face today when he'd met with that man: determination and strength, shadowed with a touch of desperation. What did it mean? Evan Hammer hadn't gotten back to her on Reese's sketch or on the CivID she'd given him for the man, which meant she didn't have any new information about what Ty had been doing, or why.

"What?" she said to Ty, who was staring at her now, a frown on his face.

He hesitated a moment before sliding a hand inside his

jacket and coming out with the square of his iTeev. Unfolding it to make a larger screen, he held it out to her. "This came across my desk a month ago. I've been waiting for you to say something. Why didn't you tell me you applied?"

She stared at the words on his screen uncomprehendingly for several long seconds. Then she realized what it was: a list of ten birth order applicants. There she was in capital letters near the end of the list: LYSSA SLOAN.

"Why do you have this?" She asked, a queasy feeling growing in her stomach.

She hadn't expected anyone to know about her request, and certainly not Ty. In fact, Ty hadn't even crossed her mind. She knew why she hadn't told him, of course. Jaxon's premonition meant Ty was living on borrowed time, and his feelings about her future would never be an issue.

"Why do you have this?" Lyssa repeated. She felt violated—and more than a little fearful. Who was this man?

"The Regulator's office always sends out questionnaires to employers for potential birth candidates," Ty said, his voice low and steady. "They want to know if the candidates are in good standing or if there are issues that might bar them from being parents."

The idea seemed ludicrous. "You mean every applicant depends on their employer for a review before being considered? I thought it was a lottery. I mean, what if someone's slow at their job, or the reviewer has a grudge against them?" Or if a woman happened to be dating the reviewer. Her sense of violation increased.

"It is," he said, "or at least I think so. But apparently, they weed out potential problems first. Don't worry. I gave you a clean review." He paused and added more softly, "I always give everyone a clean review." He allowed a small smile to cross his lips. "Even if I don't like them. And I like you . . . a lot."

Lyssa glanced down at the names on the screen, recognizing another woman in dispatch and two enforcers. The others she didn't recognize, though that wasn't much of a surprise. Amarillo City Enforcer Division was the largest in Dallastar. All of the applications except hers had been submitted jointly with the applicant's spouse.

"Why didn't you tell me?" he pressed. "I had no idea you wanted . . . I wish you would have . . ." He trailed off, as if unable to find more words.

"It's not like I have an actual chance." Lyssa handed back his iTeev in part to cover her shock at being found out. "I thought it would be good to start submitting. So many people submit dozens of times until they're accepted. I don't expect to be approved, especially since I'm single."

Ty pocketed his iTeev and moved his chair around the small table until it was next to hers. "It can happen. I've seen it." He glanced furtively around before adding in a voice that was so soft Lyssa almost didn't hear, "There might be a way to increase your chances. I-I know someone who knows a guy in the Regulator's office. I could talk with him. There might still be time. The list won't come out until Friday."

Lyssa's heartbeat shot into overtime. One of the things that had always bothered her most about Ty was his apparent subservience to the CORE rules. Every single one of them. This confession completely and utterly surprised her. He might disappear when she was following him or hand out cash credits to the drunken saucebags that hung out at bars, but neither of those were illegal. She'd never heard him say anything against CORE policies or recount stories about family members who'd had issues with the government.

He glanced around again and then whispered, "Do you have an idea of who the father would be? Because . . . I-I would be willing."

In that second, understanding dawned on her. No wonder he'd been pushing for a change in their relationship. He'd made no secret that he wanted her to move in with him and to tell everyone they were together. He wanted her, but now it was clear he also wanted a baby. Did that mean he wanted *her* baby, or would any baby do? She'd heard of people submitting birth orders together to increase their chances, even if they weren't in love and didn't want to marry.

As if interpreting her thoughts, Ty closed the space between them, bringing his lips to hers. If he did anything right, it was this. Ty Bisset kissed like all her romantic fantasies coming to life and set her body quivering for more. For a brief second, she let herself live in an imaginary world, where she loved Ty more than anything. He wasn't going to die, they would marry, he would pull favors to get a birth order, and she'd openly be a mother to his child.

Too soon, she became aware of other people around her. She also noticed Ty's satisfied smile, and she dismissed her imaginary world for the lie it was. Because even if her request for a birth order were ever granted, the baby wouldn't be hers. She and Lyra would trade identities outside the home like they did inside it, so Lyra could get pregnant and finally have her own baby. Lyra certainly wouldn't continue dating Ty during the pregnancy, which meant Lyssa's relationship with Ty would end. Then when they switched back after the baby was born, Lyra's child would officially be Lyssa's, just as Tamsin belonged to Lyra and Kansas.

At any rate, the baby's father would be Kansas. Not Ty. Never Ty. He would be dead by then.

Ty tried to kiss her again, but Lyssa pulled away. Ignoring the disappointment in his dark eyes, she said, "I'd better go. Lyra and I are leaving early tomorrow for the seminar." When he started to protest, she added, "We'll talk about this when I get home from Estlantic." They wouldn't, of course, because she wouldn't win the birth order.

"That's not exactly a response to my proposal."

"Proposal?" She felt stupid as she repeated the word, and for a moment, she simply stared at him. "Wait a moment. Offering to be my hypothetical baby's father isn't exactly a proposal." She couldn't help the censure. This was not a cheap Teev film where she could believe everything would work out because he wanted to be her baby's daddy.

To her shock and horror, he started to slide from his chair and go down on one knee. She shook her head and pushed at him before he could make it very far. "No," she said, aware that her voice sounded strained. "Please don't. Now is not the time."

He nodded, a frown covering his face. "I know. I'm sorry. There's still so much up in the air."

That's right. Like how you don't know about my daughter or my secret life. And I don't know about yours.

"If there's anything you ever want to talk about," he said in a low voice, leaning closer and taking her hand between his, "I'm here. I know there's a lot going on with the changes in the CivIDs and the crackdowns in the empty zones. Not to mention that fringer break-in at HED. It's a lot for everyone to think about."

It was, but she couldn't exactly talk to him about her part in any of it. Not about the break-in or the fringers she was currently helping to rescue. "Yeah, okay."

There was no salvaging the evening after that, and curfew was pending, so Lyssa offered Ty a ride home in the Department of Transportation employee shuttle she used courtesy of Kansas. Ty accepted, for which she was glad, because she didn't want to have to follow him to make sure he wasn't attacked on the way home. A very real part of her lived in fear that he'd die after being with her—because of her.

Ty took her hand the instant they were in the shuttle, pulling her close, and she clung to him tightly. They kissed all the way to his apartment, but she didn't go in despite his repeated urging. She needed to be there for Tamsin in the morning.

She arrived home, going once around the block to make sure no one was staking out the house. It paid to be careful with Special Forces hot on the trail of fringers and sixers. After making sure no one was around, she exited the shuttle and sent it back to the garage at the Department of Transportation.

The night air was crisp in her throat and the streets were utterly still. She hadn't reached the short flight of steps leading up to her apartment building when a movement in her peripheral vision brought her to a halt. For a long, terrifying second, she felt frozen. Then, as she reached for the gun in her bag, she recognized Evan Hammer, the CSI unit leader, who even close friends called by his last name.

"Hey, Lyssa." He paused, looking down at her hand holding a gun half out of her bag. "Oh, sorry for startling you. I thought you saw me. I know it's late, but didn't you get my text?" Hammer was a large man with an expressive face and a black ponytail. He wore enforcer blues, complete with weapons and emergency equipment. Despite his impressive bulk and the power in each of his compact movements, he was surprisingly light on his feet, as she'd learned in her bi-weekly hand-to-hand combat training sessions with the man. His presence always felt a little overwhelming to Lyssa, but she chalked that up to lack of trust rather than his size.

"Guess I've been a little busy." She and Ty certainly had been too occupied on the way home to hear anything but a loud emergency signal.

"I have the information you wanted. I was going to leave it with Lyra if you didn't answer in the next little while."

"You could have sent me the file."

"No. Even encrypted, I didn't want to risk the feed. And it couldn't wait. Not with what I've found."

"Have you told Brogan yet?" she asked. Hammer had been involved with Brogan and the underground since before Lyssa and the other sixers were recruited. For months, she'd worked with him without suspecting a thing, which made him the best liar she'd ever known, except for maybe herself.

His lips pursed briefly as he shook his head. "No. I'll have to, though."

Her eyes lifted to the camera on her apartment building. They couldn't be heard, but they could be seen if anyone was watching. Not that they were doing anything illegal. It was close to curfew, but as division employees, they had leeway.

"Come on inside."

Unlike Ty, who had never set foot in her apartment or met Tasmin, it wouldn't hurt to have Hammer come in. He knew about her daughter, as did all her crew and Captain Brogan. Lyssa was still wary of Hammer, however, a sentiment he didn't seem to have about her. Until he'd learned she was dating Ty, he'd asked her out for a drink on more than one occasion.

They rode up the nine floors in the elevator in silence. Unlike New York, where so many of the tall buildings had been flattened during Breakdown, and where they now had an eight-floor limit, a few tall buildings still existed here in Dallastar. Disappointingly, the only view their building showed through its several windows was that of other similar buildings.

The apartment was utterly silent, which told her Lyra and Kansas must have already gone to bed. Lyssa led the way to the kitchen, where she double-checked that the feed was shut off before sitting at the table.

"Want some brew?" she asked. "I have the good kind."

"No, I want to sleep tonight." As if he still didn't trust her setup, Hammer laid a device on the table and turned it on before sitting.

She smiled and poured him a glass of chotks instead. She was already feeling a little light-headed from drinking with Ty, so she opted for a glass of water.

"Like you expected, the man's CivID is definitely a fake," Hammer said, pulling out his iTeev. "It had an identity linked to it, but it was flagged today as false and deleted. I can't access anything about it, not even the info provided on the original bio. Reese's drawing, however, did give us a valid hit. It matched up with a man called Fletch Teller." Hammer unfolded the iTeev to the largest screen possible—as wide and slightly longer than his large hand—and tapped the unit to show an official image of the man she'd seen today. In the corner of the screen, an icon blinked a warning that the device was not currently connected to the feed.

"Nothing stands out in his background," Hammer continued. "He was a mediocre student when he was in school. He completed a certificate in manufacturing and went right to work for the CORE in Teev manufacturing. No arrests, though he did have an uncle who was sentenced to a colony for theft. But here's the big red flag: he left his old job two years ago and currently works for Kordell Corp."

The KC, Lyssa thought, a knot forming in her stomach. Kordell Corp was the largest non-CORE owned company in all of CORE Territories, and their main product was readymeal manufacturing, the carton meals nearly every CORE citizen consumed every day. The three hundred thousand captive consumers in the colonies alone would have made them powerful, but the fact that the rest of the CORE also depended on their product made them that much more dangerous. Reese had once helped convict one of their executives for producing juke, and their revenge had been swift and nearly fatal.

What was Ty doing meeting with the KC? she wondered, passing the iTeev back to Hammer.

"We knew they'd crop up again, after we heard they'd taken control of the Estlantic underground," Hammer said. "But I don't like the fact that this man attacked you here in broad daylight. We need to find out how he's connected with Ty—and fast." He paused a moment and added, "They could be the ones who kill him."

Lyssa was thinking the same thing herself. The KC was a force to be reckoned with, and if Ty was communicating with them, he was probably working for them or passing information. Whatever they planned, he was in over his head. Currently, El Cerebro had an uneasy truce with the KC, but that could end at any moment.

Hammer sipped his drink. "You know, when we do succeed in taking down the Elite, the KC will be like vultures. We'll have to make sure they don't swoop in and take over."

"They control the food," she said bleakly. The raw food came directly from the captive colonies, which the KC then packaged for the entire CORE.

He sighed. "Yeah."

That was when she noticed Tamsin standing behind him in the kitchen doorway. Lyssa was about to send the child back to bed with a promise of a snuggle when Tamsin glided over to her without moving her feet. The edges of her body were soft, as if she were made of a poor hologram.

She's not really here, Lyssa thought. Fear gripped her, making it hard to breathe.

"Mommy, why is he here?" Tamsin asked sleepily. "I don't know him. He looks scary."

She wanted to comfort her daughter, but she couldn't with Hammer staring at her. He couldn't hear Tamsin, of course, but Lyssa hadn't controlled her reaction very well.

"I'd better go," Hammer said, glancing awkwardly around the kitchen.

"Right. The morning will be here soon enough, and I do need to check on my daughter. She's supposed to be in bed, but sometimes she doesn't stay there." This last bit she said with a pointed glance at Tamsin's traveling form.

Hammer downed the rest of his drink, standing as he set the cup back on the table. "I'll see myself out." He pocketed his blocking device and left the room.

"Go to bed," Lyssa whispered urgently to Tamsin. "Now. I'll come in a minute."

The child nodded and faded. Lyssa sat lost for a few seconds before finally pulling it together enough to catch up with Hammer at the door. "Thanks for coming," she told him. "I appreciate it."

He turned and faced her. "You need to start carrying your weapon in a more accessible place than your purse. And you need to wear a vest. You could have been hurt this afternoon."

She nodded. She'd never noticed before how kind his eyes were—or maybe it was the upward sweeping of his brows. He had the most expressive face.

"This isn't going away," he continued. "It's only going to get worse." He reached out to her, as if to touch her arm, but pulled away at the last moment. "See you in the morning."

"Okay," she said without thinking. Then, as his meaning set in, she added, "What? No, I won't be in tomorrow."

"Oh, you didn't know? I'm going along with your crew. I'm the best at navigating the Newcali T-link feed."

"But that doesn't leave Captain Brogan with anyone at division." Any undergrounders, she meant.

Hammer shrugged. "He'll make do. He always does." With a smile and a nod, he left, leaving Lyssa to stare at the back of his head and his black ponytail. She wasn't surprised when he took the stairs instead of the elevator.

When Lyssa entered her room, Tamsin was lying in bed with her eyes closed. As she snuggled in with her daughter, the child curled into her. "I had the strangest dream," she murmured. "Were you in the kitchen talking to a man?"

I need to tell her, Lyssa thought. The time had come.

But not on the evening before she went to Newcali. She needed more than a hurried explanation in the dark. She'd need demonstrations and Lyra's help to explain the importance of secrecy.

"Shh, honey," she said. "We'll talk about it later, okay? But that man is a friend, so you don't have to worry. He'd never hurt you."

She said the words and believed them. Why? She wasn't sure. How was it that she could be sure about Hammer and not about Ty, the man she was dating? A man who'd sort of proposed this evening.

"And remember, if you ever have a dream like that when I'm not around, just think of being back in bed, okay? And hold onto that thought."

Tamsin, apparently too tired for argument, buried her forehead in Lyssa's chest with sighs of contentment. Within a few minutes, her breathing was normal again. But all sleep had fled from Lyssa's mind.

Ty was collaborating with the KC, Tamsin was traveling, and tomorrow they were going to Newcali into what might possibly be a trap.

CHAPTER 6

Reese Parker's doorbell rang early Wednesday morning while she was still getting her bag ready for the journey to Newcali. "Who is it?" she asked the Teev, which was connected to the feed and showing a half-sized holo of the news in the middle of her sitting room.

"Your visitor is Detective Jaxon Tennant," came a woman's voice that still sounded mechanical to Reese, though she'd installed the latest upgrade everyone raved about.

A smile spread across Reese's face. Her partner was supposed to meet her at division this morning, where the entire crew would take a shuttle to rendezvous with Dani in the empty zone northwest of Amarillo City. But since they'd started officially and not-so-secretly dating, he'd been unpredictable.

She hurried to the door and let him in. Automatic entry was one upgrade of her refurbished, pre-Breakdown apartment that she had refused. She liked having a door that locked no matter who might take over command of a connected Teev feed.

"Hey," she said, stepping into his arms. It was meant to

be a brief hug, but he clung to her, burying his cold face in her warm neck. She didn't object but instantly recognized that something was up, because this needy display wasn't like him. Not at all. His hands went to her back, pulling her tightly against the length of his body.

For long moments, they stood in the doorway like that, until his nose warmed and her back was beginning to protest its awkward arch. At last, with a little sigh, he drew away and stepped into her apartment, closing the door behind him.

The Teev holo reporter was now talking about the increase of beasts encroaching from the North Desolation Zone into Estlantic and Special Forces' capture of dangerous fringers. Reese didn't know how much of it to believe, however, as the Controller recently announced that Dani had been captured, which was far from the truth. But if monsters were encroaching on the empty zones and inhabited lands in Estlantic, how long would it be before they had the same problem in Dallastar? With a downward sweep of her hands, Reese shut off the Teev. Then she also manually disconnected the Teev's connection to the feed, just in case.

"What is it?" she asked Jaxon. "Is something wrong?" She couldn't think of anything that would make him act this way, except maybe if something happened to his adopted father, a former beat enforcer who'd rescued him from the colonies and sponsored him through the rest of his education.

"No." Pause. "Yes." He frowned at her open bag on the couch. Her clothes were packed, but she still had her weapons and emergency supplies to throw in. "You should finish packing. We can talk later."

"What is it?" she insisted.

He pulled his iTeev from his pocket. "All night, I've been feeling a little off, like something's going to happen, and I thought maybe I couldn't get a clear premonition because of

Doc Kentley's treatment, or maybe because we were with him yesterday and he has that calming effect. Anyway, I was sure it was related to our trip today, but then this morning I received a message from HED."

"HED?" Her heartbeat went from normal to agitated in the space of a second. Headquarters Enforcer Division, or HED, was the home base of the Controller and his Special Forces. They'd nearly been killed twice by Special Forces, so a message from them couldn't be good.

"What does it say?"

For an answer, he handed over the iTeev, and she read hurriedly.

Detective Enforcer Jaxon Tennant,

We are happy to inform you that you have been chosen to become a part of Special Forces. During your career as an enforcer, you have shown the four qualities that set you apart for advancement: capability, initiative, dedication, and loyalty. We invite you to become a member of our elite rank of enforcers. Unlike your current job that is limited to one locale, Special Forces are assigned all over CORE Territories under the direction of Controller Warrick Ramsey, who in turn answers only to the Director. We are tasked with assignments that are vital to the continuing peace of the CORE. This is a special honor afforded only to the chosen few.

Acceptance would require a transfer from your current locale to HED, located in New York. You will retain your detective status, but your eventual postings and assignments will rotate as needed by the Controller. We eagerly await your response.

Sincerely,
Zale Walsh, Captain of HED

Reese handed back the iTeev in disbelief. She'd known he had once wanted to be in Special Forces, but she felt betrayed that he'd requested to join when he knew Special Forces and the Controller had murdered so many of their people. "You applied?"

Jaxon shook his head. "That's just it. I didn't. Sure, I wanted to be a part of them once, but not at all since I came here and learned the truth. Special Forces is the last group I'd want to be a part of. Especially because of Ramsey."

"Because of what he is to you." Reese's hurt subsided. Of course Jaxon hadn't applied to leave her and the crew. Not now. Maybe not ever.

"Because of what he *might* be to me," Jaxon corrected.

It was true they weren't sure exactly what the Controller might be to Jaxon, but Reese knew Jaxon wondered if the man was his biological father, or perhaps knew who was. There was at least some connection. Twenty years ago, when they were kids, the Controller's half brother, Bensell Summers, had visited Jaxon's mother in Colony 6 a week or so before her murder. At the time, they'd thought he'd been one of the many men who paid for her illegal sexual services. But three months ago, Summers and a group of Special Forces had come for them. Before Jaxon had been forced to kill him during the confrontation, Summers had hinted that he'd visited Jaxon's mother at another man's bidding, someone who wanted him to take Jaxon to Estlantic alive. Both Summers and Controller Ramsey had blue eyes, a rare genetic trait Jaxon shared.

There was also the fact that Captain Brogan and Hammer had been able, with the help of tech from Dani's friends in Newcali, to alter the citizen database to remove signs of their crew having been born in Colony 6. Except for Jaxon, whose records had been specifically protected from tampering, yet in the months since Summer attempted to kidnap him, no more Special Forces had come for Jaxon. Then during their last op, Ramsey himself had reacted to seeing Jaxon. When Jaxon had taken the hallucinogen juke to activate his premonitions, which also amplified the sixer madness, he'd seen glimpses of talking to someone about his father. He hadn't experienced the premonitions since Dr. Kentley started treating him, but that didn't mean it wouldn't come true. All of Jaxon's premonitions came true.

"Maybe this is their new way of rounding up sixers," Jaxon said, taking her hand and pulling her over to the couch. He picked up a stack of readymeals and set them inside her travel bag, next to a medical kit.

"You mean instead of with assault rifles." Reese picked up her own assault rifle, protected by a canvas case, and laid it inside the bag as well, followed by one of her pistols and extra ammo. Her other pistol and knife would go with her. Dani hadn't forbidden them from bringing guns, so she was going in prepared.

Jaxon sat where the readymeals had been. "If Kentley hadn't developed that treatment, I would have had to turn myself in . . . or something."

Or die, he meant. Reese would have been willing to turn Jaxon in to save his life, but she had never admitted as much. "It won't come to that."

"It will if we can't find a cure. If we can't make them give us a cure. We're too much of a danger."

She shook her head slowly. "We shouldn't be. Not with how many sixers they've already killed."

"That's exactly why we're a danger." All traces of his upset had vanished, and now he sounded determined and confident, like the boy he'd been back in the Coop. Except, underlying the confidence, she could hear a clear note of menace that had never been a part of his child self.

"Have you eaten?" she asked.

He shook his head. "Not yet."

"Come on." She led him to the kitchen, where she inserted two flat cartons containing breakfast readymeals into the narrow opening of the microwave embedded in her wall. Within minutes, they were ready, and she set one down in front of Jaxon at the table.

"I don't like being kept in the dark," he said. "If the Controller knows me, or knows who my father is, why doesn't he just say?"

Reese pondered for a moment as she peeled back the lid of her meal and removed the attached plastic fork. "There must be something we're not aware of. Some plan he hasn't put into motion yet. But we know he tortured Dani's brother and other sixers, and that his men exterminated ten thousand people from Colony 6."

"He answers to the Director," Jaxon said. "And maybe they didn't know what else to do in the beginning. Maybe they didn't yet have the cure." Then as quickly, he added, "Not trying to defend him or anything."

Reese understood the urge. She'd wanted to excuse her own father for ripping her life apart. But for some things there were just no excuses.

Reese gazed at the holograph of the land outside the hovercraft, created by the T-link she wore over her eyes. They'd long ago left behind everything she was familiar with and were now more than halfway to Newcali, heading toward the valley pass that would lead them to a filling station in an abandoned city called Gila, where they would refuel. Their journey had taken them dangerously close to the southern tip of the North Desolation Zone. The hover was adequately shielded, but skirting around radiation areas helped Dani's people preserve the life of their machines.

The empty zone stretched out in all directions around the hover, as if Reese sat on top of the vehicle instead of inside it. The area was completely abandoned, having been destroyed by the bombing during Breakdown and being too close to the desolation zones for rebuilding. During the first few hours of their trip, the emptiness had given Reese hope for new growth, but now the half-buried steel girders and chunks of concrete only reminded her of what humanity had lost. How many people had been buried in their cities? Too many to count, with no one left to really mourn them.

For a time, they'd followed the remains of the sky train line, but it had disappeared along with everything else. Dani had told her there were numerous sky train sections still intact throughout the empty zones and the desolation zones, but the expanse between them was too vast for her people to repair.

Hovercraft could travel at one hundred and ninety kilometers an hour, similar to the high-speed sky trains, which exceeded the speed of the best enforcer shuttles by at least twenty kilometers. The hover could sustain that speed over unpaved terrain as long as it wasn't vastly uneven. They did have to slow to a crawl over the rougher areas, and in some cases, they searched for an alternate route. If they could have gone at full speed, they would have arrived in Newport, Newcali's capital, in under eleven hours, but Dani estimated it would take them between fourteen and sixteen, depending on whether Dani drove herself or used autopilot, which always took longer. Even when the hover went slow, hovering about two meters over the earth, it was far better than a shuttle, whose tires never would have held up.

Another ruined city was coming up on the north as they neared the pass, too close to the North Desolation Zone to sustain life. Once, the city must have been huge; now, piles of rubble loomed like mountains. Unable to bear witnessing more destruction, Reese pulled off the T-link and folded it into her pocket next to her deactivated iTeev.

She looked around the interior of the hover, realizing with surprise that seating had changed while she'd been occupied with the exterior. With two three-seat rows of front-facing seats and one rear-facing row, the windowless main cabin had felt crowded when the trip began but was less claustrophobic after someone had retracted the first front-facing row of seats into the roof and replaced them with a narrow table that rose from the floor.

Jaxon was in one of the three back seats opposite her, his T-link over his eyes, looking pensively at the same holo of the outside that had engrossed her. Next to him, on his left, was Thane. Eagle sprawled near the boy, taking up more than his share of the room with his tools and the 3D printer he never seemed to be without. The twins sat on Reese's right, opposite Eagle. Dani was at the controls in the cab-like alcove at the front of the hover. A small window showed a slice of the outside terrain, but she wore a helmet that, like their T-links, would enhance her view of the outside. As usual, she wore her light gray, Newcali soldier uniform that complimented her very black skin. Near her, across a small aisle, Hammer filled up the other front seat to overflowing with his muscled bulk. They were talking, but low enough that Reese couldn't make out what they were saying.

The four enforcers—Reese, Jaxon, Hammer, and Eagle—wore a variety of bulletproof civilian clothes instead of their uniforms. The men wore all black, as if they couldn't bear to be without something close to their customary uniforms, while

Reese had chosen a gray jumper design for its similarity to Dani's cement-colored Newcali soldier uniform. If they ran into trouble, Dani's soldiers might think twice before shooting in her direction.

"Ha, it works!" Eagle crowed triumphantly.

"You sure?" Lyra said. "Where is she then?"

It took a moment for Reese to realize they were talking about Lyssa, who lay slumped over the table with her head on her crossed arms. Like Lyra, she wore black pants and a bright blue, long-sleeved shirt that played up their alikeness. In CORE Territories that always unsettled people, as current birth orders never allowed twin births, and maybe they thought it would confuse the Newcalians as well. Lyssa appeared to be sleeping, but Reese decided from the context of the conversation that she was traveling. But to where?

"She's sitting on the table in front of Jaxon," Eagle said without hesitation. "With her knees curled up to her chest. No, now she's standing and her legs are cut off where they disappear under the table."

"What is she saying?"

"Saying?" Eagle asked. "I can see her mouth moving, but I can't make out words. Her whole head is a ball of light."

Lyra shook her head. "I meant with the Handspeak Dani uses with her brother."

It was a great idea. They'd been so impressed with how the language had helped them in Estlantic that they'd all learned the basics.

"Oh, that." Eagle concentrated. "Lyssa, you need to hold your hand away from your body so it doesn't mix in with the rest of you. Okay, now I see it. She's saying, 'You see me.' Well, it's not so much seeing you as it is your energy, but yep, I do."

As if on cue, Lyssa raised her head. "That's fantastic."

"It might become even clearer once I adjust a few more

settings, but I don't think I'll ever be able to see skin or hair or clothes like you do because you're not really there. You must have some mental link as well. Anyway, I could see the shapes you made with your hands, though they tended to run together. That's the part I might be able to tinker with."

"Couldn't you adjust your glasses to help you hear?" Lyra asked.

He shook his head. "I see all forms of light and energy, which helps me diagram and judge distance, velocity, depth, weight, and such, but I can't see sound. I mean, I can sometimes detect the waves, but my ability doesn't translate them into images for me like it does with other light." He frowned. "I'd need another device altogether. I'm just not sure what kind."

"It's amazing you can do that much," Reese said.

Eagle's hand slapped down on the table. "That's right. We should learn more terms. We can practice now. Not much else to do."

Thane's eyes were curious, and Reese thought it was because of the Handspeak, but the boy's next words surprised her. "You can see so much," he said to Eagle, "but what about the sunset, or a flower?"

Reese had wondered the same thing but had never dared ask.

Eagle gave them a slow smile. "Take what you see and multiply that by a dozen other colors. No, I can no longer see what you do, but I wouldn't give up what I have now. It's like having another sense. I see so much more."

Reese understood in part what he meant because she'd grown accustomed to seeing sketches from other people's minds, but for her it wasn't a continuous process, and it never happened when she was alone.

"Nice," Thane said, nodding in satisfaction.

"While we're asking weird questions," Eagle countered.

"What about you? Has dying changed anything?"

Thane shrugged. "I don't really remember it. I don't feel slow or anything, if that's what you're asking, and my dad says I seem normal." He paused before adding a bit more slowly, "I do sometimes have weird dreams, but I mostly don't remember them, either."

"Good," Eagle said. "Not about the dreams but the rest." It was a sentiment Reese knew all of them echoed.

"We'll be coming up on the filling station soon," Dani said. "I'd like you all to put on your T-links and help me look for anything out of the ordinary."

"What do you mean?" Reese asked, unease spreading through her.

Dani flipped up her visor, twisted around, and leaned over into the aisle between her and Hammer. "Just a precaution. We've already gone more than half the way, and we need to charge our fuel cells or we won't make it all the way to Newport." Her dark lips twisted humorously. "It would be different if there were somewhere near Amarillo City that we could drive the hover to and fill up."

Amid the ensuing chuckles, Reese asked, "What exactly are we looking for?"

Dani barked a laugh. "You'll know what I mean if you see it. I'm hoping we don't."

Okay, then.

"You're talking about the beasts, aren't you?" Thane asked, paling slightly. "The big ones."

Reese had seen the monsters, had fought them at the northern borders in Estlantic as a new academy graduate, but they hadn't been the really huge ones Eagle had told her he'd seen in the Santoni empty zone, the ones that could swallow a man in a single gulp, or cut through a body with a simple chomp.

"We call them cazadors," Dani replied without apparent concern. "But they're not the worst things out here." She turned back to her display.

Reese was relieved when less than ten minutes later, Dani announced, "Welcome to Gila. At least that's what we call the place. It's just a ruined city now, like all the others, but it was the best location for the station."

She slowed the hover, curving around a ruined building where a small but state-of-the-art refueling station appeared like a mirage. The fat hydrogen tank was at least double the height of a man and was anchored in place by three curved, vertical columns of metal. The metal anchors were nearly a half meter thick, and six bands of thinner metal encircled both the columns and the tank, spaced evenly along the height.

Eagle whistled. "You don't want anything getting into that, do you?"

Dani brought the hover down in front of the tank with barely a jolt. "Yeah, we protect it really well. There's a lot of wind out here . . . and the cazadors. The actual fuel is underground." She removed her helmet, revealing a shock of short, white hair that stuck out from her head at seemingly random angles. Sliding from her seat, she moved into the main cabin, heading for the door.

"You can get out and stretch your legs," she said, setting her hand on the pad near the door, which instantly retracted into the hull of the hover. "Seven hours is a long time with no activity except a trip to the toilet."

Eagle pushed a control on the side of the shuttle, and the table retracted into the floor, leaving them more space to get to the door. "How long do we have?"

"Fueling won't take more than ten or fifteen minutes, tops," Dani said. "Once the fuel is in, we're leaving. It's not safe to be here long. In the meantime, keep a weapon handy, your T-links on, and at least one earbud in, so we can alert each other in case of a problem. We've taken great care to install T-link towers all along our usual routes, so communication shouldn't be a problem. If you see anything out of the ordinary, get back to the hover. If you can't get back safely—hide."

"What about radiation levels?" Thane asked warily.

Dani shrugged. "They're okay here, as long as the wind isn't blowing. Wouldn't want to live here though."

Reese followed the others out of the hover, her limbs stiff and aching from the long hours of inactivity. By the time she was on solid ground, Dani had already used her handprint to open a panel in the tank and was drawing out the fuel line. The others scattered, but Jaxon stayed near the hover.

"Something's off," he muttered. "It's the same feeling I had last night."

"What kind of feeling?" Reese eyed him with concern.

He shook his head and gave her a wry grin. "Not sure. Could be a precursor to a premonition. Makes me wonder how many I missed because of my treatment with Kentley."

Reese frowned. "Some things are better missed."

"Not if I should have had a premonition last night that would help us today. Or last week." He scanned the area uneasily. "Anyway, let's not go far."

"We'll keep our eyes open," she agreed.

Aside from the typical ruined buildings of an empty zone, Gila held an austere, untouched beauty. Scatterings of rare trees, brush, and grass filled the valley, indicating the presence of a stream, lake, or underground water source. After the recent cold spell in Amarillo City, Reese enjoyed the delicious warmth of the sun beating down on them. She and Jaxon wandered up a small hill where they found a tiny lake, ringed by more trees. Most of the trees were stunted,—as they always were in the empty zones—but that they were growing at all meant someday it might be livable here. Maybe it already was habitable a bit farther south.

"Think the water's safe?" Jaxon asked, pushing his T-Link up on his head for a better look.

A smile tugged at her lips. "Maybe, but we don't have time for a swim."

He chuckled. "I guess not."

A shout from below called their attention, and they hurried back down, drawing their weapons, only to see Thane waving his hands in front of a ruined building. Lyra also moved toward him, a crease on her brow, the blue of her bright blouse shining in the sunlight. When she saw their pistols, she awkwardly drew one of her own. While Brogan had insisted the twins be trained, Lyra hadn't progressed nearly as far as her sister, Lyssa.

"Look!" Thane called excitedly as they approached. He held up a coil of yellow, plastic-covered wire. "I found a bunch of this! Even this close to the refilling station. I bet there are rooms full of treasures here that haven't been scavenged. Do you think Dani could bring my people here? This far out, we'd be safe from Special Forces. At least for a time."

"It's too close to the desolation zone," Eagle said, appearing from behind a pile of rubble. In his hands, he also carried an electronic gadget he must have found in the wreckage.

"A little farther south then," Thane insisted.

Jaxon turned to Eagle. "Can you calculate how far they'd need to . . ." His words trailed off as the color drained from his face. Without further warning, he doubled over.

Reese immediately reached for him. "Jaxon! What do you see?" She recognized all too well the onslaught of one of his stronger premonitions.

She hadn't needed to ask. Already, she could see the sketch from his mind. Monsters were coming, beasts twice as large as the extinct elephants viewed now only on ancient Teev films. But these weren't anything like those animals. They were covered in long red fur and had mouths as large as a shuttle, and the sharpness and length of their white, pointed teeth seemed to be matched only by the black claws on their four feet. Or were they paws? Reese couldn't tell, but each foot was considerably longer than her arm.

With a few hand motions, Reese began transmitting on her T-link. "Dani, Jaxon is seeing some really nasty-looking beasts," she said. "I don't know if that means they're coming now. Or if it's a future event."

Dani's response was immediate. "Better get back here."

"How dangerous are they?" Lyra asked, her voice coming from both next to Reese and from Reese's wireless earbud.

"Dangerous enough," Dani said. "But what follows the cazadors is even worse. Get back here now. I think we have enough fuel to get us most of the way. I'll keep the line in until you make it back."

"Okay." Reese tugged at Jaxon. To Thane and Lyra, she added, "Help me with him."

"No!" Jaxon said. "It's too late."

His last words were nearly obliterated by a terrifying roar that seemed to slice into Reese's head. She gazed around but didn't see where the sound was coming from. At any second, she expected to see one of the beasts from Jaxon's premonition.

Jaxon convulsed again but this time didn't collapse. "We need cover," Jaxon gritted. "No time to get to the hover."

Thane whirled and started back into the building he'd just left. Jaxon leapt for him, grabbing his shoulder. "Not that one. It'll collapse."

Even as he spoke, another sketch appeared in Reese's mind of this very building stomped to rubble. "We need something that can withstand a lot of force," she said. "Eagle, help us!"

"There's nothing here, but I saw something back there that might work." Eagle motioned, and they began running.

Jaxon had shaken off the effects of the vision far more quickly than Reese expected, so she left him to guard the front of the group while she dropped to the rear. That was when she caught sight of the first gigantic beast, appearing behind the building where Thane had found the wire. It lumbered awkwardly around, lifting its head to bellow out something between a roar and a scream. The creature was followed by two more beasts that were every bit as massive.

"They're coming!" Reese shouted as she ran. "How much farther?"

Eagle's panting voice came through her earbud. "Not far."

"What's going on?" Dani's voice crackled with interference. "Do you see the cazadors? How many?"

"Three beasts on our tail," Reese said.

She glanced back over her shoulder to see that one of the creatures had stopped and was sniffing at the building. Its body was far too large for the jagged opening, but it reared up on two back legs and pounded its forepaws into the structure, which collapsed in a burst of debris and dust. The beast roared triumphantly as it clawed at the remains. Reese had the sinking feeling it was searching for food—for them.

The other two animals lumbered past the first beast, uttering more horrendous screams. They were surprisingly fast despite their awkward bulk, and within a few heartbeats, they were gaining on the humans. Reese paused to lay down cover fire. The cazadors halted momentarily, but then roared louder and sprang forward in a loping run toward her.

"There!" Eagle pointed. The building ahead was more ruined than the others, but an immense length of sky train girder had collapsed on top. "Even given their bulk, we should be safe under the girder," Eagle said. "That is, if we don't get squished by any debris they might send sideways when they try to crush us."

Reese had no time to answer. She'd used all the rounds in her magazine and was shoving in another—and pulling out her backup weapon. She thought longingly of her assault rifle, left back in the storage compartment of the hover. The bullets from her nine mil seemed to do little but slow and annoy the creatures.

"Only two, now," she reported. "Not sure where the other one went."

Jaxon was firing from behind her now, right outside the cave-like opening where the others were disappearing inside. Reese ran to catch up, diving into the hole after Lyra. She fired again with both her pistols as Jaxon scooted past her inside. They fired together for a few seconds, and then turned and hurried deeper into the building. The others were nowhere in sight, though it was difficult to see through the gloom.

A loud crash came from behind them, followed by a furious roar and a shower of debris. A chunk of something slammed into Reese's back. Breath whooshed from her, but she kept her footing.

"Here!" Eagle appeared in front of them, a glow of artificial light in his hand.

He disappeared to the right, and Reese plunged after him, hopping over debris. A short distance ahead, Thane and Lyra huddled in an alcove made by a huge girder. As big as the monsters were, Reese felt relief. They couldn't damage that length of steel, not even more than a century after its creation.

Reese activated her T-link, this time with the holo feature. "Dani, come in."

"I'm here." The interior of the hover came to life in front of her.

"As you can see, we're okay." Reese panned the area so Dani could see them all.

Dani's black face twisted in a scowl. "Wait. Lyssa and Hammer aren't with you?"

"They didn't make it back to the hover?" Reese's stomach clenched.

"They aren't here." Dani paused a moment. "Let me try to raise them." A few seconds ticked by. "Neither one is answering."

"Wouldn't we get at least a signal from their T-links?" Lyra asked.

"I'm getting a faint signal from Lyssa's T-Link, but nothing at all from Hammer's."

More screams from the beasts drowned out any response. The building around them shook thunderously, and clouds of dust billowed into their hiding place, but the metal remained solid.

Reese looked at Lyra. "You go find Lyssa," she said. "See if she needs help. We'll keep you safe."

Lyra nodded, her bottom lip caught between her teeth. She closed her eyes as another violent quake hit the building. This time the metal around them moved slightly, but Lyra didn't appear to notice. Maybe she was already traveling.

Reese remembered what Dani had said about something following the beasts. What could possibly be worse?

She had the feeling they were about to find out.

CHAPTER 7

Lyssa was sitting on a red boulder, basking in the warmth of the sun, when her T-link earbud flared to life with chatter. At Dani's order to return to the hover, she jumped to her feet and began running. The ensuing roars of the beasts and the panicked comments from her companions as they ran from the animals drove her even faster. Heeding Dani's earlier warning, Lyssa hadn't gone far from the hover, but each of her steps now seemed to take place in slow motion. She hoped she wouldn't trip. Now she regretted giving in to her need to be alone after being crammed for so long in the hover, thinking and worrying about Tamsin. And about Ty.

More screams reached her, sounding louder now. With a sudden start, she realized the sounds were no longer coming from the single earbud she was using but from around her. She came to a halt, her chest heaving. Something was moving in the debris ahead. She slid her pistol from the concealed holster at her hip and pointed it ahead, finger close to the trigger, her muscles poised to run if the rumors about the beasts' size turned out to be true. But instead of a monster, Hammer came sprinting from around a chunk of broken concrete. Relief waved through her.

"Thank the CORE," Hammer murmured. Louder, he added, "I saw you go off this way and was worried. Come on. Let's get back to the hover."

Had he been checking up on her? Probably. She told herself that he'd be equally worried about any of the rest of the crew, but it seemed odd that when people had started away from the hover, he'd chosen the same direction she had.

"I can hear them," she said, her breath still labored.

"Yeah, but we'll beat them to the hover."

She'd started to smile at his confidence when a creature as tall as Hammer and four times his bulk appeared behind him. *A cazador,* she thought. The beast was a pale reddish color, like the boulder she'd been basking on. Black eyes glittered under the matted fur on the creature's misshapen head. Its mouth was a huge maw, stretching wide and lined with jagged teeth. The cazador wasn't nearly as large as Lyssa expected, but far, far more terrifying. It reared up on its hind legs, angling down on Hammer, as if to take off his head with a single gulp.

Lyssa stepped to the side to get a little better view and fired. Once, twice, three times. The shots hurt her ears and echoed through the valley. Still, the creature barely staggered backward. Hammer whirled, bringing up his own gun. The cazador was coming forward again. He fired two shots at its chest. No effect. Lyssa shot twice more, and then again as Hammer continued firing. The creature howled its ghostly cry but still lumbered forward. Then Lyssa understood. Whatever this monster was, it was bulletproof. She stepped backward, firing until her bullets were gone. As she checked for another magazine, she tripped on a weed growing in the rubble. Her T-link and earbud went flying as her head hit the ground hard. Dazedly, she forced in the magazine and came to her knees.

Hammer was still firing as he retreated toward her. The beast fell to all fours and leapt after him. No way could they outrun it. Not for long. Unless . . . unless she could find a way to get past that hide. Maybe the eyes. Still kneeling, she took careful aim, all too aware that the monster was a mere leap away from Hammer. She pulled the trigger.

At first she thought she'd missed, and that she'd be forced to watch Hammer die. Then red ichor welled from its eye, and the beast's steps slowed and stopped. Screaming in outrage, it toppled over, twitching so violently, one of its legs hit Hammer. He flew past Lyssa, but she didn't dare take her eyes from the creature to see if he was all right. Her hand was shaking now, but she knew she needed to get close enough to make sure the beast wasn't getting up. She forced herself to her feet and took a step.

A hand fell on her shoulder. "I'll do it."

Lyssa nearly collapsed with relief. Hammer strode forward, limping slightly. He came within three feet of the cazador, carefully avoiding its thrashing limbs. He fired three more shots at the creature's eye. At last, it lay still.

He turned and hurried to join Lyssa. "Tough little pus bag," he muttered. "Thanks for having my back."

"Thank Eagle. He's the one who taught me to shoot."

"Yeah," Hammer said. "He says you're a natural."

Lyssa hadn't believed it before today, but maybe it was true. She bent down to recover her T-Link, but it didn't register a signal. Folding it, she shoved it into her pocket. Her earbud was nowhere in sight.

Hammer's hand went to his head, presumably to check for his T-Link, but the device was gone. He glanced toward the beast. "I think it fell off when he hit me. We don't have time to look for it. Not if there are more of those around."

They gave the creature a wide berth as they continued forward. They were about to round a building when more screams cut through the air. Horrendous, unnatural screams that seemed to tear something inside Lyssa.

Hammer reached out to her and held her back. "Wait," he said. Hugging the building, he scooted to the edge and peered around it. What he saw froze him in place.

"What is it?" she asked.

When he didn't reply, she crept next to him and tried to see around his bulk. He shook his head, made her back up, and traded places. More screaming curdled her blood.

She peeked around the building and saw what had shocked him. There in the clearing between mounds of rubble was a beast that was taller and more massive than any creature she'd ever seen, even on the ancient Teev films. The cazador made the smaller one they'd faced look like a baby in comparison. But like the smaller one they'd killed, it was covered in red fur, though two shades darker. Its teeth and claws each had to be longer than the span of Hammer's huge hand.

The cazador screamed again, only to be answered by other screams. What was it she'd heard Reese say before? That there were three beasts? She didn't know if that meant three plus the little one they'd found, or four altogether. Maybe there was an entire herd.

Terror filled Lyssa. Stark, mind-numbing terror that threatened to turn her legs to puddles of useless jelly. *I'll never get to teach Tamsin about traveling,* she thought. *I'll never get to tell her the truth.*

Hammer pointed at something, and it took long seconds before Lyssa's frozen mind understood what she was seeing. A dozen small humans stood in front of the monster, each with a long, jagged spear. As the cazador opened its huge maw, they jabbed the spears inside. Two of the fringers also shot arrows into the beast's mouth. The cazador screamed in obvious pain and flipped its head up. Two of the people, still clinging to spears embedded in the creature's mouth, went flying into the air. One landed in the monster's mouth and disappeared in a crunch of bone and spray of blood. The other fringers shouted at each other, though Lyssa didn't understand any of the words.

The cazador came down for another bite of the remaining fringers, but this time, as the ready spears pierced its mouth, two more humans appeared near the monster's rear, spears tied to their bodies. The fringers scurried up the beast's furry legs to its back, and there they clung like miniature bronco riders as the humongous creature screamed and whipped its head up, trying to dislodge the spears from its mouth. Three spears remained, but the humans holding them let go, falling to the earth before the beast could flip them away. Landing on the rubble in a crouch, they missed being stomped to death by centimeters before scurrying back out of reach. The fringers on the creature's back stubbornly held on.

"Are they crazy?" Lyssa yelled at Hammer over the din.

"I don't know if they're even human," he said. "And I'm pretty sure those are radiation sores on their skin."

She looked closer. While their general appearance was humanoid, a few had extra appendages. Their bodies were twisted, their faces asymmetrical, as if someone had flattened their faces and twisted the resulting mess. Their bare, skinny limbs were too long, their foreheads pointed. Open, pus-oozing sores covered their exposed skin. What little clothing they wore were either dirty rags or woven from red fur.

"Radiation-crazed fringers," she murmured. This was what the Elite showed residents of the CORE, especially when they talked about lumpers—the term for people stupid enough to wander close to the desolation zone and be captured by fringers. This was why most people were so afraid of fringers.

These were the true fringers, not those in the CORE who lived in the empty zones. Not the Newcalians.

The fringers divided and retreated, dancing around the beast, who whirled in anger. A huge paw came down on one unfortunate fringer. The monster sucked up the broken body in a blink and continued the chase.

They're all going to die, Lyssa thought. *Then it'll come for us.*

She pushed at Hammer, urging him away, but he stared over her head, his eyes fixed on the beast. Following his gaze, she saw that the two fringers on the back of the cazador had climbed near the base of the misshapen head and were holding their spears. As Lyssa stared, each put one hand onto a single spear and plunged it into the monster. This was followed, lightning fast, by the second spear.

Without so much as a whimper, the cazador stumbled and fell to its knees. The huge head crashed to the ground. The body convulsed twice, nearly dislodging the fringers on its back. Then the creature lay still. The scattered fringers cheered.

"Now what?" Lyssa muttered.

"My guess is they eat it," Hammer said. "Or take as much of it as they can before other beasts come to eat it."

"There's at least one more." Lyssa glanced around her warily.

"Yeah, let's get back to the hover. We'll have to go another way, though. The last thing we need is to get caught up with those, uh, people."

Lyssa agreed completely.

They went back the way they had come, wandering through the ruins. Another inhuman scream pierced the air somewhere to the east, but it was far enough away that Lyssa was beginning to hope they'd get to the hover without further incident. Had the others also made it? What about Lyra? She was tempted to travel to her sister but doing so while running wasn't exactly smart. She was currently vaulting over crushed and broken concrete, pieces of worn and shattered wood, and metal of all sizes. That was mostly what remained in the eighty years since Breakdown, at least out in the open like this. She rounded another building that would put them on the homestretch.

All at once, three fringers with spears rose up in front of them. Lyssa stopped short, pulling her gun. Hammer bumped into her, causing her to stumble before regaining her balance. The fringers were even shorter than Lyssa, though two were as wide and muscled as Hammer. Their twisted faces were hideous, each different from the others—a caricature of a normal person. The smell they emitted from their unwashed clothing and bodies made her want to gag. At this close distance, she could see the ends of their spears, which seemed to be made of salvaged metal, pounded thin and shaped into wicked points.

Hammer turned his back to hers. "They're behind us too."

She risked a glance and saw six more fringers, who quickly spread out around them, spears pointed in their direction. "I don't have more than a few rounds left," she said, grateful for his comforting bulk against her back. "Maybe three."

"I have about the same. But I'd rather not kill them. They probably have families."

This surprised Lyssa. In morning training sessions, he wasn't one to show mercy, and he'd once broken his own hand to help the crew get away from Special Forces. He was also skilled with weapons, so she'd assumed he'd think to shoot first and ask questions later. Instead, she was the one advocating killing these twisted-faced humans. Maybe that was why Hammer was a crime scene investigator and not a beat officer or a detective.

"If we shoot enough of them, we might get away, but maybe we should let this play out a bit," Hammer added. "They're obviously intelligent, at least to some extent."

"They don't seem to know what guns are," Lyssa said. "Or they're not afraid of them."

Before Hammer could respond, the fringers began talking among themselves. Lyssa could almost recognize words, but they were so changed and distorted that she couldn't be sure she understood at all. Something about fur. Perhaps.

One of the fringers in front of Lyssa removed a small tube from a pocket. He brought it swiftly to his mouth and blew. Something bounced off the vest she wore under her shirt, but the next dart jabbed into her neck. Swift numbness began spreading to her limbs. Her knees buckled. She turned as she fell, trying to warn Hammer, but he was falling with her. They landed in a heap, his ponytail under her cheek. It smelled fresh and clean and soft between her skin and the debris on the ground. She'd never guessed how soft his hair was. Then numbness took over and she felt nothing, not even the rock that had been digging into her side. She tried to look at the fringers, willed herself to pull the trigger, but her gun slipped from her useless fingers.

"Saca!" Hammer swore. Whatever else he said was unintelligible as numbness must have claimed his throat.

Lyssa was aware of hands on her, but she couldn't really feel their bony fingers. She couldn't move, not even to close her eyes.

"Lyssa?" It was Lyra's voice.

"Run!" Lyssa tried to shout, but all that came out was a grunt.

Lyra walked through one of the fringers grabbing Lyssa's arms. *She's traveling,* Lyssa thought with relief.

"Hold on," Lyra said. "We're pinned down by a couple beasts, but I can get Dani here. What did they do to you?"

This time not even a grunt came from Lyssa's throat, but she felt energy leave her body in a rush. Then all at once, she was standing by Lyra, which she would have thought impossible a few days ago, since Lyra's body wasn't anywhere close by.

Did that mean they could also travel to the location of the other one's energy? Or did it mean her body was so relaxed that she was able to go wherever she wanted?

"It was some kind of dart," she told Lyra. "A poison. Not sure if it'll kill us or if it's meant to hold us."

"I'll be right back," Lyra said. "I'll go talk with Dani."

"I'm going with you." Lyssa looked down at the bodies, hers and Hammer's. The fringers were carrying them now, dragging them back in the direction of the clearing where they'd killed the beast. "It's not like I can do anything here."

"Let's try it then." Lyra reached out her hand and clasped Lyssa's.

For the first time when traveling, Lyssa felt something solid, though it didn't feel like skin. It was warmth and safety. And love. She met Lyra's gaze and smiled. They started gliding along the rubble-strewn path, and Lyssa was surprised they hadn't snapped immediately to Lyra's body.

Lyra had the same thought. She pointed back at the disappearing fringers. "Look at us. We can't see either of our bodies, and yet we're traveling. You think it's because we're together?"

Lyssa had no answer. "I don't know, but we'll have to figure it out later. Even if we can walk back to where you are, I don't know the way, and there isn't a lot of time. Keep hold of my hand and let's concentrate on where you are now."

The next instant, they were back with Lyra's body, and Lyra was sitting up. "Fringers have Lyssa and Hammer," she said, words tumbling fast from her lips. "The kind of fringers we grew up hearing about. They've darted them with poison that makes them unable to move. But Lyssa can still travel. She's here with me, by the way."

Inhuman screaming shook the collapsed building where they stood, but Lyssa could see that the location had been chosen wisely.

"Dani," Reese said, "you get all that?"

Not wearing a T-link earbud on her physical body, Lyssa didn't hear Dani's response, and she gestured to Lyra to put Dani's transmission on speaker so she could hear. "Tell her we're a little southwest of the hover," Lyssa said. "Maybe a minute on foot."

Lyra repeated the information. "Can you fly to them? Maybe drive the fringers off? We're kind of pinned down until these monsters lose interest."

"Unfortunately, I've just been surrounded by a few dozen fringers myself," Dani said. "They've thrown a net of some kind over the hover, and a couple have climbed on top. I can break loose, but it's going to take a minute. We've had run-ins with these guys before, and they're very persistent. I might have to leave and fight my way through to you."

Lyssa didn't miss the tinge of excitement in Dani's voice. She knew if anyone could fight her way through fringers and cazadors, Dani could. Her sixer ability to utilize oxygen to enhance her physical prowess made her faster and stronger, and gave her more endurance than ten strong men.

"I'm not worried about them damaging the hover or getting inside," Dani added after a slight pause. "They don't have the right tools or knowledge. But they are completely capable of hurting Lyssa and Hammer. Last time some of my soldiers were captured, they sacrificed them to the cazadors. They worship them."

"But I just saw them kill one," Lyssa protested. She recounted the story and waited impatiently for Lyra to tell Dani.

"Yeah, it's a strange sort of worship." Even over the comm,

Dani's voice dripped irony. "They kill one when they need food, but they sacrifice their weak and aging to the beasts. Fortunately, the beasts prefer live prey, so we may have time."

"It's amazing they figured out how to kill one," Reese said. "The beasts were barely fazed by our guns."

Dani snorted. "They may be backwards and stupid, but they've survived. You do what you have to. The cazadors' weak spots are their eyes and the base of their skulls."

"The eyes, huh?" Reese said. "Jaxon and I can do that."

"Actually, I think they're leaving." Jaxon stood and started over the rubble. "Don't they sound more distant? And they haven't hit the building for at least a minute."

Eagle cocked his head. "Is that a horn of some type?"

"I hear it," Dani said. "Half of these people are leaving. I'm going to slip out and cut the ropes. I'll let you know when it's done. Oh, and shoot to kill if you have to. Don't bother with a temper laser. They're all immune."

Lyssa felt a strange tugging sensation in her chest. "Something's happening."

"Go," Lyra said. "We'll be there as soon as we can."

Instantly, Lyssa returned to her body. She lifted her head to see that while she'd been gone, the fringers had tied her and Hammer to a steel girder buried in the earth, rising to at least a meter taller than Hammer. The numbness was leaving her body, so she could feel the coarse red ropes digging into her arms and stomach. No, not ropes but woven beast hair.

One of the fringers was blowing on a horn that looked suspiciously like a black claw from a beast, burnished to a high sheen. The sound that came out was loud and haunting. The squat, dark-skinned man with the claw was naked except for swirls of designs on his body and a fringe of matted red hair that hung around his waist. His stomach pushed out impossibly each time he sucked in air, like a grotesque balloon.

They weren't the only ones tied to the steel girder. A dead fringer, his body obviously broken in many places, was secured on Lyssa's other side. She guessed he had been killed earlier in the attack against the beast but somehow hadn't been chomped and swallowed.

In front of them lay the dead adult beast, and the stench of the monster this close was enough to make her eyes water. Dozens of fringers roamed over the enormous corpse, cutting and carrying armloads of meat to a growing pile next to the dead fringer. Others were slicing long sections of red fur from the animal's back and stuffing it into woven bags of the same red color.

"Welcome back," Hammer said, looking relieved. "Don't start worrying yet, but I think we're meant to be dinner. For the beasts, I mean."

Lyssa shuddered as a faraway roar punctuated his words. "Dani thinks so too."

Hammer's brow rose. "So you weren't knocked out."

She tried to shake her head, but pain shot through her, rippling down her spine. Now that she thought about it, every part of her body hurt, whether from falling or from being dragged, she didn't know. As she tried to shift to a more comfortable position, a group of fringers passed by with a dozen or so red, liquid-filled skins balanced on a hide carried between two poles. They cast uneasy glances at Lyssa and Hammer as they passed. No, not at them but at the space behind them, as if expecting something terrible to show up at any moment.

"Can you reach what I have in my hand?" Hammer asked. "I'm at the wrong angle to use it, but you might be able to. They took our guns, but they didn't find everything."

She strained toward him, expecting to feel the tip of a piece of metal he'd salvaged from the rubble when they were tying him, but instead she felt the tip of a heat laser. "You came prepared," she said.

"Always."

As she strained for the heat laser, the fringers with the skins stopped before the humongous pile of cazador meat and began pouring the contents of the skins over it, as if seasoning it for a feast. A pungent copper smell reached her nostrils. Another fringer poured liquid from a skin over the dead man.

"Is that—"

"Blood," Hammer confirmed. "But it didn't come from the cazador. They brought it in. My guess is that's an offering for the beasts. Maybe they aren't cannibalistic, so the fringers are trying to pass the meat off as human."

"You mean that's fringer blood?"

He made a face. "Or another animal. They put some earlier on these ropes. I don't think we have a lot of time. The fringers will probably leave and wait until the cazadors eat us before coming back to finish their harvest." His last words were nearly drowned by the scream of a beast.

Lyssa wriggled harder, pushing herself back and forth against the ropes until she felt a trickle of blood running down to her hand. She couldn't tell if the blood was hers or coming from the ropes. At last, she felt Hammer's laser in her fingers. "Got it. You can let go."

"It should burn the ropes, if you can focus it at the right angle," Hammer said. "Be careful—it'll burn flesh too."

Lyssa felt for the switch. "Maybe I should check and see what Lyra and the others are doing."

"I'm right here," said a voice beside her. "We're close, but I'm afraid the beasts are closer." Her sister's eyes showed panic.

"Just hurry," Lyssa said.

Lyra nodded. "Use the laser." She disappeared.

Lyssa had already turned the laser on, angling it for the rope securing Hammer's hand. He was their best bet to fighting their way free. Smoke began curling up between them, but like the hides themselves, the fur was tough. This was going to take a while.

They felt the beasts before they came into sight, their lumbering strides rippling through the ground like earthquakes. The fringers stopped what they were doing, scooped up armfuls of beast fur, and scattered, disappearing into various buildings or holes. Why the fur seemed to be more important than the food the beast's flesh represented, Lyssa didn't know.

The inhuman screams grew louder, and the pounding of the footsteps more pronounced. Hammer strained against the ropes while Lyssa tried to keep the laser aimed in the correct direction.

Hammer surged from the bindings as two beasts came into sight. They were of the large variety, like the one that lay dead in front of them. Lyssa had dropped the laser, but Hammer swept it up and aimed it at the ropes securing her. His muscles bunched as his free hand pulled at the bloody cords he was trying to cut.

Lyssa's gaze went to the beasts. She felt mesmerized by their sheer size. She tumbled forward as the rope broke, but Hammer pulled her to her feet, and they ran.

More screaming cut the air behind them.

Close behind them.

With a sinking feeling, Lyssa realized there was no way they would make it to cover.

CHAPTER 8

All at once, miraculously, the screaming stopped. Lyssa dared a glance around and saw that the monsters had paused in front of the mound of meat. With large, huffing mouthfuls, one began on the offering while the other crunched into the dead fringer before helping its companion finish off the cut meat.

All the eating had taken less than a minute, and now, with sickening roars, the beasts turned in their direction. Toward them, and not toward the carcass of the dead beast, so Hammer must have been right about the purpose of the blood. As they ran, Hammer swept up a spear one of the fringers had dropped.

"Go," he ordered. "Down that narrow alleyway. I'll stop at the entrance and distract them."

"Are you crazy?" she shouted. "You're not stopping!"

The monsters were now that much closer. Lyssa swept up a jagged piece of metal that was far too short for comfort, but she was going to stand with Hammer and go out fighting. She didn't let herself think of Tamsin.

As one, they stopped running and whirled to face the beasts. Lyssa's heart pounded wildly. They were so incredibly large. "We have to run," she said, gasping to drag air past the lump of fear in her throat. "It's our only chance."

Hammer nodded but didn't move. Neither did she.

The cazadors bellowed their horrendous screams, sending ice through her veins. But another sound cut through the unholy din, catching Lyssa's attention. Gunfire. Lyssa glanced behind her to see Reese, Jaxon, and Eagle laying down cover fire.

Behind them, Lyra motioned to her. "Hurry!" she shouted. "This way to the hover."

Lyssa caught Hammer's gaze. As one, they turned and ran.

"Remember," Jaxon was shouting to Reese and Eagle as they passed. "The eyes. Go for the eyes!"

More heart-wrenching screams as Lyssa pushed her sore body to go faster. Ahead of her, Lyra glided along instead of running. That told Lyssa she was traveling—and hopefully that meant she was already safe. Lyssa could see the hover waiting at the end of the narrow aisle, but the mounds of rubble were too tall and close together to let it through. Behind them, one of the beasts roared, and a huge crash told her it had fallen.

"Retreat!" Jaxon shouted. Lyssa glanced over her shoulder to see her team scurrying backwards, still firing at the remaining beast.

Ten meters before the hovercraft, six fringers appeared, stepping in front of Lyssa and Hammer and pointing with their spears. Two let off warning arrows.

Lyssa stumbled to a stop, but Lyra ran right through them and disappeared. Hammer blocked an arrow with his spear, cursing under his breath. Then, just as suddenly as they had appeared, the fringers began falling. Lyssa caught a glimpse of

Dani's grinning face as her fists slammed into them, moving too fast for the fringers to react.

Hammer actually chuckled. "Always wanted to see her in action."

"Get inside the hover," Dani ordered as the last fringer fell into an unconscious heap.

Reese, Eagle, and Jaxon had given up all pretense of shooting and were running toward them at a frantic clip. The remaining beast followed, its huge limbs scattering debris as it waded into the narrow space, forging a new, wider path. Eagle ducked as a chunk of concrete flew at his head.

Dani, not waiting to see if her orders were obeyed, grabbed a spear from a fallen fringer and ran toward Reese and the others, her figure almost blurred. She passed them, not heeding their shouts.

Reaching the hover, Lyssa paused at the door and watched in dreadful fascination as Dani sprinted toward the cazador. As its mouth came down to chomp her, she angled to the side and jumped nearly all the way up its foreleg, clinging to its fur. As the animal swung its head in confusion, Dani scurried up the rest of its leg and climbed onto its back, somehow holding on. There, she balanced a terrifying moment before shoving her spear deep into some vital spot only she could see. The beast went down hard, shaking the ground and sending Dani tumbling over its head. She landed on her feet at a run.

Obviously, this was something Dani had done many times before, which made sense since she was always crossing the empty zones to smuggle people and goods to Newcali.

Dani made it back to the hover at the same time as Jaxon, Reese, and Eagle. Lyssa dove inside before Eagle, breathing a sigh of relief when the others joined her and the door slid shut.

"Everyone here?" Dani demanded.

"Yes," Lyra answered from one of the front-facing seats as Lyssa sank into the seat beside her.

Dani vaulted into the pilot seat, pulling on her helmet. "Good, because here come the fringers. They're not going to be happy we killed their gods." Her voice now came from both the front and the internal speakers inside the main cabin.

The hover rose from the ground and turned around. Sure enough, fringers were popping up in front of the hover. Arrows and spears flew like rain, and some were stretching a rope across the way. Dani barreled through it before it was secure, and in seconds, the fringers were far behind them.

It still didn't make sense to Lyssa why it was okay for the fringers to kill the cazadors, but not them. "They'll have food for a while, at least," she said.

"And fur to make clothing to hide their scent," Dani agreed.

Hammer sighed. "So that's why they wanted the fur. And why they soaked the ropes they tied us with in blood."

"It's their blood," Dani told them. "They make their whole village cut their wrists and drip it into bladders before the hunt, which they mix with a plant that prevents coagulation. It's a whole night-long ritual. But whenever the beasts come, the fringers are always close behind, even if they aren't hunting. Between the beasts and the fringers, the fringers are far more dangerous—and not just because they kill all outsiders. Better get out the med kit and check our radiation levels. I'm guessing we're all going to need a few hypos."

"They live in the desolation zones?" Thane asked from the passenger-side seat next to Dani. The boy's face was flushed and excited.

"They go wherever the cazadors go," Dani told him, "and since food is growing scarce in the north, they're all migrating south. Just like in Estlantic."

"But how did the fringers end up in the desolation zones?" Lyssa asked. "We've met all kinds of fringers in the past few months, but these are the only ones who show signs of radiation mutations."

"As near as we can figure, this is what happened to the people who wouldn't comply with the Elite orders when the CORE was created," Dani said. "Those who didn't have property and wouldn't go into the colonies were driven into the desolation zones. Everyone expected them to die. Many did, but some survived and so did their descendants. These particular people, and those like them, weren't just changed by the radiation, they adapted to it. The only reason my people in Newcali aren't exactly like them is because they had a place that wasn't destroyed or made uninhabitable. And they were strong enough to fight the CORE's efforts to force them into the desolation zones."

Lyssa was about to ask Dani how many times she'd fought the beasts when her eyes fell on Hammer, who was seated on her left, his bulk taking up some of her space. Beads of sweat stood out on his brow, accentuated by the way his long black hair was still pulled into his customary ponytail. His jaw was clenched tight.

Her eyes ran over him, expecting to see blood. There wasn't any, but maybe the first smaller beast had caused internal damage when it tossed him around as if he weighed no more than a packaged readymeal. Then she saw his arm, the one that had been near the laser when she cut the rope. The flesh poking out of his long black sleeve was reddened and angry looking.

"Let me see your arm," she demanded.

Reluctantly, he held it out to her. "Might need a little burn cream."

Lyssa took his elbow and pulled the arm closer. "Can you move your fingers?" She touched the digits in question, but he nodded without moving them. "Well enough to pick up a spear, but I'd rather not move them if I don't have to."

"Big baby," she taunted, more through habit than anything else, but also because she was suddenly very aware of how close they were. How her knee brushed his leg, how her fingers tingled where they touched his. Usually, his muscled bulk made her uncomfortable, but at the moment, she felt anything but uncomfortable. She felt alive and safe, and . . .

Stop, she told herself. Aloud, she said, "Where's the med kit? I'll need something better than what I brought."

"In the compartment above the bathroom," Dani said over the comm. "The radiation hypos are in there too. Along with the meter to check if anyone needs the medication."

The bathroom was wedged between the front passenger seat and the rear-facing seat in the main cabin where Reese sat. She stood and dug into the compartment above the bathroom, wresting out a case. As Reese set the case on the table and pushed it over to Lyssa, her hands shook. Her face had that stressed expression that broadcasted her need to record the sketches she was seeing, sketches Lyssa bet came from all of them. She was about to comment on it when Jaxon shoved Reese's drawing pad into her hands with a hard stare. Reese nodded and sat back down, opening the pad.

"Only Hammer and Lyssa need the medication," Eagle said, cocking his head as if measuring the light emitting from them. "Both need pain meds too."

"Great," Hammer said.

"It's not that bad," Eagle assured him. "Your exposure wasn't long and it was only secondhand. The fringers don't create radiation, they just live in it. But we should test everyone with the monitor just in case. Dani was radiating some of the same light, but it's gone now. Probably because of her ability."

Hammer patiently endured both the pain and radiation

hypos, and the bandage Lyssa wrapped around his arm. "Should be all right tomorrow," she told him. "This cream has nanites."

"Only the best for my crew." Dani turned and gave them a smile.

Lyssa didn't know if she was talking about her soldiers who normally rode in the hover, or them, her Colony 6 crew. Dani cared about them, of course, but like with Brogan, Lyssa suspected her cause might be even more important than a few individuals.

"Thank you." Hammer's voice somehow glided over her skin like a caress.

"What about you?" Lyra asked. "You have blood on your arm."

Lyssa examined her arm. Under the blood, she could see scrapes, and bruises were already visible, but there were no deep cuts. "Not mine," she said. "Or not most of it."

Before she could ask for a cleansing cloth, Hammer was already reaching for her arm with his unbandaged one. He held her hand and slowly cleaned off the blood with one of the cloths, his touch so light that her arm barely hurt, though the pain meds might have helped with that. His circling motions were hypnotic and sensual. They were surrounded by their crew, yet it almost seemed as if they were alone. Blood rushed in her ears. Their eyes met and held. Too long to be a casual glance. Unbidden, she remembered the softness of his hair and the way it had felt on her cheek.

Then it was over, and he released her arm, tucking the cleansing cloth into the disposal unit on the wall next to him. All at once, she could hear the others again. Lyra was pointing to the blood stains crisscrossing Lyssa's shirt where the ropes had been tied, showing up on her blue shirt far more readily than Hammer's black one.

"Guess I need a shower," Lyssa said, wrinkling her nose. She could smell the blood now, even if the others couldn't. With it came the memory of the blood the fringers had poured over the freshly slaughtered meat—and that same meat as it was devoured by the beasts.

"The bathroom is equipped with a sonic cleansing unit," Dani told them. "It's not great, but it'll get off most of the blood."

Eagle retracted the table while Reese put the med kit away. Lyssa stiffly made her way to the cargo space behind the pilot's seat to retrieve a change of clothes, and then to the minuscule bathroom. As she ducked inside, she caught Hammer watching her. She found it difficult to look away.

Inside, she peeled off her clothes and waved on the holo-screen embedded in the wall, requesting her reflection. Her body was bruised, but she saw nothing that wouldn't heal on its own in a few days. Stuffing her dirty clothes into a plastic bag and then placing both her clean and dirty clothes in a side compartment, she turned on the sonic cleanser. The dirt and grime and blood slipped away, suctioned into the filters embedded in the walls. Dani was right that the unit wasn't strong, but at least she wouldn't stink for the rest of the journey. When the unit finished, she dressed, combed and braided her long hair, and left the bathroom.

As she put away her dirty clothes, Hammer passed her, with his own fresh clothes in hand.

Lyra gave Lyssa a smile as she walked back to the seats. "Better?" Lyra asked.

"Yes." Everything was always better in clean clothes.

"That reminds me," Lyra said to the others in a voice that was too quiet to carry to the front of the hover, as if she didn't want Dani and Thane to hear. Lyssa didn't know how well that would work, because with her helmet on, Dani had still been able to participate in earlier conversation.

Reese looked up from her drawing pad, her expression calmer, and Eagle and Jaxon let their conversation about the beasts slide to a halt. When Lyra had their attention, she continued, "Lyssa and I learned that we can both leave our bodies at the same time and travel together at least some distance. We're not sure how far we can go, but it might be a workaround to increase our range until we figure out how to go wherever we want."

Eagle was immediately interested. "You could try it now," he said.

Lyssa was about to agree when Lyra shook her head. "We already know our traveling range to each other isn't much over a hundred and fifty kilometers. At the speed we're going, I don't want to risk getting stuck too far away from our bodies. We could be snapped back once we've gone too far, but we don't know for sure that will happen. There may be that moment where we hold off too long. What if we can't make it back or find the hover? And we don't have the fuel to stop and go back."

"Right," Eagle said. "Later then. But this is a huge break-through because one of you doesn't have to be in danger for you both to go somewhere useful."

"Well, we only did it for a little while," Lyssa said. But she was also hopeful.

Lyssa closed her eyes and settled in, letting the conversation drift over her. Yet when Hammer emerged from the bathroom, she was instantly alert. His long hair was hanging free instead of in the ponytail. He looked strong and sexier than she would ever admit. Why was she thinking of him in this way? Was it because of how they'd nearly died? Because of how they'd fought the monsters and saved each other? That had to be it. Something between them had changed.

So where did that put her with Ty? But she knew the answer

to that. He was going to die, probably because of his connection to Kordell Corp.

Hammer settled back in his seat, smiling at her. "Amazing what a little cleaning can do."

Eagle stood and pulled some readymeals and a bag of his favorite pretzels from the storage compartment. "Food, anyone? I don't know about the rest of you, but I'm famished." He slid a meal into the narrow microwave slot above the storage unit.

Lyssa's stomach growled at the mention of food, and everyone laughed. The tension she'd felt between her and Hammer dissolved. "I do," she said. "In fact, I'd like two meals."

Somewhere along the rest of the journey, Lyssa drifted off to sleep. She awoke to find her head against Hammer's arm. Embarrassed, she righted herself and looked around. The others were putting on their T-links.

"What is it?" she asked, carefully not looking in Hammer's direction.

Lyra grinned. "We're here. Or almost. Dani just stopped at a fuel station on the outskirts of Newport, and now we're heading to their city administration building. They call it the Circle."

Excitement spread through Lyssa, and her embarrassment was instantly forgotten. This was the moment they'd been waiting for, ever since they realized that rumors of Newcali were true. Dani hadn't given them much information, not even population size, but she'd dropped plenty of hints that Newcali had greater technology, as it encouraged free-market science, unlike the CORE Elite, who kept a tight grip on advancements, picking and choosing only those that enhanced their agenda.

"My T-link isn't working," Lyssa said.

Hammer gave her another one, apparently also having found a new one for himself as well. Lyssa unfolded the screen and pulled it over her eyes, giving the hand signal to link to the outside. The world opened up around her. At first all she saw in the quickly fading light were the ruins of an empty zone, similar to any empty zone near the CORE, but slowly the ruins gave way to houses and apartments, all with the squarish bottoms and high-peaked roofs that had dominated pre-Breakdown architecture. This was similar to the CORE's larger cities, but every so often, a house would appear with a dome roof, the construction so foreign and striking that Lyssa stared. New construction in the CORE was basic, not beautiful, but these houses had been created with an eye for beauty. They had large windows that shone with interior light, asymmetrical angles, and trim of various colors that attracted the eye. These windows rose to opaque, crystal domes that sparkled in a blaze of glory in the twilight. A variety of grasses, trees, and flowers decorated the exterior grounds of all the buildings, both new and old, and plants adorned their fore-fronts and various balconies. Overhead, the familiar lines of a sky train arched across the sky, but the periodic supports had been accentuated by colorful trim and crystal domes, creating a trail of brilliant light that was more noticeable as true night enveloped the city.

Lyra's hand reached out to grip hers. Lyssa knew what it meant to her sister that the city existed and appeared so peaceful. It meant someday having her own child.

For a time, they saw no people, but as they neared the center of the city, cars and hovers shared the roadway, and people appeared on the sidewalks. Lampposts topped with miniature crystal domes lined the streets, vying with vehicle headlamps for the crew's attention. But nearly all transit stopped several kilometers away from their destination, giving way to people standing or walking on moving walkways.

Dani laughed at their astonishment. "We found plans for

these sidewalks in the empty zones south of here. At some technofirm. The company was destroyed like most of the rest during Breakdown, but the Teev drives were intact. We've had the tech for over a decade now, before I came here. In the middle of town, it's more practical than cars or hovers."

"Are all your cities like this?" Lyra asked.

"We all have the same technology," Dani said. "And we don't have work colonies, so everyone here pulls their own weight."

"What about your leaders?" Jaxon asked. "Who have we come to meet with? Can you give us more information now?"

"You'll be meeting with the Presidents' Circle," Dani said. "The Circle consists of five people who change every six years on a rotating basis. By popular vote. They can serve a total of two terms."

This was more information than Dani had ever given them about Newcali. Since Elite leaders were appointed for life or until they voluntarily retired, the concept of rotating leaders seemed impossible. The Elites always appointed other Elites, often from the same family. The crew began asking more questions, except Eagle, who was mumbling under his breath. To Lyssa, it sounded like counting.

"Here we are," Dani said as they approached a huge glittering dome that stood like a blazing beacon in the darkness. "This is the Circle." Unlike the domed roofs they had passed so far, the material of the Circle reached all the way to the ground. "During the early years of conflict with the CORE, we built this dome to house our administration office, our T-link servers, and our library database. This is where you'll be staying. I'll be here too, though normally, I'd be staying at my own place."

"Can't wait to see where you live," Lyra said.

Dani's hesitation was obvious. "Um, just to be clear, I'm

not sure how much you'll be allowed to see. The Presidents' Circle is very careful of outsiders coming from the CORE. We're aware that the Elite want this land, and any information getting back to them is a risk."

"We're not telling anyone anything," Reese protested. "Especially CORE Elite."

"I know that," Dani said, "but they don't. Give it a little time. Let's see how the discussion goes."

"There are a lot of empty zones between Newcali and Dallastar," Lyssa reminded them. "Why would the Elite come directly here? I'd think they'd want to repair the sky train line first so they'd have adequate transportation."

"Right," Jaxon agreed. "From an enforcement standpoint, they'd be at risk so far away from lines of support."

Dani didn't answer. Lyssa saw a movement in the dome ahead of them and watched as a gap opened to let them into a hover bay. They slowed further before flying to the end of a row of hovers and settling on the ground.

Dani stood from her seat, removed her helmet, and faced them. "Because," she said, "if the Elite built on our coast, they wouldn't need support. Our entire coastline is undamaged by radiation, and that means food and water and a lot more. That's why our ancestors fought so hard to keep this land and repel the Elite after Breakdown. And why we'll continue to fight them for as long as we're able."

"Maybe we can do that together," Eagle said, pulling off his T-link.

Dani gave him a cryptic smile. "I hope so."

As they started to remove their bags from the storage compartment, Dani spoke again. "You can take all your equipment, including your iTeevs, which can't connect to the feed here anyway, so they aren't an issue. But the weapons stay. I'll make sure you get them back."

"Are you serious?" Reese demanded, anger flushing her face.

"You're here to see our leaders," Dani said. "Do you really think they're going to let you in with weapons? Does El Cerebro allow newcomers to bring weapons into the subway? Of course not. This is my personal shuttle, and everything will be safe here. You have to trust me. If I think you're in danger, I will get you out."

For a moment, no one spoke, and then Jaxon pulled out his gun from the holster built into his clothing and set it on his seat. Lyssa wasn't surprised. He had never lost faith in Dani. "I trust you," he said. A second gun followed, and also a pile of extra magazines.

The others began removing their weapons, Lyssa included. Back in the Coop, Dani had saved their lives dozens of times, especially after Reese and Jaxon had left the colony. A lot had changed since then, but there wasn't really another choice, so Lyssa handed over her backup gun that was in her bag and the extra ammunition. Her main weapon was probably a play toy for some fringer child by now.

Dani set her palm on the panel, opening the door. "All right, let's go." She preceded them into the bay, pausing after everyone was out to shut the door after her. "Open only to my handprint," she told her onboard T-link. The panel by the door flashed a message that Lyssa couldn't read from her position.

Lyssa didn't have any expectations about their reception, except maybe a nice meal and a good night's sleep before meeting with the Presidents' Circle in the morning, but as they rounded the nose of the hover, her stomach twisted. Two dozen armed soldiers in light gray uniforms awaited them. The front half of the group were in a ready stance, their rifles in both hands, though pointed upward, while the second row quickly spread out to encircle the crew. A female soldier with close-cropped brown hair stepped forward and saluted Dani by stamping her foot on the cement with a snapping motion, her arms pointing downward, her hands in tight fists.

"Welcome back, General Balak," the woman said. "We trust your journey went well?"

Dani returned the salute. "Yes, thank you, Nara."

"Is this really necessary?" Jaxon asked, his gaze scanning the soldiers.

Ignoring him, Dani gave an order. "Search them and then accompany them to their quarters." To the crew, she added, "Don't resist."

Dani stalked off, leaving them surrounded.

CHAPTER 9

"**N**ot exactly the welcome we hoped for," Hammer said in the guest quarters.

Lyssa had to agree. They had been unceremoniously searched, as had their bags, with most of the time being spent on Eagle's equipment. Not one soldier had spoken to them, except to give orders during the search, during which they had confiscated Reese's hidden knife. Eventually, they'd been cleared and brought to these guest quarters. No, locked in them. Because the door definitely didn't open from the inside.

Eagle was already busy unpacking his equipment. "No listening devices," he announced after a few minutes. "I mean, as long as we keep their T-link feed off in here as well as the portable devices Dani gave us. Since the T-link is a sister device to the Teev and iTeev, we should assume that anything we say around it might be recorded."

"Nothing hard-wired?" Jaxon asked.

That provoked another search, which turned up negative.

"Well, so maybe things aren't as bad as they seem," Lyra said, settling on one of the two pale blue, synth-leather couches.

Blue seemed to be the theme for this common room, which was divided into two medium-sized areas, a sitting room and a kitchen. In the sitting area, a sky-blue carpet cushioned the middle section of the gray-blue, rock floor, the squat table in front of the couches was topped by the same gray-blue rock, and the image receptors on the wall depicted deep blue oceans and windswept beaches. The kitchen had more of the gray-blue rock, a built-in stovetop, an oven, and a refrigerator in all white with blue trim. The plastic form table and eight chairs had a slight blue cast. The room wasn't extravagant but comfortable.

"They took our weapons," Reese said, slumping onto the other couch and bringing out her drawing pad. She began sketching with short, violent strokes, while Jaxon kneaded her shoulders from behind.

"I'll print you a knife," Eagle said. "They didn't take my raw materials, and while they deleted some of the programs I've saved, they obviously didn't realize I can create another one in my mind and download it to my printer. I'll make you all knives."

"Dani knows that," Jaxon said.

No one responded.

Lyssa walked to what she'd thought was a window behind the grouping of couches, realizing as she approached that it was a holo. Whatever the area looked like outside, they didn't have access to it.

"Did anyone notice how few people there are in the city when we were passing through?" Eagle carried his printer and a block of printer plastic to the kitchen area. "I'll have to double check my numbers once they give us access to their database, but—"

"If they give us access," Reese said dryly.

Eagle nodded, his dark glasses giving him an impassive air. "If they give us access," he amended. "But on our way in, I was calculating the houses and apartments, versus the shopping and eating areas, the cars and hovers. Extrapolating from what I saw, if this is the middle of the city, as Dani indicated, I calculate that there aren't more than fifty thousand people here. And maybe only thirty."

"Fifty thousand is only the size of a colony," Jaxon said.

"Right." Eagle fell silent, his head slightly twitching in a way that told Lyssa he was looking at something only he could see, perhaps some 3D image in his brain. "Of course, just because it's their capital, doesn't mean it's their largest city."

Jaxon crossed over to the kitchen. "Maybe not."

"What does the size matter?" Lyssa asked. "We're here only to access their archives and pick their brains about how to change our government, right? Well, and to see if they have any tech they're willing to share."

"Because the smaller they are, the more danger the CORE represents to their autonomy," Hammer answered. "The Elite haven't been twiddling their thumbs for the past sixty years. They may not have hovers, but they have at least a few helicopters, and plenty of enforcers and weapons, including those stronger temper lasers. And they have ways to build more. All that gives us leverage because the people here may need us more than we need them. You heard what Dani said about the coastline. If they can't protect that, it'll be all over."

"That coastline and its resources is probably the only thing that has kept them strong enough to repel the Elite in the past," Lyssa added.

Nods all around, and then Hammer said, "I might be able to get into their system. Even if they don't allow it. Dani and I have worked together with codes she's provided to back doors into the Teev feed. I might be able to reverse the flow." He gave them a flat grin. "I'd have to turn it on first."

"Wouldn't that be seen as an attack?" Lyra said. "We're here to ask for help, not to challenge them."

Hammer met her gaze. "I won't be obvious. I can cover my tracks. I have practice at that."

"I think he should try," Jaxon said, a thin smile ghosting his lips. "After all, they're the ones who met us with armed guards. Are we finished saying anything we don't want them to hear?" When everyone agreed, he nodded at Hammer. "Do it, then. While you're working, the rest of us will take our things to whatever serves as a bedroom here."

A short investigation found a hallway that led to a narrow room where ten single beds lined one of the walls. Opposite them were built-in shelves to hold their belongings. The floor was marble, the same gray-blue swirl as in the main room. There seemed to be windows on the walls above the beds, but they were actually holos depicting more beach scenes.

"Kind of like the academy," Eagle said.

Reese slapped a mattress. "Actually, these aren't made of rocks like the ones at the academy."

"Guess we're not going to find any privacy here," Jaxon grumbled, bumping Reese's shoulder.

"Definitely not a luxury suite." Lyssa dropped her bag onto the bed next to the one Lyra had claimed.

Thane sat on the bed closest to the door. "This is nice," he murmured. "Of course, I'm probably not the best judge. I've been sleeping on the floor for weeks in the tunnels back home . . . I mean back in Santoni." He stopped talking and frowned at the small pack he'd brought, as if it had suddenly hit him that he was never going back to Santoni again.

Lyssa gave him a sympathetic smile and stepped close to her sister. "We should try traveling together."

Lyra nodded. "Maybe we can find Nova."

"Nova?" Thane perked up. "You think we'll see her tonight?"

Jaxon threw his bag onto one of the shelves. "Nova will be here soon," he said with certainty.

Lyssa arched a brow at him. He wasn't mopping the floor with his face, so it was probably a hunch and not a full premonition. "Good," she said into the expectant silence.

Further conversation was cut short when a doorbell sounded a series of light-hearted chimes. They were hurrying down the hall when Hammer appeared in the doorway to the main room. "Two workers are here setting up a meal in the kitchen. We'll have to move your equipment, Eagle. They brought a lot of food."

"Good. I'm hungry!" said Thane.

Lyssa followed him back to the main room, where a man and a woman in blue jumpsuits were taking covered dishes from a waist-high, multi-layered cart. Eagle cleared his equipment from the table as the workers spread a feast fit for a group of important Elite. They cast surreptitious glances at the crew as they removed the domed covers from the steaming food. The smell made Lyssa's mouth water.

"Thank you," Lyra said as the two workers finished.

The woman dipped her head low in a graceful bow. "Good appetite," she said.

They started to leave, but Reese blocked their retreat. "A friend of ours is here," she said. "Nova Cerebro. We'd like to see her. Tonight, if possible."

The man gave a small shrug and shook his head. "I'm sorry. We can't help you, but we will be happy to pass on your request."

"Do that please," Reese said icily. With a sigh, she hurried away and retrieved her drawing pad from the table. She was scary when she was angry, and Lyssa didn't envy the workers.

But it was possible she was less upset at the Newcalians than she was irritated at any sketches she might have received from them.

Lyssa sank down at the table to eat. Everything appeared freshly cooked. It was so foreign from the CORE readymeals or even her own meager attempts at cooking that she hardly knew where to start.

Thane didn't have that problem. He grabbed something resembling a roll with one hand, bringing it to his mouth, and with the other began scooping a heaping ladle of some kind of savory stew into the nearest bowl. Lyssa followed his lead. The rolls were slightly sweet and so soft they practically melted in her mouth. For a long time, they busied themselves eating. The many flavors were unusual and amazing, causing Lyssa to eat far more than normal. By the sated look on their faces and the near-empty dishes, the others felt the same.

At last, Thane climbed to his feet sluggishly. "If Nova's coming, I'm going to find a shower." He hurried out of the room as the others grinned after him.

"He's got the right idea," Reese said. "We could all use a shower."

"I'm just going to have one more piece of this tart," Jaxon said. "Want one?"

Lyssa left Reese and the men eating tarts and joined Lyra on the couch. "You ready?" Lyra asked.

"Let's do it?" Lyssa stifled a yawn. "If it's sleep or relaxation that fuels our gift, now's the perfect time."

Lyra looked at her sympathetically. "We can wait until morning."

Lyssa shook her head and squeezed her sister's hand. "The more we discover tonight, the more ammo we'll have for the discussions tomorrow."

They leaned back and closed their eyes. The transition

from their bodies to energy was instantaneous, and before she could take another breath, Lyssa stood looking down at their bodies. She was aware of her physical self and felt a strong tug as it called to her, but at the same time, all the weariness she'd felt drained away. Whatever effort it took to move her energy around, it was a lot better than dragging her actual physical body.

She also became aware of an equal pull to Lyra's physical body and a lesser one to the energy her sister was projecting. Was that how her energy always knew how to find Lyra? As identical twins, they were biologically the same, so it stood to reason that her energy would connect with either body.

"Let's give it a try," Lyssa said. She willed herself toward the door, not bothering to fake actual steps.

Lyra followed. "It's different than appearing where you are. Or walking along with your body."

The largest difference was that Lyssa had to think about the direction they were heading. She paused the briefest of seconds before walking through the door. So far, so good. They continued down the corridor that curved gently to the left in a continuous arc. They passed the occasional door, and after about a meter, a series of large windows looked out into a well-lit courtyard of lush trees and grasses, crisscrossed by cobblestone walkways. The design was simple, but the colorful stones, rows of bright flowers, and the healthy, luxurious green of the shrubbery made it appear magical. A man and a woman were together in the courtyard on a patch of short grass. The man sat while the woman lay on the grass, her head in his lap. They were both eating some kind of fruit, and with his free hand, he stroked her hair. Lyssa couldn't remember seeing anything so perfect and peaceful, except maybe Tamsin sleeping as a baby.

As if by unspoken consent, she and Lyra stopped to stare. The tug of their physical bodies was stronger now, but Lyssa still felt the lesser pull toward Lyra's energy, which seemed to prevent her from snapping back to the guest quarters. "It's working, I think. But it's getting harder to go forward."

Lyra nodded. "For me too."

"Maybe if we put ourselves at different ends of this building, we could walk between us."

"Maybe." Lyra thought a moment. "If they ever let us out of the room to try."

"They will. They want something from us, remember?"

They stood for a few minutes, and then without realizing that she was moving forward, Lyssa was through the wall in the courtyard. She took a deep breath—only to realize she couldn't smell anything. "Why can I see but not smell it?"

Lyra shrugged. "Maybe it's the same reason Eagle can see us but not hear us? We receive the visual signals but not the olfactory ones?"

"But we see and hear, even without physical eyes and ears, so somehow we transmit that information. Maybe it's more a matter of us never having needed to smell. Have you ever tried?" Lyssa took another deep breath—and was aware of her chest back on the couch expanding.

And all at once she smelled the perfume of the flowers, the woodiness of the tree bark, and the unidentifiable scent of green and growing things. Or rather, her body did back in the guest quarters, but it was really the same thing as being there. It smelled as perfect as it looked.

"Do you think the earth always used to be like this, with greenery and trees and flowers?" Lyra asked. "Before Breakdown, I mean. That's what I noticed most as we flew in—the plants. Even that refilling place in the empty zone had so much green. It's different than the occasional tree or the city gardens in the CORE." Her voice grew quiet. "Those are pretty to look at but far too valuable to touch."

"They must have an ample, uncontaminated water source here." Lyssa sighed. "If the Elite found out, it would make conquering Newcali that much more important."

A line of concern appeared between Lyra's brow. For long moments, they didn't speak, and then she said, "I told Kansas the truth about where we were going."

Lyssa stared at her. "I thought you didn't want to put him in danger."

"He's already in danger." Lyra's eyes glinted with anger. "If anyone knew what we've done . . ."

Shame washed over Lyssa. *My fault,* she thought. *It's all my fault.* "I'm sorry. I just meant with the rest."

Lyra's ire faded. "I'm not mad at you. You know I'd do what I did a million times over. I love you, and I love Tamsin. But I think . . . I think he's going to leave me when he finds out."

"Finds out what?"

"I'm pregnant."

The words slammed into Lyssa, sending her reeling. "H-how? You have an implant. Everyone has an implant."

"After we brought Dr. Kentley back, I asked him to take it out." The statement was matter-of-fact, but Lyssa knew her sister well enough to understand the painful decision behind the words. "And that's why I can't go back to Amarillo City," Lyra added. "I won't pass the next required physical."

"What about Kansas . . . and Tamsin?" *And me.* But Lyssa couldn't say this last bit.

Tears made wet tracks down her sister's face. "I don't know. I wasn't thinking that far ahead."

It was a huge admission that, despite the seriousness of their conversation, made Lyssa smile. "You, the planner, didn't think?"

Lyra's responding laugh held no real mirth. "From the moment you had Tamsin, I wanted her to be mine. No, that's not fair. I wanted my own baby. Kansas's child." She paused. "Now I'll have that, even if I lose him." The mask was off her pain now, the words raw with emotion.

"Never. He loves you." It was the one truth Lyssa knew. "Whatever is going on between you two, he'll always choose you." She reached out to clasp her sister's hand. "And so will I."

"If it doesn't work out that way," Lyra said, her free hand going to her abdomen, "Tamsin must come first. I understand that." Of course she did, which was why Lyssa knew her sister was willing to leave Kansas and Tamsin for her baby.

They walked a few more paces in the garden, and then Lyra said, "I haven't been outside yet, but the feeling is good here. It'll be a good place to raise my baby."

Lyssa couldn't consider leaving Lyra behind. Not now. "Let's go on." Lyssa turned resolutely back in the direction of the corridor and willed herself through the glass.

They continued forward, trying to ignore the increasing pull of their bodies. They checked inside a few doors they passed, finding only small offices with attached one-room living quarters that were obviously lived in but deserted at the moment. There was also a large kitchen, two meeting rooms, and a cafeteria. The few people they encountered went about their business of eating, talking, or watching holo films. In one room, three women supervised a dozen children of all ages.

"Look," Lyra whispered, pointing to a couch on the far side of the room. "It's Dani."

Lyssa looked to see Dani, still dressed in her uniform, nestled on a couch with two little boys whose skin was as black as hers. One had white hair like Dani, while the other had pale brown. For a long moment, Lyssa stared, watching her cuddle the boys, her contented expression unguarded.

"Do you think they're hers?" Lyra's expression was as surprised as Lyssa was feeling.

"Must be. Or maybe her brother's."

"How can they be hers?" Lyra asked. "How could she have let herself get captured in Estlantic knowing they were here waiting, even if it was to save her brother? What if the Controller had killed her?"

But Lyssa understood. It was the same reason she'd left Tamsin to come to Newcali. The same reason she and Lyra both risked working with the underground. "She's doing it for them," she said. "For their future."

Lyra frowned for a moment, looking ready to protest, but then she nodded. "Right. I guess I know that only too well."

"Dani!" a deep voice called, drawing Lyssa's attention again to the door where a tall man with skin nearly as dark as Dani's was entering. His hair was thick and dark, and his muscles bulged, but he wasn't a handsome man. The left side of his face was misshapen, with severe burn marks blotting the skin. More burn scars covered the whole of his left forearm and hand, and several fingers on his right hand were missing. He walked with a noted limp, as if the very act pained him.

"You're back," he said as Dani stood to greet him. His glad tone contrasted sharply with his rough appearance.

"I'm back," she agreed, hugging him. Dani wasn't exactly a beauty, either, but she was nothing if not compelling. She had good, well-formed features and a tall, strong figure that exuded power. Taken separately, Lyssa would never have put Dani with this ruined shell of a man, yet as he took her in his arms and their lips met in a fiery kiss, she seemed to belong in his embrace.

The two boys stood on top of the couch, clamoring for attention. One catapulted himself onto the back of the scarred man, as if his frightening visage was nothing out of the ordinary.

Lyra touched Lyssa's shoulder. "Come on. Let her have this privacy."

Lyssa suddenly felt like a voyeur. Nodding, she turned to go, still feeling stunned at the peek into Dani's private life.

In the hallway, neither she nor Lyra talked about what they'd seen. "That's odd," Lyra said, motioning a short way down the hall. "Are those two soldiers guarding that door? I wonder what's in there."

"Let's go see."

But they glided only half the way before Lyra came to a stop. "I can't seem to go farther." She sounded breathless.

"Me either. I can feel Dani, though," she said, tilting her head toward the room they'd just left. "Or at least I assume it's her."

"Yeah, it's only the faintest tug, though."

"At least it's something."

"Maybe." Lyra didn't seem too sure. "But right now—" She broke off as she disappeared.

Lyssa let the pull take her too. In less than a breath, she was back on the couch in the guest room, sitting up and blinking at her sister. The tears Lyra had shed while traveling were still drying on her cheeks.

Reese was sitting on the couch across from them, openly studying their faces. Eagle and Hammer were in the kitchen—Hammer at the holoscreen, and Eagle at his 3D printer.

"I was beginning to worry," Reese said, regarding Lyra's face solemnly. "Are you both okay?"

Lyssa nodded, though she felt far from okay. Lyra was illegally pregnant, Dani had a family she was hiding, and soldiers were guarding something in the building. "We managed to go some distance down the hallway."

"Find anything of interest?" Hammer shut down the holoscreen in the kitchen, stopped at the T-link controls in the wall briefly, and joined Reese on the couch. "Because I haven't managed to get past their firewall. And don't worry, I just disconnected the T-link feeds. No one's listening."

"What about Jaxon and Thane?" Lyssa asked. "Shouldn't we wait for them?"

Reese laughed. "Apparently, they have real water baths. Thane still hasn't come out of his, which is just as well, since we don't know how much we should tell him, and Jaxon's in the other. We can fill him in later."

Lyssa was about to recount their journey when a two-note chime sounded in the room. All eyes snapped to the already opening door. Half expecting Dani, Lyssa was surprised to see a familiar figure with curly, dark hair pulled partially back into a semi unruly mess that cascaded with abandon halfway down her back. Instead of her customary street-wise underground attire, the girl wore a casual, fitted, yellow sheath dress and matching sandals. Lyssa could almost smell the sea on her. She looked tanned and rested and had put on much needed weight. At least two kilos.

"Nova!" Lyssa exclaimed, coming to her feet and hurrying forward with Reese to the door. The gladness she felt at seeing the girl surprised her. On Nova's best days, the four-teen-year-old was sassy and belligerent, but she had also helped them in the past, showing uncanny bravery and resilience that somehow made up for her disobedience.

Nova grinned. "Yep, it's me." She gazed down with a self-conscious air, as if realizing how different she looked. "I came as soon as I got a text from Dani telling me you were here."

"Why haven't you returned to Amarillo City?" Reese shot a pointed glance at the soldier who had accompanied Nova. "Are they keeping you here?"

"No, they aren't." Nova stepped into the room, leaving

the soldier in the hall. When the door closed behind her, she continued, "I'm free to go whenever I want."

Reese's face flushed now. "Well," she said acidly. "Your uncle is going out of his mind. Did you ever think about what your decision to stay would do to him?"

A look of regret passed over the girl's face. "I'm sorry about that."

Reese nodded, some of the ire fading from her face. "Is this because of what happened to . . . back in Santoni?"

"No, of course not."

Did Nova's denial hold too much emphasis?

"Then why are you still here?" Lyssa asked, so Reese wouldn't have to. Reese was closer to Nova than the rest of them, and Nova generally showed her more respect than the others, which was key to taming her wild nature. It was a relationship Lyssa felt they should maintain, and she knew from personal experience how long kids could hold grudges.

Nova went over to the T-link controls in the wall by the adjoining kitchen, checking them before nodding in satisfaction. "Because they're hiding something," she said. "Something big that involves CORE Elite. I don't know what, but I couldn't leave until I knew. My uncle would want me to find out, wouldn't he?"

They all knew the answer to that. "Yes," Eagle answered for them, leaving his 3D printer on the kitchen table. "Tell us everything."

CHAPTER 10

Silence fell in the room, making Nova wish she could have told them in some other way. Or that maybe she should have led up to it more gradually. But here they were waiting expectantly for more, and she'd have to tell them everything. Why did her suspicions suddenly feel like nothing more than her gut instinct? It wasn't like she had any solid proof.

"When my uncle sent me here, he told me to keep my eyes open," she said, coming over to perch on the armrest of the couch where Reese was settling. "So, of course, I did."

"He shouldn't have sent you at all," Reese said, scowling. "That wasn't fair."

Nova lifted her chin. "I was glad to come. It's the least I could do with you all being in danger in Estlantic. And we needed the hover." She scanned their faces, noting suddenly that Jaxon wasn't among them. "I thought Jaxon was okay. Did he—?"

"He's fine," Reese said gently. "Thanks to you."

Nova was glad, even though she no longer had a crush on

the enforcer, who was too old and in love with Reese anyway. Besides, she didn't want anyone now. Not since Thane—

She broke off that train of thought before it could derail her. She waited until Eagle settled into a chair he'd brought from the kitchen table before continuing. "In the beginning, I was only collateral, so I stayed here at the Circle, mostly under the care of President Shala. I'm still living here, but now that I've told them I want to stay, they make me work in the kitchen or in the nursery to pay for my room. Anyway, I asked questions, hid around corners, listened in on their conversations, and searched their database. You know. I spied." Nova quit talking, realizing she was explaining too much, that it must appear she was trying to convince them. And they would be right.

She'd suspected all along that her uncle had sent her here more to cheer her up than for any secrets she could uncover. Knowing this, she hadn't bothered with any spying at all, but instead, she'd thrown herself into enjoying what Newcali had to offer, especially the long stretches of pristine beaches and the water full of marine life. She'd explored the inlets and rocky shores, picked up shells, and gathered shellfish to cook on a fire right there on the beach. She'd watched the seagulls winging across the incredibly blue sky, and played with the sand crabs and seaweed. The feel of the water on her body and being able to bask in the sun without questions or cameras scanning her CivID was nothing short of a miracle.

She'd tried not to think about how much Thane would have loved it.

She only had to avoid the beach on days that the long-distance buoys broadcasted radiation danger after a storm or on days of mysterious underwater current change, but the swimming prohibition never lasted long. Meanwhile, there were the miraculous moving sidewalks, public hovers, and markets full of everything imaginable, from culinary delights to salvaged art and tech.

For three lovely weeks, she put her uncle off and basked in the sun, but on one of the sea warning days two weeks ago, all that had changed. She had overheard President Shala talking with another Circle member about a trade with the CORE. Shala had also mentioned El Cerebro and sixer abilities, and the threatening intent of the words had sliced through her lethargy, and since then, she'd been actively doing what her uncle had expected of her all along.

"What makes you suspicious?" Lyssa asked now, gently pulling Nova back to the conversation at hand.

Today, Lyssa's voice held far more gentleness than was customary, and Nova stored that away for future thought. Of the twins, she had always thought of Lyssa as the hard one, the one who talked more and who had more guts. Maybe that was because she wasn't a mother yet, like Lyra, although something wasn't quite right about that either—some secret no one had let her in on yet because they never talked about the child around her. That wasn't a surprise. There was a lot El Cerebro and his top agents didn't talk about around her—and probably wouldn't again for a long time since she'd followed the sixer crew without permission on the last mission.

"Was it something in the database, or something someone said?" Lyssa pressed.

"I heard two of the Presidents' Circle talking about trading with the CORE," Nova said. "At least one person for sure is part of the Circle. They were both kind of excited and talking really fast. I didn't think anything of it at first, because they often talk fast when they're in council, but this time it was just the two of them. When they said something about a treaty with the CORE, I started paying more attention. They also talked about the Controller and Colony 6 and abilities. And my uncle." Nova frowned, angry at herself for having wasted those initial three weeks. "They said the word betray when they talked about him. That's when I knew it was serious."

"Who were the Circle members?" Reese turned her whole body toward Nova as she asked the question, bringing one of her knees partly up on the couch cushion.

"President Shala, I recognized her because of her voice, but I don't know about the other member." Nova sighed. "Might not be one of the presidents at all, now that I think about it."

"Man or woman?" This from Lyra.

Nova shook her head. "I couldn't tell. Their voices were too low. And I was somewhere I shouldn't be—in the Circle chambers—so I couldn't exactly step out and confront them. Besides, they know I'm El Cerebro's niece. If they knew I'd heard them, they probably would have locked me up or something."

"Maybe they were planning to keep you," Lyssa said. "And that's the betrayal."

Nova thought a moment. "I don't think so. I mean, they need people here. That's part of what they do—send missions out to rescue people who want to escape from the CORE. They even have a Teev site all set up that only certain people find. But they don't force people to stay."

"We know about the Teev site," Reese said. "We found it ourselves. That's how we reconnected with Dani in the first place."

They had known, and once again, no one had told her. When was her uncle ever going to treat her like an adult?

Nova decided to pretend it didn't bother her. "Then you probably know Dani's also rescuing people from the colonies and buying babies from them too. The Circle has a nursery here where they keep the babies before adopting them out. They want adults and older children more, but they'll take anyone who will come with them."

"It makes sense," Reese said. "They need people to be strong enough to fight against the CORE, if they come here."

"When they come here," Eagle corrected.

"They give the newcomers land in a city south of here called Beach City," Nova continued. "Or there's also another city farther away. Angels. There are houses and houses in those cities. Like our empty zones, only they're not destroyed. They're just empty. Like everyone simply left after Breakdown—or were taken away. And the cities aren't close to radiation zones, either, so they're safe."

No one said anything for a long time, but Lyssa and Lyra exchanged a subtle glance and a very brief mouthed conversation that no one else seemed to notice. Something else to remember and maybe ask about. Nova was tempted to add that she never wanted to return to Dallastar, even to make her uncle happy, but she didn't want to deal with their disappointment right now. There would be time for that later.

"Are there a lot of people here with abilities?" Reese asked. "Dani's been helping them escape Colony 6 for ten years now."

Nova shook her head. "That's the puzzling thing. I thought there would be a lot of them—and there are a lot of former colonists, including those from Colony 6, but no actual sixers. A few times they brought a couple people in that I thought were sixers because they were acting weird. But it's strange . . ." She wrinkled her nose. "I only saw them once and then never again. Even Dani's brother was only here for a day or so when he came back. He brought me a package from my uncle, but I don't know where he went after that. He just disappeared. Maybe to one of the other cities. Anyway, I couldn't exactly tell my uncle any of this," Nova concluded. "I don't have proof, and I don't know how to find out more information."

"You've done a great job." Reese smiled up at her and squeezed her arm.

After weeks of no physical human contact, the touch came as a shock, but not an unpleasant one, and the burden Nova had been carrying lifted. She wasn't alone in this anymore, and the fate of her uncle and the underground no longer rested with her. Maybe now she could go back to basking on the beach and forget about the underground altogether. Maybe she could still figure out a way not to go home.

That was the biggest secret of all. Because enjoying herself or spying wasn't her real reason for staying in Newcali. Staying away from those she loved was far, far more important, especially her uncle. Her mother had died when she was only a child, and she'd watched her father fade away from radiation sickness. Others from the underground had met abrupt deaths.

And Thane, of course.

She didn't pretend that she'd loved Thane. There hadn't been enough time for that. But he'd given her that first real kiss, and they had a shared past together in Santoni, back when her dad died. They might have also shared a future.

Not anymore. She was finished with all that. With caring. And she certainly wouldn't stand by and watch her uncle die.

"Do you have access to the T-link database?" Hammer asked. "You mentioned searching it."

"Yeah." Nova pushed off the armrest. "I can show you. When Dani returned with her brother, she gave me access. She said I should research the database for anything that might help. And I have been. They have a lot more history than we do. From before Breakdown, but after too, and the after is really different from ours. They claim there were a lot of protests about the colonies and that some people disappeared after they spoke out against it."

"They were right to be worried," Lyssa said quietly. Nods all around.

When no one said more, Hammer climbed to his feet.

"Show me, then. If I have your access, I can maybe dig in deeper."

Nova shook her head. "There isn't any more. Well, unless you're talking Circle business, maybe. Everyone in Newcali has access to the information library if they're in distance of the feed towers. Nothing is by special permission. I've collected a lengthy file on wars, and especially bloodless revolutions."

Reese arched a brow. "Did Dani tell you to look for that?"

"No, President Shala did. We've talked a lot about how to beat the Elite without killing everyone else. She thought maybe we'd get ideas from history."

"That's what your uncle was hoping," Reese said.

"Well, President Shala is a lot like him," Nova admitted. "I used to talk to her a lot until I realized she might be pumping me for information. But I promise I never said anything about the location of the underground or about any of you. I was careful about that." Her voice faltered a bit before she continued. "But I know President Shala suspects El Cerebro has contacts within law enforcement. She mentioned several times how easily he is able to control Dallastar, and especially Amarillo City."

Hammer snorted. "It hasn't been all that easy, but we do have a lot of sympathy in our division. He's handpicked most of the employees, even those not actively working with the underground."

"I'm sure you didn't tell her anything," Reese said. "You're good at keeping secrets. But please show Hammer what you've researched. It'll help."

"I don't think it will." Nova headed over to the T-link controls. "Because the only way it worked in the past—a bloodless revolution, I mean—was when a huge number of enforcers or people higher up with a lot of power staged a coup. If a large number of people with guns and power take over, they can do it without sacrificing people to win. My uncle may have people in enforcement helping him, but not nearly enough to go up against Special Forces."

Silence fell over the room. She could tell they wanted to protest but no one could think of anything to say. Finally, Reese nodded. "We could start with what we have, but it might take months or years to find enough enforcers. And I remember back in the academy thinking that so much of the training we went through was to weed out enforcers that might think differently. I was so grateful to be out of the Coop and able to use my gift without anyone knowing that I just played along."

Nova allowed herself a small smile. "I think it would take years too." No one else spoke, so she turned on the controls and showed Hammer how to get in to the T-link feed. She was showing him her files when a figure appeared in the doorway that led to the sleeping quarters.

The figure of a ghost. A very sleepy, flush-faced ghost with wet, uncombed black hair that hung in his dark eyes. With a horrified gasp, her breath caught in her throat and stayed there. Was she going crazy? How could Thane be here?

Somehow, Reese's hand was on her shoulder. "I meant to tell you before now, but he wanted to surprise you. He showed up in the subway in Amarillo City yesterday. We thought we'd bring him along, just in case we needed help convincing you to come home."

Nova heard Reese but didn't take her eyes from the figure in the doorway. The figure who had stopped short and was staring at her with a silly grin on his face. He was still thin and gangly. Had he really been that tall?

"Thane?" The word ripped from Nova's throat.

"It's me," he said.

She didn't move toward him, still not quite convinced.

He swiped his hand across his forehead, removing the hair

from his eyes. She remembered that motion. "You told me to come visit," he said. "Well, here I am."

She took a few steps toward him and stopped, barely feeling Reese's hand drop away. "So, they didn't use you for parts."

"I woke up before that happened. Thankfully."

She hurried toward him then, and he met her halfway in a brief, awkward hug that didn't begin to show how her heart was singing inside. He smelled fresh, not like the boy from her childhood that she'd become reacquainted with five weeks ago in the Santoni tunnels. He smelled far too good to have come back from the dead. But here he was.

No thanks to her.

She stepped back. "You were dead," she said with growing horror. "I told them to leave you behind in the empty zone." If Eagle had listened to her, Thane wouldn't be here now. Tears pricked her eyes, but she refused to let them fall.

Thane chuckled. "*I* would have left me. I don't blame you. I'm just glad to see you again." His voice lowered so only she could hear. "It's all I've thought about since I woke up."

A single tear trickled down her right cheek. Was it silly to be happy that she was clean and wearing nice clothes? That her hair was halfway tamed? She looked older than fourteen when she wasn't playing an urchin, which was good, since she'd lived a lifetime in those few short years.

He reached for her face but stopped at her expression that told him he'd better ignore the tear and her weakness. His grin grew just a bit wider. "We have some catching up to do," he said.

She nodded, but all the time she was thinking that Thane was a miracle, and if one miracle could happen, maybe there could be more. Maybe her uncle was right and the underground could win against the Elite.

Behind her, Lyssa cleared her throat, her arms folded over

her chest. "Nova, can you contact Dani? It's time we get some answers."

Nova's stomach clenched as it always did when she thought of Dani. The woman was frightening and also entirely awesome.

"I agree," Reese said. "If someone here is thinking of a treaty with the CORE, we're in big—"

A loud *thump!* in the hallway leading to the sleeping quarters cut off whatever Reese had been going to say. Nova hurried forward with the others and was surprised to see Enforcer Jaxon in the hallway, one hand braced on the wall for support, his torso bent slightly, his face drained of color. Like Thane, his dark hair was wet, but his was combed. When his eyes met Nova's, they were more startling blue than she remembered. Or maybe that was the resulting shock of whatever vision he'd just experienced.

Reese pushed past Nova but stopped before getting close, as if afraid of any sketch she might receive from him. "What is it?" she demanded urgently.

Nova also wanted to know, but her voice had frozen in a mouth that tasted like death.

Jaxon took a deep breath and straightened. "I think Kentley's influence has worn off. I've had two really strong premonitions since we arrived."

"We expected that," Reese said. "And after what happened today in the empty zone, it's probably a good thing."

Jaxon nodded, swallowing hard. "I know. But I can also feel the insanity returning."

The crew exchanged glances warily, and for a moment, Nova wondered what it was like to be a sixer. To have an ability that slowly led you to madness. She had never envied any ability before, until she'd met Dani.

"What did you see?" Lyssa asked into the silence. She was

using the hard, determined voice she normally used, and Nova was glad that someone could do it.

"In the first one, I was talking to one of the enforcers I know, Ekan Donnel. He was recently promoted to a team leader with Special Forces. He was in Amarillo City talking about killing fringers and about Queran, that sixer who heats things up. I sensed Donnel felt bad about some of what he was doing."

"Good," Eagle said. "It's about time some of them questioned their actions."

"I also saw the Controller," Jaxon went on, as if he hadn't heard Eagle. "And myself."

Everyone waited. There was more. A lot more. Jaxon's eyes told them that.

"I was telling him about the sixers and the underground," he continued, his voice thin and defeated. "Me. And I saw El Cerebro lying unconscious. I don't know why or how. Maybe it's connected to that weird invitation to join Special Forces, but somehow I betray El Cerebro. Maybe I betray you all."

Nova could barely believe the words. Jaxon wouldn't betray them, and yet his visions always came true. Even if a couple times there had been slight alterations, which could very well be caused by perception.

"What now?" Nova asked, managing to find her voice.

"Now," Lyssa said. "Jaxon tells it again to Reese, so she can get a sketch for us to see. Then, Nova, you need to call Dani."

CHAPTER 11

Early the next morning, Lyssa became aware that she hovered over a bed in an unfamiliar room. She stifled a yawn and started to look around—only to blink with shock as she realized she'd never seen this room before. Dani was in the bed curled up next to the misshapen man she'd been so happy to see last night. They weren't asleep but talking quietly. He leaned forward and kissed her nose in a gesture that was both sweet and intimate.

So unlike Dani.

Then Lyssa was back in the guest bed, her eyes open.

I found Dani again, she thought. And this time Lyra hadn't been with her. The tug toward Dani wasn't nearly what she felt toward Lyra or her own body, but it was still there. As she lay pondering, she realized there were other pulls weighing on her, coming from her team in the sleeping quarters, signals she couldn't exactly identify, except to know they were familiar. As she thought about them, they began to feel distinct somehow, each becoming someone she knew. She sat up, sleep fleeing—and the signals vanished. No matter how she concentrated, they didn't return.

Grabbing clothes from her bag, Lyssa left those who were still sleeping and quietly went to get dressed in the bathroom before making her way to the main room in the guest quarters. Despite Nova's call, Dani hadn't appeared last night, so they'd finally gone to bed. On one hand, Lyssa understood Dani's absence. She'd been away from home for weeks and would want to spend time with her family. There had been moments when Lyssa had also ignored work to spend time with Tamsin, but with Jaxon's strange vision and Nova's suspicions, Lyssa found herself irritated at the delay. There was more at stake here, and Dani knew that probably better than anyone else.

She found Hammer sleeping on the table in the small kitchen, his head resting on one outstretched arm, slicing through the still-live holoscreen in front of him. His black hair was loose, hanging far below his collar, and it glistened under the overhead light. He looked peaceful, his angular features softened by the beginnings of a beard.

She waved the holoscreen off, and Hammer awoke instantly, his hand going to the knife she knew he'd hidden in the folds of his black shirt. The 3D-printed knives Eagle had made for them last night weren't metal, but they were as strong as they could ever need. Lyssa felt better having one, even up against Newcali guns.

"Oh, hi," Hammer said, changing his motion so it appeared he was only rubbing his hand along his shirt.

"Anything new?" Her stomach rumbled, and before she remembered that they didn't use readymeals here, she started looking for a dispenser. When that failed, she looked around for the remains of last night's dinner, but at some point, workers must have cleared the food away. Too bad. She'd like some of the tart now.

"No," he said. "Nova's right. I've gone through all the information she's collected, and I'm coming up against a brick wall. We've been doing it all wrong. Instead of gathering people to the underground all these years, we should have been putting them in place as enforcers or in government. We should have been recruiting enforcers."

"That would be a lot of recruiting," Lyssa said. "With ten enforcement divisions in Estlantic and five in Dallastar, plus the six subdivisions in the colonies, that's an awful lot of enforcers."

"Right. Fourteen thousand, give or take. So even if we infiltrated different divisions and drew in all our current allies, including the KC, who we know has a hidden agenda, we'd need more people than we currently have to take the Director and Controller into custody, not to mention the Administrator and the Regulator, who probably also have their own set of guards."

"What does El Cerebro say?" Lyssa asked. By way of a backdoor to the Teev feed that Dani had put on their T-links, they could communicate with Brogan, but the messages would need to be short and encrypted in order to stay secret. Because they were supposed to be in Estlantic and not in another territory altogether, Brogan was also screening the messages sent to their personal accounts and forwarding anything that was timely or important.

"I sent him two messages late last night. I haven't checked for a reply." Hammer smiled sheepishly. "I guess I fell asleep."

She grinned. "You should have come to bed with the rest of us. The beds are actually quite comfortable."

"I wanted to see if I could find anything." The way he said it, she understood that he meant *break into* anything. "Besides, someone had to keep an eye on these two." He motioned toward the two couches where Nova and Thane sprawled separately. Nova was curled in a ball on her side, her face covered with her wild dark hair, while Thane lay on his back, one skinny arm thrown over his eyes and his mouth wide open. If they hadn't started out with blankets, someone had pulled one over each of them. Lyssa was betting it had been Hammer.

"She's still only a kid," he added, "and her uncle would never forgive me if I let someone take advantage of her."

Lyssa reached out to pat his shoulder, the mother in her grateful, while at the same time understanding that if Nova put her mind to something, no one except El Cerebro could stand in her way—and maybe not even him.

Hammer's gaze went to her hand, which somehow still lingered on his shoulder. The muscles in his jaw worked as his eyes traveled up to her face, pausing on her lips before meeting her eyes with an expression she couldn't misunderstand. A buzz of electric shock seemed to creep up the length of her arm, burying itself into her body and igniting something inside her that started to spread even more rapidly.

He hadn't changed from one day to the next. He hadn't suddenly grown smaller or less intimidating, but as she suspected before, things were completely different between them. His height and bulk didn't bother her. She didn't feel overwhelmed. Maybe it was their shared experience. Maybe she trusted him enough now that nothing else mattered.

Hammer tried to speak but gave a false start before words finally emerged, slightly hoarsened. "There's food in the fridge and the cupboards, by the way. It's mostly snack items they left last night when they cleaned up dinner. At least they aren't going to starve us."

Lyssa held her place for a moment more, not wanting to appear to be running away, but also not wanting the moment to end. The pressure built between them until she wondered who would explode first. Finally, after far too long, she nodded and stepped away.

Opening the refrigerator, she saw a pitcher of some kind of juice. Curious, she poured a glass and then cut a slice from the loaf of bread lying on the counter under a cloth. Her mouth watered. Besides last night, she hadn't eaten bread this fresh since her last restaurant dinner with Ty.

Ty. She hadn't thought of him much, not with everything that had happened, and now a flush of guilt followed the usual remorse she experienced whenever she remembered how he would die. To cover the emotion, she gulped the orange liquid in her glass. An unexpected flavor tantalized her taste buds.

"Mmm." She closed her eyes in near ecstasy. "It's orange juice. Real orange juice. Maybe even freshly squeezed." She'd had real oranges before, but they were extremely rare in the CORE, as most of the orange groves and places that could sustain them had been destroyed during Breakdown.

Hammer chuckled. "Never thought I'd see *that* expression on your face."

Lyssa's eyes whipped to his, her mouth falling slightly open in surprise. "Oh?" she asked, trying to hide the spurt of desire that filled her at the comment. She couldn't decide if he was flirting or being inappropriate. "And what expression is that?"

His teasing grin vanished, and his eyes fell to the table. "Um, nothing." He stood and rummaged in the cupboard for a glass. "I'd better taste it myself before you drink it all."

Lyssa frowned. It was just like a man not to say how he really felt. How was a woman ever to know where she stood?

Hammer gulped his juice, sighing with pleasure, and then poured them both some more. "Now, that expression," he said, glancing at her, his voice carefully nonchalant, "that's more what I'm used to."

"What are you trying to say?" she pressed.

"I'm saying, I know you're dating someone."

"Yeah, maybe." She really didn't know after Ty's offer the other night. "But you also know he's going to die."

Hammer nodded. "For what it's worth, I am sorry."

She knew he was.

"This is really good." He refilled her glass again.

"We should save some for the others," she said half-heartedly.

"No, we shouldn't. They should have gotten up earlier."

Silence fell between them, but it wasn't awkward as she would have expected after their previous comments. "I was traveling," she said after a time. "That's why I woke up."

He cocked his head to the side. "Oh?"

"I think I've made a break-through of sorts. Because of what Lyra and I learned to do yesterday. But it does seem to be relaxation that's the trigger."

Hammer rubbed the tiny hairs on his jaw thoughtfully. "Maybe try using a sleep-aid."

"Maybe. Not sure how I could report back if I ended up completely out."

He laughed. "There is that." After another minute of silence, he said, "I'd better check my messages."

"Me too." Lyssa didn't expect to see anything, but an encrypted message waited for her. Clicking into it, she found a text from Ty that was dated the day before.

Look, sorry about last night. I know you have your reasons for keeping me out. Maybe it won't always be that way. In regard to what we discussed, I'm calling in a few favors. No strings attached. See you when you get back.

Lyssa had to read the message three times before she understood that he was making a deal with the KC to help her with the birth order, and she couldn't stop him.

"Bad news?" Hammer asked.

She shook her head. "At least, I don't think so." If Ty was successful, Lyra might not have to stay behind in Newcali. Why then did Lyssa feel only dread? Maybe she should ask Jaxon to see if he could glimpse some new information about Ty.

They had finished the entire pitcher of juice by the time the other adults rolled out of bed. Fortunately, Dani showed up in her uniform shortly after, at seven, with two male kitchen workers, who pushed a trolley of foods that included two more pitchers of juice. Lyssa was too full to eat anything, but she pulled up a chair next to Dani, who apparently came to eat breakfast with them.

"You took your sweet time getting here," Hammer said after the workers had been dismissed.

Dani shrugged. "It was late. Everyone needed sleep." She scanned their faces as she took a bite of unidentifiable breakfast casserole. "Did something happen that required my presence sooner?"

Lyssa, the only one not eating, recounted Nova's story. When she finished, Dani carefully set down her fork, with a bit of food still attached. The movement was calculated and slow, as if Dani was forcing herself to be calm. That control was the only clue Lyssa had that Dani was worried. It was the calm before the storm. Lyssa recognized her reaction from their time together in the Coop, and it triggered a memory.

Once, when they were thirteen, three years after Jaxon and Reese had disappeared from the colony, the remaining crew had gathered on top of the water transfer station where they had been swimming, and Lyra had told them how the oldest Jammer brother had cornered her earlier in one of the hallways, threatening her with violence if she didn't join his crew and give them sexual favors. Things might have ended badly if the math teacher hadn't come along right then. Lyra was safe for the moment but worried about the future. Dani had listened intently from her perch, carefully restowed her things in her pack, and had left them without a word.

The next day, both Jammer brothers had come to school with bruises, black eyes, and a broken finger each. They claimed Dani had come with a crew to their room at night and hurt them, but no proof had been found except for a lone image from the outside camera of a blurred figure moving fast and averting its face. Lyssa had no doubt it was Dani, and for a long time, the Jammers hadn't even looked in their direction. It wasn't the first time Dani had saved them, and it was far from the last.

With measured strides, Dani walked to the couch and roused the still-sleeping Nova. Lyssa, Reese, and Hammer hurried after her, leaving the others at the table. Nova squinted up at Dani, coming awake quickly like most people who lived a life on the run in the underground. Across from her on the other couch, Thane did the same.

"Tell me exactly what you heard President Shala and the other person say," Dani said, sitting as Nova put her feet on the ground and came to a seated position.

Nova scrunched her eyebrows together. "They were talking really fast, but I'm sure I heard Shala say, 'A treaty with the CORE might sound good, but we would need assurances.' Then there was a lot of mumbling before one of them—I'm not sure who—said something about Colony 6 abilities and trading with the Controller. I think in exchange for something." Nova tucked the hair that had escaped the clip behind her ears, but it immediately popped free. "After that, the other person, not Shala, talked about El Cerebro. I didn't catch much, just low mumbling, but then Shala repeated his name and the word 'betray.' That's all I can tell you."

"Okay," Dani said. "Let's go through it again. See if you can remember which one talked about the Controller. Were their voices raised? Were they arguing? Was the second voice more like a woman or a man?"

Nova shook her head, recoiling. "I don't know more. That's it. Period. I'm not like you or other sixers. I don't have an ability, and it wasn't like I could hear that well up in the air shaft."

Thane coughed at that, casting an admiring stare her way. "You didn't say you were in an air shaft."

Nova shrugged. "I was trying to find a way out of the dome, just in case. I don't like not having a back door." Lyssa found herself nodding along with Thane. To Dani, Nova added, "I guess you already know, there's not one."

Dani's mouth twisted into an ironic smile. "At least not one for you." She looked over at Reese, who had settled on the couch next to Thane, her ever-present drawing pad open and a pencil in her hand. "Can you help? See what she saw?"

Reese shook her head. "She didn't *see* anything. She only heard. I can't sketch that." She paused long enough for Dani's nod and then continued, "But what could your people have that they could give the Controller in order for him to promise to stay away? Food? Land? Or do you think it was hypothetical? A discussion rather than a plan? Maybe there isn't anything to worry about."

Dani's lips pursed. "There is something. But I'm not supposed to tell you."

"Well, if your T-link feed has anything like our TAD-Alert, someone's listening," Lyssa said from where she stood behind the couch. "The T-link is still on."

Dani turned and stared up at her. "No one is listening. We don't have a TAD-Alert, and we don't have cameras everywhere. Our ID cards are carried, and they do not emit tracking signals. The Presidents of Newcali do not spy on their people."

"And you know that how?" Hammer asked, his tone more curious than challenging.

Dani stood so swiftly that Lyssa didn't see her move. "Because I'm one of them."

They all stared at her. "You mean, you're President Balak?" Lyra said from the table where she was still eating. "I thought you were a general."

"They call me general because I'm that too." Dani's brow creased. "And up until this moment, I trusted President Shala with my life—I trusted all of them with my life—but she has said nothing about this conversation, and that concerns me."

"That doesn't mean she's plotting behind your back," Lyssa reminded her, because Dani looked ready to explode. "Maybe she was brainstorming ideas. We've all done that before."

"Maybe," Dani said. "But what you don't know is that the CORE did approach us. They came in a helicopter and landed outside the range of our missiles that run all the way up and down the coast. When we met with them on the border, they asked to build a colony here on the sea. At first we considered it because of the trade possibilities. They promised they wouldn't interfere with our autonomy, but someone we have in their government let us know there would be a division built as well, with a thousand armed Special Forces. That's when we understood that if we allowed a colony to be built here, it would only be a matter of time before all of Newcali was part of the CORE."

Eagle rose from the table and pulled his T-link from his pocket. "By my calculations, you don't have more than fifty thousand people in Newport. And I'm guessing it's a lot less."

Dani grimaced. "That's right. Counting all three of our inhabited cities, we have just under fifty thousand people. Only thirty-two here. It's a good number for a growing population, but to withstand the advances of the CORE, we'll need more people. We encourage births, and we recruit fringers, colonists, and anyone we can from the CORE, but the Elite are on to that now. They've tightened security everywhere and are rounding up all the fringers they can."

"So that's why they're cleaning out the empty zones," Lyssa said.

Dani nodded. "I think so. Once that problem is taken care of, there are only two things standing in the way of their coming here."

"El Cerebro and the Dallastar underground?" Nova asked.

Dani regarded her without expression. "That's one. The other is Kordell Corp."

"The KC?" Reese spat. She looked ready to explode, but Lyssa understood why. After someone tries to kill you, you are allowed to hate them.

"Yes, the KC," Dani said with a frown. "Now that they've taken over the underground in Estlantic, they're a concern. They make the readymeals, which means they have a lot of power and money. They've even approached us about making meals for us at a severe discount in exchange for fishing and water rights. To know that much about us means they have someone planted in the Director's office as well."

"Of the two, the KC might be the lesser evil," Jaxon said from the table, ignoring the glare Reese cast in his direction.

Dani shook her head. "I disagree. We've tested the ready-meals they send to the colonies, and they're more plastic filler than real food. And the Elite have permitted them to add in all kinds of additives and mind-altering drugs. Have you ever considered how easy it would be for them to drug the entire territory? Newcali will not permit sole reliance on readymeals or allow a monopoly like that. We don't need them. We have plenty of food and water here. Maybe it was too dark when we got here for you to see all the green, but we rediscovered pre-Breakdown tech to desalinate water cheaply, so everyone can grow food. We aren't dependent on contaminated water coming from the North Desolation Zone."

"If the Elite know that," Lyssa said, "they'll be even more

anxious to come here. Clean water is always an issue in the CORE, especially in the colonies." As a child in Colony 6, several times they'd gone without any water except whatever skins were handed out at school.

"What you're saying is that even if we find a way to change CORE leadership, we'll have to deal with the KC," Reese said to Dani, but she was looking at Jaxon as if to make a point.

Dani nodded. "Whatever choices we make about how this revolution takes place, we can't position the KC to seize power. Currently, the KC gets all of their food and the fillers directly from the colonies, but it's the CORE that the KC pays for the goods, not the colonies themselves. The KC then manufactures the readymeals, which they sell back to the CORE and to the rest of society at a huge profit. All the colonists get are substandard readymeals, their tiny houses, and a few credits to spend on sauce or clothing. Once we overcome the Elite and the colonies can trade with CORE restaurants and manufacturers directly, that will be a huge detriment to the KC. As will our ability to do the same." She gave a mirthless laugh. "We already sell directly to several dozen CORE restaurants through your underground."

"But the KC doesn't have an army." Jaxon pushed back his plate, still half full, and joined those standing near the couches. "They have one sixer that we know of, and maybe a hundred thugs, but that's nothing against CORE enforcers or even your soldiers."

Dani gave him a flat stare as she rose from her place on the couch. "They have an exclusive market with two million captive consumers—three hundred thousand of whom are trapped in a colony. I'm certain they have their own plans to take control of the enforcement divisions. Or maybe just Special Forces. Remember, they have someone inside the Director's office— or at least the Controller's office, which is probably more dangerous since he's the man with the real power."

Reese nodded emphatically, and Lyssa's throat tightened as she remembered Ty's message. She should tell him not to go through with his plan to deal with the KC, but she knew it was already too late. Today was already Thursday, and with only a day left before birth orders were announced, whatever he planned to do would already be completed. Besides, if Lyssa were forced to admit the whole truth, her sister was more important.

Even if Ty's dealings with the KC caused his death?

Lyssa couldn't answer that, but she felt as guilty as Breakdown about not being able to stop him. She folded her arms across her chest. "You said there was something you weren't supposed to tell us. Does it have anything to do with what your soldiers are guarding in the room down past your nursery?" *Where your children are probably waiting for you now,* she added silently, but she would withhold that information for later, if she needed it. "What haven't you told us? You brought us here to help you every bit as much as we came to find help. Tell us."

Dani's tall form wilted slightly. "We're supposed to meet the Presidents' Circle in a few minutes, but yes, there is something. I can't tell you, though. It's better if I show you. And then we'll have a chat with President Shala."

"Wait. If you're all leaving," Nova said, leaping up from the couch and spilling her blanket onto the floor, "you need to give orders to let me take Thane out of this room. We'll go crazy in here all day."

Dani contemplated the request for a few minutes. "Okay, but you go only to the common rooms. You're not to try to leave the complex. Either of you."

"Fine." Nova stopped short of rolling her eyes, at least to Lyssa's view, but Dani didn't seem to notice. Maybe because her boys were still so young. But the fact that Nova hadn't rolled her eyes showed that if she didn't like Dani, she at least respected her.

Minutes later, the adults left the teens eating at the table. Dani dismissed the guard waiting outside and released the lock on the door. Lyssa fell into stride next to her sister and behind the others. It didn't take her long to see that Lyra was drooping.

"Are you okay?" she asked.

Lyra made a face. "Morning sickness, I think. I've been seeing Doctor Kentley, and apparently he's been helping me with more than I knew. Maybe more than he even knows. No wonder he always looks so tired."

"Jaxon's feeling Kentley's absence as well, and Reese hasn't stopped drawing since we left Amarillo City." Lyssa lowered her voice. "It's affecting me too. I traveled to Dani this morning. I saw her in bed with that man—her husband, I guess. And before I came all the way awake, I could feel everyone in the room. I felt that I could probably travel to them."

Lyra brightened at that. "Then you should stay away from Kentley. Maybe this would have happened weeks ago if we hadn't been with him so much."

"Maybe." Lyssa chewed on her bottom lip as she thought about the implications. "But I'd like to be able to control it better. Spying on Dani, at least when she's in bed, isn't very useful." She was also worried that her increased ability meant she was that much closer to the sixer madness.

The group paused at the window to the interior courtyard that today literally glittered with light as the early morning sun filtered through the overhead crystal dome. The grass was so green, it appeared to be another color altogether, and in the light, it was clear the trees grew with verdant abandon.

The courtyard was deserted, but Lyssa remembered the couple from the night before, and her gaze strayed to Hammer. He was watching her instead of the courtyard. Their eyes met, and she saw a question there—one she suspected he might never ask. Whatever happened or didn't happen between them was up to her.

He was the only man interested in her who knew her secret, but that wasn't anything to base a relationship on. Besides, there was Ty. She cared about him more than she wanted to. More than she should, given the circumstances. With a short, noncommittal nod at Hammer, she turned away.

It was much farther to the door with the double guards than it had seemed last night without her body, but at least she didn't feel the continuous pressure tugging her back. The guards stood at attention as Dani approached, saluting her with a sharp snap of fists at their sides and the customary stomp.

"At ease," she said.

Lyssa half-expected the soldiers to protest as Dani placed her hand against the lock to the door, but they only stepped back in deference, studying the group without expression. Lyssa decided they were either well-trained or they trusted Dani implicitly. Remembering how Dani had defended them back in the Coop, Lyssa leaned toward the latter explanation.

The door was a single one, and no different than any other door they'd passed, but that was the only similarity. The room it led into was cavernous, as if it had been designed to house a gathering of several thousand people. How large exactly, it was hard to determine, as the room was nearly dark, but the entrance they used must be a service entrance and not the main one. Huge chandeliers hung from the high ceilings far overhead, but they were off at the moment. The only light was a soft glow that came from the oblong cylinders set horizontally close together on the floor. Whatever the room's original purpose, those cylinders were currently the only objects in the space. They stretched as far as Lyssa could see into the gloom, hundreds of them. Too many to count.

"Nine hundred and seventy-two," Eagle said. "Each of them one hundred eighty by sixty centimeters."

"Are they weapons?" Lyssa asked. She had a sudden vision of the Presidents' Circle dropping missiles on Estlantic from a hover—never mind that flying more than a couple meters high wasn't possible with hover technology. They'd been recruiting scientists for years and had access to thousands of miles of empty zones. True flight should be within their grasp, if they hadn't recovered it already.

"About the size of a man, if I'm not mistaken," Jaxon said with an impossible surety.

Lyssa stared at him. "You saw them already?"

He nodded, while Reese winced and clutched her notebook. "We both did," she said, her voice strained. "We just didn't know where they were. We feared it was the Controller." To Dani, she asked, "But who are they?"

Dani didn't respond, and there was no more conversation as Dani waved her hands and the chandeliers came on, at least a dozen of them, bathing the room in a brilliant, shimmering light. "This way," she said.

They followed her, passing the cylinders but not close enough yet to see what they contained. Lyssa had counted twenty when Dani paused and led them closer to one of the cylinders. The glass top was opaque except for a small section on one side, where they could see a face framed by short white hair, glowing slightly from the illumination inside the cylinder. A black human face. No, not exactly a simple human but a sixer—and one they knew.

"Tauri?" Lyssa said. "Why is your brother here?"

Dani set her fingers on the glass, as if to touch his face. "He was afraid. After using his ability in Newcali to get himself free, he started to lose control. He was afraid of killing someone again, someone innocent like before. The only way to prevent that was to sedate him. More heavily than the rest here. A light sleep doesn't work for him."

"Do you mean to say all of these are sixers?" Lyssa stepped to the next cylinder and peered down into the face of a woman with medium brown hair and equally medium brown skin. The next one held a thin-faced woman with dark brown hair and brown skin. Beyond her was a pale, heavyset man with three deep creases in his balding forehead that hadn't relaxed, even in sleep.

"Yes. Some start fires, and many can read thoughts or see images like Reese. A few are strong like me, though their abilities don't come from oxygen regulation because they can't stay under the water like I can. There is a guy who can breathe water, though. And we have a woman who can hit anything with a gun or arrow or piece of concrete, and one who can hear things being said a kilometer away. I don't even know what some of them do because they were too far gone when we got to them. But as far as I know, there are no precogs like Jaxon or travelers like you. There might be, however, and maybe they don't know how to use their gifts."

The enormity of the situation rendered Lyssa speechless. These people were powerful and yet so utterly helpless. She continued her journey through the cylinders. Most of the sixers here had been born within the same generation and had similar features that were blended from the melting pot of Colony 6, but among them were the occasional misfits with too-pale skin or very black skin, like Dani and her brother. Rows and rows of unconscious people. Lyssa felt as if the walls disappeared around her as she wandered through the cylinders. Everything else faded until there was nothing but her and the cylinders full of lost souls. Nine hundred and seventy-two seemed to be ten times that amount. Betrayal filled her. This wasn't life. How could Dani keep them here?

"What have you done?" Lyssa said, her breath barely a whisper but somehow echoing through the room.

Dani met her gaze steadily, and from not nearly as far away as Lyssa felt she'd wandered. "We helped them escape CORE Special Forces, but we couldn't save them from the madness. There was no other way."

Understanding dawned. Lyssa knew these sixers represented less than ten percent of those who had been murdered by Special Forces. Dani had at least tried to rescue these.

"Are they in some kind of stasis?" Lyssa asked.

Dani shook her head. "We don't have that technology. If anyone ever had it, it's been lost, so they're still aging. We simply induce a coma and feed them intravenously. For most of them, that's enough to prevent their abilities from activating. A few, like Tauri, we have to sedate more heavily, and"—she motioned to the far end of the room— "a few we've had to put in special containers. But it's not usually necessary. We have them hooked up to oxygen and everything else they need."

"Do you ever wake them?" This from Lyra, whose face held a green tinge.

"Periodically. And often that gives them a couple days before they lose control again. It's time they can have with their families. A lot of them have young children who are being raised by others until we find a cure."

Is this my future? Lyssa wondered, thinking of Kansas raising Tamsin while she and Lyra spent the rest of their lives in a coma. "The children," she said. "They don't have abilities?"

Dani cocked her head. "Not that we know of."

"It could happen," Eagle said. "The drug they gave everyone in Colony 6 only enhanced and activated extrasensory abilities that their families already displayed. Brogan said as much when he told us his grandfather was part of putting the colony together, and the Controller confirmed it. Even without the drug, some of the children may develop abilities."

"And go crazy?" Lyra's voice was breathless, and Lyssa moved closer in case her sister fainted.

Dani held out her hands, her shoulders lifting in a shrug. "They never received the drug, so maybe not. We'll need to test them all."

"Not sure what good that will do." Reese took a few steps toward a cylinder and stared down into the face of the sixer there. "We can't use children as soldiers."

"Maybe not the younger ones," Dani said. "We were one of the last years to receive the drug, and that was twenty years ago. There were others before us, and some of their children won't be much younger than us now, especially those who were forced to stay in the colonies."

"Well, these sixers can't help us," Jaxon said. "They're as likely to fry us as the enemy. But if the Controller found out about this, he'd want to use them."

"Use them or destroy them," Dani agreed.

"This is why you wanted Dr. Kentley," Lyssa said in sudden understanding. "El Cerebro was right not to let you have him. He can help the few sixers we have, but this would kill him."

Dani's lips pursed, but any disagreement she felt was kept to herself. "We hoped he'd help us find a cure. If he doesn't, they'll die—or worse."

"What's worse than lying here getting older and never seeing your family?" Lyssa asked.

Dani's chin jutted forward. "How about fighting *against* your family and killing everyone you love?" She held their gazes, and no one refuted her.

Dani led them to the door, but she paused before exiting the room. "Besides the Presidents' Circle and two doctors, you are now the only ones who know the full secret contained within this room. Even my most trusted soldiers assigned to the room don't know the full extent of what they are guarding, though I'm sure there are rumors. The sixers themselves here aren't aware of how many others are also like them, and their children only know that they're sick and being taken care of. We tell those who only have extended families that they're on missions for the Presidents' Circle." She paused and let her gaze rest on each of them in turn. "But if President Shala was talking about the Controller and people with abilities, this is what she was talking about. That's what we need to find out. If the CORE or the KC learns about them, none of us here will be safe. They will consider them too dangerous."

A sinking sensation in Lyssa's stomach told her Dani was right. These coffin-like cylinders represented more than just people waiting for a cure—they represented an army. A currently helpless but potentially terrifying army. Aside from being sixers, they were survivors and warriors who had held out against Special Forces until Dani could bring them here. And whoever controlled them might just win the war.

Including El Cerebro and the underground.

Lyssa set her jaw. "We need to lay hands on the cure. And fast. Before anyone else knows they're here."

"That's what I'm thinking," Dani said. "I just hope it's not already too late."

CHAPTER 12

Less than ten minutes later, Lyssa and the others sat on a large circular grouping of tan couches in a room that was twice the size of the main room in their guest quarters. Four aisles separated the circular couches, and in one of the aisles stood a real wood podium with elaborate carvings that had to be of pre-Breakdown construction. Two chandeliers like those in the room housing the unconscious sixers hung from the vaulted ceilings.

Lyssa didn't know if it was customary to have guards attend the Presidents' Circle, but none of the other Presidents commented on the two who now stood by the door. Perhaps they thought Dani had requested their presence for the crew's sake, but she had only called the guards after leaving the sixers. One had first accompanied a nauseated Lyra back to the guest room to lie down, but Lyra had already returned incorporeally, for which Lyssa was glad. If needed, she could leave her own body and travel with Lyra to see more of the Circle complex.

Dani presented each of them in turn with a brief background

that covered their actions as part of El Cerebro's top team without mentioning their official work for division. Then she introduced the other presidents, only three of which were present.

President Ange Shala was a thin, bronzed woman who rivaled Dani for height, though her frame was decidedly frail. Her wrinkled face and graying hair, pulled back in a loose knot, told of her age and Newcali's lack of—or indifference to—the Nuface therapy that was so prominent in the CORE, especially among the Elite. Shala's aged face was welcoming and as bright as the brilliant blue of her flowing robe.

"We are honored to make your acquaintance," she said with a husky, almost sensual quality to her voice. "Ever since Nova came to us and we started combing the archives for ideas, I've been eager to discuss an alliance with you. She's got a good head on her shoulders, that child. Her uncle has tutored her well. I'm excited to explore a relationship with El Cerebro. I'm especially interested in the many fringers that are looking for homes. We can use new settlers here."

She meant more soldiers to stand against the looming invasion, Lyssa thought cynically, but she liked Shala. How could this old woman be responsible for plotting with the Controller?

Next was President Gita Turner, a voluptuous woman of average height with flawless skin and luxurious brown hair that cascaded around her face and down her back like a Teev film star. She wore snug black pants and a loose black duster that complimented her ample figure. She smiled and greeted them with a smile and a soft, "Nice to meet you," and then crossed both her arms and legs and fell silent.

The fourth attending president, introduced as Speaker Kinder Delsindy, wasn't a handsome man. He had a hooked nose and abnormally wide shoulders for his thin frame, but he exuded confidence and was far more outgoing than Turner.

"We should have met much sooner," he said, moving forward to where they sat on the comfortable couches to pump their hands vigorously. "Much sooner. Glad you're here. Please let us know if there is anything we can do for you."

"I'd like to see the beaches," Lyra said, but as she was traveling, Delsindy didn't hear her.

"Speaker?" Reese asked. "Not president?"

The grin on Delsindy's slightly florid face was wide and infectious. "Just an extra title like the one we use for General Balak. I'm called that because usually they make me give the public announcements. It can be confusing having five presidents." He boomed a laugh and resumed his seat. "President Turner is the smart one, Shala's the wise one, Balak is the fierce one, and I'm the talkative one."

"I thought there were five," Lyssa said.

Delsindy inclined his head. "There are. Always five so that the majority rules. President Moride Enger is our ambassador to the other cities. He was called away this morning, however. He's the planning one, always busy with the details. We can try to raise him on the T-link."

"There's no need," Dani said. "We can brief him later. But before we begin, I have some pressing business of security to attend to."

Delsindy's smile faded. "Should we discuss this alone?" He shot a pointed glance at the visitors.

"In the importance of transparency, I feel they need to be here. This involves them and ultimately the future of both our territories." All eyes riveted on Dani now, but only Delsindy spoke.

"Very well, General Balak," he said formally, "You have the floor."

Dani nodded and came to her feet, though she didn't stand at the pulpit. "You all know my stance and the reasons

I have been working with El Cerebro and his underground in Dallastar. The CORE has fourteen thousand enforcers, including two thousand Special Forces. By contrast, we have one hundred and fifty peace officers and the four hundred soldiers under my command who patrol our boarders." She paused, as if to let that sink in, and Lyssa knew the information about their soldiers was mostly for the crew's benefit and not to remind the presidents.

"With such a great disparity," Dani continued, "I believe the only reason the CORE hasn't already come for us is our greater technology, especially the hovers and our recovered missiles, as well as our distance from their main center of population in Estlantic. But rumors of newly-built helicopters with long distance fuel cells, and the CORE's official request to build a colony here, have brought things to a critical juncture. I believe more firmly than ever that helping El Cerebro and his underground in their battle with the CORE, and especially the Controller, is the only way we're going to maintain our autonomy in the long term."

"Of course, of course," Shala said. "That's why you've brought this delegation here, to see if we can come up with a mutually beneficial plan. We also agreed that allowing a CORE colony in our territory would be a mistake. Which leaves me a little puzzled at your tone. Has something happened to increase your concern?"

Dani turned and shifted her gaze solely on President Shala, who was sitting on the couch nearest her. "Yes. Two weeks ago, Nova overheard you talking with someone—someone I suspect may be in this room—about making a deal with the CORE Controller. She also heard someone talking about betraying El Cerebro."

Shala blinked, her white head jerking back a few centimeters in surprise. After a few moments of silence, she said, "I do recall that conversation. I was speaking with President Enger. If you remember, he was the only one who thought we should explore making a deal with the CORE. He worries it's inevitable we won't survive any war they might wage against us."

"We all worry about that," Delsindy said. "And we won't survive long, not without help. But we can drag it out and make them pay." His tone had lost its former easiness, revealing a surprising iron beneath.

"What was said?" This came from the quiet Turner, who was leaning forward on the couch, her expression drawn.

"He wanted to see if I would support a motion to request a revisiting of the colony issue," Shala said, throwing a look at the guards near the door. They were far enough away that they might not hear everything, but her voice lowered all the same. "This time, in addition to the payment and ongoing supplies the CORE promised, he wanted access to the cure. I argued that might necessitate telling the Controller about those we've rescued, or that he'd suspect, and we couldn't risk that. President Enger argued that if cured, they could help us protect Newcali, or at least wouldn't be a drain on our resources. With the other CORE allowances and our weapons, we might be strong enough to withstand their advances, even with a colony here."

"What did you two discuss about El Cerebro?" Dani asked. "Do you recall that as well?"

Shala flushed. "I'm sure the rest was just talk. He thought if we gave them information about El Cerebro, not only would that sweeten the pot enough to have them give us the cure, but they'd be so busy with conflict against the underground that they wouldn't be able to focus on us."

Dani stared with the same horror Lyssa felt. "He *said* that?"

"It was just talk," Shala insisted. "I told him I would not support the motion and discussed it with him until we both agreed it wouldn't work. And that it wasn't honorable. At any rate, as a Circle, we've made our decision. We can't trust the CORE with a foothold in Newcali."

"We can also never allow another colony to be built," Dani growled, with a horizontal slicing motion of her hand. "Never. Slavery is slavery no matter how they mask it."

"Agreed," Shala said, holding Dani's gaze. "Of course, my friend. We've seen how it is for those poor colonists. And you know that once they are free, we will open our lands to them."

"We'll talk to Moride when he gets back, just to have it in the open," President Turner said, folding her arms over her generous breasts and sitting back on the couch.

Lyssa had to think a moment to remember that Moride was President Enger. It was odd that Turner had used his first name when they had all thus far made a habit of addressing each other more formally. Of course, among themselves, they were likely on a first name basis, so the slip wasn't that unusual.

Silence fell over the group. After a long moment of awkwardness, Delsindy said, "Maybe we should now discuss ideas of what we can do for each other."

Dani nodded. "Very well, but I will talk to President Enger the minute he returns." To her guards at the door, she added, "You're dismissed, but please remain on call. I may still need you."

"Something isn't right here," Lyra said to Lyssa. "Can you feel it?"

Lyssa nodded, but she didn't reply. The presidents were already talking about something else, and she didn't want to alert them to Lyra's hidden presence.

"Tell you what," Lyra said. "After I see what ideas they have, and everyone starts talking at endless lengths about it all, you go find someplace quiet to leave your body and we'll go exploring. This room is much farther away than we were able to go last night. Let's see if we can travel anywhere we want between our bodies."

Lyssa smiled. It was a great idea. Let the others talk until their voices were hoarse. She and Lyra were going exploring.

CHAPTER 13

After waiting for Thane to devour pretty much everything on the table and to take a brief trip to the sleeping room for a change of clothes, Nova led him to her own modest suite, which was a much smaller version of the guest quarters. To her, it still felt like a luxury not having to share a bathroom or sleeping quarters with anyone else. It was worth slaving away in the kitchens during the lunch and dinner shifts. Not today, though. She'd found someone to cover her shift so she could spend the day with Thane.

She showered and changed into pants that reached only halfway down her thigh. Over her sleeveless red top, she threw a soft black jacket she'd found in the crate of castoffs meant for colony refugees, exchanging it with the blue one she'd used previously—one that had belonged to Wolfe, a former undergrounder who'd died in a shoot-out with Special Forces some months back. She liked not having to remember him every time she put it on. Wolfe had tried to kiss her too—mostly because she was the ward of El Cerebro and he'd had delusions of grandeur. She hadn't liked him that way, but sometimes she thought maybe he would have grown on her. But he was dead, and it didn't matter now.

"Where are we going?" Thane asked when she emerged from the bathroom, braiding her hair so it wouldn't be in the way.

"You'll see."

"Will I really need my jacket? It's warm in here." He was even wearing a short-sleeved shirt.

"Yes, just in case. It's not as if it's heavy." She led him to the door. "Did you really walk all the way from Santoni to Dallastar in that? It's December." Which meant rain and cold nights.

He shrugged. "We had fires and blankets." The closed look on his face told her he didn't want to discuss it. That, she could well understand. Talking about the hard things didn't change them, so it was better to pretend they didn't happen. Like his mother being sent to a colony and not knowing if she had died.

Well, he wouldn't be thinking about it for long. Nova was about to blow Thane's mind.

Her first stop was at the kitchens, where she loaded the pack she'd brought with food. The head cook, Ankilde, had already made bread drops for lunch, and he grinned at Nova as he gave her a container full of the still-warm treat. Her mouth watered. Fresh food always did that. How had she survived on readymeals for fourteen whole years?

"I'm going to miss your help at dinner," Ankilde said. "One of my workers didn't show up today, so we're short-handed."

A twinge of guilt made her say, "I could come in, I guess." She didn't dare glance at Thane when she said it.

"No, no. He wasn't much good anyway," Ankilde said. "Always disappearing for a smoke. You go have fun, child. While you're young. I get the feeling you won't be here long."

"Long enough," she said, giving him a smile. "See you tomorrow."

At the end of the hallway, still near the kitchen, Nova took a screwdriver from her pack and began loosening the screws on a grate in the wall.

"What's this?" Thane asked.

"It leads to the garbage chute," she said.

He stared up and down the hallway nervously. "But . . ." he began.

"Don't worry. They don't have cameras here. Only in certain public places. It's not like the CORE."

He thought about that for a moment, his body relaxing. "Okay, but why the garbage? I wanted a tour, but this seems a little too detailed."

"It's the only way out."

His eyes widened. "You mean, you did find a way out?"

She grinned. "Of course I did." The grate came loose, and she gestured him inside. "It joins up with the garbage chute, but this one is for the kitchen, and it empties only three times a day. We're safe until after lunch." She pulled the grate shut after they were inside, carefully leaving the screws near the opening. "They flush the chute itself with antiseptic, but it still smells. Sorry about that."

"Do I get to see the beach?"

She grinned. "Oh, yeah."

"Then it's more than worth it." He was crouching close to her, as if waiting for her to lead the way, but there was no way to slide past him in the narrow space.

"You'll have to go first," she said, willing her face not to flush.

The shaft led to a junction in the main chute that had a tiny connecting door that allowed air in but nothing out. Once through the door, the stench of garbage and antiseptic was immediately overpowering. "It's not far," she muttered, breathing through her mouth. She double-checked the door to make sure it was closed before duck-walking after him. The last thing she wanted was to have her way out be discovered because garbage went the wrong way at the next flushing cycle.

They didn't have far to go to reach the outside of the dome where the garbage flushed down a chute into the sewer. Nova pointed Thane to the maintenance ladder, and then climbed to it herself. She was pleased to see that the day was nice. They'd need their jackets on the beach because of the breeze, but it would be warm enough for a picnic.

Of course, she took him on the moving sidewalks. Though most of the sidewalks vanished outside of the main city, the beach was popular enough that one stretched all the way there. Thane grinned as the air ruffled his hair. Others were heading to the beach too, mostly parents with younger children, but they fit right in.

"No cameras, really?" Thane asked.

"Here I think there are," she responded, "just to make sure there's no tampering with the sidewalk, but they don't scan for CivIDs."

"Good thing, since I don't have one." His tone showed a hint of remorse. The last time they'd been together, he had been proud of the fact that he was finally getting a forged ID, which was a big deal for an illegal child. Nova had mocked him then, even understanding the value of it in the CORE. She had one she typically masked from the cameras. Doing so was dangerous, but it was a small way to rebel.

"I guess dying put that on hold, huh?" she said, keeping her voice light.

"Something like that."

He fell silent, and Nova let him stay that way. Sometimes silence was a lot better than trying to make up for something that could never be made up. Like her parents dying.

When the sand finally came into view, the blue ocean

stretching out beyond the horizon, Thane threw back his head and laughed. She understood it wasn't the view but the anticipation that made him happy. He'd seen the ocean many times, south of Santoni near the empty zone, but there, the water was poisonous.

They took the moving walkway clear to the end and then walked another kilometer to find a place with no other people. "Here's good," Nova said, dropping her bag.

"Is it always this deserted?" Thane asked.

"Most people are working. Later in the day, there will be more. But even then, there's not many people who live here, and the coastline goes on forever."

They kicked off their shoes and tossed their jackets onto the sand before running to the water together, shouting and laughing. At the water's edge, Thane stopped to roll up his pants while Nova plunged her feet into the icy water.

Thane gasped as he followed her. "It's freezing!"

"They say it's warmer during the summer, but that might only be because the beach feels hotter then. I don't know. I don't even care." In fact, she often stripped down to what the natives called a bikini, but seemed to her like underwear only thicker, to swim and bask in the sun. If any natives saw her, they laughed good naturedly but rarely joined her in the water. Today, though, Nova hadn't taken the time to strip.

Cold water hit her in the face, and she realized that Thane had slapped the water, spraying it toward her. "Seriously?" She splashed him back and even managed to trip him before dancing out of reach and back onto the sand.

They were both shivering now, despite the sun overhead, and she was glad she'd brought the heating blanket. The battery reserves were full, and as long as the sun was shining, it would keep charging. Thane pulled off his shirt and spread it on the sand to dry. Nova did the same, glad for the bikini top now.

Her pants, made of a synthetic material, would slough off the water in minutes, so she left those on.

"So this is why you haven't come home," Thane said, laying back on her blanket and pulling the edge over his side to ward off the breeze.

"It's nice here," she said noncommittally. Getting into why she'd prefer to stay here, away from her uncle and her friends, wasn't something she wanted to do right now.

But Thane got it anyway. "It would be nice," he said. "Not to worry about my dad, about our people. Or about those stupid Special Forces."

"Or your mother," she said.

He was quiet for a long moment. "Yes."

Heat from the blanket spread through Nova, and she stopped shivering. Lying flat in the sand with the edges of the blanket curled around one shoulder and Thane touching her other side, she felt content.

"Your uncle wants you back," Thane said after a moment.

"I'm out of the CORE. I thought he'd want that for me."

"Yeah, but not like this. He wants to take care of you, and he probably misses you. You have to guess that he told them not to come back without you."

"Maybe I don't care. Maybe I want to take care of myself for a change."

Thane snorted and rolled onto his side, propping his head up with his elbow and hand. "I don't think so. If anyone I know is a rebel, it's you. You have to come back with me."

"Why?" She really wanted to know. "So I can watch you die again?"

Thane regarded her for a long moment without speaking, and then he said, "That's not fair. I didn't mean to get shot."

"No, and my father didn't mean to die of radiation

poisoning. Or rather, he did mean to—as long as it freed me from Colony 4."

Thane nodded, though awkwardly with his head propped on his hand. "I heard them talking about your father. They said he wasn't born in the colony."

"No. He and my uncle were regular people, just as oppressed as everyone else."

"What happened?"

Should she tell him? How did she know it was even the truth? She knew only what her uncle had told her later. She turned toward Thane but kept low to the blanket, pillowing her hand with an outstretched arm.

"My dad was a scientist, and apparently, he tried to use pre-Breakdown tech to send messages to other continents to see if anyone else was out there."

"Was there a response?"

"Only from the Controller's office. Turns out it was illegal, both not to report that he had found the tech, and to contact outsiders. He was sentenced to Colony 4 for acts of conspiracy. My uncle had pull even then, and worked to help him, but he couldn't stop it." She sighed. "Well, at least he made it so my father wasn't medically enhanced." Though maybe that was the lie, because a missing section of his brain might explain why he had been willing to sacrifice himself later. "Anyway, when he married my mother, there was really nothing my uncle could do. Even if they'd let my dad out, he wouldn't leave her."

"Colony 4 is where they sent my mom."

Nova nodded. "It's an awful place." The colony mined oil and produced raw plastics. The only thing Nova remembered about it was the constant smell of the factories. "They worked sixty hours a week just like the rest. But Mother got sick and died." A tear formed in her eye, and she pressed her face against her arm to blot it away. "I was seven or so, I think. Anyway, that was when my dad started talking to someone about the desolations zones and how he could find tech for them. He'd gone before, only not very far in, and it hadn't hurt him. He did a couple trips for them, and the next thing I know, we're in Santoni celebrating my eighth birthday. Two years later, after a bunch of trips into the desolation zones, he died."

"And that's when we met."

"Yes." She closed her eyes.

Her uncle had put a tracking chip in her foot and had taken her to an empty zone, to a woman who hid illegal children. Nova hadn't been illegal, but she'd been out-of-her-mind insane with ideas of revenge. She'd stayed there two years before convincing Brogan she wouldn't do something crazy, and he'd taken her to the underground. She could have lived with him above ground as Captain Brogan's niece, but she preferred to be known as El Cerebro's ward.

Thane's hand reached out and ran a finger along her cheek. A delicious shudder rippled up her spine at his touch. "That's why you'll go back," he said softly. "Because of your dad. And because of every other person trapped in those colonies."

Like his mother, who was probably already dead.

Nova didn't respond right away, but after a moment, she whispered. "We'll see."

Tired of the painful memories, she jumped to her feet. "Let's walk. There's a place I want to show you."

They pulled on their jackets, stuffed the blanket back in her pack, and picked up their wet shirts, letting them dangle as they walked. There were some rocks a few kilometers away that they could spread them on.

"You can walk all the way to Beach City," she said after a time. "I mean, it takes a while, but I've done it before."

"Let's do it." He looked down at his bare feet, smiling.

She laughed, understanding instantly. The feel of the sand between her toes had fascinated her for days. Not to mention the long stretch of sand with no sign of death and seagulls circling overhead, cawing without a care in the world.

"We wouldn't get back in time to make Dani happy," Nova said. But maybe she didn't care. Now that she'd told the enforcers about what she'd heard, they could deal with it. Thane was wrong about her. She wasn't a rebel, and she wanted to live here forever—or at least until summer, so she could swim in warmer water and camp out overnight under the stars.

"Do you hear that?" Thane asked, coming to an abrupt stop.

"Hear what?" She cocked her head to listen, but only the cry of the gulls met her ears.

"A thumping sound. It's gone now."

"It's probably just the waves hitting those rocks." She pointed ahead to a long, rocky expanse that stretched out into the water like a part of some natural bridge. "Come on. Let's run. I'm hungry, and it's a lot farther than it looks."

They were out of breath and Nova's side was aching when they finally reached the rocks that loomed several stories over their heads. Thane squinted his eyes. "Little windier here. Be hard to eat with this flying sand."

"On the other side, there's a little cove," Nova told him. "The rocks curve around. It's protected from the wind, and it'll be warmer."

"How do we get there?" He looked inland, where the line of rocks continued to the edge of the sand.

"We can go around, but I like to climb." Nova put her now-dry shirt back into her bag and slipped on her sandals. "It's sharp on your feet," she explained. Thane didn't object, so she began climbing. She couldn't wait for him to see the view. Of course, she'd have to beat him to the top.

Despite her lead, he was gaining on her before she reached her goal. But now she was hearing a strange *thump, thump, thump* that definitely wasn't the water. She stopped and waited for him to come level with her. "I hear it now," she said, her voice sounding small to her ears as the wind whipped it away.

Thane nodded, held a finger to his lips, and pointed upward. Nodding, Nova shrugged off her pack and stuffed it in the rocks before she continued climbing. She moved carefully now, stopping every few minutes to crane her neck and see if she could catch sight of whatever was making the noise. When she reached the top, she barely poked her head over the rocks. At first she didn't see anything, but another step upward showed her the top of something she'd previously only seen on the Teev.

"A helicopter," she breathed, not nearly loud enough for Thane to hear, but they exchanged a frightened look. As far as she knew, the only person who had access to a pre-Breakdown flying machine like this was the Controller. In fact, if hovers had been taken to the CORE, they would have been confiscated immediately. The skies and all they represented belong to the CORE—or rather, the Elite who made the rules, as her father had discovered the hard way.

Nova moved closer to Thane at the same time he moved toward her. Nova didn't have time to think about how their cheeks touched before they bounced awkwardly apart. "We have to see who it is," she said. He nodded in agreement.

Hugging the rocks, they crawled onto the relatively flat top, where chunks of broken concrete told her that at some time humans had used this place more frequently. Nova ignored the pain of the rocks and concrete slicing into the flesh of her hands and knees.

The whole of the helicopter was in view now, and Nova could see a half dozen people gathered. At least two wore

CORE enforcer uniforms. As they watched, the people began climbing inside the machine. Her heart pounded. What were the Controller's people doing here? Nothing good, she was sure.

She was about to inch closer to see if they had left anything on the beach when a strong hand closed around her forearm. She whipped her head around to see a man rising partially behind her, most of his torso down among the rocks. His other hand was clamped on Thane's arm.

"What . . ." she began, falling silent as she realized she was staring into the tanned, lean face of President Enger. His expression was thunderous, and as she tried to pull away, his grip tightened cruelly.

That was when she noticed his assistant balanced on the rocks behind him. In his hand was a gun.

CHAPTER 14

Lyssa's mind was about to burst. They'd discussed historical examples found in the Newcali database. They'd rehashed numbers of enforcers and current distribution, which both Reese and Hammer had researched intimately. They'd talked about the fringers fleeing Estlantic and the increasing controls issued by the CORE. Hammer had even divulged that El Cerebro's own personal access to fighters was over two hundred strong, not counting any of the refugee fringers, but his people were spread out across Dallastar. Even together, their forces paled in comparison to the enforcers in the CORE, especially if the confrontation took place in Estlantic, on the other side of the continent.

If El Cerebro and Newcali succeeded in arming and transporting their soldiers to New York, where the Director and Controller and other Elite leaders resided, the heavily-populated area would mean numerous civilian casualties.

"That won't bother the Controller," Dani said with disgust, "but how can we in good conscience do that?" She was pacing again, but everyone here was accustomed to her inability to remain still for long, especially after the long journey through the empty zone in the hover.

"It might be," President Turner said, turning an enigmatic stare on them, "that blood will need to be shed. On both sides." She had a mug of brew in one hand, and though her voice was tired, she didn't look any worse for wear than when they'd started that morning.

"What we need to do is kill the Elite," Hammer countered. "They're the ones who've hurt so many people."

About the only thing they agreed on was that the fringers who'd been uprooted from the empty zones should be transferred to Newcali, where they could live without fear. At least until the CORE enforcers arrived, which Lyssa knew wouldn't be long. With the rioting and crimes that had begun taking place every time birth orders were announced, and the increasing undertone of discontent, the Elite needed some way to appease the people while tightening their hold.

"We'll all be in a colony soon," Jaxon muttered darkly. Lyssa hoped he wasn't saying that because of any vision he had seen.

Hammer sighed and rubbed a hand over his weary face. "Given that for each colony of fifty thousand, they maintain an average of only one hundred enforcers—or one enforcer to every five hundred colonists—compared to one enforcer for every one hundred and twenty-seven people outside the colonies, I'd say that more colonies are the only way the Elite can hold onto power if they want to increase the population and take over Newcali. The colonists are overworked and undernourished with food that is likely drugged, so fewer enforcers are needed to maintain order. More colonies would permit controlled growth."

Reese looked up from her drawing pad. She'd filled nearly half the book in the hours they'd been here, stopping her sketching only when lunch and a late-afternoon snack had been served in an adjoining dining room. Lyssa had glimpsed only one image, and it was of President Turner talking with a man she didn't recognize.

"The Elite have plenty of incentive," Reese said. "More colonies mean more credits and control."

"And more slaves!" Dani stopped pacing, her dark eyes flashing anger. "Maybe we could take our missile launchers to Estlantic. With good intel, we could take out the top leaders at least. Although I don't know how we could stop the collateral damage."

Reese frowned. "Taking out the leadership without having something else in place could mean the KC takes over. They already have a lot of control over the food colonies."

With that, they were back at the beginning, but something Hammer said had piqued Lyssa's interest. The colonies required only a hundred enforcers. The tall walls, inadequate nutrition, and constant work did the rest of the job.

Tall walls. Those could be made just as hard to get inside as they were to get out. Colonies 1 through 5 were responsible for most of the primary industry in the CORE. That meant most of the food, fuel, raw textiles, and mining were inside those walls. Colony 6, the most expendable of the colonies, processed materials from the other colonies before sending them to outside companies for finishing. Most of those companies were automated and owned by the CORE, of course. But what if the CORE or Kordell Corp didn't have access to goods from the colonies?

Lyssa had only a moment to ponder this when Lyra, who had given up following the conversation and had returned to her body, reappeared standing inside the couch next to Lyssa. "They still at it? I thought you were coming to get me so we can investigate."

"I'm ready now." Lyssa excused herself from the others who were once more talking about the unconscious sixers, and made her way into the adjoining room, where the remains of lunch had been cleared away. She sat at the large oblong table, folded her arms on the burnished wood, and laid her head down.

Sliding from her body was easy. Together, they glided through the walls and into the corridor. "Which way?" she said to Lyra.

"Right. That takes us beyond both our bodies, so we won't be able to go far, but we should try anyway."

They checked rooms as they went, finding nothing besides a few storage closets before the building came to an abrupt end. Their attempt to leave the building failed, and Lyssa was yanked back to her body.

Lyra showed up a few seconds later. "I was able to walk for a bit more back toward the council chambers," she informed Lyssa, "but when someone passed, I lost my concentration and snapped back here."

Lyssa slipped from her body again before saying, "Hey, it's progress."

This time, they chose the left corridor, which would keep them between their physical bodies. They began checking rooms with only a slight tugging urge in both directions.

"Nothing new here," Lyra said with a frown.

"No, but it's not as much strain. At least we know we can travel easily between our bodies. We're almost back to the guest quarters now."

"Where they locked me in again." Lyra's annoyance was clear.

"I'd better get back to the meeting," Lyssa said. She'd already been gone long enough that she was worried one of the presidents would come looking for her.

Lyra sighed. "I really thought we'd find something."

"Me too."

Lyssa was about to allow herself to be pulled back to her body when Nova and Thane appeared at the end of the curved hallway, marching toward them. They weren't alone, and the upset on Nova's face froze Lyssa in place.

Next to Nova walked a man whose resemblance to one of the drawings Reese had made back in chambers was immediately obvious. He was a well-formed man in his early forties, his body accustomed to hard work and exercise. His hair was a light blond, an oddity in the Core and also in Newport, and his oblong face was flushed. His sand-colored clothing was stained with sweat.

Beneath her wild hair, Nova looked ready to cry. "President Enger," she was saying, "please let us go back to my room. We won't be any trouble. I promise."

Whatever Enger replied was lost on Lyssa as she noticed a second man behind Thane and Nova. He was tanned and strong-looking, with black hair and a face half-hidden with a trimmed beard. In his hands was a gun with a shiny metal barrel that gleamed under the light.

Lyra's hand grabbed Lyssa's, her eyes flushed and panicked. "Go tell Dani! I'll stay with Nova."

"You won't be able to. Remember the last time?"

"But I can feel Nova. Can't you?"

Lyssa could. The pull wasn't nearly as strong as that of her body or Lyra's—or even Lyra's essence—but it might be enough to anchor her sister here. Then again, it might not be. "Let's follow them to at least see where they're going. Maybe they're heading to the Circle chambers."

They glided along after the man with the gun. Lyssa hoped someone would speak so she could understand what had happened and how Nova and Thane had come to grief with Enger, but no one spoke. When they turned down another corridor before they reached the Circle chambers, Lyssa felt she could wait no longer.

"Okay, I'd better get Dani," she said, noting a picture on the wall so she could mark the place. "Focus on Nova and try to go with them to see where they go, if you can. When they get wherever they're going, come to me. Or I'll find you." Without waiting for a reply, she allowed herself to be pulled back to her body.

Entering her body, Lyssa leapt up from the table and sprinted to the chambers, where the others were still talking. Lyra hadn't yet reappeared, so maybe she'd been able to stay with Nova. "Dani," Lyssa blurted, "Nova needs help."

The conversation in the room cut off as all eyes turned on her. "What happened?" Dani asked, coming to her feet.

"It's President Enger. He's got Nova and Thane. And a gun."

"Where?"

"He's taking her somewhere inside this building." Lyssa pointed to her left. "They turned up a corridor near a picture of a beach. Lyra's following them."

Dani was at the door before Lyssa had finished speaking. "We have many beach pictures," she said. "Show me."

Lyssa hurried after her, aware of the others following.

"I don't understand," President Delsindy said. "Your other delegate isn't with us, and you don't appear to be using a T-link. How are you communicating?"

Dani shot him a pointed look. "She's from Colony 6, like me. They all are." That wasn't quite true, since Hammer wasn't a sixer, but no one corrected her. "Do you think I would bring anyone here who didn't know firsthand what we are fighting for?" She glanced at Lyssa, who motioned up the hallway. Dani hurried forward.

"But the madness," Delsindy called, looking askance at them as he hurried through the door, twisting his wide shoulders so he didn't hit Shala, who was also trying to get through. "To have active sixers inside the Circle is a severe security breach."

"I said I vouch for them." Dani's voice dripped disdain. "That should be enough."

Delsindy fell silent, but Lyssa understood his concern. They were all okay at the moment, mostly because Dr. Kentley had used his ability to help them, and because their abilities had a natural tendency to let off the pressure that exacerbated the madness. Still, Lyssa, like the others, felt it waiting behind a fast-approaching corner.

She sprinted after Dani. Periodically, Dani slowed to let them catch up, her muscles bunched and her face tight with fury. Lyssa guessed that if she had been able to identify the picture, she'd leave them all behind.

Lyra appeared within minutes. "Good," she said. "You're almost there. I was able to stay with Nova. She's okay. But Enger is furious about something." She glided ahead and waited by the beach painting.

When Lyssa identified the painting, Dani scowled. "This corridor leads to our offices. Why is he taking her there?"

"He won't hurt her," President Shala called from somewhere behind Lyssa. "You know Moride." Lyssa noted that Shala was also now calling President Enger by his first name, as if protocol had been thrown out the window.

Ahead, the new corridor intersected with two others on the right, angling separately in a V. Dani continued past the first corridor before Lyssa could indicate that Lyra had turned up it.

"Here." Lyssa pointed.

Dani was next to Lyssa in a heartbeat. "This doesn't go to his quarters. It leads to mine and Turner's."

Lyra glanced back to see how President Turner was taking that, but only Eagle, Hammer, Shala, and Delsindy were behind them. Before she could ask where Jaxon, Reese, and Turner had gone, Lyra disappeared inside a door.

Lyssa stumbled to a stop. "In here."

"That's Turner's office."

Dani had her gun out, and instinctively, Lyssa felt for the knife Eagle had made for her. Dani tested the door, but it was locked. How had Enger gotten inside?

Lyra reappeared through the door. "They're not in the office, but in the adjoining bedroom. Enger is tearing the place apart."

"Where's Turner?" Dani demanded, her eyes searching the hallway behind them.

"Never mind that. There's three of us here." Shala strode forward, punched in a code on the flat lock screen, then placed her hand on it. A light flashed as the machine read her print. Immediately, Dani placed her hand, followed by Delsindy's. The door beeped and accepted the override.

"Wait here!" Dani ordered. "I've called for my soldiers. Tell them to come in when they get here." She disappeared inside, and Lyra with her.

Hammer pulled his knife. "No way in Breakdown am I letting her go in alone."

Eagle put a restraining hand on his shoulders. "Without a gun, you'll only be a target."

Hammer and Lyssa hesitated, but ensuing shouts from inside compelled them through the door. They ran through an office to a small but well-furnished sleeping quarters. Enger was half inside a closet, his hands in the air, but Dani's gun wasn't pointed at him. Near a shelf next to the bed, Nova and Thane stood in front of another man holding a gun. Currently, it was pointed in the air.

"Get his gun," Dani ordered.

As Hammer sprang forward and relieved the unresisting

man of his weapon, Nova, who was standing by a shelf, stepped forward. "Wait, you got it all wrong. The gun is for protection." The hands Nova held up to them were scraped and bleeding, but otherwise, she seemed all right.

Delsindy and Shala appeared in the doorway. "What is going on here?" Shala demanded of Enger.

But it was Nova who told them. "We saw a helicopter! It had to be sent by the Controller."

Shala's swift intake of breath mirrored that of Lyssa's own. "So you decided to contact them," Shala snapped at Enger. "Well, it won't work. None of the rest of us will agree. No matter what they throw at us."

"It wasn't me," Enger said. "My discussion with you was only meant to verify my own feelings. It was Gita who was pushing for it. She asked me to approach you." Gita, meaning Gita Turner, and his use of her first name seemed to linger intimately in the air.

"President Enger saved us," Nova put in. "When the helicopter was taking off, they would have seen us. He had a camo tarp. He did make us come here with him because he was afraid we'd tell someone before he found what he needed, but he saved us."

"They would have killed them." Enger's voice was hard. "Now can I please put my hands down? I think I know where we can find proof that she's been in private discussion with them."

"Do it," Dani said, moving to help him.

Enger lowered his hands. "She has a safe in this closet. I found it one night when we were here together, but I could never figure out the combination. The evidence has to be in there, because I've checked her home. To give the helicopter access, she would have needed my traveling codes and a communication device that piggybacks off our T-link feed."

Dani spoke into her T-link. "Find President Turner," she said. "Last sighted in council chambers. Do not allow her to leave the Circle. Detain with force, if necessary."

"Don't worry," called a voice from the next room. "President Turner isn't going anywhere."

"Reese?" Lyssa asked.

She pushed past Shala and into the office, where Reese and Jaxon each stood with a hand on President Turner's arms. Reese also held something at Turner's back that Lyssa guessed was one of the newly 3D-printed knives. Hammer was on Lyssa's heels, immediately raising his confiscated gun and pointing it at Turner, though it would probably be useless unless the fingerprint reader had been disabled.

"I caught her throwing something in the disposal chute," Reese explained, not relinquishing her hold. "Some kind of T-link, I think. Something I'm betting she doesn't want the rest of the Presidents' Circle to know about. But she's been sending me odd sketches all day, and I knew something wasn't right, so when all of you took off, Jaxon and I stayed behind."

Delsindy hovered uncertainly in the doorway between the rooms. "Now, let's not be rash."

"We're way past rash," Moride Enger said, glaring at Turner as he squeezed past Delsindy, forcing him aside. "What have you done! I knew something was happening today when you tried to get me to stay inside the Circle. So I took one of the hovers and went up and down the coast. I saw the helicopter and tracked it. Below their sensors apparently. They were too busy salivating over our land to notice much of anything else. Looked like they were doing a survey. That means they got past our missile launchers on the border. You did that. Don't deny it."

Turner's beautiful face flushed. "It's just one helicopter, and the codes change weekly, so they won't have them next week.

I was trying to show them what we have to offer, so we could make a better deal."

"You used me," he spat at her. "You used our relationship to get the codes. And now they'll be back for sure."

Turner sighed. "We can't hold out forever. You all know that. I was simply seeking more information. If they can give us assurances . . ."

"They aren't to be trusted," grated Dani. "Haven't you understood that yet?" Her gaze turned to Shala. "You should have let me take her to Colony 6. She needs to see firsthand."

At that moment, two of Dani's soldiers appeared, looking flushed, their weapons drawn. "We're good," Dani said, glancing down at her own gun, which she still had in hand. "But please wait outside. You may be needed." The men shot calculating stares at Reese and Hammer, who were still armed, but Dani waved them off. "Put away the knife, Reese. Hammer, give me the gun."

With a disgusted snort, Reese's knife vanished, and Hammer passed the gun with a wink at Lyssa that told her he was having fun. Reese and Jaxon backed away from Turner, and Lyssa didn't think it was an accident that they kept themselves between the woman they saw as a traitor and the door.

"Look," Turner explained, "I was buying us time. And it's working. I knew if we told them right off that we wouldn't deal with them, things would heat up. Now, with delays and stringing them along, we can stretch this out years before we need to confront them. We'll be in a better position then."

"Some people don't have years," Reese countered. "Those sixers you've sedated are losing more of their lives with every day that passes. Death rate in the colonies is six times what it is in the rest of the CORE. The birth rates are equally high to create expendable human slaves. You may be Newcalians, but those are your people too. Or relatives of your people."

"I know all that," Turner said dismissively, "but my primary concern must be the people here in Newcali. Besides, the sixers, as you call them, are part of the plan. If we can treat them and make them healthy, they can help both us and their people."

Enger's face drained of blood. He stepped over to Turner and set his hands on her shoulders. "Did you tell them about the sedated colonists? Please say you didn't. We voted not to initiate that conversation, regardless of any other discussion we might have with the CORE."

Turner shrugged him off. "I simply asked for twenty doses of the cure as a goodwill gesture before we begin serious negotiations, so we can treat any stray people with abilities who may wander into our territory. They agreed to consider the request. With that much, we should be able to reverse engineer it. Even if we only manage to create a treatment and not a cure, it will help. The answer is no, of course I wouldn't hint that we have nearly a thousand potential soldiers on ice, so to speak. I know how their Controller is anxious to find those with abilities. I wouldn't betray them to him."

"What if they guess?" Lyssa asked. For being billed as the smart one, President Turner appeared to see only one issue. "That would put an even bigger target on your back. Not only because using the sixers would be to the Controller's advantage, but because none of the Elite can risk our people learning the truth about the colonies. Especially when they are planning a new one and want to entice people to willingly join it."

"How could they guess?" Turner retorted with derision. "I gave them very little information, and they didn't have codes to come near our main cities. They won't know our population, or our numbers. They weren't even supposed to come anywhere this close."

"Yes, they will," Enger said. "They'll know it all."

"What do you mean?" Turner demanded. "I was careful, I tell you."

Enger gave her a flat stare. "Because I know why they came this close. They picked someone up."

Turner stared at him. "Picked someone up?"

"Yes, between here and Beach City. I suspect when they sent that first delegation earlier this year, the two we talked with weren't alone. And with you asking them about the cure, as sure as Breakdown, whoever they left behind that first time will have been busy learning why we would ask for it."

Turner reached for her pocket in an abrupt gesture that had Dani lifting her gun, but Turner shook her head and removed her T-link from a pocket of her black pants. "We need to check if any of the Circle workers have gone missing. If not, then there isn't a problem. No one else would have access to information about the sixers."

Dani nodded assent and Turner pulled her T-link over her eyes. She waited a few moments, and then began speaking. "I want all Circle personnel contacted and accounted for. Everyone, from the cook to the guy who washes the windows. Let me know if you can't reach anyone, or if anyone didn't show up for work today. Call me when you have the answer. Priority red."

Nova stepped forward. "There was a kitchen worker who didn't show up today. Ask Ankilde."

"I'll send my men." Dani marched to the door and began talking with her soldiers.

"Even if the person wasn't employed here, they'll still have intel on your population," Lyssa said.

Eagle nodded. "I figured it out, and it was dark when we came into town."

Turner sighed. "I was trying to buy us time."

"There's a reason there are five presidents," Enger said. "This was not your decision to make alone."

She nodded, and when Dani returned to the room, she added, "I know you'll need to arrest me."

"Yes," Dani said. "But first, tell us everything."

There wasn't more, except a few details, which Turner told them in the Circle chambers after sending Nova and Thane back to their quarters under guard. Lyra had also joined the crew in the chambers, in person this time. By the time Turner had finished going through the explanation twice more, with everyone listening in mostly tense silence, Dani's guards verified that the missing kitchen employee's apartment in town was cleared out and vacant.

"We have to assume the Controller knows," Dani says. "No matter how we look at it, this is going to speed up his plan. He's coming for us."

"How long do you think your missiles could hold out?" Jaxon asked.

Dani exchanged a look with Delsindy and Shala, who both nodded their permission to share the information. "We have a large arsenal and can make more weapons," Dani said. "In the past fifty years, we've made it a priority to search most of the empty zones around us for useful items. We also have special suits for trips into the desolation zones, so we've harvested weapons and tech from there as well. We should be able to stand a full assault from the CORE for six months, or maybe a year, if they can't match our firepower."

"Impressive," Hammer said.

Lyssa thought so too. But she began to think of what might happen if some of those missiles and launchers were moved to the colonies.

"Food and water won't be an issue for us, but a possibly big one for them, so that might add to the time we can hold out," Dani said. "But after that, we'll be as vulnerable as babies. The CORE could use the colonies to manufacture anything they need." She paused, her expression grim, and Lyssa thought of Dani's two boys and the danger they would soon be in. "You must all return to Amarillo City," Dani continued, "and tell El Cerebro that not only have we failed at finding a solution, but that very soon, we're going to need your help."

"Unless," Lyssa said, her two thoughts finally merging into a solid plan, "we go on the attack."

Turner snorted. "We've been through all that today," she said, her face twisting into something not beautiful at all. "Weren't you listening?"

"Shut up," Dani ordered. To the guards that had brought news of the kitchen employee, she added, "Please escort President Turner to a holding cell."

When Turner was gone, Hammer winked at Lyssa, setting her pulse pounding at an unnatural pace. "Let's hear it. What are you thinking?"

Lyssa grinned at him. "Well, first off, Jaxon is going to betray El Cerebro. But that's only the beginning."

CHAPTER 15

Lyssa's plan was far from simple, though it took her less than five minutes to explain. Everything began and ended with the colonies. If the underground, with the help of the Newcali soldiers, could overcome the enforcers at each of the six colonies, they would effectively bring all production to a halt in the CORE, as well as severely strangle Kordell Corp. That would give the underground leverage to demand the surrender of the Elite. Someone would have to step into the leadership vacancy, but Lyssa knew Brogan would be more than capable to either lead or appoint interim leadership to make sure the KC didn't gain control. One of the Newcali presidents could be involved in the reorganization as an ambassador, with the idea of encouraging more freedoms and trade between the territories.

What Lyssa didn't spell out in front of the presidents, but which the crew very well knew, was that as captain of the Amarillo City Enforcer Division, Brogan also supervised two of the three Dallastar colony enforcer subdivisions, namely Colonies 5 and 6. Taking over those wouldn't be a huge challenge, as orders that put the enforcers at those locations at a disadvantage wouldn't be suspect until far too late. The other four colonies would need to be taken by complete surprise and possible bloodshed, but the secret passageways Dani had used to smuggle people out could just as well be used to smuggle people in.

One snag in the plan was gathering enough people to hold the colonies for the length of time needed to convince the Elite to turn over power. Newcali's portable missiles and the CORE's own reluctance to destroy their primary industries should protect the colonies from complete annihilation, but enforcers would likely surround and siege each of the colonies. That meant both the unconscious sixers' abilities and armed presence would be vital to controlling what happened.

Once again, Dani was pacing. "To make the sixers useful, we still need to treat them."

"Yes, but now that the Controller knows about them," Lyssa said, scanning the group, "I think we can lure him to Amarillo City and get the treatment directly from him. Or at least enough temporary doses that Dr. Kentley can use to create more treatments, and eventually a permanent cure."

"It won't be easy luring him there," Dani said.

"No, but doable." At least, Lyssa hoped it was. "Here is what I propose. First, we get President Turner to communicate with the Controller to say that she no longer needs any dosages of the cure, perhaps indicating that the sixers are no longer a problem."

"Assuming we can trust her to do that." Reese scowled, folding her arms tightly over her stomach and sitting back on the couch where she sat between Jaxon and Eagle.

"We can," Dani said. "She believed what she was doing was best for us. But we'll make sure she complies." Delsindy and Shala nodded in agreement.

Enger was noncommittal, but he asked, "What good will her communication do?"

"We let him stew for a day or so," Lyssa said, "wondering if someone else has a cure, or if the sixers died. Then Jaxon contacts him."

Jaxon leaned forward, his face tight. "I'm assuming this has something to do with my premonition and betraying El Cerebro?"

"Yes." This was the trickiest part of her plan, but Lyssa hoped her grin hid her nervousness. Their action had to be bold to get the Controller to expose both himself and the cure. "We all know there's some connection between you two. Or him and your mother. He has to know you're a sixer. Not everyone gets an unsolicited invite to join Special Forces."

"Make that no one," Eagle cut in.

Lyssa nodded. "Right. No one in regular ranks. Although maybe other sixers have received such invites, and we just don't know about it."

She paused, gathering herself for the final step of her plan. She believed this could work, but success depended on if the others believed in it too. Especially Jaxon, so she focused her attention on him. "In your premonition, you were betraying El Cerebro, and that's exactly what you need to do. You respond to your invitation and say you want to be in Special Forces, but also say that you might need a mental evaluation, because you had a strange vision of El Cerebro with an army of soldiers with special abilities. Maybe a thousand of them. Firestarters, mindreaders, people with abnormal strength or spying abilities. People who can't die. Well, maybe that's too much, but you get the idea. It's probably better to be more subtle. Anyway, you also say you recognize the place where they are—in the empty zone outside Amarillo City. He'll guess that you've seen this because of your ability. I think if we play it right, he'll come."

"For the sixers," Jaxon said. "To decide which he'll murder and which he'll recruit."

Lyssa nodded. "And he'll come for El Cerebro. But the Controller won't be able to transport that many crazy people, so he'll bring the treatment as well."

"And we're going to take it." Hammer looked eager to do just that.

"Right. Of course, the sixers won't really be there, but the Controller may assume Newcali sold or gave the sixers to El Cerebro."

Silence fell over the room. Lyssa waited for objections, waited for someone to point out overwhelming flaws in her plan that would send them all back to the drawing board. But not a single person objected, not even Jaxon. That meant they were either hopeful or desperate. More likely, they were a little of both.

"There will be a lot to work out," Dani said finally, "especially keeping in mind that we'll have to keep the peace inside the colonies when we take over, every bit as much as we'll need to protect them from the CORE. But I know good people in each of the colonies, and they will rise to this opportunity. I think it's our only option."

That reaction wasn't as good as Lyssa hoped, but maybe coming from Dani it was all she'd get.

"I can take two hundred of my soldiers," Dani added. "That leaves a bare minimum to guard our border."

"El Cerebro will use all of his two hundred," Hammer said. "And we can find maybe sixty more fringers from the refugees. In case of siege, we'll need food stores for the colonies that don't produce food. They should have several weeks of readymeals already on hand. We've learned a lot of them raise animals to supplement their diet, even in the non-food colonies, but we'll need more."

"We can supply a lot," Shala responded. "We can give them water too. As much as they need."

Lyssa hadn't thought about water. "How soon can we get all this in place?" she asked. "Is it believable that Jaxon would wait weeks to respond to the invitation?"

"I'm feeling pressure about it already," Jaxon said with a shake of his head.

Hammer squared his big shoulders. "I think we should do it as soon as possible, while surprise is on our side. With use of some of the larger hovers, we could do it in a week working around the clock. Less, if we had additional transportation once we got the sixers and supplies to Amarillo City, but we have access to only so many shuttles, and I can't see us transporting unconscious sixers on the sky train."

"Doc Kentley could help some of them," Jaxon suggested. "At least those worse off or those who can lead."

"That's a good point," Hammer conceded. "We need to talk to El Cerebro and figure out how fast we can do this. He may have other contacts who can help."

Dani nodded. "We'll leave for Amarillo City first thing in the morning." She turned to Shala. "I'll need a dozen extra hovers this time. And for the next trip, as many more as we can spare. Even public ones. We'll start moving the sixers now. And the missile launchers. Two per colony should be plenty of deterrent."

"Will we move the sixers awake or asleep?" Shala asked. "We can fit more if they're awake."

"Awake," Dani decided. "At least this first batch. I'll hand-pick those I want to send ahead to the colonies to help spread the word among my contacts there. They'll be better at working with the colonists than my soldiers, and we want those colonists ready. Dr. Kentley will be able to treat several dozen sixers at least. The rest will go sedated. We'll get them in place near the colonies and wake them once we have a treatment."

"We'll need guns too," Reese said.

Hammer shook his head. "That's one thing we have plenty of in the underground. We've been gathering them for decades. Most are so old they don't have fingerprint readers on them, but they work just as well. We've plenty of ammo."

"We'll make sure our soldiers and the sixers are armed," President Enger said. The former anger and betrayal in his voice had given way to determination. Lyssa was pleased that even he seemed to support the plan.

Dani finally sat on a couch, leaning over to rest her elbows on her knees. "Each colony has a self-contained public announcement system. They normally use it to extend work hours or announce medical enhancements, but we'll use it to inform colonists what's going on after we take over. Hopefully, we can keep internal rioting to a minimum. We don't need to be fighting the colonists as well as the CORE."

"Let them riot," Lyra said darkly. "They deserve to protest after the horrors they've endured. In fact, we should arm them and let them help guard the walls. And once we're done, I say we give the colonies back to the colonists permanently. The cities belong to them, and they should be in control of their own products."

"Yes," Dani agreed. "But they'll need help negotiating in the beginning. And they'll need protection from people like the KC."

"One other thing we need to figure out," Hammer said, "is how to notify the Elite of the takeover. I'm envisioning a public announcement that details the history of the colonies and especially the extermination in Colony 6. We'll also announce that the Regulator's office is defunct and people can have as many children as they want. That alone will put the people on our side."

For the first time, Dani grinned, and it made her look a

little crazy. "Those codes we gave you to change the crew's background should work to get us into the public feed. They'll likely shut our broadcast down within a minute, but that'll be long enough to direct viewers to the backdoor to our T-link network, where they'll find all the information they ever wanted."

"They'll send out enforcers to arrest people who go to the link," Reese said.

Dani laughed. "Let them. There are still more people than enforcers, and I'm betting most of those enforcers will be following the link as well."

They continued to talk long into the night, making lists and plans. Hammer wrote down everything and condensed it to send to Brogan, who answered back two hours later with a green light. Near midnight, Lyssa excused herself, more for her sister's benefit than anyone else's. Lyra was drooping. Dani sent one of her soldiers to lead them back to the guest quarters, though after their exploring today, they were perfectly able to find their own way.

"Can we really do this?" Lyra asked in a soft voice as they walked down the curved hallway.

"I don't know," Lyssa answered. "But we have to try. If we wait much longer, we won't have any chance at all."

The next morning, Lyssa tumbled out of bed shortly before six, Newcali time, feeling more rested than she'd expected. A bustle of activity filled the guest quarters as the rest of her crew packed their bags in preparation for departure.

"Hey, sleepyhead," Hammer said with a note of affection in his voice as she came into the main room where someone had spread a feast. "Better hurry. Dani's sending someone for us as soon as she's ready to take off."

Lyssa made a face. "I hope we don't run into any more cazadors."

Hammer laughed. "Me too. Dani says it's unlikely. She says by now the fringers will have carried away all the meat they can use back to wherever they currently have their camp, and the remaining carcasses will warn off other beasts for a time."

"Good," she muttered. Then curiosity drove her to ask, "Any more from Brogan?"

He sobered immediately. "No, we don't dare risk any of this getting out. We're keeping communications to a minimum. For now, only those of us in the room last night and Brogan will know the whole plan. Not even Turner, Nova, Thane, or El Cerebro's top guards will be privy to everything. They'll know their part, but not what everyone else is doing, especially in the colonies. But after Sixer Day, everyone will know."

"Sixer Day?" she asked with a bit of a laugh.

He shrugged. "Hey, we gotta call it something, and why not? They—you—deserve it."

With those words the easiness between them vanished. The tension that took its place made her want to reach up and touch his face and run her fingers down the muscles of his chest. Quickly, she averted her eyes.

"Where's Lyra?" she asked.

"Bathroom. Is something wrong with her? She looks sick."

Nothing another eight months won't take care of, Lyssa thought. "She's fine."

"Well, she says she's not coming back with us. She and Reese had words about it a few minutes ago. Reese is concerned your ability won't be as useful without Lyra, and she doesn't want Jaxon to face the Controller alone."

The point was a valid one. "I'll talk to her."

"Wait, there's something else." Hammer followed her into the hallway. "Something important."

She faced him. "What?"

He glanced over his shoulder at the others in the main room, as if making sure no one was paying attention to them. "Birth orders came out today."

She sucked in a breath, and her heart started pounding. She'd checked before rolling out of bed, but there hadn't been any forwarded message from her personal account. She reached for her T-link to check again, but Hammer was already handing his over, as if knowing she needed to see it for herself.

With only a point five percent birth and death rate outside the colonies, just over twenty-one hundred birth orders were announced each quarter. Lyssa had to scroll most of the way through the list to see her name near the end. She'd been approved. *Ty*, she thought, both grateful and sad at the same time. This meant the end of their relationship. Unless maybe she could tell him the truth. With the underground revolution so close, birth orders would be a thing of the past. Maybe there could be a future for them.

Until Jaxon's prophecy came true.

"Thank you," she said, her voice scarcely a whisper.

Hammer didn't comment on her luck, and she thought that odd. Didn't he wonder how a single woman could get a birth order on her first try? Didn't he wonder who she would choose for the baby's father?

"Do you think it'll make a difference?" he asked when she started to turn away. "With Lyra wanting to come back, I mean. It's for her, isn't it?"

She blinked at him. "You knew?"

"I figured. She helped you, and it's only natural you want to help her. We all know how much she wants this. So, congratulations."

She nodded and turned without responding. She felt . . . what? But she knew. She wanted the baby herself, to raise a child in the open, something she hadn't been able to do with Tamsin. It was silly but true. Squelching her emotions, she marched to the bathrooms. Regardless of what happened with the revolution, this baby was for Lyra, not for her.

"I need to see a doctor," Lyra said after she answered Lyssa's worried knock and let her into the bathroom. She was pale and moving very slowly.

"You can see Kentley when we get back," Lyssa said.

Lyra closed her eyes and leaned against the wall. "I can't risk it. You know it'll take weeks, possibly a month or more to get things in place."

"Not if we can find additional transportation. We need to trust Brogan. His people have been planning something like this for a long time, and Dani knows her way around the colonies. With the hovers, we can do it fast."

"Not before my next physical." Lyra raised her hand to stop the words that threatened to pour from Lyssa's lips. "Will you please tell Kansas where I am? Tell him I hope he'll come too. And you and Tamsin—" Her voice broke.

"I got a birth order," Lyssa said. It wasn't the way she'd wanted to tell her sister the news. Well, to be honest, she hadn't expected to tell her anything since being accepted had been such a long shot.

Lyra gaped. "You're on today's list?"

Lyssa nodded. "It came out this morning. If the revolution doesn't go as planned, we'll have to change places, and maybe see if the captain can pull a few strings to get the doctor to look the other way about the date, but you can come home. Reese is right, we need you."

A sob burst from Lyra's throat, and tears began down her face. "How? How did you do it?"

Lyssa shrugged. Now wasn't the time to tell her about Ty and his connection to the KC. "I don't know. Maybe it was just luck."

"I don't believe that for a moment. And neither do you. Whatever you did, thank you!" Lyra hugged her, and for a long moment they stood in the bathroom, clutching each other.

Finally, Lyssa pulled away. "I had a thought just now when we were talking. Since you've told Kansas about the colonies and the underground, do you think he might be able to help with transportation? If we can use shuttles to get Dani's soldiers and the sixers to the Estlantic colonies instead of making the hovers go through the desolation zones, it'd cut the time in half. Or more."

Lyra shook her head and said bitterly, "I don't think he'll risk it. He's too afraid."

"You might be able to convince him. Or maybe Brogan could."

"No!" Lyra's face flushed with anger. "Don't mention him to the captain. What if he decides to *make* Kansas help? You know what the captain is capable of if he refused. I can't see Kansas hurt."

Lyssa swallowed hard. She understood Lyra's fear, but at the same time, a part of her *wanted* Brogan to force Kansas to use his position in the Department of Transportation to help. It could mean the difference between success and failure. But her loyalty to her sister won out.

"Okay, but at least give him the chance. Kansas loves you, and he's going to love this baby."

Lyra didn't look convinced. When they heard Dani calling from the other room, she splashed her face with water and hurried with Lyssa to the main room.

"It's done," Dani began when they arrived. "We had President Turner use her device to contact the Controller. She was put right through. She didn't let on that we know about the spy he planted here, but she told him the rest of the Presidents' Circle is willing to reopen the discussion about building a colony here. Then she added casually that we no longer needed any doses of the cure."

"You think he bought it?" Jaxon asked.

Dani nodded. "I asked her to say something about finding a doctor who was able to help instead. Since the Controller knows El Cerebro has Dr. Kentley, we agreed that would also pave the way for Jaxon's story later." She paused, her mouth turning up in a smirk. "He wasn't happy to hear that, of course. In fact, he was so unhappy that he mentioned a raid he's planning on the Amarillo City subway, which he anticipates will lead to information and possible capture of El Cerebro. He very solicitously said she should be aware of this in case El Cerebro contacted her for help. He would be horrified if she were somehow caught in the middle."

"You think he is planning a raid?" Hammer asked, his brow furrowing.

"No," Dani said. "At least not yet. Not until he finishes with the Estlantic empty zones and the subways there. He was fishing, plain and simple."

He was fishing. The phrase sounded wrong to Lyssa. There was only one place in Estlantic where ocean fishing was safe, and all streams had to be tested regularly. Water pipes were now the primary source of water in the CORE. But here in Newcali, fishing was commonplace. Would it ever be like that in the rest of the CORE? Lyssa believed it would, maybe for her grandchildren, but if the Elite remained in charge, the people might never make it to the oceans or streams. They'd be trapped behind the high, thick walls of a colony, working away their short lives so the Elite could remain in control.

Not while her crew still lived.

"Ready?" Dani asked. "It's time. It gets darker sooner in Amarillo City than here, so we should hurry."

Lyssa grabbed her bag and hurried after Dani. Once back in the hovercraft, she was relieved when Dani handed back their weapons. Lyssa didn't remember the bulk of her gun being so comforting, but it was now.

"This time when we refuel," Dani said, "everyone stays in sight of the hover."

With that warning ringing in her ears, Lyssa sat down and strapped in.

CHAPTER 16

Unlike their journey to Newcali, their trip back to Amarillo City was without incident. In Gila, where they'd refueled, there had been no sign of the fringers, and only one of the adult beast carcasses, virtually untouched, remained where Dani had slain it. How the fringers had managed to cart away the other three beasts, bones and all, in a matter of forty-eight hours, Lyssa didn't care to guess. The huge red stains on the ground, however, convinced her to remain close to the filling station. Only Nova risked Dani's wrath to venture away from the hover, coming back with a box of jewelry she must have stashed the last time she'd come through.

They arrived in an empty zone outside Amarillo City after ten. The other hovers that had accompanied them dropped off their sixers and missile launchers, leaving this first batch for El Cerebro to somehow ship to the colonies. The hovers then returned to Newcali bearing loads of refugee fringers—especially women with children, who could not stay and fight. By the time Lyssa and Lyra took a shuttle into the city, it was nearing eleven, and Lyssa was sure Tamsin would already be asleep. Even on a Friday night.

She was tired and her muscles were stiff, and she could see her sister was sagging from exhaustion, even though they'd both tried to nap in the hover. Lyssa thought about Kansas. Lyra would have to tell him about the baby.

Or would she? It would be a mistake not to. Because if there was one thing Lyssa knew, it was that Kansas loved Lyra more than his own life. Even more than he loved Tamsin. She knew because she'd pined away for him for far too long.

But now, as Kansas opened the door to the apartment before either set their palm on the reader to unlock the door, the old familiar rush at seeing his bronze face and curly hair was missing. Instead, she was thinking about Ty and what she would say to him. If she were completely honest, she was also remembering how Hammer had tried to save her from the beast in the empty zone and the delicious tension between them.

Kansas's gaze slid past Lyssa to rivet on his wife. "You're back," he said, relief apparent in his tone. He started to hug Lyra, and then stopped, as if nervous to do so, which meant they'd been fighting before she'd left. Nothing new there. But Lyra stepped willingly into his arms.

Kansas's open display of affection told Lyssa that Tamsin was definitely in bed, so when an excited squeal came from the hallway, she was surprised. "Mommy!" Tamsin appeared, rubbing one eye tiredly. She hurtled herself at Lyssa, and warmth filled the emptiness in her heart.

Lyssa scooped her up and turned the child's back to Lyra and Kansas, but the two had already parted. "I missed you, baby," Lyssa said.

"I'm not a baby," Tamsin protested, her voice muffled against Lyssa's shoulder.

"I know. How did things go?"

"Okay. Do you have to work tomorrow?"

"For a while." Not for her regular shift, but she had work to do in a secret room behind dispatch. "Come on. Let's get you to bed."

"Night, Daddy. Night, Aunt Lyssa."

There it was again, her name on Tamsin's lips. Now with the baby on the way, what would they tell her? Some convoluted story about Kansas being a sperm donor and the baby being both her cousin and her brother? Lyssa's head ached.

"Night, sweetie." Lyra smoothed Tamsin's hair and leaned in to kiss her hair-covered cheek.

"Night," Kansas echoed.

Lyssa hurried away, going into Tamsin's room and shutting the door firmly behind her.

"Was it fun?" Tamsin asked sleepily.

Nearly being eaten and planning a coup wouldn't be high on anyone's list of things to do on a trip, but Lyssa also remembered the mouth-watering food, growing closer to Hammer, and learning more about her ability. Truthfully, she'd never felt more alive. Only Tamsin had been missing in all that.

"Yeah," she said. "I'm glad to be back with you, though. I missed you."

That won her a grin. "I missed you too. I told my class you went to Estlantic, and they asked if you were going to bring me anything."

"I did." Lyssa shed her coat, tossing it over the only chair in the room, and dug in her pocket for one of the necklaces Nova had recovered from the empty zone. The piece had cost Lyssa all the cash credits she and Lyra both carried with them, and it was a discount at that, according to Nova. Lyssa didn't know if that was true, but as she hadn't left the Circle or done any shopping, it was her only choice. At least the links on the silver-colored chain looked strong, and the butterfly charm sparkled with different colored gems that might or might not be real.

"It's so pretty!" Tamsin immediately tried to put it on.

Lyssa started to object but thought the better of it. If the necklace had survived Breakdown, it would survive a night on her daughter's neck. She helped fasten it and then stripped off her outer clothes and lay down next to Tamsin.

The little girl's arms wrapped around her neck. "Thank you so much for my necklace," she whispered, her voice already becoming sleepy again. "I love you, Mommy."

"I love you too."

Within minutes Tamsin's hold relaxed as sleep claimed her. Lyssa knew she should get up and move to her own bed, but the enormity of what she and the rest of the crew planned to do plagued her. Not acting wasn't an option, because there was no way she would allow Tamsin's children to grow up in a colony. But if the coup didn't work, if Lyssa were caught, what would happen to Tamsin? She needed a plan for her daughter in case of failure.

Tamsin's increasing ability was another issue. She needed protection, and that might mean telling Kansas. She and Lyra had briefly discussed that possibility during the day, and they hadn't come to a conclusion. Would he insist on doctors that would bring the notice of the Elite down upon them? No. He was sensible, and he loved Tamsin. They'd have to figure something out.

What if Dani tested older sixer offspring and found they had abilities without the madness? If many of them had survived childhood, that would be another boon in the underground's favor, and they would need everything they could get if they were going to make it through this.

Her iTeev vibrated, sounding impatient. Lyssa didn't have

to look to know who it was. Since they had come back into range of the Teev feed, she'd received three texts from Ty, all of them asking how she was, when she'd be back, and if he could see her.

Did he expect thanks for the strings he'd pulled?

The last thing she wanted to do after traveling hundreds of miles across an empty zone was confront him. She really did have to work tomorrow, and though she didn't have to be there early, her body craved sleep.

Still, she dragged out the iTeev and looked at the message. *Please, can we talk? You're home now, right?*

Sighing, she rolled from the bed and scooped up her pants, shoving her legs in reluctantly. Her undershirt would be enough to get her to her room modestly, even if Kansas happened to be in the hallway. She kissed her daughter's cheek before gathering the rest of her things and easing the door open. The hallway was deserted.

In her own room, she ran her fingers through her hair before reconnecting the room's Teev connection to the feed and giving it the signal to return the last call sent to her iTeev. After only a few seconds, Ty's face appeared in front of her, looking as if he were right there in her room. He looked handsome, his hair combed and slightly spiked, and unlike her, he was wearing dress pants and a shirt that looked fresh out of the closet.

"You're back," he said, sitting in a chair in his living room.

"Yeah, we're back." She settled on her bed, hoping that with only one low light on, he couldn't see her few remaining bruises from the beast attack.

"Tired?"

She nodded. "It was a couple of long days."

"I bet." He regarded her for a couple minutes and then said, "Congratulations on the birth order."

"Look, you shouldn't have—" She broke off. The feed was always monitored, and if she wanted a private conversation with Ty, now wasn't the time. If he pushed, she'd have to beg off, claiming exhaustion, which wasn't far from the truth. Then again, if he was working with the KC, he wouldn't trust the feed any more than she did.

"What I said before," he said. "Have you given it any more thought?"

She'd thought about almost nothing else on the drive home. She didn't want to break up with Ty, but with Lyra pregnant, they'd soon have to change places in the real world.

"It's late and I'm exhausted," she said. "Let's talk later, okay?"

He nodded. "You're working tomorrow?"

"Just to catch up on some reports," she lied.

"Maybe we can get together for dinner."

"Can I text you when I see how it goes? Sunday might be better. I might have to watch my niece." She couldn't exactly say she wanted to spend time with her daughter.

"Sure." He hesitated a few minutes before adding, "Look, I get the feeling there's something you aren't telling me."

That was an understatement, if there ever was one. "Ty," she began, getting ready to play the exhaustion card, "I—"

He held up a hand to stop her. "I know it's a crazy time with CivID changes and rebel fringers being chased from the empty zones. But it'll all be over soon. I just want you to know that I'm always here for you. No matter what."

All be over soon? What did he mean? Could the KC have their own plan, as Dani had suggested? Or was he simply referring to the Elite rubbing out the fringers? Lyssa's numbed brain couldn't decipher any of it, but she felt guilty at his offer. She knew he meant it, and she wished she could have been more honest with him.

"Thanks," she said. "Goodnight, Ty."

His lips pursed momentarily, as if in frustration, but then he gave a nod. "Goodnight, Lyssa."

Lyra was happy to see Kansas, and he seemed equally happy to see her. After Lyssa and Tamsin had vanished into Tamsin's bedroom, he'd kissed her for real. One thing had led to another, and they'd ended up in her bed. Lyra was happy to let everything else slide away. Everything except the feel of her husband's body against hers. Even thoughts of the baby in her belly, yet unseen and unfelt, vanished in their lovemaking. She was glad she'd come back, if only for this moment. It might very well be one of their last together.

They slept in each other's arms all night, and when they awoke Saturday morning, he kissed her neck again, ready to repeat their passionate night, but the sudden movement destroyed the fragile peace of Lyra's stomach. Gagging, she bounced from the bed into the small adjoining bathroom. She hugged the toilet, vomiting repeatedly until her heaves brought up a tiny amount of yellow bile.

"Do you need a doctor?"

She turned to see Kansas staring down at her anxiously, med kit in hand. "No," she said.

"I have anti-nausea meds. One hypo ought to stop the vomiting. It's probably all that hover travel."

Lyra knew what she really needed was food. "I'm fine." She waved him away.

Rising unsteadily, she rinsed her mouth and started for the kitchen. There, she popped in a breakfast readymeal, wishing instead for the fresh bread she'd eaten in Newcali. When the readymeal was finished, she staggered with it to her bedroom where Kansas, his curly hair mussed, waited by the bed as if wondering what to do with himself.

Ignoring him, Lyra climbed on the bed and rested a moment before opening the readymeal. The scent of fake eggs almost made her vomit right there on the bed. But there was some kind of bread, too, and it was warm. She chewed it slowly and steadily, and after finishing the bread, the urge to puke was almost gone. She sighed with relief. She'd have to get something from Dr. Kentley, or maybe just spending time with the man would help again.

Kansas sat on the bed, staring at her. "What's going on? This isn't like you." His gaze sharpened. "I remember when Lyssa was . . ." His voice trailed off, and the color drained from his face.

Lyra nodded. "I'm pregnant," she confirmed. "And yes, it's yours." She held her breath.

His jaw dropped. For a long moment, he stared at her, mouth agape. "How long?"

Lyra let out a sigh. "About a month I think."

For a long time, he remained quiet, not voicing the questions in his eyes. Finally, he said, "This is why you . . . all that talk about Newcali."

She nodded, not trusting her voice. She'd expected anger, not this . . . whatever this was.

He slid over to her and put his arm around her, carefully pulling her close. His hand went to her stomach, his warmth transmitting to her through the thin material of her night dress. "But you have an implant."

That was where things got sticky. She wasn't going to tell him about removing her implant. Not yet. Maybe later, when everything was okay—if things were ever okay. Implants rarely failed, but they did occasionally, which was why there had recently been talk about requiring an implant for men as well.

She shrugged. "It doesn't matter. I'm happy about it, and I'm keeping her."

"Her?"

Lyra hadn't even told her sister what Kentley had been able to determine with a simple scan. "Yes, her. I've been to a doctor."

Kansas frowned, but his hand didn't leave her stomach. "That's a huge risk. What if the doctor reported you?"

"He won't." She hesitated before adding, "They're after him already. He's with the underground."

"Oh." More head shaking. "I can't believe it." Then a wide smile spread over his face. "I'm going to be a dad." He sounded happy.

Happy? Lyra wasn't sure she could trust her ears.

"So now what do we do?" he added.

We, he'd said. Not *you.* Relief poured over her, retriggering the urge to heave. "Lyssa got a birth order," she whispered, swallowing hard. "We'll trade. Like we did before."

He hugged her then, and she was shocked to feel the tears on his cheeks. "I know you've wanted this for a long time," he said against her neck. "I don't know how we're going to pull this off, but we will. Like we did before. And I'm sorry."

"Sorry?"

His hold tightened. "I haven't been there for you. After we argued . . . I began to worry that you weren't coming back."

"I almost didn't," she said quietly.

"I've done a lot of thinking about what you said. You're right, no one should tell us when we should be able to have a child. And no one should be sentenced to a colony because they want a baby." He kissed her cheek. "So I'm sorry."

She laughed, a touch of hysteria to the sound.

"Tamsin's going to be thrilled," he said. "Wait. What can we possibly tell her?"

"I don't know, but maybe for now let's wait. We might be able to tell her the truth soon."

He pulled away from her, his expression both interested and wary. "Why do you say that?"

"I can't tell you."

"Yes, you can." He released her and rubbed at his scalp with a frustrated hand. "You can trust me."

"It's for your safety. And for the plan's safety. Everyone can only know their part, except a few of us."

"You and Lyssa?"

She nodded.

"We'll wait then."

"You don't understand." She put a little space between them, wanting to study his reaction. "There's going to be fighting. And probably rationing until things are settled. It might become dangerous here. And if we fail . . ." She shrugged because she simply didn't know what would happen then.

His tongue wet his lips. "Do we need to leave?"

"I can't. They need my ability. But you and Tamsin can. I can arrange for you to go to Newcali." Tears formed in her eyes. "It'll be good for us there. So many empty zones with houses that aren't destroyed. Maybe when it's over we won't even want to return."

"Let me get this right." Kansas gave her a hard stare. "You're suggesting that I run away while my pregnant wife stays here to start a rebellion?"

He had seemed perfectly willing to bury his head in the earth before, but she probably shouldn't point that out. "I'm asking you to take care of our daughter." Ours, because Tamsin was hers too.

For a long time, Kansas didn't speak. He simply studied her. At last, he leaned forward, kissed her forehead, and pulled her tightly to him. "We'll make sure Tamsin's safe, but my place is with you. I don't want to be on the outside anymore. I want to know it all. I want to help. Tell that to your friends. Tell them if you're in this, then so am I."

Lyra thought about that for a moment, and also about Lyssa's suggestion about asking Kansas for his help. Maybe he could help and remain safe.

"There is something," she said. "We need transport. A lot of it. Can you get us shuttles that won't be noticed? It has to be off the books, without their trips being recorded or tracked."

Kansas nodded slowly. "Yes. I believe I can. We have vehicles in for maintenance that I can deviate, as well as a sizeable group of new shuttles that we need to ship to Estlantic. With some creativity and a little help on your end with the TAD-Alert program, I think I can get fifty or so."

Lyra smiled. For that brief moment in time, everything was right with her world. "How soon can you get them?"

All Saturday and Sunday, the empty zone north of Amarillo City was a hive of activity. As Dani's hovers brought in the sixers, water, food, and missiles, the shuttles Kansas had appropriated moved them out. Each batch of supplies and sedated sixers were accompanied by a group of Dani's uniformed soldiers, heading to the three colonies in Estlantic. All of Dani's soldiers would end up at those three colonies for the coup, along with a handful of El Cerebro's most trusted guards. The last groups of sixers would go to the closer colonies, joined by larger groups of undergrounders and refugee soldiers. Once the cure was in hand, trusted soldiers would rush it to all the colonies in more borrowed shuttles.

Then Sixer Day would begin.

Even with the hovers and shuttles running constantly, it would take until Tuesday to place the sixers, soldiers, and supplies bound to Estlantic. Then they'd start on the Dallastar colonies that were much closer. The Tuesday deadline was far earlier than Lyssa had predicted, but the worried expression in Brogan's eyes told her it might not be soon enough. Every day that passed meant more risk of exposure. So far, Jaxon had delayed responding to his Special Forces invitation, but much longer than Monday or Tuesday might be suspect, and how soon the Controller would come to Amarillo City after that was anyone's guess. They wanted all their people who could be spared in place before then.

Each of the sixers had been awakened briefly before transport for a briefing and to be strapped into a seated position with hastily sewn harnesses. Only three had been kept back due to medical concerns. As Dani had predicted, all were willing to fight. Dr. Kentley helped as many of the initial loads of sixers as possible, and he was looking near death when Brogan finally ordered him away from the empty zone. They needed him rested when they finally took possession of the medicine.

Meanwhile, the bulk of El Cerebro's black beanie-wearing guards and several dozen refugee fringers prepared to confront the Special Forces and steal the medicine. A carefully subdued excitement radiated through the crew, soldiers, and undergrounders alike as each dutifully bent to their tasks.

When they exhausted the shuttles Kansas had provided, Brogan dug up a half dozen more. He also used several police shuttles and borrowed enforcer uniforms for his undergrounders to move missiles and launchers near the three Dallastar colonies, where they would wait for the rest of their soldiers before being smuggled inside. Watching his impassive, mask-covered face as he gave orders, Lyssa realized the captain had as much to risk as anyone if their plan failed. There would be no second chances, especially for him and his under-grounders. Only success or death.

When she wasn't with Tamsin, Lyssa spent all her time in the small, secret room on the backside of dispatch. Unlike inside the dispatch room, where the TAD-Alert interface consisted of mostly holoscreens, the secret room housed the bulk of the super Teev's hardware. Brogan had connected backup holo emitters that would allow the crew to use the TAD out of sight of prying eyes.

Lyssa's current job was to make sure no enforcers were in the immediate vicinity of the empty zone, and that any disturbance calls in the inhabited areas nearby were forwarded to Reese and Jaxon, instead of normal beat enforcers. They couldn't have anyone catching sight of a hover or shuttle entering the empty zone. As it was the weekend, and dispatch often switched up the TAD's enforcer recommendations, anyone monitoring the TAD-Alert shouldn't catch the difference or become aware that Lyssa was inputting information from a secret terminal rather than from inside dispatch itself, where the regular employees worked in blissful ignorance.

Early Sunday afternoon, Hammer came into the secret room to relieve her, his long hair in his customary ponytail. "Hey," he said. "I hear you've been working all night."

"Someone had to run interference, and Lyra's not feeling well."

He nodded. "I figured."

He wasn't the only one who had guessed about the baby. Everyone had noticed how sick Lyra had been on the way home from Newcali.

"Besides," Lyssa added, "she was here most of yesterday afternoon so I could be with Tamsin. She should be in soon. Dr. Kentley gave her something for the nausea, and it's easy enough work. There aren't that many calls coming from near the empty zones."

As she finished rerouting another call, Lyssa was acutely aware of him. How he unfolded the extra chair propped against the wall and sat, oddly graceful despite his bulk. How his hair, drawn tightly back, exposed the defined outline of his cheekbone. She could also feel his gaze on her.

"What?" she said finally, tearing her eyes from the holoscreen.

He gave her a slow, compelling smile that burned heat in her gut. "I'm wondering what you are going to do with Tamsin. She doesn't know anyone in the underground, and I heard Kansas refused to go with her on one of the hovers back to Newcali."

"He can't go, not while he's managing the shuttles. If we get caught . . ."

"Right." He gave a solemn nod.

Something of the expression on his chiseled face reminded her of their capture by the fringers in the empty zone, and how he'd offered to stay behind and fight the beast so she could run. She believed he would have fought alone to save her, even if it had meant his death. Maybe he would have done that for anyone, but she wasn't just anyone, not to him. She could see that. Now she had to figure out what her feelings were—and what to do about it.

"I've been thinking," he said after a moment of awkward silence, when she was crazily considering how his cheek would feel against her hand. "Remember Reese's aunt in Big Horn? Theena Parker?"

"Yeah, her great-aunt, right? We had Reese's birthday party at her place. But you weren't there."

"No, but I've met the lady, and you said Tamsin loved her chickens, and that they got along well. Why not take her there? The aunt isn't an Elite, but her grandfather was a city manager.

She has pull in the community and is a pretty smart woman. From what Reese says, she has leanings to our cause, even though they don't discuss it. Plus, it's far enough away from Amarillo City and the colonies to avoid the fighting. We could go tonight and take her."

The suggestion made Lyssa feel suddenly emotional. She and Lyra had discussed Tamsin at length, but neither had come up with a solution. She'd thought they'd have a week or more to figure something out, but with that now carved down to days, she was running out of options. That Hammer had not only taken time to consider Tamsin but had offered to go with her, even if she didn't need him, made his suggestion that much more thoughtful.

"It's a good idea," she said. "I'll talk to Reese."

They stood at the same time, her to leave and him to take her place in front of the screen. For the briefest second, their bodies brushed. The resulting jolt made her mouth dry.

"Be careful," he said, the silkiness of his voice sending a shiver up her spine. "And let me know what time you're going. I meant what I said about going with you."

"I'd like that," she somehow managed to say. "Probably after dinner. I need to figure out an excuse for keeping her away from school."

"I'll wait to hear from you."

Lyssa had paused to make sure the door was locked behind her when a movement down the hallway startled her. She whipped her head around to see Ty Bissett.

"Lyssa," he said, his voice pleased.

"Um, what are you doing here?" She moved down the narrow, dimly-lit hallway and into the main one where he stood.

"You weren't answering your iTeev, and since you had to watch your niece yesterday and we didn't end up having dinner, I decided to stop at dispatch to see if you were working."

"Just catching up on those reports I told you about," she said.

He craned his neck, looking past her. "I've worked here ten years and I never knew this hallway even existed."

"It doesn't," she joked. "Hey, what about a late lunch? I haven't eaten yet, and I'm starved."

That meant she'd have to talk with him now about where their relationship was heading. Or not heading, rather. But in light of her increasing feelings for Hammer, and the impossibility of telling Ty the truth, it was better for both of them to get it over with.

"Sure." His smile lit up his whole face, and the bittersweet rush of emotions that followed made Lyssa wish she didn't have to say goodbye. Maybe if they made it through these next few days, she could tell him everything. Maybe that would change their future and his destiny. But even if a miracle happened, would she be able to stay away from Hammer? She didn't think so.

"I can't stay long," she said. "My sister's coming in for work, and I promised to watch her daughter again."

"I'd like to meet her sometime," he said as they started down the hallway. "I can't believe I haven't. You talk about her so much. It's obvious you're close." He paused, as if expecting her to say something, maybe to invite him over, but when she didn't, he shrugged and remained silent until they stepped outside the front door of division.

"Where would you like to go?" Ty asked as they began strolling down the sidewalk.

Before Lyssa could respond, two men fell into step on either side of them. A hand that seemed made of iron clamped around her upper arm. She whipped her head around only to stare into the broad face of Fletch Teller, the KC minion that Ty had met with less than a week before.

He grinned. "Hello again."

CHAPTER 17

Lyssa tried to wrest her arm from Teller's grip. "Let me go."

"Stop, or I'll make this more unpleasant than it has to be." He opened his long leather jacket to show her the glint of a weapon.

Well, Lyssa was armed too. And Hammer's combat lessons had taught her a lot. These men couldn't hijack them outside division on a street full of witnesses. But a glance at Ty showed her that a rough grip on the arm wasn't their only concern. The brown-haired man accosting him wasn't as tall or as broad as her attacker, but he was walking entirely too close. He must have a gun at Ty's back.

Ty's expression was angry, and his dark eyes sparked as she looked at him. "Run," he urged.

She debated following his advice, but the clenched jaw of his attacker left no question that he wouldn't think twice about shooting Ty. Jaxon's premonition had shown Ty with a broken neck, not a bullet. Did that mean he wouldn't die from the shot?

In the next instant, all chance of action was taken from her as she was pushed into an oversized black shuttle. She felt Teller check her for weapons and remove her gun.

Saca! she cursed silently as Ty was forced into the shuttle after her and the doors slid closed.

"Drive," the second attacker told the man at the shuttle controls. The shuttle jumped forward with a little screech of wheels.

Immediately Lyssa closed her eyes and slipped from her body.

"What did you do to her!" she heard Ty screaming.

"Nothing," came Teller's guttural reply. "We're just going to ask her a few questions. If you'd done your job, we wouldn't have to."

"She has nothing to do with this," Ty retorted.

"She has everything to do with this."

Lyssa didn't linger further. As the shuttle drove away, she glided back into division. *Hammer, Hammer,* she thought. She had to get to him. He was the closest, and he could give chase. If she'd found Dani in Newcali, by Breakdown, she'd better be able to find a man she was considering letting into her life.

An instant later, she was back in the secret room with Hammer. "The KC," she said, not wasting time on her triumph at reaching him. "They grabbed Ty and me outside division."

The words barely escaped her mouth when Lyssa realized her own stupidity. Of course, he couldn't see or hear her. He wasn't Lyra or even Eagle. What was wrong with her? Her attraction to him was getting in the way of good sense. Cursing at herself, she traveled to Lyra, instantly appearing by her bed in their apartment. Lyra was sound asleep.

"Lyra, wake up!" she said, clapping hard for additional sound. "Wake up. The KC. They've grabbed me."

Lyra moaned softly, but her eyes didn't open. Instead, she

appeared incorporeally next to Lyssa. "What's wrong?" she asked. "I hear you calling, but I feel all foggy. Like it's a dream."

"You're asleep," Lyssa said. "Why won't you wake up?"

"Doctor Kentley was here. He heard that I didn't sleep all night, so he did something. He said I'd wake up in two hours, but that was a while ago. I know I'm supposed to relieve you at division."

Lyssa shook her shoulders. "You have to wake up. The KC grabbed me outside division. Ty too. I'm afraid this is where he . . ."

Dies.

That wasn't her only concern. If the KC got wind of their intended takeover, they could lever the knowledge to their benefit, perhaps preventing the underground coup and pulling off one of their own in its place.

"I'm trying," Lyra said, staring down at her body. "But all that's there is sleep. Fogginess."

"Maybe Eagle can help." Lyssa willed herself to go to him. Nothing. Either he was too far away for her to find, or she was too flustered. When she'd traveled to Dani, they'd been under the same roof.

"Tamsin," Lyra said, snapping her fingers. "Tamsin can call Reese and Jaxon. I'll keep trying to wake up."

The words barely escaped Lyra's lips when Lyssa felt herself moving, but the location transfer was nowhere near instantaneous like it had been with Lyra. Light streamed around her and then stopped dizzyingly as she appeared next to Tamsin. The child was standing by the river that ran through town, throwing bits of seeds from the nearby dispensers to the few remaining ducks who had been smart enough to stay in Amarillo City instead of following their instinct and going south for the winter. South, where a desolation zone and death awaited.

"Tamsin," she called.

The little girl looked up, a smile spreading over her face. "Mommy, you're back! Daddy said you wouldn't be home for another hour."

Daddy. Lyssa's gaze flitted to a nearby bench were Kansas was looking at something on his iTeev. Obviously, they were between the staggered transfers, and he'd taken the opportunity to bring Tamsin here for a normal father-daughter Sunday outing. She'd had several lulls herself in the last ten hours, in which she'd slipped out for food or even napped in the secret room.

Biting back fear, Lyssa said. "Go tell Daddy I need you to make a call for me. Hurry, sweetie. This is very important. Daddy can't see me because I'm traveling. I'll explain that later, but you have to call or make him call. I'll tell you the number."

Tamsin immediately dropped the handful of duck seed on the hard-packed earth. The ducks swarmed her, but she pushed through them. "Daddy, Daddy," she called. "I need your iTeev. Mommy needs me to call someone for help."

Kansas blinked, looking around. "What do you mean? Mommy's not here."

"Yes, she is. Right there." Tamsin pointed at Lyssa.

"I don't think now is a good time for pretending." Kansas folded his iTeev and reached for her.

"Tell him it's related to the shuttles. Tell him Mommy needs help now, and Aunt Lyra is sleeping so she can't help."

"Aunt Lyra is sleeping?" Tamsin said. "Don't you mean Aunt Lyssa?"

"Just say it," Lyssa told her, trying to keep the panic from her voice.

But by then Tamsin already had Kansas's attention. He glanced once at the space Tamsin was talking to and unfolded his iTeev screen, without activating the holo capabilities. "What's the number?"

Lyssa told him and Tamsin repeated it obediently, as if talking to her incorporeal mother were the most natural thing in the world.

"If you'd have let me get an iTeev," Tamsin said, "I could have called myself."

An unexpected snort burst from Lyssa. They'd purposefully not allowed her to have an iTeev. She was already monitored enough from the constant feed access at school. "When you're older," she said mechanically.

"Who's this?" Kansas demanded into the iTeev when someone answered the line. He'd met the whole crew the day before, and he should recognize Hammer's name. Apparently, he was satisfied at the response. "Look, this is Kansas Bateman. My daughter says her mother has a message for you. I don't know exactly what's going on, but I'm figuring it's something to do with"—he coughed, perhaps biting back words he was afraid of saying over the feed—"those transport issues we're having." To Tamsin, he said, "Go ahead, sweetie." He held the iTeev up to her face.

Tamsin looked up at Lyssa and repeated diligently as she spoke. "The KC took Mommy and Ty outside division. They're in a black shuttle. There was probably a camera interruption or an ID you can follow. She says hurry. That's all. And we need to wake up my aunt." Tamsin thrust back the iTeev.

"Wait," Kansas said, looking again askance at the empty space next to Tamsin. "Why would they take you?"

Lyssa ignored him. "Thank you, sweetie," she told Tamsin.

Tamsin's eyes filled with tears. "Are you okay?"

"Yes, I am now." She smiled. "See? All better. You did so well. Now tell Daddy to go home and wake your aunt." Lyssa wasn't sure Tamsin heard the last words as she felt herself tugged back to her body.

She opened her eyes as someone slapped her face. The

numbness in her cheeks told her the slapping had probably gone on for some time, but she hadn't even tried to keep tabs on what was happening to her physically. More bruises for her collection.

Fletch Teller gazed down at where she was prone on the floor of the shuttle, whose back seats had apparently been removed. He looked like he was enjoying himself. "Welcome back," he said with a sneer. "I trust you're awake enough to answer a—"

"What did he do to you?" Ty broke in. "Lyssa, I'm so sorry."

His voice came from her right, and Lyssa turned to see him lying next to her, his face drawn in concern. She felt for his hand and gripped it tightly. "It's okay. They'll find us."

"Who will find us?" he asked.

"Enforcers."

Teller snorted. "Maybe. But first you're going to tell us what we want to know."

Lyssa tried to raise herself to see out the darkened windows, but Teller's gun pressed into her side. "Why were you following me?" he demanded.

"I wasn't following you," she protested. "I was following Ty."

Ty did a doubletake. "Me? When?"

"On Tuesday after lunch. You didn't go home."

Teller's hard fingers forced her face back in his direction. "Why did you follow him?"

Lyssa said the first reason that came to mind. "I thought he was meeting a woman. Why else wouldn't he go back to work?"

"There is no other woman," Ty said. "How could you think that? I went to them because of the birth order."

Teller shifted, glancing once at the other man, who crouched by the door, gun in hand. He shrugged at Teller.

"This is the woman you wanted the birth order for?" Teller asked.

"Of course she is. Why are you doing this?" Anger filled

Ty's voice. "I said I'll get you the records. I always have before, haven't I?"

Now it was Lyssa's turn to gape at him. "You're helping them?"

Ty shook his head, but his next words confirmed his confession. "Something has to change in the CORE before we're all nothing but mindless shells. I'm just giving them personal records of the enforcers in the colonies. Enforcers and administration employees." Ty's gaze was earnest. "You might not understand, but the colonists are really prisoners. When all this began, the KC told me they wanted to free the colonies, so I thought I was doing the right thing." His tone said that now he wasn't so sure. Lyssa understood only too well. Brogan had once given her the same opportunity. She'd come to believe in him, but what if she'd been recruited by the KC first? She didn't even want to consider that.

Lyssa's eyes went past Teller to the second attacker, hoping he'd be more inclined to believe her. "I don't know anything about that," she said. "I just want to have a baby."

She hoped this would be the end of it. If they'd helped her with the birth order, then they'd have something on her, and there would be no need to kill her for hearing Ty's information. And from what she'd heard, Ty hadn't yet given them the most recently requested information. He worked in personnel, but that kind of information wasn't something you could easily get without being flagged. You needed access to the TAD-Alert and to understand what kinds of queries to give it that wouldn't raise any flags. Now that she knew what he planned to give the KC, she could put a stop to it.

Why would the KC want the colony enforcers and admin records? She'd pulled the same information yesterday for Brogan so they could account for all the people they'd have to overcome in the colonies, but the KC didn't have the personnel to stage a similar coup. Did the KC intend to recruit those people instead? Or maybe threaten them into some kind of alliance? Lyssa couldn't begin to decipher their intentions with what little information she'd been given. Whatever the KC plan, it might expose the underground coup that was in progress.

Teller snorted again at her denial. "What is El Cerebro planning?" he gritted. "We know something big is going down. You *will* tell us."

"She doesn't know anything," Ty shouted. "It's me you want. Let her go. I'll do what you want. I just need a few more days."

Teller rolled his eyes. "Your girlfriend here is a part of the Amarillo City underground. What?" he mocked. "Don't tell me you didn't know about it."

"You're lying," Ty growled.

"Am I? Five weeks ago, when she was in Estlantic, we rendered assistance to some of El Cerebro's people. We didn't see your girl then, but since she's been back, she has been seen repeatedly sneaking off to places unknown with those we did help. Presumably somewhere down inside the ancient subway. It's where we in the Estlantic underground have our headquarters. Or where we had it before Special Forces started cleaning out the tunnel."

"You're out of your mind," Ty shot. "Lyssa, tell him."

At this point, Lyssa decided to play dumb. All she had to do was buy time. If Lyra didn't show up to pinpoint their location by the time they arrived at wherever the KC was taking them, Lyssa would travel to Tamsin and give her the address to pass on. She was also sure Hammer was searching for her with the TAD. In a city filled with Teev cameras, even a disruption would be traceable.

Tamsin chose that moment to appear on Lyssa's stomach. "Mommy," she said happily. Then her face sobered as she saw the men with guns. "What are they doing?" she whimpered, sinking closer to Lyssa.

"I'm okay," Lyssa assured her. "Go home."

"But, Mommy," Tamsin began.

Lyra appeared then, her body half inside Teller's. She grimaced and moved away. "Tamsin, sweetie, I'll stay with Mommy. You need to go back to Daddy so we can work."

Tamsin looked around uncertainly. "This is work?"

"Yes, sweetie." Lyra set her hand on Tamsin. "Go now, and don't come back until I tell you it's okay. We can't distract Mommy. We're on a special mission. When we're finished, we'll tell you all about it, okay?"

"Okay." With worry still creasing her small forehead, Tamsin disappeared. Lyssa had to fight the urge to travel with her.

"Sorry about that," Lyra said. "She was worried." She stared out the window for a few brief seconds. "They're blocking your iTeev and CivID signals, but your current location seems to coincide with the TAD's tracking of this vehicle. They disrupted cameras for a few blocks but then stopped, and we picked it out. Our people are enroute. Hold on. I'm going to check on Tamsin." She vanished.

Lyssa became aware that everyone in the shuttle except the driver was staring at her. Finally, Teller snorted. "You're not going home, lady. You're far from going home."

"Look, I don't know what any of this means," Lyssa said. "My co-workers might. Just because I go out with them doesn't mean I know everything they do."

"You were seen in the presence of El Cerebro," the second man said.

That was impossible. Lyssa hadn't been anywhere topside with El Cerebro. None of the crew had. They couldn't risk exposing the underground's connection with division. But that gave her an idea.

"Maybe it was my sister," she said. "My twin works at division too."

"Twin?" Teller spat with a mixture of scorn and disbelief. He glanced at Ty, who nodded.

"She does have a twin," he said. "They're identical."

All but a tiny mole on the right side of Lyra's neck, under her ear, but Ty couldn't possibly know that as he hadn't spent time with both of them.

This information seemed to disgruntle Teller further, and he glared accusingly at the second as-yet-unnamed man. Was he the one who'd claimed to have seen her with El Cerebro? She studied him now. Like Teller, he wore an expensive-looking jacket, but it was some kind of black linen, not leather, and instead of shiny black boots, he wore equally shiny dress shoes. His looks were only average, except his hair, which was perhaps slightly lighter than the customary brown. If she'd passed him on the street, she wouldn't have given him a second glance. He looked like a business man, not a thug. She couldn't recall ever seeing him before, but he did seem familiar.

He glared back at her, his gaze unflinching. Then, almost jerking, his eyes closed and his face contorted. When he opened his eyes again, there was curiosity in his expression.

"Ollin, are you okay?" Teller demanded. "What is it?"

"Nothing," Ollin growled. "Let's just get this over with."

Ten minutes later, the shuttle stopped. Teller produced black bags to slip over their heads and tie around their necks. Lyssa thought that was a good sign. They obviously didn't want them to see where they were heading, which meant they might live to tell the tale. But she wouldn't relax her guard. These men were killers working for killers. She could never forget that.

CHAPTER 18

Teller's big hand yanked her away from Ty and propelled her across a paved expanse. Lyssa fought panic.

"I'm right here," Lyra said from beside Lyssa, her voice sending a much needed calm through Lyssa's heart. "The team's arriving and moving into place. Looks like these men are taking you into a warehouse. There's a step in about five paces, so be careful. One, two, three, four, five—lift your foot now. Good."

After another few seconds, Lyra added, "Okay we're inside, going past an empty receptionist desk into a huge room with rows and rows of crates. Looks like they hold readymeals."

The bag was yanked off Lyssa's head at that point, and she found herself staring at huge crates stamped with the contents: beef with broccoli, chicken with rice, eggs and sausage. There were dozens of different titles, some she'd never seen before, like avocado with beans. She didn't even know what an avocado was. Probably something pre-Breakdown that was now produced in such small quantities that only specialized stores carried the readymeals.

Teller holstered his gun and pushed her past the rows of crates to a door next to a refrigerated section that was full of smaller crates. *Refrigerated?* Lyssa wondered. Readymeals were made primarily of processed foods and synthesized food substitutes. They never required refrigeration. Unless these were sold only to the Elite. A surge of anger ran through her at the thought.

"It'll be over soon," Lyra said, misreading her expression. "And Tamsin is fine. She's watching one of her favorite Teev films with Kansas. Dani and the underground took care of the last sixer transfer, so he won't be needed for another two hours."

Lyssa would have felt a lot better knowing Dani was among those moving into position, but she supposed that Reese, Jaxon, Hammer, and whoever else Brogan had sent would be enough. She didn't see a lot of KC men here, though with all the credits' worth of readymeals inside the crates, they likely had a strong security presence at the warehouse.

The door in front of them opened and a man appeared, flanked by two others. A gasp came from Lyra's throat. "It's the man from Reese's drawing, the one who gave us the scramblers and the shuttle for our getaway in Estlantic."

Xavier, Lyssa remembered. They'd all felt betrayed when the KC had responded to El Cerebro's request for aid from the Estlantic underground. It was the first moment they'd realized the leadership there had changed. Xavier had also been present the night Reese had nearly died at the hands of the KC minions. He'd been the one calling the orders and planning her murder.

"Hello," Xavier said to Lyssa, ignoring Ty completely, for which she was glad.

"Why have you brought me here?"

"You were seen in the company of El Cerebro." Xavier's

eyes flashed to Ollin and back to her. "We have detected a lot of movement in the underground of late, and we want to know why."

Lyssa studied him a moment. His eyes were dark and his hair black, cropped short like an enforcer's. His face was perfect and attractive, as if perhaps medically arranged—the kind of face that made even happily-married women look twice. His snug gray pants showed off muscular legs, and his high-collared, white V-neck shirt showed a muscled but smooth expanse of chest. A gun sat securely in an under-the-arm holster. Though he didn't seem the kind to dirty his hands himself, she bet he was capable of killing when needed.

"I don't know what you're talking about," Lyssa said.

Xavier nodded once, and Teller lunged toward Ty, wrapping his arm around Ty's throat and gagging him.

"Think carefully," Xavier said, blinking slowly. "Or your boyfriend here is going to take a nosedive from the top of the administration building. With any luck, he'll only break his neck."

Break his neck. Lyssa's stomach lurched. All this time, she'd been trying to protect Ty, but in reality, dating him had put him in deeper danger. She'd known that, but she'd been selfish. She'd been tired of wanting Kansas, tired of not having anyone who loved her for herself. She looked around for Lyra, to see what she might say, but her sister had vanished.

"Why don't you ask El Cerebro?" she said finally. "You have an agreement with him, right? Of mutual aid? At least in your capacity with the Estlantic underground."

At a nod from Xavier, Teller released Ty, who gasped out. "Lyssa, what are you saying? Do you know what they're talking about?"

"Let him go," Lyssa said to Xavier. "He doesn't know anything. I was only using him for personnel information, just like you." The lie slipped casually from her lips, and she very carefully avoided Ty's gaze.

"You'll forgive me if I hold onto him a little longer." Xavier smiled, one side of his mouth lifting higher than the other. "And to answer your question, I did reach out to El Cerebro. I didn't like his answer, which is why we are here now."

"No," came a strong voice from somewhere behind Lyssa. "We're here because you don't know how to take no for an answer."

Xavier started to reach for his gun. Ollin, Teller, and Xavier's two guards also reached for their weapons, but only Teller drew. Lyssa whirled to see Brogan in his guise as El Cerebro, complete with the skinlike mask and the C carved on his right cheek. Next to him were Hammer, Jaxon, Reese, and Eagle in bulletproof plainclothes, all with assault rifles drawn and ready. Circling around the rest of the room, some stepping out behind crates or poised atop, were two dozen underground soldiers wearing black beanies. Half of them held pistols to the heads of men who were apparently in KC employ. A grinning Lyra had also reappeared incorporcally beside Lyssa.

"There are two dozen more of my soldiers outside," Brogan said. "Carefully toss down your weapons."

Ty looked ready to speak, obviously recognizing the crew from division and wondering why they were with El Cerebro, but Lyssa gave a quick shake of her head, warning him to silence. Now wasn't the time to start slinging accusations.

Xavier's uneven smile looked sinister, but he set down his weapon and pushed it forward with his foot. His men did the same. Teller had a few guns, including Lyssa's, and she felt a little of the tension seep from her shoulders as she retrieved it.

Reese moved around Lyssa, picking up scattered weapons before coming to a stop within a few feet of Xavier. Fury glowed on her face, and her finger rested eagerly on the trigger of her gun, which was pointed at his chest. She didn't say a word, but they all knew she was only awaiting orders. She owed five months of horrible suffering to this man.

On the other side of Lyssa, Eagle had moved in closer to Ollin, taking his weapon, while Hammer focused on Teller, who to Lyssa's view was the most dangerous. Jaxon came up behind Ty, grabbing his shoulder and bringing him back away from the others. Ty resisted slightly, his mistrust of his co-worker apparent, though the two had always been friends. At least now there seemed to be no reason to think Ty would meet his death today, though the haunted expression on Jaxon's face indicated that the premonition hadn't changed.

"I wondered if you might come out of the woodwork if I acted," Xavier said when no one else moved.

Brogan's masked face lifted into the slightest of grins. "You obviously didn't expect me to show up here."

"Obviously," Xavier conceded. "Or I would have brought more men. But it means I was on the right track." When Brogan didn't respond to that, Xavier continued, "When you refused to return the favor you owe us, you said your men were tied up in an operation."

"They were, and you're interrupting." Brogan slung his rifle on his shoulder and strode forward, his brown eyes glittering dangerously. His arms looked big enough to punch Xavier into the next room. "This is *my* territory. You will not find us as weak as you apparently found the underground in Estlantic."

"We have no intention on challenging your authority," Xavier said. "But we helped you free your agent from HED in Estlantic. You owe us. We know you have allies within the enforcers here. Having them turn the other way while we approach Colony 5 should be a simple thing. Instead, within the past few days, two of our convoys have been detained by enforcers. Another delegation was denied entrance on their sky train."

Brogan barked a laugh. "Compared to the temporary use of vehicles, what you ask is too much. Colony 5 is the CORE's primary source of cattle and livestock. I don't think giving you access would benefit my people."

Xavier's jaw worked, and the prettiness of his face was lessened by rage. "Because of what you're planning?" he said coldly.

Lyssa swallowed hard. Their success depended on no one knowing what they were doing until it was too late. But apparently, while they'd been occupied in Newcali and transferring sixers, Captain Brogan had been busy fielding requests from a now-suspicious Kordell Corp.

"Maybe," Brogan said. "Maybe not. But what's important right now is what *you're* planning."

When Xavier didn't answer, Brogan lifted two fingers. A heartbeat later, what sounded like a single shot reverberated through the warehouse, and the two men flanking Xavier collapsed, red bullet-sized holes in their foreheads. Ty gasped, and Lyssa felt like vomiting.

"The other two are next," Brogan said. "Then the rest. Then you."

"Wait, boss." Eagle, his face dispassionate, gestured to Ollin. "I know this man. He's the sixer who works for them: Ollin Sarvis."

Ollin's eyes grew wide. "You know me?" He peered at Eagle, as if trying to see his face beneath the dark glasses.

Ignoring him, Eagle stepped closer to Lyssa and Brogan for a private conversation. "He's from our school. A year younger than us. We don't have a good image of him as an adult, probably because of KC tampering with the database, but his facial structure matches the kid we knew. I'm sure it's him."

"He does look familiar," Lyssa said. "But I don't remember him at all."

Brogan nodded and returned his gaze to Xavier. "I'm still waiting."

Xavier didn't speak, and as Brogan's hand started to raise, Ollin burst out, "It was me," he said. "I have visions. I know things. I saw you attacking the colonies, and they think it's going to mess up their plans." He held out his hands, palms up as if to show he had nothing to hide. "Look, I work for them, but only because they threatened to kill me. They also give me a drug to stop me from going insane like so many others."

"You have the cure?" El Cerebro said to Xavier.

Again, it was Ollin who answered. "Not a cure but a treatment. They trade a vision to the Controller for a dose." His grin flicked on his face and then away, as if more of a tick than an emotion. "They came to that agreement after the Controller tried to take me from them."

Lyssa glanced back at Jaxon, who was paying close attention. They hadn't yet met another sixer who saw the future, and this was an interesting development. No wonder Kordell Corp had managed to stay on top when every other private company had been forced to sell out to the CORE itself.

"Do you know their plan?" Brogan asked Ollin.

"No," Ollin said. He pointed at Ty. "But he was supposed to give us the count of the enforcers in the colonies. We told him we were trying to free the colonies, but I don't think that's true." He darted a wary look at Xavier. "They're the KC's largest single consumer, you know."

"I didn't though!" Ty broke in before anyone could answer Ollin. "When they told me what they wanted on Friday after the birth orders were announced, I went to Captain Brogan." Then as if realizing that his words probably weren't helping his case with El Cerebro, he fell silent. Jaxon leaned forward and whispered something to Ty that Lyssa couldn't hear.

"The plan," Brogan said again, leveling his gaze on Xavier. "Why do you care about enforcement personnel in the colonies?"

Xavier still didn't speak. Lyssa guessed that he was willing to allow all his men to die rather than betray whoever pulled his strings at Kordell Corp. She steeled herself for more shots.

"I got it," Reese said into the silence. "There's a wall safe in that room. Combination three, four, twenty, six, and then his handprint." She gestured to the still-open door behind Xavier where they could see comfortable chairs set at intervals around an elegant table. One of the chairs held a long leather jacket, which Lyssa thought must belong to Xavier.

At that moment, Xavier began choking. Foam lined with blood dribbled from the corner of his mouth. He collapsed on the ground and began convulsing.

Reese lunged for him. "No!" she shouted, grabbing his shoulders and shaking him. "You won't escape me this easily."

"Hurry," Brogan said, his tone immediately halting Reese's reaction. "The scanner must need him alive."

Jaxon surged forward and helped Reese drag Xavier into the room. He tried to resist, but Reese laughed as Eagle and Brogan grabbed his legs. "Oh, you'll live long enough for this," she said, her voice twisted into something Lyssa barely recognized. "I promise. Before you die, you'll know that you're the reason we're going to destroy your precious Kordell Corp. And I'll rest easy knowing you will never do to anyone else what you did to me."

With the distraction, Teller started to run, but Hammer hit him hard with his rifle, driving the man to his knees. Forcing him down flat on the cement floor, Hammer cuffed both his hands and legs.

Lyssa pointed her gun at Ollin. "Don't even think about running," she warned.

"I want protection," he countered, raising his hands near his face. "If that means joining the underground, I'm in. Please." His earnest expression looked so familiar right then that Lyssa felt disoriented.

Hammer came over and slipped cuffs on Ollin and ordered him to sit against the wall under the watchful eye of an underground soldier.

"You're really with the underground?" Ty took a step toward Lyssa, his gaze going back and forth between her and her gun.

Lyssa exchanged a glance with Hammer. She could see the pity in his eyes. Like them, Ty would now be given the truth and the choice to work for the underground. Or die. Lyssa turned away from him without a response.

She was almost to the room when Brogan and the others reappeared. Xavier wasn't with them. In Brogan's hand was an iTeev, unfolded to its largest size. "Looks like their plans involved Colonies 1, 2, and 5."

"The food colonies," Lyssa said, her research about the number of enforcers assigned to each fresh in her mind.

El Cerebro nodded. "They were planning to take them over. Just those three. They already compromised enough of the enforcers and administrators in the first two colonies. But they'll need Colony 5 for a complete monopoly of the food. That would force the Elite to give them whatever they want. And you can be sure as Breakdown that doesn't include freeing anyone."

Lyssa exchanged serious glances with the others before asking, "Is this going to delay our plan?"

He shook his head. "That was my first thought, but maybe if we play it right, it'll actually make it easier, at least in Colonies 1 and 2. We're ahead of the KC schedule, so we'll simply let those enforcers know there's been a change. And . . ." He trailed off, motioning to the stacks of crates. "We have all this. Plus, back in Estlantic they have extra food shipments going to the first two colonies. Obviously, they expected some kind of siege as well. So we'll let them go through with that, and we'll reroute these to the other colonies." He met Lyssa's gaze. "I'll need you and Hammer to figure out their regular supply routes and make sure we don't raise any alarms." His mask stretched into a haunting attempt at a grin. "Use any means possible when questioning his men, but get those meals in place before Wednesday."

"You're really going to free the colonies?" Ty found his voice, shooting a reproachful look at Lyssa as he spoke.

"Yes," she said.

He nodded. "Okay, then I want to help."

Brogan laid a hand on his shoulder. "We'll talk about that. You will be riding back with me."

Lyssa watched them go, wondering if this was the last time she'd see Ty. Maybe the death staring him in the face came from within her own camp all along.

Hammer touched her arm tentatively, and it was a relief to turn in his direction. "Go talk to Reese about her aunt," he said. "Then go home and be with your daughter. I can get the information from Teller and work on the shipments while you take Tamsin to Big Horn."

Lyssa focused on his face. Why had she never noticed how kind it was?

"Okay," she said. "I'll see you later."

Lyssa sat next to Tamsin on a bed in the guest room at Reese's great-aunt's house. It was way past Tamsin's bedtime, but the child was still so excited after playing with the chickens and the prospect of missing school the next day, that Lyssa had stayed to settle her down. She could always sleep in the shuttle on the way back to Amarillo City.

"When are you coming back?" Tamsin asked.

Lyssa's heart felt ripped in two with the question. "I'm not really sure. We don't know how long it will take to fix everything."

Tamsin frowned. "Then can I please come see you in my mind? Or will you come see me?"

She meant traveling, of course, and it was high time Lyssa gave the child more information. "It's called traveling," Lyssa said, "and I'll be a little far away, so I don't think I can, but I promise to come as soon as I can. I'm trying to make this world safer for you. You understand that, right?"

The little girl nodded. "And I helped today, didn't I?"

"You did. Without you, things could have gone very wrong." To say the least.

Tamsin grinned. "It's a little like magic, isn't it? That's what Daddy said. He said because you have it, you have to help others who don't."

Gratitude rose in Lyssa's chest. Her brother-in-law had purposefully ignored what was going on in the CORE for a long time, but he had finally come through for all of them, and especially these past few days for Tamsin. Lyssa was grateful her daughter was lucky enough to have him as a father. If the rebellion went well and they had the freedom to tell the truth, things might change, especially with the baby coming, but Kansas would always be there for Tamsin. And for Lyssa as well.

"Daddy's right," Lyssa said. "We're sixers, and that's special, but for now, it's our secret. A family secret. Someday, we'll be able to tell everyone."

Tamsin nodded. "But what about the baby? That's not a secret, is it?"

Lyssa gaped at her daughter. "Who told you about that?"

"I'm ten, Mom," Tamsin said with a patronizing smile and a slight roll of her eyes. "I watched something about the local birth orders today on the Teev. You should have told me."

"Okay, then. Yes, your aunt is going to have a baby. A little girl."

Tamsin's eyes grew wide. "It's a girl? Oh, I'm so happy!" She threw herself at Lyssa, hugging her. "I always wanted a little sister or cousin."

Lyssa was glad she didn't ask about the baby's father. Time enough for that explanation later. Hopefully much later. "She'll be just like a sister," she said, stroking her daughter's hair. "I'm sorry we didn't tell you sooner."

"That's okay." Tamsin snuggled into her. "Can we try to, uh, travel once together before you leave? I know how by myself, but it's a little weird."

"Sure. Just be careful that before you travel, you make certain your body is in a safe place. Like in this bed." Lyssa leaned back against the headboard and slipped from her body.

Tamsin came with her. "I feel like air!" Tamsin exclaimed, her essence shooting above Lyssa's head and doing summersaults.

Only a child would discover this kind of joy in traveling, Lyssa thought, feeling rather light herself. She and Lyra certainly hadn't.

"Whenever you're feeling homesick," she said to her daughter, "just do this and remember me."

Whatever awaited them in the future, they always had this night.

CHAPTER 19

Tuesday afternoon, Jaxon Tennant sat in his tiny office at division with his iTeev unfolded to its full size as he pondered the message he and Reese had spent most of the morning hashing out. It was a careful mix of truth and fiction that exposed him far more than he'd intended, but it seemed right for enticing a personal visit from the Controller himself. They'd waited as long as they'd dared to respond to the invitation, but now that the soldiers and sixers were in place near the Estlantic colonies, and the ones currently arriving had much less distance to travel, it was time for this phase of the plan.

Esteemed Captain Zale Walsh,

I am honored at your very generous offer. Like most of my counterparts, I have long aspired to be a part of your Special Forces. I love being an enforcer and have worked hard at my job. I am grateful to know that my work has been noticed.

Therefore, it is with gratitude that I accept your offer. However, before I begin my service, I feel it would be wise if I underwent another mental evaluation. For the past week, I've experienced vivid dreams of strange flying vehicles coming to Amarillo City from outside the CORE. In them are hundreds of men and women who are asleep, but in a later dream, these people come awake with incredible strength and power. I seem to recognize some of them, as well as the place in the empty zone north of Amarillo City where they are revived by Special Forces led by the Controller himself. There is also a man with a C carved into his cheek lying dead on the ground.

These dreams could have been caused by the many off-hours tracking I've been doing of the underground here in Amarillo City, as everyone knows that cheek mark is a signature of El Cerebro. But as you have access to my records, you will also know I was born in the colonies, and I've heard rumors of mental instabilities there. While I have never experienced such myself, I thought it only fair to make sure I'm in a condition to serve you fully. I also understand if you decide to retract your offer. The safety of the CORE is always my first concern.

Sincerely,
Detective Enforcer Jaxon Tennant

He was content with the final result, and the mention of the Controller in the dream was a particularly juicy addition because it would assure the man would come to Amarillo City himself. But so much could go wrong. What if the captain just dropped him and didn't report the note to the Controller? Or worse, what if they fired him from the enforcers altogether?

"None of that is going to happen," Reese assured him when he voiced his concerns. "The Controller recognized you when we were at HED, remember? And your records are protected.

I think that means he's been keeping an eye on you and waiting for signs of an ability."

"What if Captain Walsh does tell the Controller, and they send someone to drag me to Estlantic?" Jaxon asked. "Like he tried before."

"He won't. Not with you mentioning the unconscious sixers. He'll come, and he'll bring his treatment."

"If he comes, he won't be alone," Jaxon retorted. "It'll be him and enough Special Forces to drag all the sixers back to Estlantic."

Despite his protests, he did think the man would come. Because somehow they were connected. Summers, Controller Warrick Ramsey's half brother, had implied as much before Jaxon had shot and killed him. Ramsey might even be Jaxon's father. And if he was the man who had visited and impregnated his prostitute mother in Colony 6, Jaxon wanted to know why. Why would the man travel all the way to Colony 6 to carry out his sordid fantasies with an illegal whore when closer colonies contained equally desperate women willing to do anything to make ends meet?

Jaxon didn't want a murderer as a father, but he'd had visions of talking with the Controller about his parentage. Admittedly, these had been under the influence of a hallucinogen, and Jaxon's recollection of the exact wording was vague, but he knew it would come true.

For a dizzying instant, he felt the world around him shift and fade, as if his thoughts had triggered an attack of some kind. *Another premonition,* he thought, and then it took him.

He walks with Controller Warrick Ramsey through an empty zone. All around them, bodies lay unmoving on uneven slabs of broken concrete or on the ground, wrapped in heat blankets. Fear grips Jaxon's heart as the Controller bends down to uncover a man that looks suspiciously like Hammer. Beyond Hammer lies the prone figure of Captain Brogan in his guise as El Cerebro.

"Jaxon?" Reese's voice came from far away.

He pulled himself back, expecting her to ask what he'd seen. But she was already reaching for her drawing pad. Figures appeared under her fingers. Within minutes, she'd captured that moment from his vision when the Controller pulled back the blanket from Hammer's body.

"It's us," she said. "That's how we're going to get the meds. We replace the sixers with us. Look, that one is me." She pointed to a woman near Hammer that he hadn't even noticed. Even slightly out of focus, the figure was definitely Reese. "We'll outnumber them, and they won't even know it. We have to tell Brogan. He needs to delay sending the undergrounders to the Dallastar colonies. Instead of half of them, we're going to need them all here first."

Until that moment, the plan had been to lure the Controller to Amarillo City with enough of the treatment, find out where it was, and then steal it. During that course of action, Jaxon would have to lead the Controller into the empty zone for a fake trip to search for non-existent sixers. Brogan and half of his underground soldiers would be there to provide a distraction while Reese, Hammer, Eagle, and a few others went for the cure. It was risky both because Jaxon and Brogan were exposed and because the medication might be hidden or well-protected. Jaxon had worried about all of that, especially why Brogan—or El Cerebro, rather—seemed to be dead in his vision. Now, he understood why.

"It could work," he said.

"It will." She gave him a confident grin.

"I haven't seen the end yet. What if he brings too many enforcers?"

Reese thought a moment. "We just happen to have a lot of Newcali soldiers sitting around in Estlantic waiting to take over the colonies. What if some of them started shorting out those beautiful laser fences Special Forces have been setting up in the empty zones to keep out the beasts? He'd have to send people to fix them, right? With any luck, they'll be distracted by an actual beast."

"Divide and conquer," he agreed.

"Anyway, it's the perfect attack." Reese's face glowed with anticipation. "He's expecting hundreds of unconscious bodies. He won't be expecting them to rise up and fight. My guess is he'll secure a place here to keep the sixers and bring them to consciousness as needed. Even if he doesn't have enough doses of the treatment to wake them all right now, he'll have at least enough for an initial shipment of people—and he'll probably bring some of that to the empty zone. That will be sufficient for Dr. Kentley to reverse-engineer."

"Reverse-engineer in a day or two?"

Reese frowned. "Maybe not, but he knows how to make a treatment already, and he seems confident that with enough treatments, he can synthesize what we need. It would be better if he had the original viribus so he could find a permanent cure. But I really think Ramsey will bring enough doses of the treatment. This will work."

"We're not going to be able to simply take the meds and walk away," Jaxon said.

Reese sighed. "No. We're going to have to take Controller Ramsey and his enforcers prisoner. But that's not all bad because then they won't be around to try and retake the colonies."

"We'll lose people." Jaxon hadn't seen that happening, but they were bound to lose a few, even though in this battle they should outnumber the Special Forces troops.

"Maybe not," Reese said. "I have an idea about how we can

hedge our bets." She leaned over, connected his iTeeve to the feed, and pushed *send* on his message.

"What idea?" he said, watching the message leave his screen.

"Something I learned from those crazy fringers in Gila. I'll let you know if it looks like it'll work. First, I'll need to see Andres." With an enigmatic smile and a brief kiss, she left the small office.

Andres was their medical examiner, and an underground sympathizer. He and Reese had dated in the past, but Jaxon wasn't going to let that bother him. He didn't trust Andres with Reese, but he sure as Breakdown trusted her.

Jaxon reconnected his office Teev to the feed and stared at the holo image that appeared on his wall, one that depicted a peaceful mountain scene and a lake. The place no longer existed in the CORE, or anywhere else that he knew. The closest he'd come to seeing anything like it was the refueling station in Gila. But the image was the future, he was sure of it.

He just had to do his part and hope that he'd be around to see it.

Jaxon expected to wait all day for a response, but two hours later when he and Reese were back in the empty zone helping with another set of transfers, a reply came to his iTeev.

Detective Enforcer Jaxon Tennant,

Thank you for your message. We agree that a psychological evaluation is a responsible course of action, though we are sure the findings will be within acceptable parameters. As luck would have it, Controller Warrick Ramsey will be in Amarillo City for another matter and would like to meet with you personally about your experience in Colony 6, as you may have information that will be helpful to a project he has been working on. Please arrive Wednesday at ten in the morning in uniform at the following address.

We will inform your captain that you have been transferred to Special Forces and are no longer under his command. Stop at the AED to retrieve your personal belongings at your convenience. I am looking forward to working with an enforcer of your caliber.

Sincerely,
Zale Walsh, Captain of HED

Jaxon met Reese's eyes, waiting for her to finish reading the message. Her gaze lifted to his, and for a long moment neither of them spoke. Then in a strangled voice, Reese said, "You know what? I changed my mind. I don't like this. They seem too eager."

He didn't like it either, but now it was his turn to put a good spin on things as she had earlier. That was what they did. When one was weak, the other was strong. "That's because we set it up so well. He's coming. We did what we were supposed to do."

She nodded, a glint of moisture in her eyes that he knew she would not at all be happy to have him point out. "Right. Let's go tell the others."

Late Tuesday evening, the subway station platform that served as the main gathering and trading area in the underground was alive with activity. At one corner table, Andres, the medical examiner and fellow underground sympathizer, was passing out skin-to-skin tranquilizers to all the underground soldiers and refugee fringers who would be pretending to be sixers in the empty zone the next morning. This was Reese's idea turned into reality, and Jaxon was more than a little impressed at how fast it had come together.

In another corner, Nova and Thane were passing out heated blankets and clothing to the soldiers who were able to take their places tonight. They couldn't risk everyone converging on the chosen location at the same time the next morning, possibly alerting someone who might report back to the Controller. Across from them, Eagle and some of the newly arrived refugee fringers were finishing up making explosive devices to plant around the site where they planned to trap the Controller, but as a backup only, because explosions would attract unnecessary notice. If unused, they would be delivered to the colonies at the same time as the sixer treatment.

In the recessed space next to the platform that intersected with the tunnels, where the ancient trains had once run, Reese and Hammer were handing out weapons. The twins, of course, were back at division, taking turns in the secret room to make sure no enforcers were called near either of the important empty zone locations.

With his crew accounted for, Jaxon went to receive his own tranquilizer patch that he planned to wear on his arm as a backup when he led the Controller into the empty zone. "Make that two," he said.

Andres handed them over. "Everyone gets three, actually. One for the neck and one for each hand. Just slap them on when you're dressed and pull off the top strip right before the action. The bottom is flesh-colored, so it won't be noticed until it's too late. Just be sure you touch their skin, or that they touch you with bare fingers. It's really low tech and potent as all Breakdown, so not much margin for error. Nasty stuff. Begins to work within about sixty seconds. They'll be unconscious for at least three hours, possibly longer." Andres smiled at him as he spoke, and Jaxon was relieved to see that he didn't seem to hold a grudge at him for stealing Reese away. That might have something to do with the pretty underground soldier who was at his side, helping him distribute the patches.

Andres wasn't the only one who seemed enamored. Shadow, the fringer woman who had come from Santoni with Thane, hadn't left Eagle's side all evening. Eagle couldn't seem to keep his black-glassed gaze from her, and more than once his laugh rang out over the din. Jaxon understood the attraction. With her lithe body, long brown hair, and tanned, freckled face, Shadow was attractive, if not beautiful. Her eyes were most certainly unusual, a bright blue like Jaxon's own—a rare color among the browns or hazels that were prominent in the CORE. And the few times they'd talked, she'd seemed intelligent, if wary. Jaxon hoped it worked out for them.

"Old Eagle Eyes is totally besotted," said a voice from the table a meter away.

Jaxon redirected his attention to Ollin Sarvis, the captured KC sixer, sitting at a table, still wearing handcuffs and also chained to a heavy metal ring embedded in the wall. He seemed to be watching all the commotion with apparent enjoyment.

"I think you're right." Jaxon nodded, moving toward him. He'd wanted to talk to the man about his ability, but so far there hadn't been time. Until they figured out what to do with him, Ollin had been given the option of being locked in a cell or shackled in the station, and he'd chosen the latter.

"She glows," Ollin said, indicating Shadow. "When she talks to him. Not all the time, and just a bit. It's barely noticeable, unless you have nothing to do but watch. She's like us. A sixer."

"I heard," Jaxon said. As he watched the couple, Shadow did

seem to shine, but in the time he took to blink, the effect had vanished. "How are you settling in?" he asked Ollin.

Ollin raised his cuffed hands a bit fatalistically. "I've been better, but not recently. On the whole, I think these are good people."

"They are. And once we're finished with what we're doing, you'll be free."

"I'll hold you to it." Ollin paused, his gaze narrowing. "Look, I know you don't remember me. But I remember you. From the Coop."

Jaxon still didn't remember Ollin. How could he when he'd left at age ten? People changed a lot in twenty years. Yes, he'd known Reese instantly at their reunion, and the rest of the crew as well, but the years they had struggled together to survive had made them like family.

"I'm sorry," Jaxon said. "I don't remember you. I was young when I left."

"Naturally." Ollin's forehead creased. "I was always sorry how they talked about your mom. She did what she had to. My mother liked her, you know. They worked together in the factory."

Not a surprise since they'd lived in the same area. Everyone had the same long shifts in the factories while their children were in the schools or running wild through the streets. "I appreciate that."

"Just wanted you to know."

"Thanks." Jaxon extended his hand to shake the other man's.

The moment they touched, Jaxon's world crumpled and waved. He expected a premonition, but none came. As they broke abruptly apart, their eyes locked in shock.

After a moment of complete silence, Ollin spoke, his voice rough, "You need to shoot. No matter what he says, you have to shoot. Or it won't be over. She'll be okay."

Jaxon sank to a chair opposite him. "What do you mean? What did you see?"

"I don't know. You with a gun. A choice." Ollin gave his head a rough shake. "They gave me a dose of the meds yesterday before we grabbed your friend. It always messes me up for a day or two, so they save it until the last possible moment." His voice lowered. "And truthfully, I don't really know how to control this"—he waved his finger in a circle near his temple—"whatever is going on in my brain. I don't really see things so much as I feel them. From what I've heard from Dr. Kentley, it's different for you."

"I see it," Jaxon confirmed.

Ollin nodded. "For me, the madness is always there, ready to pounce, except right after the meds."

Jaxon understood only too well what he meant about the madness. Without the madness, there might be a way to focus, but as it was, he was at the whim of whatever future images fate chose to send him. He'd been lucky to have Dr. Kentley soothing the madness over the past weeks, but that temporary cure had also calmed his visions, and for the past few days, Jaxon had stayed away from the doctor.

"I only know you have to shoot. But you won't want to." Ollin frowned. "That's all I know."

Jaxon wondered if the man was telling the truth or still working a secret agenda for the KC.

"Thanks," he said, forcing himself to his feet.

During his conversation, a strange hush had fallen over the station platform. His eyes sought out the reason, and he realized that everyone was staring at Reese, who was now alone next to a markedly diminished mound of weapons. Jaxon made his way over to her, jumping down into the recess that led to the tunnels instead of using the stairs.

"Hammer went to relieve Lyssa," she told him quietly as he joined her. "All the soldiers have what they need."

"Then what are *they* waiting for?" He motioned to the ragged line still in front of her. Aside from a few aged men and women, the somber faces belonged to young teenagers around Nova's age who weren't allowed to participate in serious ops.

Reese's expression was stricken. "Some of them are going to be on top of the buildings with rifles. They know how to shoot, and we have to trust that they also know how to hide if things go wrong. The rest will be going to watch over the missiles and supplies we're sending to the gathering locations outside Colonies 5 and 6. With the regular underground soldiers occupied in capturing the Controller and the meds, they won't be able to get out there soon enough."

He grimaced. "I don't like that at all."

Her nostrils flared, and her eyes flashed. At that moment, she looked both beautiful and terrifyingly determined. "There is no other way. We don't dare have too few soldiers here. Warrick Ramsey has access to two thousand Special Forces—and thousands more enforcers besides. Including us and our division."

"Special Forces are already responding to the laser fence failures in Estlantic," Jaxon reminded her. "Ramsey can't bring them all at such short notice, and I don't think he'll want word of this getting out to our division or any other."

"That's what I hope. We can't allow him to suspect that Newcali is playing him. Not yet. Taking the Controller will be the biggest thing any rebel has ever done in the CORE."

Jaxon could only hope that the Controller's arrogance and many years of unchallenged control would also aid in the man's downfall. Though much rested on Jaxon's shoulders, the plan depended every bit as much on everyone in this room.

All at once he understood the respectful silence that had fallen over the underground station. That the undergrounders were willing to risk even their children told him everyone present knew and accepted that if they didn't win this battle, they would lose everything.

CHAPTER 20

Jaxon took a deep breath as his enforcer shuttle pulled up in front of the address given to him in the message from HED. The three-story building was nice but was located in a scantily populated section of town, made up mostly of offices or factories that had become unneeded as their ancestors had finished building the colonies and shifted much of the work there, or as automation took over. Those still in business needed fewer people, and those employees would remain only for the six-hour workday that was customary outside the colonies.

Though he couldn't see them, Lyssa and Lyra were traveling with him and could report back to Brogan and the others. Lyra's physical body was at division in the secret room while Lyssa's was in a shuttle on the north side of the building. They'd tested last night in a similar location and confirmed that the twins were free to roam incorporeally anywhere between their two bodies as long as they were traveling together. Once traveling, however, one of them could anchor to Jaxon while the other returned to her body, coming and going as needed. Jaxon had wanted to station Lyssa in the empty zone north of the target site, but Reese had argued that the Controller might take Jaxon elsewhere, and insisted on the shuttle. As Jaxon's position moved, presumably to the empty zone, so would Reese and Lyssa, keeping him between the twins.

That morning, Jaxon's emotions had ranged from anger and determination, to fear and anxiety. Two strands of thoughts seemed to tear him apart from the inside. First, Jaxon believed this man or his brother had been responsible for his mother's murder. Second, Jaxon had a lifelong urge to know his father, which might end up being Controller Warrick Ramsey himself—a confirmed murderer.

Since neither thought had anything to do with freeing the colonies, he pushed them aside and double-checked his suit recorder. This was a day for history, and if possible, they wanted it chronicled to the last second.

The entire front of the first floor was made of glass, and he could see into the lobby as he approached the double doors. Two receptionists sat behind a desk against the wall, and a group of six people, one reading something to the others from an oversized iTeev screen, were gathered near a hallway that led away from the lobby. All civilians—or at least they weren't dressed as enforcers. This wasn't surprising since the building was the same one the Controller came to each time he was in Amarillo City. A search of county records had shown that besides offices, the upper floor contained apartments for visiting dignitaries. A small staff was kept on at all times in preparation, though they reportedly had homes elsewhere in the city.

When the premonition came, Jaxon barely had a warning, the air only shifting suddenly around him and his stomach clenching.

The Controller stares at him. "There's something I need to tell you," he says.

"Stay away from me," Jaxon retorts. "I have nothing to say to you."

He is vaguely aware of fighting all around. But no sound comes to his ears.

Pain shoots through him.

It was over in the space of a single step, and Jaxon was relieved his practice at controlling his physical reaction had helped him maintain his balance. It helped that this premonition was one he'd seen before, and that it had been only a glimpse rather than a lengthy vision. It felt more immediate today, though—something Jaxon had come to recognize as being close to occurrence.

As Jaxon opened the door, four uniformed enforcers with Special Forces patches on their sleeves came past the group of staff and hurried in his direction. Even though he was ten minutes early, someone had been watching and waiting for him. After his vision in Newcali, Jaxon wasn't surprised to recognize one of the enforcers as Ekan Donnel, a man who had been at the academy with him. Jaxon had last seen Donnel during their big op in Estlantic, when they'd freed Dani from HED. What he didn't know was why the man was here now.

"Jaxon Tennant," Donnel said, coming forward with a smile, his hand extended. He was shorter than Jaxon by a good fifteen centimeters, but he'd muscled up since their last meeting. Ten years earlier at the academy, Jaxon had beaten him easily in hand-to-hand combat practice, but now he wasn't sure he could best the man. Donnel's face was still pointed and his face eager. His dark hair had been cropped extremely short.

"Ekan Donnel." Jaxon shook his hand. "Imagine seeing you here." They hadn't exactly been close during their time at the academy, but Jaxon considered him a friend, albeit a distant one.

"I heard you're going to join us," Donnel said.

"Yep, I hope to finally be one of the big boys."

Donnel's grin widened. "It's about time." He jerked his head toward the other men. "These are Enforcers Lindslay, Gruen, and Ahern."

Jaxon's gaze ran over the other three enforcers. They looked like standard issue, as if the Controller had handpicked them for both their alikeness and their proclivity to obey orders: dark hair, brown eyes, high cheekbones, wide shoulders. And each was very young.

Pliable, Jaxon thought as he shook their hands and exchanged nods and smiles.

"You still carry those spiked brass knuckles?" Donnel asked when the introductions were finished.

Of course he did. Growing up in the colonies had taught him to always be prepared to defend himself or his crew. Back then, before his mother's death and his removal from the colony, his brass knuckles had been a bent metal spoon stolen from one of the teachers.

"Yeah, I have it," he said.

"Good, because we're officially allowed to carry non-traditional weapons." Donnel laid a hand on his shoulder. "Come on. Let's take you back to the Controller."

Jaxon and Donnel went ahead while the other three fell in behind. Donnel leaned over and whispered. "I call them the triplets. It's uncanny how much they look alike these days. They really are good enforcers though. They know how to take orders."

Jaxon snorted softly in amusement. "How did you end up here? Last I knew, you were angling to be a team leader, not an assistant to the Controller. He must have really liked that nyckelira case I sold you." During their last op, Jaxon had provided the case to Donnel for him to gift the Controller as a way to pass a weapon to Dani.

"Oh, he loved it. It got me an assignment as a team leader. A few extra teams were called in for whatever is going on here. I'm on the greeting committee because I volunteered that I know you."

Jaxon laughed out loud this time. "You never change."

Donnel didn't take offense. "Hey, to get noticed in this business, you have to speak up."

"And you like where you're at now?"

"Oh, absolutely." But Donnel had hesitated a second too long. What that meant, Jaxon couldn't say, but he intended to find out everything he could.

"Guess you've seen a lot more action than you did as a regular enforcer."

Donnel nodded. "We've been cleaning out the empty zones and setting up laser fences so the beasts won't enter from the desolation zone. We tried electronic ones, but they break them down. The lasers kill them. Guess they've exhausted the food in the desolation zones. Or maybe the humans are easier prey than what they're used to."

A memory of the beasts made Jaxon's insides shudder. "You've fought the beasts?"

"Not personally. I've seen them, though. We have access to the new helicopters, and we basically drop explosives on them if they come into the empty zones."

That was important to know, Jaxon decided. If they could drop explosives on beasts, they could drop them on colonies. "Always from helicopters? Seems expensive."

"Well, you didn't hear it from me, but with this recent beast trouble, the moratorium on building missiles and machines capable of flight has been stretched. They've started manufacturing missiles, so hopefully in the future, we can set those up along the border."

"Are they building the missiles in one of the colonies?" If so, they wouldn't have to worry because it would soon be under their control. Otherwise, they'd need to figure out a way to prevent some overanxious Elite from using missiles against them.

"Are you kidding? Can't trust those lazy slobs. They'd probably launch them at us." Then Donnel colored, as if remembering too late that Jaxon had been born in a colony. But Jaxon had never told him as much—it wasn't something he'd been proud of back in the day—so someone had briefed Donnel.

"Didn't mean anything by that," Donnel said hurriedly. "Some awesome people have come out of Colony 6. Like Queran. I told you about him last time, right? The guy that can heat people and anything else from the inside."

"Is he here too?" Jaxon asked. "I'd like to meet him. See if I remember him."

"Yeah, but I don't think they keep him here." Donnel laughed. "When he's in a temper, things can get hot real fast."

Which probably meant they kept him in specially-lined quarters, and that was something the twins might be able to track down. If they could find Queran, maybe they could free him or at least make sure he wasn't going to be a problem. But did his presence mean the Controller had immediate plans to enter the Amarillo City subway tunnels as he'd hinted to President Turner back in Newcali? Jaxon filed the thought away for later discussion, though it seemed unlikely the Controller would do anything before Jaxon led him into the trap.

They reached the elevator, which opened the minute Donnel put his hand on the reader. "Are there a lot of fringers?" Jaxon forced himself to ask as they stepped inside. "The ones you're picking up in the empty zones, I mean."

"Not anymore." Donnel's voice was grim as he averted his face to study the number readout above the door, refusing to meet Jaxon's eyes. "We're forced to kill most of them."

"They fight back?" From what Jaxon had seen, most of the refugee fringers were worn and beaten. Not exactly vicious killers.

"No," Donnel said quietly. "They don't. But they won't stay in the colonies. They escape and they rile up the people in the process." He met Jaxon's gaze at last with eyes that hinted at remorse. "Cleaning out the empty zones is now an extermination order. Unless they're young. They send those to the colonies, mostly to Colony 6. I'm not sure why."

Jaxon knew. Ten thousand murders had left Colony 6 unable to run at full capacity until the population once again reached fifty thousand.

Having exhausted all his questions, Jaxon lapsed into an anxious silence. In a few minutes, he'd be standing in front of Controller Warrick Ramsey. What was their connection? Did the man know who'd murdered his mother?

"So, you dating anyone?" Donnel asked as the elevator doors slid open, his previous attack of conscience replaced by joviality.

The question took Jaxon by surprise. "Yeah, actually. She's an enforcer with the AED, too. I mean, like I was before today."

Donnel bumped his arm. "I know that expression. It's serious, isn't it?"

Reese was the one thing in the world Jaxon was sure about. "I've loved her since I was ten."

Donnel's expression sharpened at that, and Jaxon wished he hadn't spoken. He'd as much as admitted that Reese was a sixer. Or at least from the Coop. It shouldn't matter after today, but he regretted saying it all the same.

"How does she feel about this new assignment?" Donnel asked.

"That's still to be determined. What about you? You find someone?"

Donnel shook his head. "Not yet. I work too much."

They stopped outside a door, where this time Donnel's hand on the reader only sent a chime. After a brief wait, the door slid into the wall and they stepped inside a large office. Jaxon had expected them to conduct a search and relieve him of his weapons, but no one did. Apparently, Warrick Ramsey wasn't worried about Jaxon going insane just yet. No one checked to see if his suit camera was running either.

Ramsey stood in front of what looked like a large window. But instead of gazing down on offices or factories, his view showed Amarillo City's administration building with its majestic columns and Freedom Fountain. Definitely a holo-screen. Ramsey was tall with medium brown hair and an average build. His strong, attractive face had high cheek bones and a prominent widow's peak. His smooth, unlined skin made him look forty, contrasting with his stated age of seventy-six, an obvious result of Nuface therapy. The most notable thing about him, to Jaxon's view, were his blazing blue eyes. Jaxon shared this trait, as had Bensell Summers, the Controller's half brother. The man Jaxon had murdered.

Ramsey turned from the holoscreen and strode toward them. "Welcome, Detective Tennant," he said, extending a hand.

Instead of an enforcer uniform like Jaxon and the others, he wore shimmering black pants and a black deep V-neck shirt with long sleeves and cuffs. No buttons or fasteners in sight, so the garments obviously used the same tech as enforcer uniforms. Maybe they were even bulletproof. The clothes were so similar to those worn by Xavier, the KC employee who had killed himself, that Jaxon felt hysterical amusement bubbling up inside him. It must be what the Elite pus bag set were wearing these days. Or those who had more money than the Elite.

"An honor to meet you, Controller Ramsey." Their hands touched. Jaxon almost expected something to happen. Nothing did. That didn't mean he couldn't pretend. He sucked in a breath and momentarily made his eyes cross. He gripped Ramsey's hand with a little too much force.

"Are you okay?" asked Ramsey.

Instead of withdrawing his hand, Ramsey led him to a chair near a large table before seating himself close by at the head. Donnel settled next to Jaxon while the triplets took up standing positions around the door.

"What is it?" Donnel asked. "What did you see?"

"See?" Jaxon faked surprise. "Nothing. I think I'm just tired. Didn't sleep well last night. Maybe I need some meds."

Ramsey nodded. "The physician will be in here soon to examine you, but first, why didn't you sleep well last night?"

Jaxon stared down at the table for a few seconds before meeting his gaze. "It's just a dream I keep having."

"What dream?" Ramsey pressed.

Jaxon tried to look embarrassed. "Maybe I should see the doctor."

Ramsey sat back in his chair, folding his hands across his chest. "Detective Tennant," he said, "this may come as a surprise to you, but several people from Colony 6 have developed special abilities. Given your history, I believe these so-called dreams may have more import than you give them."

"My history?" Jaxon said.

The Controller sighed, his left cheek ticking twice. "Colony 6 was first settled with people who had a tendency toward unusual gifts. Some of your relatives showed precognitive abilities, and we enhanced those with special treatments. The fact that you could be experiencing flashes of past or future events is quite possible. Now, if you'll just tell me what you saw, we can begin to determine if this might be the case."

Jaxon debated on how to react. On one hand, if he knew nothing about the history of Colony 6, he'd ask far more questions, but it was clear Ramsey wanted him to spill the information sooner rather than later. So maybe it was better to dampen his own curiosity and speed this along.

"I've heard of a guy called Queran," he admitted, not looking at Donnel. No need to get him in trouble if he'd breached a confidence. "And my mother once told me about a relative who could predict the future." The last was an utter lie, but it seemed to fit. Jaxon injected a note of eagerness into his voice. "It would actually be a big relief if it were true. It might explain why I seem to anticipate when things are going to happen." He glanced at Donnel and added to him in a confiding tone, "My case closing rate has always been higher than anyone else's." This was true, but Jaxon suspected the Controller already knew that.

The Controller's next words surprised him. "We've suspected you have this ability for some time. I did send someone to talk with you about it some months ago, but he was sidestepped by another matter."

You mean I killed him, Jaxon thought.

"When there weren't any incidents of psychological disturbances on your records," Controller Ramsey continued, "we decided to wait and see if anything developed. Now tell me what you saw."

Jaxon nodded. "Okay. Well, at first it started out like a dream, and there were only a few unconscious people, but now it's like . . ." He made a face. "I see dozens and dozens of unconscious people inside a huge building. The building is one I've seen before in the empty zone. Except in my dream, the rubble has been cleared out, and it's packed with people. More and more arrive in a shuttle that flies about a man's height off the ground." He shook his head. "I know that sounds crazy—those don't even exist. Anyway, El Cerebro is with them. His men are carrying the people from the shuttles. And—"

"How many men?" Ramsey interrupted.

Jaxon closed his eyes, pretending to concentrate. "Maybe a dozen or a little more. Not nearly as many as the unconscious people. But I can see they're planning to give them some kind of drug. They talk about burning down New York and the admin buildings, and about people who can kill without touching you." He paused. "I guess people like that Queran guy. But he can't really do that, right?"

The Controller didn't respond, but Donnel's head bobbed in a slight nod.

"Go on," the Controller urged.

Jaxon took a breath. "Then you come, and Special Forces too. I'm with you. We take El Cerebro prisoner. And our enforcers start checking the unconscious people against the database. Or at least I think that's what they're doing. Some they wake and give medicine to. Others they're taking away in shuttles. That's what I saw last night."

"You recognize the people?" Ramsey asked.

"Some of them. I think they're from Colony 6. But it's hard to remember. I was just a child when I left there. My mother was murdered, you know." He'd hoped for some kind of reaction from Ramsey with that statement, but the man only nodded.

"And you're sure we take possession of El Cerebro?"

"I've been chasing El Cerebro ever since I transferred here. It's him." Jaxon allowed himself a smile. "They say his face is a mask. Maybe now we'll find out what's behind it."

Ramsey tilted his head, studying him, and Jaxon realized he'd gone too far. Maybe the fact that El Cerebro wore a mask wasn't common knowledge. Well, that should only confirm his ability. But for now, he'd better go back to acting the subservient detective.

Jaxon let his gaze drop to his hands that rested on the table, clenching his fingers together as if they were his only lifeline. "I can't believe this is happening. Like I said, at first it was just a dream, but the past few days, it's been different."

"Different how?" Ramsey asked, a gleam of eagerness escaping from his blue eyes.

Jaxon lifted his gaze. "There's so many unconscious people that they also fill up the space in front of the building. They're wrapped in some kind of thin heating blankets. It seemed like it might have happened last night. It was that real."

Ramsey swallowed hard and nodded at Donnel. "Go tell the captain. I want our forces ready within the hour. If anyone wakes those people, it's going to be us."

Donnel jumped to his feet, and without a backward glance at Jaxon, he moved so fast toward the door that he was nearly sprinting. He passed another man on the way out, a man in a black suit who carried a small black case.

The Controller stood. "Right on time, doctor. I want you to give him one dose so we can confirm what he's seen."

Jaxon was about to protest that the treatment would dampen his visions, but he couldn't figure out how to say it without blowing his cover. The doctor came over to Jaxon and set his case on the table, opening it with a press of his palm. Inside, cushioned with black foam, were several dozen small hypos in three rows. Most of them were green, but half in the last row were black with a white zigzag running around the top. It was one of these black and white ones that the man removed from the case.

"I'll need your wrist," the man said to Jaxon. "It's more pleasant than in the neck and only takes a bit longer to work that way."

How nice that he seemed concerned about Jaxon's comfort. Trouble was, Jaxon didn't trust either of them. He looked at the Controller and said, "When my doctor gives me sleep aids, the visions go away. I might not be able to see anything more."

A slow smile spread over the Controller's face. "Don't worry. This isn't that kind of treatment. This is what helped develop your ability in the first place. You had it as a child."

That was when Jaxon realized the white zigzag was actually the letter V running the circumference of the hypo. V for viribus, the drug that years ago had been fed to all the Colony 6 residents through the water. The knowledge didn't make him any happier. The viribus experiment had also birthed juke, the highly addictive, hallucinogenic byproduct that was now an expensive drug that killed people in the CORE in increasing numbers. The last time he'd taken juke to increase his visions, the resulting increase in his madness had nearly killed him.

There were many things Jaxon could do at this point—grab the case and run for the door, refuse to receive the injection, or submit. With the triplets standing guard, he didn't think he'd make it far, so running was out. Refusing also seemed impossible. He'd have to trust that Ramsey didn't want him incapacitated, at least not before he showed them the location.

He pulled back his uniform sleeve as far as it would go and extended his arm on the table in the doctor's direction. "What is it?" he asked.

"It's called viribus," Ramsey replied. "If you do have an ability, it will initiate a response. It's actually better as small doses over time for creating abilities, or rather permanently enhancing those you already have, but we're assuming you already have a precog ability. This undiluted dose will help it activate more clearly."

Instead of taking his wrist, the doctor pulled something resembling a headband from his pocket and fastened it around Jaxon's head.

"But . . . there are rumors of people going crazy," Jaxon said. "Is that going to happen to me? I mean, sometimes I feel a little . . ." He trailed off and let them guess at the rest.

Ramsey chuckled. "Undiluted viribus will eliminate any madness symptoms for months. After that, we'll get you regular doses of the green treatment. That's more temporary but far less dramatic. We'd use it now, but for people with mental abilities, it can cause a muting effect in the first few days."

The doctor rubbed something wet on his wrist before placing the hypo over his vein and depressing the top. A sharp pain registered on Jaxon's senses, followed by an intense heat that ran up his arm, seemingly intent to burn everything in its path. By the time it reached his shoulder and spread to his neck, though, the temperature was tolerable. He was glad they'd given it to him in his arm. The heat spread more slowly now, and it felt good. Not like any drug at all. Certainly not like the juke that had incapacitated him.

"You ever take it?" he asked Controller Ramsey.

Ramsey's cheek twitched again. "I have. My father had a gift, but I apparently do not."

Jaxon was about to ask what gift when a premonition hit him without warning. The world shifted, waving as if it were being blown about by the wind. He tried to manage it. He tried the breathing technique Kentley had taught him. He tried pushing it away, as Reese did with her sketches. He tried hitting his head with his fists.

Still, he curled over, his face smacking into the table as the world heaved and twisted around him . . . until finally, it disappeared.

He stares at two contorted bodies: Reese and Ty Bissett. Warrick Ramsey stands over them, grinning. "No!" he screams, falling to his knees in agony.

The world hiccupped again, and the same scene appeared. But different this time.

Reese stands at Jaxon's side. They stare at two dead people: Ramsey and Ty.

Always Ty.

Once before, Jaxon had seen a dual vision, and it meant a choice. Hadn't Ollin said he'd have to make a choice?

"What do you see?" a disembodied voice demanded.

You, he wanted to scream. *And you're finally dead.* But he couldn't warn the Controller. He couldn't allow the first vision to come true, because what would all the victory in the world mean if Reese wasn't with him?

"What do you see?" the voice said again.

Words started in Jaxon's throat despite his effort to stop them. He bit his tongue hard, tasting blood. Still, they came. No! He wouldn't betray Reese. Maybe he could use another word for dead, one that might be misunderstood.

"Y-you kill," he gasped, managing to swallow the "ed" from the end of the word kill.

"Who?" The word came from so close to his head that Jaxon cringed at the loudness. He clenched his jaw. *Don't say, don't say!* By the CORE, he would not say another word. But still, words came.

"Ty . . . and . . ." As suddenly as the urge to speak had filled him, it left. He was once again in control of his mouth. "And El Cerebro," he whispered. "You kill Ty Bissett and El Cerebro in the empty zone I saw before. You capture all the unconscious people."

"El Cerebro is dead? You're sure?"

"Yes," Jaxon said. "You shoot him in the head."

From somewhere far away he heard, "The reading confirms it was a psychological event."

"He's not able to lie?"

"They never can right after the viribus."

"Wake him up. We have an appointment in the empty zone."

Laughter sounded inside Jaxon's head. Crazy laughter, though his mind was as clear as it had been in months, maybe years. Oh, yes, they had an appointment in the empty zone.

He was going to shoot.

CHAPTER 21

Lyssa came back to her body in the front seat of Reese's unmarked police shuttle with a start, her mind pounding with Jaxon's words. Ty and El Cerebro would die. Ty and Captain Brogan.

Reese stared at her. "What are you doing back? Is he okay?"

"I think so. But where's Ty? He can't be there in the empty zone. Or Brogan."

"What are you saying?" Reese reached over from the other front seat and gripped her arm.

Lyssa hurriedly recounted what she'd seen the Controller do to Jaxon, knowing there was a touch of hysteria in her voice. "They'll be going to the empty zone soon, so you'd better get driving if we're going to stay ahead of them. But what about Ty and Brogan? Jaxon says the Controller shoots him in the head."

"He lied," Reese said with surety. "His other vision showed Brogan only pretending to be unconscious like the rest of us."

"He, he didn't take the viribus before."

"No, but we did for ten years." Reese's gaze was earnest.

"I trust his visions, and I trust him. I'm sorry about Ty, we all are, but you've known about him for months. We can only do what we can."

Lyssa nodded, her panic easing.

"Go back to Jaxon," Reese said. "I'll tell Brogan and the others. If Jaxon really doesn't want this to continue, he'll find a way to let us know. He knows you're watching."

"Do you know where Ty is?"

The set of Reese's face was grim. "He's there in the empty zone. But he should be hidden some distance away like the kids. He'll stay put."

Lyssa's stomach churned until she wondered if she was going to vomit. "I don't think he will."

"I'll have them look for him. Go!" Reese was already pulling her T-link over her eyes. They didn't have as good a range here in the CORE, but there would be no chance of unwanted monitoring.

Lyssa lay back in her reclined seat. As she began to travel, she could feel the bright pull of both her body and Lyra's. She focused instead on the much closer but lesser pull of Lyra's incorporeal energy. In the next second, she was back with Jaxon and her sister. Jaxon was sitting up at the table, his face flushed and his lips clamped tightly together.

"I gave Reese an update," she said to Lyra. "Anything else happen?"

"They gave him a stimulant. He was already awake, but they wanted him more alert."

"Do you think he really saw what he said?"

Lyra considered a moment. "I don't know. But if it's not a go, he won't take the Controller there."

It was nearly the same thing Reese had said, and Lyssa realized that of course Jaxon wouldn't let Brogan walk into danger. Unless maybe he'd decided that two lives were worth the sacrifice of freeing the colonies. And they were . . . unless they were *your* loved ones. Lyssa thought of Ty, whom she didn't love, couldn't love because of his future. And of Captain Brogan, who would willingly give his life for the cause.

Controller Ramsey motioned to the three enforcers Donnel had called the triplets. "Help him out to the lead shuttle," he said. "I'll be there momentarily."

They took Jaxon out the back of the building to the first of a dozen oversized, all-terrain, black shuttles topped with heavy artillery guns. Each shuttle had a row of interior seats running down the sides, and Special Forces troops, twelve to a shuttle, were already inside. All the enforcers wore blues and carried battle helmets. Once those helmets were on and the faceplates down, only their hands would be exposed. They had gloves that could also be worn, ones that still allowed them to activate the fingerprint readers on their weapons, but the day wasn't cold enough to deal with the added clumsiness. Lyssa and her crew had banked on that.

She stayed with Lyra and Jaxon in the shuttle only until they started off, then she returned to her body. Reese was talking on the T-link while the shuttle sped on automatic pilot through Amarillo City.

"I count a hundred and twenty Special Forces," Lyssa said. "Give or take a few. The doctor and his case of treatment is also in the convoy. What does Brogan say?"

"He said we're going through with it."

"And Ty?"

Reese shook her head. "No one has reached him yet. Are you sure the Controller is heading to the empty zone?"

"Yes, they asked Jaxon for directions," Lyra confirmed. "And I verified the coordinates they put into their onboard Teev."

Reese and Lyssa soon abandoned their shuttle near the edge of the empty zone, trading it for a two-wheel scrambler that would give them better and faster access to the target location. They bounced through the rubble, the low hum of their fuel-cell engine barely marring the quiet.

When they arrived, almost everyone was in place. Blanket-covered bodies were strewn over the field of rubble, roughly three feet apart to allow movement between the human columns. There had been an obvious attempt to place the bodies in lines, but human error and the remaining small mounds of rubble made that difficult. The columns bent and swayed and sometimes merged together, just as they might if they'd been unloaded hurriedly from different hovercraft. Ten underground men, El Cerebro's toughest soldiers and personal guards, wandered through the prone bodies, as if monitoring them. The sun shone down, warming the rocks, and the blue skies were completely empty of any life. For an eerie moment, Lyssa had the feeling she was back in that room in Newcali, finding the sixers for the first time. There were no containers or chandeliers, but the ominous silence was the same.

Lyssa checked briefly in with Lyra. "They're seven minutes out," she reported.

"Good." Reese climbed off the scrambler and ran to her place among the bodies as Hammer loped up to Lyssa.

With his long hair hanging free, a three-day beard, and ragged clothing, Hammer looked the part of a sixer or refugee fringer. He removed the rifle he carried from his shoulder and handed it to Lyssa. "I'll show you where to set up. You have the silenced pistol too, right? In case you need it?"

"Yes," she confirmed, slinging the rifle strap over her shoulder. When he'd climbed on the scrambler in front of her, she added, "Have you seen Ty?"

His unreadable eyes locked onto hers. "I talked to him. I tried to make him go back to the underground, but he says he's good with a gun."

"He's not out there?" Lyssa waved at the still bodies.

"No. He's on the north perimeter, farther out than I'm taking you. He's as safe as it's possible to be."

Relief flooded her. "Thank you."

He nodded and started north along the edge of the bodies, passing the building Jaxon had told the Controller was full of unconscious sixers. It wasn't really. Inside were only a few soldiers and supplies.

They bounced through the rubble on crooked pathways that had once held buildings, streets, or even parks. It was hard to tell what this place had been before the bombs had permanently shattered and twisted the city. Hammer slowed the scrambler and came to a stop near a rocky mound made of massive pre-Breakdown slabs of concrete.

"This location is secure," he said. "Only one way in, and only one person can enter at a time. If they pinpoint your location, you can pick them off all day if they try to reach you, unless you run out of ammo. And I don't think you will. From the top, you can see the whole field well. Don't leave here unless it's absolutely necessary, okay? Physically, I mean." He hesitated and added more uncertainly, "You're a great shot, but your size is a real disadvantage in hand-to-hand combat. If you do have to leave for whatever reason, just be sure—"

"To stay out of the explosion zones. I know. We went through it ten times last night."

"No doubt they'll send in drones first," Hammer continued, "to make sure it's not a trap, so keep low until the action begins."

"Go," she said. "You need to get into place."

He nodded and turned. He'd thrown his leg over the scrambler when he stopped and came back. "Lyssa," he said. "I know I said I wouldn't . . . In case something happens, I just want . . ." He stopped speaking as his big arms wrapped around her and pulled her against his body. When she didn't resist, his mouth lowered to hers, his lips eager and searching.

With a little sigh, she kissed him back, her hands going into his hair. She'd been waiting for this, perhaps from the very moment in the empty zone when his hair had pillowed her cheek from the rubble. Happiness and desire raced through her, and time stood perfectly still. He completely filled all her senses. She felt the slight roughness of his new beard and smelled some kind of soap mixed with musk. His arms around her were protective and dangerous all at once.

When they parted, she was breathing heavily. She wanted to tell him she wasn't seeing Ty anymore, but she couldn't find the words. His dark eyes held hers as his fingers, roughened with the past days' work, ran over her cheek. Then without a word, he was gone. She watched the scrambler zooming toward the soon-to-be-battlefield. Besides him, nothing moved.

To enter the hideout, she had to crawl under a slab and scale the mound from the inside. Near the top was a small, one-person indentation where a huge bag of ammunition awaited her. She could either rest the rifle on top of the highest slab and shoot out at the enforcers or crouch down and aim through a hole in the concrete to shoot anyone trying to enter her hideout. By its regular formation, she knew someone had lasered that hole. She hoped the younger teens fighting today were either farther away or had equally secure hideouts. Her location was directly north of division, where Lyra was physically, which meant they should still be able to travel anywhere within the target area.

Lyssa organized her rifle and readied some of the extra ammunition. With these preparations in place, she settled in the hollow and rested just a moment, closing her eyes and breathing deeply. Using her ability to come and go so often was taking a toll on her, and she wanted to make sure she would be able to finish her tasks.

All at once she felt them, small blobs that pulled at her: Reese, Jaxon, Hammer, Brogan, and Dani on the field. She also saw Ty somewhere off behind her and slightly to the right, farther from the field, and Nova even farther away to the east. She couldn't feel Eagle, who was in the underground watching remotely, ready to set off his explosives, but the others were clear. Holding onto this awareness, she traveled back to Lyra, who was still in the enforcer shuttle approaching the target location from the south.

"They're all in place," Lyssa told her sister, wishing Jaxon could hear the news as well. The lines of worry on his forehead had aged him ten years.

The shuttles came to a halt. "They'll have to do some walking first," Lyra said. They glided through the walls, not waiting for the shuttle to disgorge its occupants.

"Good thing. I've been worried they'd somehow manage to bring the vehicles through. Those guns mounted on top look serious."

"Don't worry. We made sure they won't be able to get them close enough to use."

"Wait a minute," Lyssa said, scanning the area. "We'd better make sure they're all here. I see only six shuttles."

"There's not enough room here for all of them, but there's another open space a kilometer back." They glided swiftly in the direction the shuttles had come, eventually finding all but one of the twelve vehicles.

"Maybe they didn't take that last one," Lyra said with a worried frown. "Some enforcers might have stayed behind to make sure no one broke into their building."

Lyssa grimaced. "Or they went for reinforcements."

"We'll keep an eye out. But you'd better report it."

Lyssa slipped back to her body and passed on the information via her T-link. "Heads up," she said. "They're approaching on foot from the south. Only eleven of the vehicles arrived, however. We went back several kilometers. No sign of the twelfth."

"We stick to the plan," came Brogan's answer.

When Lyssa traveled back to join Lyra, the troops of Special Forces, now wearing their battle helmets, were still circumventing the mounds of rubble separating them from the target location. At least two of the mounds hadn't been there three days ago, but they looked as old and settled as the rest.

"You say they have hovercraft," Ramsey said. "I can see where that tech would come in handy over this garbage."

Lyssa only partially agreed. Hovers could have flown to the field, but it would have taken some tricky flying. The place where they'd actually unloaded the sixers had been far more accessible to both hovers and shuttles.

Jaxon stared at the Controller blankly. "Hovercraft? Is that what they're called?" To Lyssa's ears he sounded completely genuine.

Ramsey laughed. "That's what I would call them," he said, "and if you saw them, they have to exist." He also seemed genuine, though his spy must have already told him about hovers and probably the moving sidewalks as well.

A short time later, behind the cover of a rubble mound, the Special Forces hunkered down long before entering the clearing. The Controller nodded at one of the men, who Lyssa had seen release several small flying drones.

"Drones show only the heat signatures on the field," he reported. "Nothing notable nearby, though there are plenty of places here that they can't reach. They also can't see inside the building. It's shut up tight. Got a few pictures of the unconscious people up close and the undergrounders watching over them, if you want to see."

The Controller did want to see. Pulling down the screen

on his battle helmet, he made a few motions, apparently connecting to the same display his soldier was viewing. Finally, he nodded, flipped up his visor, and angled his gaze at Donnel.

"Take five other men and check the perimeter," he said. "Three on one side, three on the other. We'll give you ten minutes to scan the vicinity along the field for heat signatures or signs of ambush. Alert us if you see anything out of place. If you find anyone, kill them only if you have to. We'll want to question them all. I'd like to know as soon as possible if there will be more shipments. We could use a few hovercraft of our own."

With a nod, Donnel pointed at one of the triplets and four others. They melded into the rubble. Everyone else, rifles and pistols at the ready, awaited the Controller's signal. Minutes ticked by until Lyssa felt she would scream with anxiety.

Finally, the time came. "Secure the undergrounders first," Controller Ramsey said. "Then those with me will continue toward the building while the rest of you start cataloguing the mutants. Remember, for the first shipment, we're searching for those with a family history of kinetic abilities."

Mutants? Lyssa thought. The single derogatory word clearly described exactly what the Controller thought of the sixers. *Of us,* she amended.

The soldiers stormed the field, shouting and brandishing their weapons. The undergrounders pretending to care for the unconscious immediately raised their hands and let themselves be pushed to the ground. Lyssa was relieved when no one seemed to be hurt.

"Where is El Cerebro?" Ramsey demanded of Jaxon.

"Not sure," he responded, pushing up the visor on the battle helmet someone had given him. "Maybe in the building. Unless . . . you don't think he's one of them . . . us, do you?" He holstered his weapon, leaned over, and pulled off the blanket that was partially covering one of the undergrounders. Then he went to the next person in the line, whose face was already uncovered, shook his head, and continued on to a third man. The Controller caught up with him and began checking the prone figures on the nearby column as they approached the building. The black-suited doctor followed him, as did the remaining two triplets and four others.

Around them, the Special Forces, most with their helmets off now or visors up, were already cataloguing the pretend sixers. One after the other, they checked for CivIDs with their iTeevs. During the process, a few of the undergrounders moved as if in sleep, reaching out to touch the hands of the enforcers.

Unheeding, Jaxon and Ramsey were nearing the middle of the field now, still pulling back blankets or peering into uncovered faces. Several of the men with them were doing the same. More than one of them reached out and touched the poisoned neck of an undergrounder or slapped away a hand that reached out clumsily as if to ask for help.

"Saca!" muttered one of the triplets, when a hand tried to touch him. "We need a better sedative."

"I agree," said the doctor.

Lyssa's heart hammered in her chest as one of the enforcers guarding the captured undergrounders staggered and stumbled dazedly to his knees in front of the captives. Another Special Forces troop ran to help him. They were far enough behind the Controller that he hadn't noticed.

Yet.

Only a few minutes more and they'd reach Brogan. That would be the moment everything would work . . . or not. Lyssa could feel his location pulling at her mind. Reese and Hammer were even closer.

And Ty . . . he was farther away, but not where he'd been before. He was coming toward the field. What was he doing? He was going to put them all in danger.

Or maybe he was in danger.

Instantly, she was back in her body, peering down from her perch to see an enforcer marching Ty at gunpoint toward her location. Within minutes, they'd be past her and in the field. Then he would die. She knew it as surely as if she'd seen a vision herself.

Grabbing her pistol and checking the silencer, she half climbed, half fell down the length of the cement. Lyssa crawled under the rock near the opening and was still on her stomach as Ty started past. She took a second to aim carefully at the enforcer's neck. If she hit him in the chest or shoulder instead, his blues would save him and he might shoot back.

You're a great shot, Hammer had said. She hoped that hadn't been flattery.

She fired. Once, twice. Just as Eagle had taught her.

She fired a third time to make sure, but that round missed since the soldier was already falling.

Ty turned in surprise as she wiggled out of the hole. "Lyssa!" he said, his voice strangled.

"Is he dead?" Horror spread through her. She'd never killed anyone before, especially not an enforcer who was only following orders. Tears stung her eyes.

Ty looked rather green, but he moved closer to stare down at the man. "Yeah, he's gone."

Lyssa scrambled to her feet and went to see for herself. Bile rose in her throat when she saw the gaping hole in the man's neck. No way anyone could survive that. She turned away, fighting the urge to vomit. Did he have a wife? A child?

"What happened?" she forced out. "We're supposed to stay hidden in case we're needed."

"I was trying to get a better view, and he found me."

"Well, go inside there," she said, pointing to her hideout. "It has a great view. I know another place."

It was a lie, and he knew it immediately. Strange how she'd lied to him so many times, and now he'd finally caught on. "No, I'm not taking your place. I'll be okay."

No, you won't, she wanted to scream at him.

His brow furrowed. "Why didn't you tell me you were involved with all of this months ago?"

"Because I have a daughter."

Understanding filled him. "Tamsin."

She nodded. "The birth order is for Lyra. Not me."

He gave her a rueful grin that tugged at something inside her chest. "I'm sorry I didn't figure it out."

Now wasn't the time to talk about it. "Please, go inside," she said. "For me. This could still go so wrong."

She hurried away without waiting for a response. She'd gone only five steps when a man rose up in front of her, a rifle pointed at her chest. It was the triplet that had gone with Donnel to check the perimeter. The perimeter where they now stood.

"Drop it," he ordered.

She tossed her pistol to the ground, glad that at least Ty had gotten away. She glanced backward to assure herself of his safety, only to see Donnel marching Ty toward her. Her heart gave an uneven lurch. Killing that enforcer had been a terrifying experience, but seeing Ty held at gunpoint by Special Forces was far worse.

"They killed Yorry," Donnel said in an ugly voice. To Lyssa, he added, "Give me one good reason I shouldn't shoot you both."

Lyssa couldn't exactly remind him that the Controller had said to bring any captives alive. "Hi, Donnel," she said instead. "I've heard about you."

"How do you know my name?"

"I work for AED in dispatch," she said. "I know a lot of the Special Forces. We're on the same team."

"Is that what you told Yorry?"

Had he seen her shoot him? She didn't think so. "I don't know anything about your friend," she said. "Ty and I are here on a . . . well, we're dating." She gave an embarrassed shrug. "Please, if you'll just let me call division, you can confirm that we work there."

"I don't believe you." Donnel pushed his rifle against the back of Ty's neck.

"We're supposed to take them in," the triplet said.

Donnel, still glaring at her, backed up slightly and motioned with his rifle for her to precede him. "Run," he said. "But keep your hands up. If you stop, I will shoot you in the head."

Okay, this will still work, she thought, falling into a jog. But she knew it wouldn't. Something had gone horribly wrong.

Minutes later, when they arrived at the huge building, Jaxon and the Controller were only paces away from the entrance and near Brogan's location. Donnel hurried her past the few bodies that separated them while Lyssa hoped he wouldn't notice that out in the field, his fellow Special Forces were weaving about or sinking to the ground.

"Look what we found," Donnel called, attracting the Controller's attention.

Jaxon grimaced. "What are you guys doing here?" he asked.

Ramsey flicked his gaze at Jaxon. "You know them?"

"They work for my division. She's in dispatch. He's in personnel. They don't have anything to do with this."

Donnel snorted. "They claim they're out here on a date. But I found Yorry shot dead north of here, close to where we caught them."

"They really are dating," Jaxon said.

"Really?" The Controller's voice dripped sarcasm. "More likely they're how El Cerebro is getting information about our movements. Find something to cuff them to. We'll question them later."

Donnel smirked at Lyssa, leaving Ty to the triplet. "You heard him," he told her. "Let's go toward the building. Move."

Lyssa didn't dare glance at Jaxon as he uncovered the prone body in his row. It was Reese, which meant on the opposite row, Ramsey would be reaching for the blanket over Hammer's face. She risked a glance Hammer's way and was relieved to see that he showed no signs of movement when the Controller gazed down into his face. She'd more than half expected Hammer to come up firing at Donnel to save her.

"This one looks familiar," Ramsey said, scanning Hammer with his iTeev. To the doctor, he added, "He doesn't seem to have a CivID, unless it's blocked somehow. Better put him in the first shipment."

The next person in Controller Ramsey's line was Brogan. As Ramsey's hand reached out, it seemed as if everyone on the field held their collective breaths, though Lyssa knew that was only in her mind. The Special Forces were dropping all over the field now without a single utterance, limbs flopping as they fell. Donnel finally noticed it and pulled her to a stop just beyond the Controller.

"Hey," he said. "Something's—"

Too late. Controller Ramsey pulled back the blanket covering Brogan's face. Brogan came up with the blanket, a gun pressed to Ramsey's chest. "Hello Mr. Ramsey," Brogan said, his face mask stretching in the slightest of grins. "I hear you're looking for me."

He wasn't the only one to rise. Like a graveyard horror film Lyssa had once seen on the Teev, all the prone figures in the field arose, grappling with the stumbling Special Forces or shooting them with silenced pistols. Dani was a blur, quickly taking out any enforcers who tried to shoot back.

"They're infecting us with something," an enforcer yelled. Dani hit him, and he went down hard.

Around Lyssa, those standing had remained strangely frozen for those first few surprising seconds. Now, Hammer launched himself at Lyssa, tearing her from Donnel. Ty twisted and lashed out at the triplet behind him, but the man hit him hard and Ty went down, only to be dragged back to his feet and locked in a stranglehold. Reese leapt up and shot one triplet in the face before she was grabbed by the third. Jaxon pulled his gun and aimed it at the triplet who held Reese.

"Hold," ordered Brogan. "No one move, or I shoot Ramsey."

The two remaining triplets, the doctor, and Donnel froze.

Elsewhere on the field, the few Special Forces still standing began retreating. But as they ran, shots from far away rifles slammed into some of them. Others were attacked by undergrounders or Dani. Lyssa hoped Nova hadn't been one of those who'd fired her rifle but guessed that she probably had been. The struggle lasted less than a minute as the Special Forces were quickly overcome. Only two escaped, but Dani sprinted after them.

"Okay," Brogan said. "Now let's talk."

Ramsey shot Jaxon a venomous look. "You," he growled.

Jaxon didn't take his eyes from the triplet who had his gun against Reese's head. "Me? I'm just a mutant."

Ramsey's face flushed with anger. "You're making a mistake."

"Let her go," Jaxon said.

Brogan jabbed his gun into Ramsey's stomach. "Tell your men to put their weapons down or I'll shoot you now."

"Show your face," Ramsey mocked. "Or are you afraid?"

"Who I am doesn't matter," Brogan said, his voice devoid of emotion. "What matters is that my grandfather worked with your father—to my greatest shame. I've spent my life trying to correct what he did."

"I've spent my life trying to make their work count!" Ramsey countered. "And I've done it. After I get rid of the fringers here, I'm heading to Newcali. I'll have access to all the food and water we need to expand the CORE and build additional colonies. Once I have my army of people with abilities, I can make sure nothing like Breakdown ever happens again."

"Only so you can profit," Brogan retorted.

With a sudden jerk and a groan, the doctor on the other side of Donnel fell to the ground, his black treatment case bouncing once before coming to rest at Jaxon's foot like an offering.

"And then there were only four," Reese mocked. The triplet behind her pressed his barrel harder into her skull.

"Let her go," Jaxon repeated. "You hurt her, and I promise you'll die." Lyssa could hear the desperation in his voice.

"There's something I need to tell you," Ramsey said to Jaxon, reaching toward him.

"Stay away from me," Jaxon retorted. "I have nothing to say to you."

"Tell you what," the Controller said to Brogan. "You put your gun down and I'll tell you why you're going to let me go."

Brogan shook his head. "That's not going to happen."

"No? Maybe a little demonstration." Ramsey nodded at the triplet who held Ty. With a violent twist, he snapped Ty's neck and dropped him to the ground. His black hair covered all of his face except his eyes that now stared out at them unseeingly.

"No! No! No!" Screams cut through the deadly silence, and only after Hammer's arms encircled her did Lyssa realize she was the one screaming. Ty was dead. He'd died exactly in the way Jaxon had seen. Dead. She'd never be able to tell him she was sorry for not being able to love him the way he loved her. She'd never be able to tell him the rest of the truth. She lunged past Donnel to get to the Controller, but Hammer's arms were immovable.

With only a breath of a pause, Brogan fired at the triplet,

who went down instantly, a hole appearing between his eyes. Before Brogan could bring his gun back to Ramsey, Donnel stepped in front of the Controller, his gun leveled at Brogan.

"Don't," Donnel said. "I won't let you kill him."

"You can't leave here," Brogan countered. "None of you can. You're surrounded." Sure enough, two hundred underground soldiers were converging on their location.

Ramsey edged closer to Reese and the triplet, as if seeking to consolidate his position. The Controller had his own gun in his hand now, and in an unexpected move, he jerked Reese in front of him, laying the barrel against her neck. "I believe we're at a standstill, unless you're willing to sacrifice her life as well. And all of those you might still have down in the subway."

His chilly voice broke through Lyssa's haze of pain.

"What do you mean?" Brogan demanded.

Ramsey gave them a slow smile that Lyssa had seen hundreds of times on the Teev. It was powerful and seductive, but now she also recognized the underlying evil that had always been there.

"I mean that I sent a man named Queran down inside your tunnels," Ramsey said. "I have access to the old subway blueprints, and he's going to find your hideout. With so many of your soldiers here, who have you left in charge of the children? I'm assuming you do have children." He paused before adding, "Rats always breed more rats."

Lyssa exchanged looks with Jaxon, while Brogan nodded at Hammer. Hammer reached for his T-link, unfolding them over his eyes. "Eagle, come in. Eagle?"

"Don't bother. We've activated signal dampeners, and my men have located your secondary connection as well." He smiled again and lifted his shoulders as if to apologize. "The way I see it, you have a choice. You let me and my men walk out of here, and I'll call him off. Otherwise, Queran is going to fry your children from the inside out."

Hammer traded his T-link for his iTeev. After a few hand motions, he pulled it off his face, stepping closer to Brogan and Jaxon. "We have communications topside, but I can't get through to the underground," he said in an undertone. "If he's telling the truth, we have no way of warning them."

CHAPTER 22

Eagle hated staying behind in the underground conference room, but an unconscious sixer wouldn't be wearing glasses. Besides, he had to control the explosions, if they became necessary. Only he could calculate the exact instant to blow each of the seven electronic fuses. That meant he was relegated to watching the drama from the safety of the underground instead of being in the thick of it with his crew.

Perhaps worse was that Shadow, or Shimmer, as he thought of her, might think him a coward. He'd never cared before what anyone might think of him, but he cared now. Even from that first day, underneath her angry determination, he'd felt an irresistible attraction to her, like a moth to a flame, which was literal in his case since he could see her shining. She'd been gruff and even rude in the beginning, but the past days of working together had changed everything.

Now that the explosives were finished and in place, they waited together in the underground conference room, the enormous holoscreen showing the field where the battle would soon take place. The moments ticked by slowly, and he turned his mind to other things to stave off the tension.

"Try it," he urged Shimmer. "I promise, you can do it. I've seen you."

She arched a brow. "I'm not sure how to even try."

"Instead of pushing away the light, try drawing it to you."

"What if I draw too much?"

That told him she believed him, at least. "I don't think you can. It's your ability. You should be able to draw it in or deflect it if it gets to be too much. Let's give it a try. See those lights?" He pointed at the ceiling. "Try to pull the energy to you."

Dr. Kentley's children, five-year-old Gwen and six-year-old Probert, giggled from the conference room chairs. The two had attached themselves initially to Eagle, and now to Shimmer. Old Debs, the woman who had previously looked after them in Santoni, was in the main station platform with the other underground children, passing out readymeals for an early lunch. There were thirty-one children at his last count. They had all been ridiculously good the past few days as their parents scrambled to make preparations.

"What if she breaks the lights?" Probert said.

"She won't," Eagle assured him.

"What about the holoscreen?" Gwen put in.

Eagle glanced at the screen, where he had several different views up so he could study the battle from every vantage point. One of the views was from a high-flying drone. He was quite sure none of it would be necessary.

"Maybe you're right," he said. "We have some time before things start happening. Let's go into the main room." This would give him the excuse to get the children out of here. The last thing he wanted was to have them watch the battle.

Just to be sure he didn't miss anything, he pulled up the main holo display in a corner of his glasses. It didn't matter that it was small because the images were also going directly into his brain, where he saw them as large as he needed. With a flick of an eye, he could also trigger the explosions, even if he wasn't in the conference room.

The kids scrambled out the door before them, calling excitedly to their friends as they climbed the stairs to the station platform. Some of the kids abandoned their food and gathered around Shimmer, who was trying not to limp too heavily on her still-healing leg. Eagle thought the children were attracted to her for the same reason he was, even if they didn't know it: she shone. For him, she was a kaleidoscope of color and light.

"Okay," he prompted. "Try it now."

The lights overhead dimmed immediately, and Shimmer glowed brighter. "More!" the kids shouted.

Laughing, Shimmer drew in an audible breath. All at once, the lights went out. The only visible illumination left in the underground station was the display of the coming battlefield on Eagle's glasses and Shimmer herself, who glowed.

"Ooooh!" the kids cooed.

"Shadow," Gwen said, her breath hushed. "You're all sparkly."

"That's why I sometimes call her Shimmer," Eagle said.

Instantly, the light went back on. Shimmer turned to him, grinning. "Okay, fine, if you insist. I admit the name is growing on me. And you were right. Looks like my gift does go both ways."

He nodded. "I know, it's a curse. Me being right, I mean."

She rolled her eyes, but her mouth told another story.

"Again, again!" shouted the kids.

"One more time," Shimmer called back, "and then you go finish eating. All of you." She turned off the lights again and glowed even brighter. The children cheered. "Okay," she said, bringing back the lights. "Go eat!"

The children scattered obediently, but a pounding drew their attention to the KC prisoner, Ollin, who was hitting his cuffed hands on the table. "Very nice," he said, motioning Eagle and Shimmer over to where he was still chained to the wall. Eagle didn't feel guilty in the least. Until this was over, they couldn't afford to trust him.

Eagle double-checked his glasses as Reese reported that the caravan of Special Forces shuttles were almost to the Empty Zone. Still plenty of time. He walked over to Ollin. "You need something? We're heading back to the conference room."

Ollin frowned at the almost finished readymeal on the table in front of him. "I just wanted to say that I've been experiencing a weird sensation. Like it's hot, you know? I feel something's going to happen."

"Something *is* going to happen," Shimmer said. "I should be there myself."

Eagle's stomach twisted at the idea. "I need you here. You know the explosive lines as well as I do. You're my backup, remember?"

"No, I'm here because of my lame leg," she retorted. "You don't really need me."

But he did. More than he could tell her now. Maybe he would be able to after it was all over. After they'd survived and there was a future that didn't involve hiding in empty zones.

"There are still guards down here, right?" Ollin asked. Small beads of sweat had appeared on his forehead just below his hairline.

"Yes," Eagle said. "El Cerebro would never leave the kids without a guard. Or even this place. We'll need it for some time to come, even if everything goes as planned in the colonies."

Eagle turned to leave, but Kentley chose that moment to

arrive at Ollin's table. As usual, the doctor's narrow face was on the haggard side, as if he needed a week of sleep. "I have news," he announced rather fatalistically.

"About the medicine?" Shadow asked, her figure brightening, which made Eagle wonder if she was battling the madness more than she'd let on.

"No," Kentley said. "I mean, yes, of course, I'm ready to make more treatments, though I'm a little concerned that even the pure viribus won't lead to a permanent cure like I thought." He shook his head. "Anyway, what I meant by announcement is that I finally had time to run Ollin's DNA against the other samples I've taken."

"Oh," Eagle said, losing interest. He was about to excuse himself when Kentley rushed on.

"I found a match."

"A match?" Ollin asked.

Kentley laughed. "You and Jaxon share nearly twenty-five percent of your DNA."

Ollin stared at him blankly. "What does that mean?"

"You're half brothers. Most likely through your fathers, since you were raised by different mothers. Though if they adopted you, it could be that you are related through your mothers. But any way you look at it, you're brothers. Or half brothers, as I said before."

Ollin gaped, and his eyes opened wide. "Are you sure?"

"Of course I'm sure." Kentley sounded offended.

"Makes sense," Eagle said. "Your gifts are similar."

"Do you remember your father?" Shimmer asked.

Ollin's surprised expression finally eased. "No. I mean, my mother talked about him, but he died when I was really young."

"How young?" Kentley prompted.

"Two, maybe."

"Did your mother have any other children?" Kentley asked.

Ollin nodded. "Older sister. But she's gone." The sadness in the words was unmistakable.

"I wonder," Kentley mused. "Couples in the colonies must have at least two children to maintain the population. And maybe the Elite haven't been so particular about them getting pregnant on their own time. I'm going to need to test all the sixers. There could be other half-sibling matches."

"You're saying maybe they inseminated women?" Shimmer was aghast.

"Or implanted embryos. We know Colony 6 was an experiment. They probably did a lot of both."

Eagle didn't know how to respond to that. His parents were gone, and they had always seemed like his real parents—he'd even looked like his father—but neither of them had admitted to sharing even a part of his ability. They hadn't gone blind either.

"Look, that's really great," Ollin said, giving an exaggerated flourish with his cuffed hands. "I'm glad to know I still have a relative in this crazy existence, and I look forward to getting to know Jaxon. He seems like a great guy." He brought up his hands and rubbed the tips of his fingers against his face, mopping off the sweat. "But right now I'm more concerned about the here and now. Can someone just check in with the guards? I think something's wrong. Or about to be wrong."

Eagle looked at Kentley, who nodded. "Okay, we'll check," Kentley said. "It can't hurt. They're due to check in soon anyway. With everyone else gone, I'm the one monitoring." He stalked away a little awkwardly, and Eagle wondered if he was a little hurt that none of them had seemed more excited about his discovery. Eagle felt more numb than anything. With so many betrayals and issues with the Elite, this latest injustice was simply one more on the heap. Later, after they processed, maybe they could feel more. Maybe the resulting anger would fuel them when the pending battle with the Elite wore them down.

Eagle checked the display sent to him by his glasses. The cameras they'd set up in the empty zones showed that Special Forces had arrived and were climbing out of their vehicles. But even as he watched, the display went black. He tried rebooting. Then he tried connecting to the Teev cameras in the city using his regular enforcer credentials—a danger that might possibly allow him to be traced.

Nothing.

That was when Dr. Kentley came toward them at a run. "I've tried to raise the guards, but they aren't answering my messages."

"My connection just went black as well," Eagle said.

Shimmer gasped. "Something's gone wrong then."

"Let's check the Teev." Eagle turned on his heel and sprinted across the station platform, vaguely aware of the curious gazes of the children. Shimmer and Kentley hurried after him.

"Hey, what about me?" Ollin called. "I can help! I'm the one who saw it."

Ignoring him, Eagle hurtled down the steps in the direction of the conference room. Before he'd even gone inside, he could see the huge holoscreen was black. He waved a holo keyboard to life as he rushed into the room. His hands danced over the keyboard and swiped the screen. Images came up, but nothing registered from the outside.

"What is it?" Shimmer asked.

"We're cut off," Eagle said. "There's no connection to the outside. If they need help, I won't know which of our traps to blow."

Kentley had brought up his own keyboard. "It's worse than that," he said. "The cameras on the entrances are completely out, both the west and east. That's where our guys are—or were—and there's no other way into the inhabited part of the underground."

That wasn't quite true. Eagle had mapped every inch with his 3D images, and he'd discovered there was at least one other secret exit that no one knew about. Well, no one except Brogan. The underground king hadn't gotten where he was without having a backup escape. Unfortunately, the escape tunnel was in Brogan's impregnable underground quarters.

"Now what?" Shimmer asked. The glow had completely left her now, as if she were already trying to hide.

"I'm going to check on our guards and the Teev connections." Eagle strode to the back of the room where a loaded equipment table filled the back wall. He was already armed, and his civilian clothes were made of the same material as his enforcer blues. "They could put dampeners to stop signals from the iTeev and the T-link feeds from getting through, but we also have a hard-wired connection to an outside waystation because the concrete is always interfering with the signals. There are only a few places the relay is accessible down here. I want to know if any of those are cut, or if the problem is topside." Cut down here would mean someone was in the tunnels with them, but Eagle didn't want to elaborate on that.

"I'll come too," Kentley said, reaching for one of the extra guns on the table.

"No." Eagle shook his head. The doctor had been with the underground in Santoni, but he wasn't trained. Before he'd had to hide from Special Forces five weeks ago, he'd been working out of a normal office and going into the empty zone only at night to spend time with his adopted children. The doctor would be a liability. "Debs can't deal with all those kids by herself. You and Shimmer stay with them."

Shimmer picked up a pistol, popped out the magazine, and

checked the chamber. "I'm going with you," she said. "You need backup." She racked the pistol and stuck it in her belt before reaching for extra ammo and a rifle.

She was right about the backup, and he knew that a lifetime of living in the empty zone and fighting to stay alive had made her more than capable, but he didn't want her in danger. "I can see in the dark," he said.

"I can make dark," she retorted. She was a good head shorter than he was, but she looked far taller somehow with her upraised chin. "I'll just follow you if you don't let me come," she added.

"Fine," he growled, both frustrated and impressed with her determination.

With his agreement, light gathered once more around her, so subtle that he knew no one else would be able to detect the glow. It swirled and brightened, evoking emotions and reactions inside him that had nothing to do with his current fear. That decided him. If they lived through the revolution, he was going to do something about whatever this was growing between them. Maybe she felt it too.

"Put this on," Eagle said, tossing her a protective vest. "You might be invisible, but you aren't bulletproof." Then he turned to Kentley. "You'd better hide the children. We'll hurry back as soon as we can."

Kentley, his face ashen, nodded and watched them leave.

Within thirty meters, the lights that signaled their proximity to the main station ended, and they were in the dark. Usually, they'd switch on lights they always carried in the subway, but not this time. Shimmer walked close to him, her glow unmistakable and bright to him. She carried her pistol in one hand, and every now and then he heard the tiny rustle of the rifle slapping against her side. After a moment, she switched the pistol to her other hand and reached out to grab onto his elbow. He responded by taking her hand in his. Not exactly the way he'd envisioned their first purposeful physical contact. Her hand was cool and slender and felt exactly right.

There was still no light ahead. Nothing that told him there were intruders. But something was out there.

CHAPTER 23

Jaxon's whole world had shifted into a nightmare. Reese was in danger. Controller Ramsey had ordered Ty's death as easily as he had requested Jaxon to take the doctor's drug, as if he had no doubt that those under him would do his bidding and be grateful for it. The remaining triplet and Donnel, still standing in front of Ramsey, didn't seem the least bit afraid of giving their lives.

"Please, Donnel," Jaxon said to him, low enough that maybe the Controller couldn't hear. "Please move."

Donnel glared at him, but Jaxon held his gaze. Then understanding seemed to fill Donnel as he glanced backward at Reese and the pistol the Controller held at her neck. "It's her, isn't it?" Donnel said softly.

Jaxon moved his head in the slightest of nods.

Donnel's glare softened, but his next words sent betrayal coursing through Jaxon, "Be careful," he said to Ramsey. "She's gifted."

"Why you—" Jaxon shifted his gun to point at Donnel.

Controller Ramsey laughed. "I see how it is," he said. "If you want her and those rats in the underground to remain alive, you'd better let me go. I'll even drop your girl off after we get away."

Like Breakdown, he would. If there was any chance of Reese being a sixer, more likely he'd keep her and begin experimentation. Jaxon shifted his gun back toward the Controller. The man was hunched slightly to use Reese as a shield, leaving Jaxon only the tiniest window that he could shoot Ramsey through to avoid both Donnel and Reese, though he didn't much care about Donnel at the moment. He knew he could make it. Maybe. What was it Ollin had said? To shoot. If he didn't, would his other vision about Reese being dead come true?

Yes. Even now, Jaxon could see the split vision of Reese and Ramsey dying. As far as Jaxon was concerned, there was no choice.

But if he did shoot, he'd sacrifice all those children—and Kentley and Eagle.

"Let her go," Jaxon said, his voice gruff and tight. "Or I'll shoot you right here and now."

Reese frowned at him. "Someone needs to get down to the tunnels. Find Dani. She might be able to make it there in time."

Ramsey only smiled. "Time is almost out. Say the word and I'll turn off the dampeners and tell Queran to stop. You can contact your people too. Otherwise, Queran will kill every man, woman, and child you have in the tunnels."

"Just like you've done in all the empty zones?" Jaxon's finger tightened on the trigger. He had to pull it soon or lose Reese forever.

"No. Some of those children we kept to work in the colonies. The death rate is so high there, you know."

Jaxon willed his hand to remain steady. "Because you work them to death."

"Forget them," Ramsey barked, spittle flying from his lips. "They don't matter. Think of this. If you shoot me, you'll never know who you are."

"Did you kill my mother?" Jaxon retorted.

Controller Ramsey shook his head, but Reese's eyes widened. "Yes," she said. "He sent Summers."

Rage filled Jaxon, hot and dark and all-consuming. His finger tightened on the trigger.

Ramsey didn't notice him. He was too busy studying Reese. "Well, well, well," he said. "So you *are* gifted. I wonder who you really are?"

"I told you," Donnel said. "She could be useful." He glanced once at Jaxon and then away.

Jaxon realized with a start that maybe this was what Donnel had intended all along. Maybe he thought knowing she was a sixer would convince the Controller not to kill her as he had Ty. But Donnel didn't know Reese like Jaxon did. She'd sooner die than let Ramsey take her.

That meant they were back to the same two choices. Jaxon had to shoot. Or watch her die.

Or could there possibly be another option? If only he could see it. If only he could control his sixer ability and see some other way. Even as he thought about it, a stuttering image crossed his vision . . . something about the case containing the viribus hypos. The viribus and a glowing figure. He tried to reach for more, pulling out images and hoping his delay wouldn't seal Reese's fate.

"I knew you were responsible for killing my mother," he said to Ramsey, to keep the man talking. "I knew it all along. Why would you do such a thing? I was a child. She was everything to me."

"Your mother was nothing," Ramsey said with a sneer. "She was a vessel, a means to an end. Like all the colonists."

"A vessel for your seed?" The idea sickened Jaxon.

"Not mine," Ramsey said disparagingly. "My father sometimes had glimpses of the future. He believed if he crossed his genes with others who were also gifted that something more would come of it. He was right. So that makes you my half brother." He gave a light laugh. "At least one of them."

"So is Ollin," Reese said, her face tight not with fear but disgust. "And I see at least two more from the colony. They're dead."

Controller Ramsey shrugged. "Couldn't be helped. And it's not as if they're really kin to me."

Not like his half brother, Summers, Jaxon thought. Bensell Summers had been an Elite pus bag just like Ramsey.

Ramsey leaned forward until he was practically touching Reese's cheek with his lips. "If you can see all that in my head, you really would be useful. Too bad your boyfriend over there doesn't seem to care if you stay alive."

A new wave of anger coursed through Jaxon. *I need to shoot,* he thought.

Reese jerked away, but the gun jabbing into the side of her neck prevented her from moving very far. "You're jealous of your brother," she muttered. "Of both of them. Because you'll never have any kind of ability."

Ramsey's face flushed as he moved his head behind Reese's again. Jaxon knew her comment had put her that much closer to death.

"Well, what will it be?" the Controller demanded.

"Jaxon, you can't." Reese said.

"Yes, I can." Jaxon met her gaze. Because he'd finally seen the end of the premonition. "But first, I want Controller Ramsey to know it was me who shot that pus bag Bensell Summers. I killed him for my mother. And now it's his turn." Jaxon would kill the Controller for Reese.

Ramsey jerked, as if slapped in the face, giving Jaxon that much more of a target to hit. "Why you—"

Jaxon fired at the same time Reese pulled away. The Controller tried to yank her back, but he was falling, falling to the ground, a small round bullet hole under his left eye. Jaxon fired again at his exposed throat. Making sure. Controller Ramsey's face relaxed into emptiness, but his open eyes showed horror. Blood pooled around his head, leaking into the rubble under him.

Brogan also fired, and the remaining triplet crumpled. Only Donnel remained standing with his gun wavering between Brogan and Jaxon uncertainly.

Jaxon shifted his gun in Donnel's direction. "Drop it."

When the man still hesitated, Reese stepped up behind him, her knife in his ribs. "You heard him."

Donnel dropped the gun.

"Call it off," Jaxon told him. Inside he was thinking, *She's okay. She's okay. She's okay.*

Donnel shook his head. "I can't. They won't listen to me." His face went from one to the next, and then he added, "There's also a contingent of Special Forces east of us. Our backup. They'll be here soon. Once they determine we're down, they'll kill everyone here." He choked on the last words. "I-I can't stop any of it." His statement was punctuated by a drone that buzzed past, followed immediately by a whining whistle.

"Move!" Brogan shouted to his soldiers. "Take cover!"

People scattered. As they did, a missile exploded only meters away, sending debris raining over them. A hand-sized piece of concrete sailed into Jaxon's shoulder, knocking him over near the Special Forces doctor. The doctor's skull was crushed now by a piece of rubble larger than Jaxon's chest.

"Come on!" Reese tugged at him.

Jaxon swept up the black case still lying on the ground and ran with her toward the nearest large mound of debris on the west side of the clearing. He'd lost sight of Donnel. Was he dead, or had he taken the opportunity to bolt? It really didn't matter. But a moment later he noticed Donnel ahead of them, running toward the same mound of cement rubble.

"Another drone," Donnel called out as they slid behind the mound.

From a kneeling position behind the mound, Lyssa shot it down. "What about the underground?" she yelled. "We have to warn them. Where's Dani?"

Brogan shook his head. "She's circling around the rear of these new enforcers. She can't make it below in time, but she can make a difference here." Remorse filled his voice, and guilt—a horrible guilt that Jaxon shared. But there was still a chance. His vision had shown him that much.

He holstered his weapon and grabbed Lyssa's hand. "You can find Eagle and warn him. You and Lyra."

Her face lost all color. "He's too far. I can't feel him. It will take too long for us to find our way there."

Jaxon shook the case in her face. "With the viribus, you can find him." If not, he'd sealed the children's fiery fate.

Understanding at once filled Lyssa's face. "Do it," she said.

Jaxon tried to open the case, but it was locked. "I'll have to shoot it off."

"You might destroy the hypos," Hammer said. "And any chance we have of a cure."

Donnel's eyes went from Jaxon to Hammer. "Cure? There is no cure to the madness, at least not one the Controller ever found. The viribus lasts a while, but the madness always returns. And eventually . . ." He shook his head. "They all die."

"Shut up," Brogan ordered, pointing his gun at Donnel. "Just tell us how we open it."

"You need the doctor's handprint," Donnel said.

Despair threatened to overwhelm Jaxon. "He's dead." He'd made his choice in saving Reese, but now they were all going to pay.

Donnel hesitated for a moment before saying, "It's a simple reader. Not linked to his heartbeat or temperature. Get his hand and it'll still work."

Hammer leapt to his feet. "I'll be back."

He ran into the clearing, pulling something from a pocket. Sun glinted off metal. With the boulder on the doctor's head, there would be no chance of bringing the man's entire corpse, and Hammer was obviously prepared.

Another whistle signaled an incoming missile. Beside Jaxon, Lyssa whispered, "No!"

An instant later, an explosion knocked Hammer off his feet, pulverizing at least three unconscious Special Forces. But Hammer jumped up immediately and kept running. Seconds later, he skidded to his knees. Everyone seemed to hold their breaths as he sawed at something they couldn't see but could imagine only too well.

Gunfire filled the east, and Jaxon had to wonder how much of that was from the teen undergrounders, and how much was from Special Forces. Where were Nova and Thane in all that? He looked to Brogan, who had his T-link on.

"Move a half kilometer south," he was saying to someone. "Just beyond the range of the explosives. You can hold them there. We'll come to you. No. We don't have access to the explosives from here, but we can try to do it manually. Just get through it quickly." A single tear rolled down the fake skin of his cheek.

Another vision took Jaxon. *Shadow drawing light. An explosion in the east. Zone seven.*

"He's coming!" Lyssa said, bringing him back from the vision.

Another explosion hit as Hammer loped toward them, but it was too far away to hinder his progress. Less than a minute later, he arrived with the doctor's hand still dripping blood. He slapped the hand on the lock, and it opened.

"Tell him Shadow needs to draw the light," Jaxon said, placing a hand on Lyssa's arm and gripping it so hard she winced. "And tell him to blow the seventh zone."

"Not until the teens are in place," El Cerebro countered. "They have to run through that area first."

With a nod, Lyssa reached in for the viribus hypo. She jabbed it against her wrist before Jaxon could tell her where to put it. *Of course,* he thought. *She watched when they gave it to me.*

One second passed. Then two. Abruptly, she slumped into Hammer's waiting arms.

CHAPTER 24

P ain burned up her arm. Even before it subsided, Lyssa slid from her body where Lyra waited for her.

"I can't find him," Lyra said, her voice panicked. "We can't do anything. You shouldn't be leaving your body. You need to retreat. Or go save Nova and Thane."

"Just give the viribus a moment," Lyssa said, as the tugging sensation she recognized returned to her awareness. Already she could feel more people than before, some she vaguely knew and others she'd never met before.

She gripped Lyra's hand . . . and felt . . .

"Kansas," breathed Lyra.

It was true. Lyssa could feel Kansas, who awaited the next shipment from Newcali at the drop site some distance away. And not just Kansas but also Tamsin all the way in Big Horn. She could even feel Reese's great-aunt. If she could find them, she knew she only had to look downward for Eagle. Past the rock and debris. Past the metal.

She had to save the children. She'd purposefully stashed Tamsin far away from Amarillo City because of possible danger, so why hadn't she insisted on moving the underground children as well? Guilt burned bright at the thought. She hadn't though, and now those innocents, including Dr. Kentley's two adopted children were in the very danger she'd made sure her own precious daughter wouldn't face. Every one of their parents who had heard about Queran would be in terror right now.

She had to save them. Or warn Eagle so he could save them.

"There," she said, finding Eagle at last.

Eagle wasn't alone. He was with Shadow, moving away from the others in the underground. But also moving toward someone that could only be Queran and Special Forces. Moving toward danger.

Still gripping Lyra's hand, they traveled. Images flashed around them, barely registering. Faster and faster as the viribus penetrated every section of Lyssa's body. In seconds, they were next to Eagle, who walked in the darkness. Even in the dark, Lyssa's energy form could see quite well.

"Get in front of him," she told Lyra. "He has to see our energy before he'll stop and listen."

They willed themselves ahead of Eagle and Shadow. At first Lyra thought they would walk right through her, but at the last second, Eagle halted as if hitting a wall.

"What?" Shadow whispered.

"Someone's here," he said. "Lyssa? Lyra?"

Lyssa raised her hand to make the yes sign. Would he understand?

"It's them," he said.

"I don't see anything," Shadow whispered.

"They're traveling." Eagle didn't take his eyes from their energy. "What's going on? Why have communications been cut?"

"The Controller is dead," Lyssa signed. She didn't have a sign for Queran, so she spelled out the letters of his name.

"Queran is here?" Eagle asked.

"Queran?" Shadow repeated, sounding horrified. Eagle put a comforting arm around her.

"Yes," he said. "And I'm betting he's the reason we can't get to the outside. The others have killed the Controller, though, so that's something."

"Queran will burn us all." Shadow's breath was coming fast. "I've seen him. I was there."

Eagle cocked his head at her. "You were there? How close?"

Lyra waved for his attention, and Eagle reluctantly turned in her direction. Lyssa spelled out, *Blow zone seven on cue.*

"They want me to blow zone seven," Eagle explained to Shadow before responding to Lyssa. "I can do that. But we're totally cut off down here. I'll have to make it to the secondary system relay first. If Queran's down here, that's where he's cut the lines. I can blow it from there."

Where? Lyssa asked.

"Up the tunnel about a kilometer, then turn right and down another half kilometer. I can make it in about ten minutes."

Wait, Lyssa signed. To Lyra, she added, "Don't let him go. That's where I feel Queran—or at least I think it's him. I'll go see." She felt herself pulled away, even as she spoke. Seconds later, she came to an abrupt stop in a familiar tunnel where she knew the guards usually challenged those coming into the inhabited part of the underground.

"Where'd they go?" a voice boomed in the darkness. The man speaking was big and glowing with a heat Lyssa felt even in her current form. Every inch of his body was covered with body armor that was so thick, Lyssa suspected he could walk an entire line of automatic fire without injury. It had to be the sixer, Queran.

"I don't know." This hesitant admission came from one of eleven Special Forces hovering down the tunnel three meters. "They took off another way. This place is a maze. Should we follow them or continue ahead?"

"They're inconsequential," Queran said. "Let's continue following the blueprints. We'll find their nest and burn it out. Then we'll look for the rest of the guards."

Rest of the guards? Lyssa's heart lurched as she tried to decipher what he might mean. She could see no sign of any captive they might have. There was nothing but a blackened patch of ground and wall, where even the cement was rippled. Had something happened there? Her heart already knew the answer.

Lyssa returned to Eagle. "Queran's near the relay," she said to Lyra. "Him and eleven Special Forces. They're armed with assault rifles, but from the berth they're giving Queran, they won't need to use them. At least some of the guards on this end got away, but Queran's coming."

Lyra began signing, and between the two of them, they managed to convey the message to Eagle.

He turned to Shadow. "Look, you have to get back to Kentley and the children. Tell them to hide. And you hide with them."

"What will you do?"

"I'll duck down one of the tunnels, and after he goes by, I'll get to the relay."

"No!" Shadow whispered. "They have heat sensors. They'll detect you."

Lyssa was swept up in the hopelessness. Everything was going wrong. Even if the undergrounders escaped Special Forces topside, would they have the will to fight on if their children were killed? She wasn't sure she could in their place.

Lyra put her hand on Lyssa's arm. "Jaxon said 'shadow needs

to draw the light.' I thought he was talking about some kind of darkness, but he had to mean her." She waved toward Shadow.

"What if he didn't?"

"There's no time to check. They're coming."

Nova scaled the mound of rubble without loosening her tight hold on her rifle. Below her, Thane was leading the other teens north into Eagle's explosion zone seven. Once they got through, they'd have to stop and fire, to keep Special Forces inside the zone until someone could blow it.

She was relatively sure the teens would get through and could hold off Special Forces for at least a few minutes. But what if her uncle couldn't get someone to blow the explosives?

Back in Newcali, she hadn't wanted to return to Amarillo City, but if she hadn't, Thane would be facing this alone, and she was glad to be here with him. She'd killed three enforcers today, and she'd shoot all of them if it meant keeping those she loved safe. If she saved even one of her friends, it would be worth coming home. This was where she belonged. She finally understood why her father had given his life to free her from Colony 4. Some things were worth dying for.

"Nova?" came a voice in her ear. Her uncle.

"It's working," she said. "At least half of them are following us. And it looks like Dani has caught up to those that stayed behind. She'll take out the missiles." She slithered down the rubble mound, landing on her feet, and ran to Thane, who had dropped behind the others and was motioning to her. "I'll let you know when we're clear."

"Lyssa and Lyra have made contact with Eagle," Brogan responded. "He's heading toward the relay. We're working our way around the missile barrage too, but he has a better chance of blowing it. Just hold on." When she didn't reply to that, her uncle added, "I love you, Nova. Be brave, child. I'm doing everything I can." For the first time she could remember, he sounded beaten and afraid.

"I know." Her voice choked. "And I love you too. Don't worry about me. I'm glad I'm here. It's where I belong."

As she approached Thane, she released a volley of shots into the air to keep Special Forces coming after them. Though all her instincts warned her to disappear into a million hiding places she'd staked out over the past four years, hiding wasn't an option. This was her fight. She would do her part and trust that Eagle would do his.

Lyssa heard the sound of hurrying feet. Queran and his men were making no attempt to be quiet as they raced through the subway tunnel toward Eagle's position. There wasn't much time. Not remembering the words for shadow, she spelled the letters when she reached the word. *Jaxon says, shadow needs to draw the light.*

Eagle stared, shaking his head. "No," he said, his voice faint.

"What is it?" Shadow demanded.

He dragged his eyes from Lyssa. "You said you saw Queran. How did you survive? Heat is just another form of light. Did you push away the heat?"

She nodded. "He couldn't touch me, but he killed the others." She fell silent and then added in a voice that was scarcely a hoarse whisper, "I can protect us both. But after he gets by us, he'll find the children. We have to go back now. I can try to protect them too."

Eagle's mouth tightened. "We'll never get the children out in time, even if Special Forces hasn't found the other guard station."

"We have to try." Shadow's chest heaved and tears began rolling down her cheeks. "He'll burn the tunnels, but some of the kids might escape."

"What if . . ." Eagle shook his head, paused, and then started again. "What would happen if instead of pushing away Queran's heat, you pulled it toward you? Could you take it in like you did the light in the station? Would it hurt you?"

Shadow sucked in a breath of air. Fear radiated from her face, but when she spoke, it was with a courage that filled Lyssa's heart to near bursting with pride for her people—for the sixers.

"I'll try," Shadow said. "It might save the children. At the very least, it'll distract him long enough for you to get through to blow zone seven. But don't touch me while I'm trying. I don't know how well I can control it."

Eagle looked ready to change his mind about the whole idea, but after far too long, he nodded. "Hide us then, until he's close enough." The two hunkered together against the wall, and Lyssa barely heard him say, "Shimmer, listen. If it becomes too much, you can always push it away. Push it toward him. I'll try to sneak past. Don't worry about me."

He calls her Shimmer, not Shadow, Lyssa thought. That was how he saw this woman. She thought of Hammer back in the empty zone protecting her body, of Ty lying dead, his neck snapped. Neither of them had left her, and Lyssa knew that whatever Eagle said, he wouldn't leave Shimmer. They would both die or survive here. Tears stung Lyssa's eyes, but when she tried to wipe them away, she felt no wetness in her energy form.

"He's here," Lyra said. "Can he hurt us do you think?"

"I don't know. But go back and check on the others, okay? And on my body. See if they're ready to blow zone seven yet." It was a genuine errand, but she was glad to send Lyra away to make sure the baby she carried wouldn't somehow be affected by Queran's heat.

Lyra nodded, her eyes searching Lyssa's. "Promise me you'll leave if it becomes too much. For Tamsin's sake."

"I will. I'll go down the tunnel the other way right now." And she would. Because dying here with Eagle wouldn't help anything.

"I feel his heat," Shimmer whispered.

Shimmer's ability had hidden her and Eagle from Lyssa's senses, but she could also feel Queran's heat and see the lights carried by the Special Forces. The walls began to glow everywhere except where Eagle and Shimmer crouched. Lyssa willed herself past them and back down the tunnel in the direction of the main station as she'd promised Lyssa. She would be a silent witness here.

Queran was only ten paces away when Shimmer left Eagle and sprang forward. "Stop!" she called, raising her hands, palms out in front of her chest. "There's nothing for you here." Already to Lyssa's energy eyes, the woman was glowing.

Queran laughed. "Why don't you save yourself and show me where the others are? If you're helpful, I can find a use for you."

"No." Shimmer's voice trembled, but she held her ground.

"That's what one of your underground guards just told me a few minutes ago. He wouldn't lead me to your people because his daughter is there. Now he's a permanent black decoration on the wall of this tunnel."

"We're your people," Shimmer pleaded. "Why are you still carrying out the orders of a dead man?"

Lyssa noted that Eagle was no longer masked by Shimmer's

darkness, but he was either out of range of the Special Forces' light or all their attention was on Shadow. His assault rifle was aimed on Queran. The bullets might not penetrate Queran's armor, but that wouldn't stop Eagle from trying.

"Dead?" Queran snorted. "Controller Ramsey will never die, and I don't care who you are. I do what he asks so I get the drugs. Period. That means I don't go crazy."

"There's another way," Shimmer said. "I don't take his drugs, and I'm not crazy."

Queran threw back his head and laughed again. "From where I stand, you are obviously insane. And now you're going to be dead."

The big man thrust out his fists, as if focusing his energy. Lyssa felt herself being sucked inexplicably forward. She skirted backward out of Queran's range.

No, it wasn't Queran but Shimmer who was pulling in energy. Queran grunted in frustration, but Shimmer glowed brighter, until even the lights held by the Special Forces winked out.

"It's not working," boomed Queran. "Shoot her!"

Instantly, shots rang out, both Eagle's and from the Special Forces rifles. A sizzle and a pop reached Lyssa's ears as each Special Forces bullet entered the glow around Shimmer, but she remained standing. Several Special Forces collapsed from Eagle's shots, either from hits to the throat or from the pain of broken ribs through their enforcer blues.

"I can't see," shouted one of the men. "It's too bright! Stop it, Queran. You're killing us!"

"It's not me," Queran growled and staggered forward, arms outstretched. Would reaching Shimmer mean he could hurt her?

As if reading her mind, Eagle shouted, "Throw it back at him!"

In a wide sweep, Shimmer threw back her arms, whirling them down and forward in a swift, windmilling motion. A pulse of brilliant light slammed into first Queran and then the Special Forces behind him. They all flew backward like birds caught in a tornado, even those already on the ground. When Queran finally hit the gravel, there was another bright flash before the tunnel went utterly dark.

Lyssa's energy was propelled forward with the last flash. And so was Eagle. He landed beyond Shimmer but struggled immediately to his feet. "Shimmer," he called, rushing back to her.

"I'm okay," came a weak voice.

Lyssa scanned the area, shocked to see that Eagle and Shimmer were the only ones remaining in the tunnel. Queran and the Special Forces were gone. Only the flattened, melted hull of Queran's suit remained some distance away, lying atop the now-glowing rock of the tunnel.

Violent sobs filled the silence. Eagle pulled Shimmer to him, comforting her. "You're okay. You're okay. You saved the children. You saved everyone."

Shimmer's cries calmed almost immediately. "Not yet," she said with a shudder. "You have to get to the relay. Leave me. I'll be here when you get back."

Eagle looked around and Lyssa waved at him. *Lyra went to see if they're ready,* she signed.

Eagle nodded, but when he spoke, it was to Shimmer. "I'm not leaving you." He pulled her to her feet, and they hurried down the tunnel, with Eagle half carrying her.

They were halfway to the relay when Lyra appeared. "They're ready," she said. "But Dani wants zone six blown too. To stop the missiles. If it works, I have to get back to dispatch and start making up excuses about the explosions. Donnel has promised to send a report to HED that should delay any investigation. But that's only if we win this now."

"Go," Lyssa said. "I'll let you know when it's done."

Lyra nodded and disappeared.

Lyssa caught up with Eagle. *Blow six and seven now,* she signed.

He hurried faster until he was in sight of the relay. There, he finally left Shimmer and sprinted the rest of the way. He threw open the panel in the wall. Dismay hit Lyssa at the disarray of wires, but Eagle thrust both hands in and began working.

"Got it," Eagle said, less than a minute later. "I'm blowing them now."

CHAPTER 25

The rest happened so fast that later, Lyssa wasn't sure of the exact timeline after Eagle blew the explosives. But everyone did their part. Dani cleaned up straggling Special Forces that weren't killed in the blasts; undergrounders imprisoned the drugged Special Forces who had survived the so-called friendly fire; Nova reported in to let a relieved Brogan know that while there were many wounds among the underground teens, not one had been killed; and Lyra made a public announcement from the Amarillo City Enforcer Division about a training exercise in the empty zone. Within an hour of the explosions, Ekan Donnel sent in a falsified report to HED, and in twenty more hours, Dr. Kentley had synthesized enough doses of the treatment to wake all the unconscious sixers.

They had won their first battle with Special Forces. Completely and totally. A dozen underground soldiers had been hurt in the missile barrage, but only the single guard in the underground tunnels had been killed defending the children. When Brogan broke the news to the undergrounder's wife and his six-year-old daughter, he promised they would erect a monument near the blackened wall.

"He's a hero," Brogan told them.

Lyssa had to agree. And anyone who died in the next few weeks would also be a hero. The monument might not be much comfort to his family now, but maybe someday it would be.

When the excitement died down, Lyssa, still under the influence of the viribus, traveled to Tamsin to give her the good news.

Two days later, Lyssa and her sixer crew took the sky train back to where it had all begun. When the huge walls of Colony 6 came into view, instead of feeling sick, Lyssa felt hope. *We're coming,* she thought. *I know it took us a long time, but we're finally back to free you.*

With them was Captain Brogan, Hammer, Shimmer, and fifty underground soldiers dressed as enforcers and carrying fake CivIDs. They walked right into the Colony 6 Enforcer Division on the pretense of giving the local enforcers a well-deserved vacation, courtesy of Captain Brogan. Laughing and joking, the crew accompanied the enforcers back to the sky train that would take them from the colony.

Fifteen minutes later, the sky train was stranded in midair some distance outside the colony and would remain so until a repair crew could be dispatched—probably long after the fate of the rebellion had been decided. Colony 5's enforcers shared the same fate.

Lyssa called in colony administration leaders and all Elite employees, and they were promptly secured in the holding cells deep in the recesses of division. Then it was time to talk to the people. Dani, who was known to most of them, even if only by rumor, spoke to the entire Colony 6 population through the colony's public communication system. After she announced the takeover, a rioting crowd of colonists converged on the colony division, but tempers quickly cooled when she announced a holiday, extra rations of sauce, and passes for everyone to the outside as soon as the situation was in hand. Her second plea for volunteers to man the tops of the walls was met with enthusiasm and grateful tears.

Moments after the takeover in Colony 6, Lyssa sat at the colony's TAD-Alert's display, watching the news from the other colonies come in. Colonies 1 and 2, whose enforcers had been compromised by Kordell Corp, had fallen almost as easily as Colonies 5 and 6. There had been far more rioting within, however, and it had taken sixer abilities to subdue the people long enough for them to realize they were being saved.

The remaining two colonies faced a larger battle, but by the time enforcers realized what was happening, the sixers and soldiers were within the walls, hundreds of prominent colonists were armed, and all communication to enforcers on the outside was cut off. At first enforcers holed up in the colony division, but when given a demonstration of the sixer abilities and their certain death by burning or the asphyxiation that Dani's brother offered, most of the enforcers willingly threw down their arms and walked into their own prisons. The rest were forced into the cells. Only six enforcers were killed in Colony 4, and just one Newcali soldier was wounded in Colony 3.

"Yes!" Lyssa punched her fist into the air as the last report came in. "The colonies are ours," she announced. "Entrances have been secured, missiles have been moved inside the walls, and food is being distributed. Looks like all teams are making good progress on finding leaders to represent each colony."

Sitting next to her, Lyra and Kansas grinned. "We did it!" Lyra said, jumping up to hug her husband.

"It's not over yet," Kansas reminded her.

"No," Lyssa said. "But almost." She motioned for the Teev to open the public announcement system. "All the colonies have been successfully freed," she announced to the now-peaceful crowd waiting outside. "It's time to send our message to the Elite." Even through the thick walls, cheers came to her in a thundering roar.

Minutes later, the rest of their crew arrived in dispatch. Hammer and Dani brought up holo keyboards and together put in codes that would hack into the feed and release the pre-recorded message.

"We're in," Hammer said, casting Lyssa a grin. Even two days after the confrontation in the empty zone and several nanite treatments, his face still held numerous cuts and bruises, some of which he'd gained protecting Lyssa's body.

He's alive, she thought with a rush of joy. *And so am I.*

The recorded message began as an image of Controller Ramsey taken from Jaxon's suit recorder flashed onto the screen. "Colony 6 was first settled with people who had a tendency toward unusual gifts," he said. "Some of your relatives showed precognitive abilities, and we enhanced those with special treatments."

Then it switched to a later conversation with Jaxon.

"Some of those children we kept to work in the colonies," Ramsey said. "The death rate is so high there, you know."

"Because you work them to death."

"Forget them," Ramsey barked, spittle flying from his lips. "They don't matter. Think of this. If you shoot me, you'll never know who you are."

"Did you kill my mother?" Jaxon retorted.

A rapid fast-forward took them to Ramsey's reply. "Your

mother was nothing. She was a vessel, a means to an end. Like all the colonists."

This was followed by a black screen that lasted a half second before Brogan appeared in his El Cerebro disguise. "I'm El Cerebro," he began, "and I represent all the colonists, who for sixty years have been kept as slaves behind the walls." He pulled off his mask and wig. "I'm also Captain Brogan of the Amarillo City Enforcer Division. I hereby publicly denounce the Elite and invite you to the Teev address below to learn the full truth."

He paused for a breath before continuing. "Your Controller is dead, killed in self-defense by those of us determined to take back our freedom. As of now, the colonies are under their own control. That means we own ninety percent of all food and raw materials. If you attack, we will shoot back. We have missiles, soldiers, and a thousand people with incredible abilities, and we will fight any attempt to approach our walls. Know that we would rather destroy all our crops, our greenhouses, our animals, our factories, and our mines than have them stolen from us. However, we are willing to let you buy our goods in fair trade. The only demand we have is the complete and immediate resignation of the Director and the two surviving Elite leaders under her, the Regulator and the Administrator. Only then will our food and raw materials be available for purchase." Brogan allowed a slow smile. "Please join us in demanding the Elite's surrender. It's time for their control of our lives to end. There will be no more slavery. For any of us. No more cameras, birth orders, or—"

The feed was cut then, severing the rest of the message, but already the bandwidth was crammed with people following the Teev address that led to the backdoor and into the T-link feed where the rest of the information was stored, including an uncut version of the Controller's final moments.

"I bet the Elite will turn off the feed in the next few seconds," Reese said. She stood next to Jaxon behind Lyra and Kansas, her arms folded across her chest. "They'll want to prevent people from getting to our site."

Hammer looked away from the holoscreen. "That was my guess, but maybe they'll wait a while longer. Shutting down the feed will also shut down everything else, including their cameras and communications. I'm betting they'll cut it eventually, though. Especially if rioting begins. In the meantime, with all the people visiting the site, there aren't enough enforcers to take them into custody."

"So now we wait," Lyssa said.

Brogan motioned for a holo keyboard. "I'm going to contact our division and see what the reaction there is. Jaxon, why don't you have your buddy Donnel call up a few more people from HED to see what he can find out there?"

"You trust him?" Reese asked, narrowing her eyes.

Jaxon shrugged as he started for the door. "I don't know for sure, but I think so. You can always stand outside the cell and shoot him if he does something stupid."

"Now that sounds like a perfect idea." Reese hurried after him.

One by one, everyone left Colony 6's dispatch office until only Lyssa and Hammer remained. She wondered how many people going to the Newcali T-link site would witness the recording of Ty's violent death at the hands of the Controller, and she shuddered at the memory. She wasn't aware of Hammer moving toward where she sat until he leaned down and encircled her with his big arms. In that instant, within the safety he represented, the horror was held at bay.

"You loved him," he said quietly.

Lyssa thought about that for a moment. She wished she could agree, but he was wrong. She hadn't loved Ty enough to trust him. Maybe if she had, if they'd both shared their secret lives, he'd still be alive.

"I didn't love him enough," she said.

"He knew about the vision," Hammer told her. She felt his gaze on her face like a physical touch.

"What?" She came to her feet, swiveling in his loosened embrace to meet his stare with one of her own.

"Jaxon told him. After what happened with the KC, he told Ty everything. He asked him to leave town, but Ty said if it was going to happen, he wanted to go down fighting."

Lyssa smiled through her sudden tears—tears that somehow were just as much relief as they were a sign of her grief. "He certainly did that," she said, leaning into Hammer and savoring his touch, his smell, his strength. "Everyone will know his name. And they'll know what kind of a man he was."

Amarillo City Enforcer Division dispatch operator Gemma Drexel's round face fixed in horror at her home holoscreen as she drank in the information on the T-link feed. She groped blindly for her husband's hand as they watched the Controller order Ty Bissett's death. How could poor Ty be dead? He'd worked for what seemed like forever in personnel and was one of the nicest men at AED. He always asked how Jimmy was doing and always commiserated each time she told him they'd refused to let her see her little boy.

As a mental invalid, Jimmy had been put in a hospital soon after his birth, presumably for his welfare. But how could it be good for a baby to be without his mother? He was three years old now, and she could count on four hands the times she'd been allowed to see him.

Gemma had once been tempted to tell Ty that she thought they were experimenting on her son, maybe testing some kind of disease treatment. She hadn't, of course, because there was nothing he could do. There was nothing anyone could do.

Except now someone had done something.

Not only had Captain Brogan come out against Elite, but so had her two coworkers in dispatch, Lyssa Sloan and Lyra Bateman. And Lyra was pregnant without a birth order. No wonder Gemma had been called in to work extra shifts all week, with the rebelling and morning sickness that had been going on right under her nose. Also involved in the rebellion were two detectives from her division's Violent Crimes Unit, the big CSI Unit Leader who wore his hair in a ponytail, and the new weapon's expert, the one who wore the dark glasses even inside the building.

"Can you believe it?" she whispered, her voice even more husky than her normal masculine timbre.

Her husband shook his head slowly back and forth, as if dazed. "I don't know what to think. I thought all fringers were insane with radiation poisoning, and now they're inviting us to leave the CORE and settle with them?"

A few more minutes ticked by as she flipped through sites on the Teev, watching excited announcers talking about women pouring into doctor's offices, demanding removal of birth control implants or CivIDs. Still more reporters showed images of crowds knocking Teev cameras from their high perches, using rocks, shoes, and even iTeevs.

Had the whole world gone crazy?

Yes.

And she was glad.

"Well I know what I'm going to do." She pulled her hand from her husband's and smoothed her long shirt over her voluptuous figure. "I'm going to see my son, and I'm going to stay there until they let me bring him home. They can't keep him anymore. He's mine."

A determined smile spread across her husband's face. "Yes," he agreed. "Let's go."

Twenty-four hours after the colony takeover, the Teev feed had gone down, but a group of disgruntled employees raided the CORE communication building with the help of a couple rogue enforcers, and the feed went back up within eight hours and remained that way. As a former communication employee, Lyssa liked to think that her public plea on the T-link site had helped that happen.

When rioting broke out around the main administration buildings in New York, Brogan hacked into the feed again and pleaded with everyone to stay in their homes. Many citizens listened. He also begged enforcers to keep the peace and to stay away from the colonies.

"The Elite will surrender," he promised. "Please do not interfere." Enough enforcers appeared to be listening that the remaining rioters were taken into custody.

The next day, despite his plea, five hundred enforcers attacked Colony 2. Newcali soldiers launched a missile, but the enforcers still managed to break through the main entrance. Soldiers and colonists repelled the attack long enough for sixers to use their varying talents to deafen, blind, and confuse the enforcers, who were pushed back and held until the gates were reinforced. By the time the fight was over, a hundred enforcers lay stunned or dead. The rest fled the gunfire coming from the top of the walls. Only six colonists and two soldiers sustained non-life-threatening injuries.

On day three, Colony 6 received a half-hearted demand for surrender from two dozen enforcers—enforcers not from Brogan's division in Amarillo City. Dani and the sixers walked through the gates to face them. When enforcer bullets couldn't penetrate the shield three of the sixers created, they immediately retreated. Two of the sixers were adult children of sixers who had been murdered by Special Forces. So far, Dani had found over two dozen children of sixers, and they were not afflicted with the madness.

The largest attempt to retake the colonies was on the fourth day when several thousand enforcers surrounded Colony 1. These included hundreds of Special Forces who were already weary from hastily replacing shorted-out laser fencing along the North Desolation border. They had missile launchers with them, but Dani's soldiers destroyed them with missiles of their own that exploded in their midst. When sixers came upon the walls and caused a violent wind and rain that froze into razor-sharp slivers of ice, many of the enforcers who managed to escape the barrage disappeared without a backward glance. The others reassembled at a safe distance, leaving all their equipment and three hundred wounded behind.

No one tried to retake the other three colonies.

Later that same day, the Teev feed reported that thousands of enforcers had encircled the Director's impenetrable iron-fenced residence in northern New York, where she and her top people had retreated. However, after only minutes, they realized these enforcers weren't there to help the Director but to demand her resignation. Civilians also marched on the residence, and a few hurtled rocks through her windows or at the cameras posted on every iron fencepost. Other enforcers continued to patrol the cities as Brogan requested, and Lyssa could see that the reports coming in from the division were different now. Several enforcer captains had refused to obey orders from HED and were instead contacting Captain Brogan for instructions.

Six days after the announcement, reporters began covering stories about shortages. Food mostly, but other factories that depended on raw materials from the colonies were shutting down. Displaced workers joined the throng of growing protesters around the Director's residence.

"It won't be long now," Brogan said.

Lyssa hoped he was right.

Eight days after the takeover, Lyssa was in the cafeteria with Hammer, Reese, Jaxon, and Captain Brogan when Dani burst into the room, her short white hair standing up even more than normal.

"She's on the Teev!" she declared, waving the holoscreen to life. "The announcement just came through dispatch."

"The Director?" Lyssa asked.

"That's right. Actually, she sent out her Magistrate Assistant with a recorded message to hand over. They're going to play it now. But rumor has it, she's stepping down."

Even as Dani spoke, a plump woman in a yellow, long-sleeved dress appeared on the holoscreen. Her hair was dyed brown and her round, red cheeks were unnaturally smooth, but her spine was curved, and she moved with the air of the very aged.

"I was not aware of any of this," she said with a tragic sigh. "I am as devastated as you all are by the great betrayal perpetuated by Controller Warrick Ramsey. But as requested by the colonists, I will step down from my long-held position, to which I have dedicated over fifty years of my life. So will those

under my direct command. They will all forward their administration files to Captain Vic Brogan, and he can give them to
whoever will be in charge. Please go home now and leave me
alone. I have no further comments."

Short, but not so very sweet.

"Finally," Lyssa said with a long breath, rising from her
chair. "But can we believe her?"

Jaxon shook his head. "Not in the slightest. Without the
support of Special Forces and the Controller, she simply knows
she can't fight back."

"Killing Ramsey was the right thing to do," Reese said,
taking Jaxon's hand.

"It was the only thing," Brogan agreed. He nodded at
Dani. "It's time. We need to get to New York before the KC
tries something. We currently control the food and ultimately
their profits, but we need to consolidate remaining enforcers
and appoint interim leadership. While you send for the
hovers, I'll let those who are coming know." These included
President Ange Shala from Newcali, Dr. Sam Kentley, the
Amarillo City Manager, two Estlantic enforcer captains who
were long-time underground sympathizers, and representa-
tives from each of the six colonies.

"We'll have two armed contingents ready to go within the
hour," Jaxon said, jumping to his feet. "Not that we'll need
them on this trip. We're going to make this work—all of us
together." He and Reese hurried to the door, where he almost
ran into Dr. Kentley, who waved a yellow hypo in his hand.

"Good news," Kentley said, his eyes bleary from lack of
sleep. "Donnel might have been right that the viribus alone
wouldn't lead me to a cure, but I found antibodies in the adult
sixer children. This should work for all sixers. Permanently."

Jaxon met his gaze with a solemn nod. "It will."

Reese rolled her eyes and groaned. "Seriously, if he wasn't

hard enough to live with before, now that he's no longer going mad, he's impossible." She pushed past the doctor and strode from the room with feigned indignance.

Jaxon grinned and pointed after her. "She loves me, can't you tell? With that pure viribus still in my system, the cure isn't going to make much difference for me right now, but Reese definitely needs it. Come on. Let's catch up with her."

Lyssa shared a grin with Hammer as the room emptied. While half the crew traveled to Estlantic to form a new government, the other half, Lyssa and Hammer included, would remain to keep the peace in Colony 6 until new leaders from among the colonists could be appointed. Already, without the constant influx of behavior modification drugs in their ready-meals, forerunners were becoming apparent: the manager at Factory One, the groundskeeper for the administration building, and two of the school directors.

They were free. The CORE was no more.

There was so much she planned to do in the immediate future. She was going to walk on a beach with Tamsin in Newcali and swim in the water. They would sail on a boat, climb a mountain with Hammer, and sleep in a tent. She would track down equipment and send out communication signals to see if anyone across the oceans had also survived Breakdown. And beginning today she would announce from the rooftops that Tamsin was hers. Tamsin would finally know her mother's true name.

Hammer reached down and pulled her to her feet. "We should probably help them get ready," he said, wrapping his arms around her.

She shook her head and stood on tiptoe, pulling his face to hers. "They have it under control," she said, kissing him. "Right now, we have something more important to do."

He kissed her back, trailing fire from her cheek down to her neck. "Oh?" he said against the sensitive skin under her ear. "I like the sound of that."

She laughed. "We're going to Big Horn to get Tamsin. I want you two to meet. We have a lot of plans to make."

GLOSSARY OF TERMS

Birth order – permission to have a child. You must first submit a birth application to be awarded one of these. The application process takes three months with a six-month waiting period between rejected applications. This means couples can apply every nine months until they have two children.

Blues, or enforcer blues – the black, bulletproof uniforms worn by enforcers with built-in iTeev connectors and heating/cooling units.

Breakdown – total economic collapse and nuclear warfare that occurred in what was formerly known as America in 2198. Sometimes used as a curse.

Breathers – gas masks.

Brew – a stimulating drink made from the guardana plant grown in Colony 2. There are two versions, a rich, tasty brew that comes from the leaves and a bitter drink derived from the stems that has the same kick.

C-lodges (capitalized) – Commonwealth lodges owned by the CORE.

Cash credits – plastic card encoded with different credit (money) amounts.

Cazadors – Newcali term for animals changed by radiation who live in the desolation zones. Called beasts or monsters in the CORE.

Chotks – an expensive, light-colored alcoholic drink that is slightly sweet.

CivID – identification that must be carried by all CORE citizens. CivIDs constantly emit a signal that can be easily picked up by surveillance cameras. There are blockers sold on the black market to mask this signal. A CivID allows access to the sky trains.

Clean spots – used to obscure online Teev activities. Use is directly against CORE law.

Cleaners – boxy, Teev-driven, automated cleaning machines that are roughly sixty square centimeters in circumference and one hundred and twenty centimeters tall. Used to vacuum and clean the floors in many large buildings. Often people who have been medically enhanced will follow these cleaners to help them navigate any difficult objects, but the job is basically nonessential. Because of this, the term "walk with the cleaners" is both a reference to a mental condition and as a comment on a person's low intelligence.

Clipper – derogative nickname for an enforcer.

Clud – a mild curse.

Colonies – settlements created to support the poor, needy, and displaced after Breakdown. There are six colonies, three in Estlantic and three in Dallastar, and each is assigned to a primary industry, except Colony 6. In Estlantic: Colony 1, farming and forestry; Colony 2, farming and fishing; Colony 3, mining and metals. In Dallastar: Colony 4, oils and plastics; Colony 5 (also known as the Sty), cattle and livestock; Colony 6 (see below).

Commontongue (capitalized) – language of the CORE.

Coop, or Colony 6 – as in chicken coop. They create raw textiles, metals, or plastics from materials created by the other colonies. Located southwest of Amarillo City in Dallastar Territory.

CORE Elite – wealthy people who lead the government of the CORE. These include the Director (overall ruler), Controller (over all enforcers), Administrator (finances and city affairs), Regulator (controls population and gives out birth orders) and all their highest advisors and underlings.

CORE Identification Unit, or CIU – an enforcer unit that specializes on discovering the identities of criminals. Serves all of Estlantic.

CORE, or Commonwealth Objective for Reform and Efficiency – name of the country and government of Estlantic and Dallastar territories, short for. Often used as an exclamation in sentences like, "Thank CORE."

Credits – money, method of exchange, normally transferred via iTeev or Teev feed.

Crew – gangs in the Coop.

Dallastar – smaller territory of the CORE, located in the mid-south of the continent and borders Fringer territory.

Data square – a tiny, thin, square, flash drive.

Desolation zones – areas affected by nuclear fallout during Breakdown.

Ditch digger – a person who does dirty work for someone powerful

Empty zones – rubble-filled areas destroyed during Breakdown and not yet inhabited or reclaimed.

Enforce weapons – weapons used by enforcers, pre-Breakdown tech that uses fingerprint identity to enable the weapons.

Enforcer – Police officer. Usually called enforcers. Besides their normal job hours, they must log three to six hours of physical efficiency training per week, depending on their location.

Enforcer divisions – like police precincts. There are ten in Estlantic and five in Dallastar, with subdivisions. Some important divisions are Amarillo Enforcer Division (AED), New York Enforcer Division (NYD), Headquarters Enforcer Division (HED).

Enhancement, or enhancing – a medical procedure where lasers are used on aggressive centers of the brain. Worse than a lobotomy.

Estlantic – largest territory of the CORE, located on the east coast of the continent.

Freedom Fountain, or the Fountain – a fountain erected in the plaza outside CORE buildings in Amarillo City to celebrate the CORE's victory against fringers during the fight for Amarillo City. Famous in all of the CORE, and almost revered in Dallastar.

Fringers – people who separated from those who created the CORE after Breakdown. Viewed as crazy and dangerous rebels suffering from nuclear radiation, fringers still fight to undermine the CORE. There are different bands of fringers living in various empty zones. A large band of fringers, population unknown, inhabit Newcali on the west coast. People in the CORE often use fringer as a derogatory term, such as "half-witted fringer."

Gathering limit – public and private gatherings are limited to twenty citizens, unless a permit is acquired from the city manager.

Handspeak (capitalized) – sign language

Holos – holographs; pre-Breakdown technology used by Teevs and iTeevs.

Hover, or hover car, or hovercraft – a small personal flying ship, a technology believed to have been lost after Breakdown.

Hypo – a small cylinder used to inject medications. A hypo can hold several doses and can be used on different people without fear of cross-contamination. Certain colors of hypos are often used to hold a specific medicine, so they can be found and used quickly. Common ones are blue for a painkiller, red for a stimulant, and white for a sedative.

Image receptors – a nearly indestructible, reusable screen the thickness of a paper. Receptors are pre-Breakdown tech that are now only available within the enforcer divisions or by CORE Elite. Images can be loaded into the receptors.

iTeev – a portable Teev (see Teev description below) that can be held in the hand or used over the eyes like glasses to communicate or view holo feeds anywhere, even outdoors, without the use of holo emitters. Normally activated and used by direct touch on the foldable screen, through hand signals, or verbal commands. Limited eye movement controls are also supported but rarely used by the general population. Has a mini earbud connected with a thin wire that can pull out of a compartment for more private communication when used over the eyes.

Juke – a recreational hallucinogen, an addictive drug that was originally discovered as a byproduct of viribus, the experimental drug used in Colony 6. Outlawed in all of the CORE. Provides thirty or more minutes of rush or high followed by exhaustion or unconsciousness unless a counter agent is used. Juke enhances the development of abilities found in Colony 6, and also speeds up onset of the madness. Often sold in a black hypo marked with a white J.

Jukehead – a juke addict. Sometimes also called a "cotton-headed juke addict" or a "warthog-faced jukehead," which are mild curses.

Level – nursery or school grade that corresponds exactly with a child's age. When a child graduates, they "level out."

Lumper – a person who ventures into the empty zones or

edges of the desolation zones and is stupid enough to get taken by fringers (or presumed taken). This has evolved into Terms like "I lumping hate you" or "I don't give a lump."

Magglue – glue for metals, contains magnetic nanites.

Marriage band – a wedding band that can't be removed until the marriage is broken. Not mandated by the CORE but growing popular among the residents. Breaking a union isn't against the law, unless you have a child under eighteen, but couples must receive permission. Affairs by those in valid unions are punishable by huge fines and even psychological reconditioning when minors are involved.

Nanobots – used to be common for fixing ailments pre-Breakdown. More rare now. A similar tech is used in Nuface therapy.

Nanoparticles – the less effective little brother of nanobots. Nanoparticles can fix internal wounds if injected near the damage, but it's mostly hit and miss since the CORE has lost the technology to program them.

Newcali – A territory that is home to a large group of fringers who live outside CORE control. Located on the west coast of the continent. Little is known about the territory's size or population, but the people are powerful enough to have resisted CORE attempts of takeover. They allow free study and invention. After leaving Colony 6, Dani Balak became associated with them and now considers them her people.

Newcali bread drops – small rolls that are very soft and lightly sweetened, cross between a doughnut and a roll.

Newport – principal city in Newcali.

Nuface therapy – nanite treatments to preserve youth.

Nyckelira – a sixteen-string fiddle-like instrument with dozens of keys intersecting the strings. Strings are played with a short bow and the keys are played with the fingers. A modified version of current day Swedish nyckelharpa. A current rage among the youth of the CORE, bought at local furniture shops, though no one seems to know exactly who is manufacturing them.

Pressure pad – pre-Breakdown tech now utilized only by Newcalians. A thin, clear pad with sensors connected wirelessly to a transmitter that signals whenever it senses pressure, such as the weight of a person stepping on it.

Punk – person who didn't finish school, works on the underbelly of society.

Punk bucket – any job that sucks, related to the buckets of waste a punk had to carry away from the work settlements when the colonies were being built.

Pus bag – derogative term for a CORE Elite (leader).

Pus licker – derogative term for a person who does the bidding of a Core Elite.

Readymeal – a flat carton of mixed processed foods and synthesized food substitutes, similar to current-day microwaveable meals. Usually heated in a microwave or inside a readymade dispenser. Often tasteless compared with fresh food but inexpensive and convenient. Primary sustenance for daily use throughout the CORE. Each carton contains immunizations and vitamins and comes with a plastic fork. Substandard readymeals are distributed in the colonies.

RealSkin – used as bandages over repaired wounds.

Reconditioning – psychological therapy for people who have disobeyed minor CORE laws.

Saca – a mild curse.

Sauce – a stiff alcoholic drink made of equal parts coarse alcohol and synthetic fillers. The drink of the poor. The taste is tart and the sour smell tends to linger on the breath.

Sauced or sauce-crazed – drunk.

Scramblers – enforcer motorcycles equipped with pre-Breakdown tech that uses fuel cells for power. Scramblers are fast, maneuverable, and can be used for a month without refueling. Mostly used in Estlantic (New York in particular).

Shuttle, or automated shuttle – a roughly tetrahedron-shaped blue car that is a Teev-driven taxi. All CORE residents outside the colonies have a limited monthly allotment of time they are permitted to use the public shuttle without cost. There are also automatic ambulance shuttles people can call for assistance. The doors on all shuttles slide back into built-in door pockets and the windows are normally darkened for privacy. Shuttle use pre-Breakdown fuel cells for power. Unlike the public shuttles that are a calming sky blue color, enforcer shuttles are silver with black and red stripes. They are also larger and faster, and their metal tops can fold back inside the rear compartment for use as a convertible. Instead of only being driven automatically by Teev, enforcer shuttles have optional manual controls.

Sixers – newly coined word for those with abilities that are from Colony 6.

Skin – a collapsible membrane with a flip top that can hold water, sauce, juice or other liquids.

Skin sealant – a powdered substance used in emergency as a temporary fix to slow or stop bleeding.

Skin tag – a circular patch of indeterminate color that immediately takes on the skin color of the user. Once activated, a tag will distort the wearer's face on any electronic recording. Activated with one long press of a finger. A two-fingered long press will distort both appearance and override any active CivIDs, including implanted ones. Three short taps with one finger turns it off. Wearer experiences a tingle as it is activated. Skin tags last up to two months and are nearly imperceptible to the naked eye.

Sky train – free, pre-Breakdown public transport that runs throughout the CORE. Runs on solar energy.

Smeg – a mildly addictive drug like marijuana that heats the entire body, giving the user a sexual reaction that emulates the flush of sex. Not outlawed in the CORE, but use is not viewed favorably.

Smegger – a person who often uses or is addicted to smeg.

Sonic cleansing – the no-water cleaning system used by most of the CORE.

Stunner, or stun – a weapon similar to a taser.

T-link – fringer version of the Teev. Also has holo capabilities and a portable wearable version that is nearly indistinguishable from an iTeev, except for the wireless earbud.

Cleaner – a boxy cleaning machine with gently rounded edges. Roughly a square meter wide and several meters tall.

Teev (capitalized) – television, Internet, and phone hardware/software combo. You can view, search, call, or read on the Teev. Teevs provide holographic feed indoors through holograph emitters embedded in the walls and are found in every household. Hand motions are used to activate or deactivate. Guests can normally access a certain feed on any Teev, but to access all the abilities, a password can be required.

Teev Aided Dispatch Alert System, or TAD-Alert – an enforcer system that tracks callers, prioritizes calls, and suggests names of enforcers to respond to any emergency. It can link to most home or work Teevs to have immediate eyes on any situation where enforcers might be called.

Teev feed – the connection between all Teevs and iTeevs, owned and controlled exclusively by the CORE.

Temper laser – mood altering laser that will calm most people. Effects last about fifteen minutes. However, 1% of people in the CORE are immune.

Ultratemp – larger, more powerful temper laser.

Underground, or the underground (not capitalized) – black market organization that skirts CORE law.

Undergrounders (not capitalized) – people who live underground in old metro tunnels. They usually work for the underground leader and trade on the black market.

Viribus (not capitalized) – the experimental drug placed secretly in the water at Colony 6 over a period of fifty-two years, about twenty-two to seventy-four years after Breakdown. Viribus enhances inborn psychic and physical abilities. The hope was to create stronger, more resilient humans, but if a person with abilities is exposed and left untreated, the universal side effect is madness and violence.

Voice modulator – a device worn at the throat to disguise your voice.

Whore wrangler – someone who visits a prostitute, which is illegal in the CORE.

X-Fang – a popular band in the CORE.

Teyla Branton grew up avidly reading science fiction and fantasy and watching Star Trek reruns with her large family. They lived on a little farm where she loved to visit the solitary cow and collect (and juggle) the eggs, usually making it back to the house with most of them intact. On that same farm she once owned thirty-three gerbils and eighteen cats, not a good mix, as it turns out. Teyla always had her nose in a book and daydreamed about someday creating her own worlds.

Teyla is now married, mostly grown up, and has seven kids, so life at her house can be very interesting (and loud), but writing keeps her sane. She thrives on the energy and daily amusement offered by her children, the semi-ordered chaos giving her a constant source of writing material. Teyla grabs any bit of free time from her hectic life to write. She's been known to wear pajamas all day when working on a deadline, and is often distracted enough to burn dinner. (Okay, pretty much 90% of the time.)

She loves writing fiction and traveling, and she hopes to write and travel a lot more. She also loves shooting guns, martial arts, and belly dancing. She has worked in the publishing business for over twenty years. Teyla also writes romance and suspense under the name Rachel Branton. For more information or to join her mailing list and get a free ebook, please visit http://www.TeylaBranton.com.